ODYSSEY

THE FRACTURED KINGDOM

ODYSSEY

M.L. FERGUS

tundra

Tundra Books, an imprint of Tundra Book Group, a division of Penguin Random House of
Canada Limited, 320 Front Street West, Suite 1400, Toronto, Ontario, M5V 3B6, Canada
penguinrandomhouse.ca

Published simultaneously in the United States of America by Tundra Books
of Northern New York, an imprint of Tundra Book Group, a division of
Penguin Random House of Canada Limited

The authorized representative in the EU for product safety and compliance is Penguin
Random House Ireland, Morrison Chambers, 32 Nassau Street, Dublin D02 YH68, Ireland,
https://eu-contact.penguin.ie

Library and Archives Canada Cataloguing in Publication
Title: Odyssey / M.L. Fergus.
Other titles: Fool's errand
Names: Fergus, Maureen, author
Description: Series statement: Fractured kingdom ; 2 |
Substantially revised edition of: Fool's errand.
Identifiers: Canadiana (print) 20240432037 | Canadiana (ebook) 20240432045 |
ISBN 9781774886090 (softcover) | ISBN 9781774886106 (EPUB)
Subjects: LCGFT: Fantasy fiction. | LCGFT: Novels.
Classification: LCC PS8611.E735 F66 2025 | DDC jC813/.6—dc23

Library of Congress Control Number: 2024942434

Edited by Lynne Missen (original) and Margot Blankier (updated)
Designed by Sophie Paas-Lang
Cover art: ~ Bitter ~ / Adobe Stock
Typeset by Kianna Mkhonza
The text was set in Adobe Caslon Pro.

Printed in Canada

1 2 3 4 5   29 28 27 26 25

Penguin
Random House
tundra   TUNDRA BOOKS

For Nick,
because you are exactly like Azriel
only handsomer, funnier and more charming.

You are about to enter a dark and dangerous kingdom. Over the course of your journey, you will encounter or hear mention of sexual situations as well as the abuse, kidnap, murder, enslavement, imprisonment, brutal torture, illness, death and grief of people of all ages. The mistreatment and death of animals are also a part of this harsh world. Readers who may be sensitive to these elements, please take note before joining the adventure.

One

DROPPING TO ONE KNEE, the pockmarked servant looked up at Persephone with a reverence bordering on awe and said, "I know nothing of what the Seer may have said about any Methusian king, Your Highness. I know only that you are the lost royal twin and rightful heir to the Erok throne."

THUD, THUD, THUD . . .

Persephone could hear the Regent's soldiers slamming something ponderous against the barred door of the palace chamber in which she and Azriel had cornered this servant who spoke of dead queens and burning baby flesh. She could see that the heavy bar was about to splinter, and she understood that when it did, the door would give way and the soldiers would fall upon them, cutting and slashing.

She knew there was no escape.

Yet as she stared into the face of the woman who knelt at her feet, Persephone felt as removed from the moment as if she were a silvery specter hovering high above the firelit chamber, gazing down upon a world that could no longer touch her.

THUD, THUD, THUD . . .

Indeed, if she'd not seen the proof with her own two eyes, she'd never have believed the tale told by this servant who, eighteen years past, had helped the desperate, dying queen mark her newborns as twins. The queen's purpose had been to ensure that if the tiny, squalling infant princess condemned to death in secret by the Regent Mordesius somehow survived and returned to claim her inheritance, she'd have proof of who she really was.

Me! thought Persephone with a sudden jolt. *An emptier of chamber pots, an enslaved girl most recently purchased for one small bag of coins and a pretty piece of stolen jewelry—I was the infant princess condemned to death!*

As if in a dream, she ran her fingertips along the whiplash scar that crisscrossed the outside of her forearm, the scar that so perfectly matched the one that young King Finnius had borne upon his arm for as long as anyone could remember. Mere moments earlier, when she broke off dancing with him to beg for the lives of the handsome chicken thief and the Methusian orphan they'd risked everything to rescue, everyone in the Great Hall had seen their matching scars. The king, the nobles in attendance at his birthday feast, the servants who catered to them, the musicians who played for them and, of course, the Regent, who now sought to break down the door and see Persephone's heart cut out so that his long-ago treachery might yet go unproven—and unpunished.

Of course, he might also want my heart cut out because I toyed with him and generally played him for a great fool, she acknowledged with the barest of shrugs.

THUD, THUD, THUD . . .

The sudden feel of warm fingers cupping her elbow yanked Persephone back to reality with an abruptness that made her gasp like a drowning woman coming back to life.

Azriel.

Persephone turned toward the one-time chicken thief. As ever, the sight of his long, lean body and broad, well-muscled shoulders caused her pulse to quicken, but her gaze did not linger here. Instead, it flew upward past his wide, sensuous lips, past the fading scar upon his chiseled cheekbone, which she herself had given him, all the way up to the twin oceans of his very blue eyes.

THUD, THUD, THUD . . .

As their eyes met, Persephone felt the ground shift beneath her. Since that first night she'd confronted him in the owner's barn, she'd seen Azriel's eyes blaze with many things—hunger, heat, hurt, humor, hardness. But she'd never seen them look like this. No longer twin oceans but instead, pieces of midwinter river ice: impassive, unyielding and cold enough to make her shiver. And though she thought she could see shadows moving far below the surface, she could not make out what they were.

Persephone's heart went into free fall. Instead of speaking words of reason to Azriel, she'd let him believe that he was the Methusian king come to unite the five clans of Glyndoria and set things to right for all people.

He'd told her that he loved her and needed her; she'd lied to him and run out on him.

Now she had taken from him not just a great destiny but also a past and a brother.

"Azriel . . ."

THUD, THUD—

CRACK.

The barred door across the room flew open so suddenly that the soldier who'd been holding the front of the makeshift battering ram stumbled and fell. The battering ram, a twelve-foot log that had been destined for one of the massive fireplaces in the Great Hall, hit the floor with a mighty crash. As it did so, a second soldier stormed into the room.

At the sight of his raised sword, the pockmarked servant, who'd thus far seemed frozen with terror, screamed shrilly and tried to scramble away from him. He responded by viciously kicking her onto her back and pressing his dirty black boot down upon her heaving chest that he might more easily run his sword through her guts. Without thinking, Persephone plunged her hand into the torn pocket of her disheveled gown. Snatching from the scabbard at her thigh the blade she'd managed to hold on to after her recent near-ravishment, she hurled it across the room. As ever, her aim was true, and the dagger was buried to the hilt in the soldier's throat before he knew what was happening. For an instant he just stood there, eyes bulging. Then his sword slipped from his grasp and he staggered backward three steps. Gurgling and clawing at the hole in his throat from which the blood had begun to stream, he slowly collapsed to the ground.

Even as he did so, two more soldiers ran into the room. The first ran straight at Persephone with his sword extended. Azriel launched himself at the man without fear or hesitation, driving his fist into the soldier's temple with such speed and force that the man was lifted clear off his feet. As his limp body hit the ground, Azriel lunged for his sword, but the second soldier, whose nose Azriel had broken just moments earlier in the Great Hall, was upon him before he could reach it. Grabbing the back of Azriel's shirt collar, he pressed the point of his knife under Azriel's chin, yanked him around and forced him to his knees. By the time he'd done so, the young soldier who'd tripped when the door had first flown open had managed to stagger to his feet and catch Persephone by the hair. She struggled valiantly, but having no weapons left but her teeth, nails, words and ability to punch, squirm and kick, she was soon knocked to her belly.

For an instant, no one moved, and the only sounds to be heard were the hiss and crackle of the dying fire, the panting gasps of the soldiers and Persephone's fierce grunts of resistance.

Then, and only then, did the Regent Mordesius lurch into the room.

From her place on the floor, Persephone was treated to a most unwanted glimpse of the bare legs that were otherwise concealed by his long, fur-trimmed robe of velvet. Grimacing, she craned her neck that she might instead look up into the shockingly handsome face of the monster who'd ordered her death all those years ago and who was about to do so again.

His head bobbing as though the delicate stalk of his neck was too frail to hold it high and steady, the Regent returned her stare with eyes so dark and fathomless that they were like pits into which one might fall without end.

Lurching a little farther into the room, he stumbled and nearly tripped over the legs of the soldier with the dagger in his throat. Forced to jerk his twisted body upright to avoid falling, the Regent was unable to bite back a cry of pain.

"Useless imbecile!" he snarled, glaring down at the body as though it had purposely put itself in his way.

"Lady Bothwell murdered him," reported the smash-nosed soldier, digging his knife a little deeper into the flesh beneath Azriel's chin.

Mordesius's eyes slid from Persephone's thickly lashed violet eyes to the amethyst necklace that dangled above her breasts, then down the length of her pinned body to where her long legs lay sprawled wide beneath her bunched skirts.

"That faithless whore is no lady," said Mordesius, his thin chest heaving. "She is a meddling complication who does not deserve a quick death but shall yet receive one."

At these words, Persephone began to struggle with renewed vigor. Mordesius ignored her in favor of addressing himself to Azriel, at whom he was now staring with undisguised loathing.

"Attempt to play the hero and I will order her punished so brutally and at such length that death, when it eventually comes, will seem a most welcome escape. Am I clear?"

"You are," said Azriel through his teeth, as he slowly unclenched his fists.

With a smile that showed his own perfect teeth to their best advantage, Mordesius shifted his gaze to the young soldier who was kneeling on Persephone's back. Licking his lips, he said, "Lift her head higher that I may watch her eyes—first as you end the miserable life of this Methusian cockroach with whom she so brazenly defiled herself, and thereafter as her life's blood drains from the mortal wound that you shall presently inflict upon her own pretty white throat."

The young soldier on Persephone's back hesitated for only a moment before twining his fingers tighter in her wild, dark hair and lifting her head so high that her back was arched almost to the waist.

Mordesius leaned his bobbing head a little farther forward. Then, without taking his eyes off Persephone's face, he breathed, "Do the Methusian."

The smash-nosed soldier holding Azriel nodded.

"No, please! Your Grace, I'll do *anything*!" begged Persephone as she twisted and squirmed with all her might.

Mordesius sighed softly at this but did not rescind his order. The smash-nosed soldier, meanwhile, struggled to get a proper hold of Azriel's recently shorn auburn hair. Upon finally getting the grip he sought, he growled with satisfaction and raised his blade.

With a lopsided little grin, Azriel looked over at Persephone— his last goodbye.

Desperately, though in a voice as haughty, cold and noble as could be, Persephone cried, "As a princess of the blood, I order you to release that man at once!"

In spite of himself, the smash-nosed soldier froze.

"Do it!" bellowed Mordesius in a sudden rage. "Do it now, you worthless piece of—"

His last words were lost in the strangled shriek he emitted as a strong hand yanked him backward by his hair, and a dripping dagger was pressed against his throat.

"I b-believe that you forgot about me again, Your Grace," stammered the pockmarked servant.

"Unhand me at once, you interfering lowborn nobody!" screamed Mordesius. "Unhand me or I will see you slaughtered without mercy!"

In response, the trembling woman adjusted her grip on the hilt of the dagger she'd pulled from the throat of the dead soldier. Fixing her colorless eyes upon the soldiers that held Persephone and Azriel, she said, "Release the princess and her lover—"

"He's not my lover," squeaked Persephone.

"Or your master is dead."

"Release them and *you* are dead!" shrieked Mordesius as he feebly struggled against the humiliatingly iron grip of the woman made strong by years of toil. "Unless . . . unless, of course, this woman releases me," he added in a deliberately less deranged voice. "If she releases me, you may release them."

At this, the servant cast an uncertain glance toward Persephone. "Your Highness?" she asked.

"Do not release *or* kill him," said Persephone, who knew that she, Azriel and the servant were finished the instant the Regent was dead or beyond the threat of death. To buy time to figure out what to do, she added, "I would ask the Regent some questions before deciding what to do with him."

At these words, Mordesius stopped struggling and looked down at her.

"By the scar I bear upon my arm, you know me to be the elder twin of the king," she began.

"Yes," replied Mordesius.

Persephone's heart leapt at the admission. "The night I was born, you could have murdered me in the birthing chamber and told the world I'd been born dead," she continued. "Instead, you ordered a lackey with mismatched eyes to spirit me beyond the castle walls, there to kill me and dispose of my body. Why?"

"It was an error," admitted the Regent as he impatiently thrust his gnarled, shiny pink hands into the pockets of his robe. "The Methusian Seer had promised old King Octavio a son, and it never even occurred to me that she might have been telling a half-truth. Since Methusians are known to be liars of the highest order, this was an exceedingly foolish mistake on my part, but that's as may be. The instant you slithered from between your mother's legs, I knew I had to get rid of you. It was that or risk having the nobility challenge my right to rule the kingdom on behalf of the weakling prince born second. Believing that disposing of you in plain view of those who'd attended your birth was too dangerous, I made alternate arrangements. In hindsight, of course, I see that I ought simply to have held a pillow over your tiny face and been done with it."

"Since you later disposed of all who'd attended her birth anyway," said Azriel coldly.

"Not all," corrected the Regent with a sinister sideways glance at the servant who still held him fast. "Only all who mattered."

"Including my mother," said Persephone.

"Oh, I had no hand in her death," demurred the Regent. "The queen died of childbed fever. So in truth, Princess, it was you who killed your mother—you and your brother, the king."

As he spoke these last words, Mordesius yanked his hand out of his pocket and drove it back toward the belly of his captor. Azriel bellowed a warning, but Persephone didn't even have time to do that. She saw a brief flash of steel and then heard the surprised grunt of the servant as the Regent's hidden blade was buried to the hilt. With a grunt of his own, the Regent awkwardly twisted from the woman's failing grasp on his beautiful dark hair. Turning, he stabbed her again and again, punctuating each knife thrust with a jubilant cry.

"FOOL! IMBECILE! TO THINK—THAT YOU—COULD BEST—THE MIGHTY—REGENT—MORDESIUS!"

It went on and on and on. When he finally finished punishing the lifeless body at his feet, straightened up and turned around once more, the Regent was beaming and splattered with gore. "That useless, lowborn nobody thought she could best me," he panted. "But she could not! And neither can you, Princess!"

"I don't care about besting you!" burst Persephone, who was shaking with horror. "I don't care about being a princess or about anything that goes along with it. I only want my companions and me to be allowed to live!"

"Your companions?" spat Mordesius, his happy countenance vanishing at once. "Do you perchance mean this smug cockroach and the Methusian brat you stole from my dungeon? Are these the *companions* of which you speak, Princess?"

"Yes," gulped Persephone, relieved that he did not appear to know about the girl who was currently hiding in the stables, or about the dog, the horse and the hawk who'd followed her so well and so far.

With a snarl, the Regent gestured for the young soldier to haul Persephone to her feet. Plucking the dagger from the cooling hand of the murdered servant, Mordesius thrust it so close to Persephone's face that she could smell the tang of fresh blood. "If you'd kept this blade to protect yourself instead of using it to save the life of the drab that now lies dead before you, you might yet have had a fighting chance," he hissed. "But you did not, and so you and your so-called companions are doomed. Which is as it should be, Princess, for though I tried valiantly to make you see that servants are replaced as easily as smashed dinner plates, you are as stubborn as your peasant-hearted brother when it comes to understanding that there are those who matter and those who merely take up space. And that is why I know I will be doing the kingdom of Glyndoria a glorious service by sending you both onward into whatever dreary afterlife awaits you."

"Wait—what do you mean 'both'?" gasped Persephone. "You . . . you can't possibly mean to kill King Finnius as well?"

"I can and I do," said Mordesius silkily. "How else am I to become king except by disposing of the one whose backside currently warms the throne?"

"But it would be a wasted effort!" she cried. "The Erok nobility would never accept you as king!"

Mordesius smiled gloatingly. "You are wrong, Princess, for Lord Bartok has promised that as soon as I announce his daughter's betrothal to the king, he will force the king's Council to name me heir apparent and to accept me as such. Thereafter, if the king should die—and I assure you that he will die, most agonizingly—I shall ascend to the throne."

Knowing from experience that those in positions of power rarely responded well to being spat upon, Persephone bit her lip to keep from doing so as she frantically searched her mind for some way to save the king and the kingdom, even if she could not save herself and her companions.

Before she could come up with any clever ideas, however, Azriel made the situation a thousand times worse by giving voice to what he had to know must be the Regent's greatest agony.

"Even if all that you say is true, Your Grace, you still can't be king. From the neck up, you look the part well enough. But from the neck down, it is another story entirely, isn't it?"

Two

AT AZRIEL'S WORDS, Persephone felt the blood drain from her face. There were easy ways to die and hard ways to die, and drawing attention to the Regent's terrible injuries must certainly guarantee the very hardest death of all.

"Azriel," she breathed, giving her head the tiniest of shakes.

"It's true, Princess," insisted Azriel with a provocative roll of his own powerful shoulders. "Even if he had other than base blood running through his veins—which he does not—how could he ever be accepted as king? Look at him! He can hardly hold up his own head!"

At this, the gore-splattered Regent lifted both his head and Persephone's bloody knife as high as he was able. Slowly, he began slouching toward the kneeling Methusian and the smash-nosed soldier who yet held him by the hair.

Inwardly cursing Azriel for a reckless fool, Persephone hissed his name again, but he took no notice.

Instead, careless of the knife that was still pressed against his throat, he deliberately ran his hand from the sculpted ridge of his chest to the hard flatness of his stomach, and kept talking.

"His Grace hasn't the strength and vitality to set him above other men," he explained as he gazed placidly up into the livid face of the madman who was advancing upon him. "There is not a nobleman alive who believes that he could wield a sword in defense of the kingdom or ride a great hunter or even dance at his own banquet. And certainly none believe that he could ever get an heir upon a suitable wife, for there is not a noblewoman in the realm who would willingly lie with him the way he is now. It matters not that his face is handsome and that he is powerful and rich. When even the lowest lowborn slattern in the kingdom looks at him, I promise you that all she can see are his dark heart, his scarred limbs and his limp, useless—"

"Silence!" screamed the Regent. Savagely wiping spittle off his chin with the back of his shaking hand, he panted audibly and stared down at Azriel as though trying to decide what piece of him to slice off first.

Seeming bizarrely gratified by Mordesius's reaction, and looking so fearless that Persephone decided he was not reckless but utterly insane, Azriel leaned forward and whispered, "Let us go and I can change all that, Your Grace. Let us go and I can change *everything*."

With an animal noise somewhere between a howl and a snarl, Mordesius slashed with the dagger.

Azriel jerked his head to the side so quickly that the point of the dagger missed him entirely and instead sliced open the cheek of the soldier who held him. As it did so, Persephone lunged against the hold of her own captor. When he did not let go, she flung her head back as hard as she could and was savagely pleased to hear the sound of his nose breaking.

Unfortunately, Azriel did not use the moment of distraction to try to escape. Even more unfortunately, he resumed speaking.

"Your Grace, I can see to it that you are healed so well that it is as though you'd never been burned at all," he murmured in a voice so seductive that Persephone found herself responding to it in spite of the rather distracting moans of pain issuing from the freshly injured soldiers. "Imagine your back strengthened, your legs straightened, your chest broadened. Feel the raw power of your fists and the fleetness of your feet. See yourself leading the hunt astride the fiercest beast in the royal stables, bringing down a ten-point stag at full gallop with one arrow shot from your mighty bow. Envision yourself striding briskly through the halls of the imperial palace with your head held high with ease, drinking in the admiring gazes of noblemen and setting every noblewoman in sight panting with lust, ready to claw out her own sister's eyes that she might lie with you next. Not for gifts or wealth or position but for the sensual pleasure of knowing you as the man you were ever meant to be. Imagine it all, Your Grace, and know that I—and I alone!—can make it happen."

For a long moment after Azriel stopped speaking, Mordesius smiled down at the handsome Methusian but did not seem to see him, so lost was he in the breathtaking vision of what could be.

Then his smile faded, and his dark eyes refocused and hardened.

"Do not play with me, cockroach," he snarled, "for I know your Methusian tricks will not cure injuries as old and as great as mine. Not even your blood will cure them—not even the blood of the very youngest of your clansmen will cure them!"

Persephone saw Azriel flinch at the Regent's offhand reference to the monstrous crimes he'd committed upon Methusian infants, but his voice was steady when he said, "I do not speak of tricks or blood, Your Grace. I speak of the healing Pool of Genezing."

Pressing her lips together to keep from groaning aloud at the folly of attempting to tantalize the Regent with that old Methusian myth, Persephone waited for the damaged man to scoff or stab or scream. To her surprise, however, he froze as though stunned.

Then, in a careful voice, he said, "Since the day Balthazar stumbled into his own funeral babbling about having found the healing pool, General Murdock has searched endlessly and never found a trace of it. Moreover, I personally interviewed all those in whom Balthazar might have confided, and I did so using the most persuasive interview techniques at my disposal. Indeed, I interviewed many of them to death! I even interviewed Balthazar himself to death—him, who could have stopped the slaughter of his people simply by naming the pool's location. Tell me, cockroach, if it really existed and Balthazar had found it, why would he not have told me what I sought to know?"

"Because he was not a fool," replied Azriel. "Do you imagine that he believed for one instant that you would stop the killing? You are the one who goaded the old king into murdering my people in the first place. How would telling you the location of the healing pool have changed the old king's fear that my people intended to use its power to become richer and more powerful than he?"

"So," murmured Mordesius in a wondering voice, "Balthazar denied me the location of the pool because he did not see any advantage to be gained by doing otherwise."

"Plus, I do not believe he liked you overly much," admitted Azriel.

Mordesius narrowed his eyes. "You, on the other hand, must like me uncommonly well, cockroach," he said menacingly, "for you are the first Methusian who has ever offered to reveal to me the location of the pool."

"That is because besides Balthazar himself, I am the first Methusian who *could* make such an offer," said Azriel. "For you see, Your Grace, Balthazar was my father."

Persephone, who'd been told that Azriel had no memory of his life before having been abandoned to the Methusians as a child, felt a stab of betrayal at the thought that it had all been a lie.

Mordesius appeared genuinely shocked. "But . . . but that is impossible," he spluttered. "Balthazar never took a wife!"

"A man needn't take a woman as wife to get a child upon her," observed Azriel mildly.

Mordesius said nothing to this, but his dark eyes roved over Azriel as though seeking confirmation of his remarkable paternity. Apparently, he found it, for at length he sighed and said,

"You're a bastard, then."

"Yes," said Azriel without shame, "and I was but a little bastard when my father returned with news of his great discovery. A little bastard beneath the notice of one as great as yourself, Your Grace, but one with ears to hear my father's whispered words and a memory to hold them safe all these years."

With a shuddering gasp, Mordesius let Persephone's dagger slip from his fingers and reached his shiny pink hands toward Azriel as though he meant to squeeze the words and memories right out of him. Halfway to Azriel's throat, however, he drew his hands back to his chest and gave his heavy head such a violent shake that he winced in pain.

"If you speak the truth, your father's whispered words were his legacy," he said harshly. "Why would you betray him now? For love of your own worthless hide? For love of the little cockroach you stole from my dungeon? For love of the princess you defiled?"

"He didn't defile me," clarified Persephone without thinking.

Neither man looked at her.

"I would do so for all of the reasons you mentioned," said Azriel, "as well as a sizable bag of gold."

Persephone's insides curled at this, but Mordesius nodded as if a demand for gold was at last something he could understand. Then he cocked his head to one side and said, "You do not seek a promise that the persecution of your people will end?"

"I do not see the point of seeking empty promises," said Azriel, looking away.

Mordesius laughed loudly. The young soldier holding Persephone immediately joined in but stopped in a hurry at the look Mordesius gave him.

"Freedom for a chosen few and a bag of gold it is, then," nodded Mordesius, his dark eyes glittering in anticipation.

Before Azriel could nod back, sealing the bargain, Persephone suddenly realized what was missing. "Wait!" she blurted, stepping forward so forcefully and so unexpectedly that she nearly broke free of the young soldier. "There is one more thing! As a further condition of Azriel revealing the location of the healing pool, you must abandon your aspirations for the throne *and* your plans to murder the king. You must leave my . . . my brother to rule the kingdom. You must content yourself with seeing your injuries healed that you might become desired above all others!"

At the mention of being so desired, Mordesius lowered his unblinking eyes to Persephone's cleavage. Then his gaze slid sideways, and for a long moment he stared into the dying fire as though carefully considering this new condition that had been set for him.

"Very well," he announced at length. Shuffling over to where Azriel yet knelt with his hair in the grip of the older soldier, he breathed, "Tell me, Methusian: Where is the healing Pool of Genezing?"

"I don't know," said Azriel.

Persephone and the wounded soldiers inhaled sharply; Mordesius's dark eyes bulged in outrage.

"I do not know *yet*," amended Azriel calmly, before the Regent could hack him to pieces. "My father's whispered words were not of the location of the pool but rather of the clues that would lead to it. Release the princess, the boy and me, and we will follow the clues and find the pool."

"Never!" snapped Mordesius. "Give me the clues, and I will find the pool myself!"

"No."

"GIVE ME THE CLUES, YOU SLY COCKROACH, OR YOU AND THE PRINCESS ARE *DEAD*!" screamed Mordesius.

"Kill us and you will suffer your terrible injuries to the end of your miserable days," said Azriel bluntly.

Mordesius's eyes bulged again. He opened his mouth as though he meant to scream in protest, then snapped it shut again at once. "Fine!" he snarled through gritted teeth. "I will release you, the princess and the boy to find the pool—"

"And you will not harm the king," interjected Persephone.

Mordesius rounded on her. "Oh, I wouldn't *dream* of it, Princess," he sneered. "For you see, I could not imagine a better way to guarantee that you and the cockroach will deliver that which has been promised than for you to know that your dear, *dear* brother is in my power, and that if you make trouble for me before leaving the imperial capital or fail to return with proof that you have found the Pool of Genezing, then he will die in mortal agony."

Three

THE BARGAIN STRUCK and the consequences of failure made abundantly clear, Mordesius nevertheless ordered the soldiers not to release Persephone and Azriel.

At least, not yet.

"I shall fetch General Murdock," he informed them as he turned, lifted the hem of his robe and began fastidiously picking his way around the gore and bodies strewn about the small chamber. "Upon his arrival, you will release the princess and the cockroach into his custody, assist him in cleaning up this mess and receive your reward for a job well done."

"Thank you, Your Grace!" cried the younger soldier, grinning eagerly in spite of his badly mangled nose.

"Wait!" Persephone called after the departing Regent. "I wish to speak with my brother, the king."

"You may speak with him tomorrow," said Mordesius without stopping or looking back at her.

"I would speak with him now."

Mordesius did not offer further reply to the woman he'd once known as Lady Bothwell. Indeed, he'd barely trusted himself to speak to her at all. His loins yet stirred at the memory of her on the floor at his feet—struggling futilely, begging him not to kill the cockroach, promising him that she'd do *anything*. Mordesius bit back a groan at the thought. He knew he should hate the princess for all that she'd done to him, and yet he found himself lusting after her all the more. The king was no longer a rival for her romantic affections, and though she was clearly willing to go to some lengths to prevent the death of the cockroach, she'd made a point of insisting that they were not lovers. It made no sense unless . . . unless the unusual appetites that Mordesius had detected in her from the start had been genuine. His cold heart beat a little faster at the possibility. Although she was unquestionably a princess of the blood, the fact that she'd murdered one of his soldiers and broken the nose of another suggested that she'd been raised in the gutter. Who could say what she'd seen and done down there? Who knew the depths to which she'd sunk in her fight for survival, and how the act of sinking had twisted her soul?

His mind swirling with the images these thoughts inspired, Mordesius breathed heavily as he lurched down the otherwise deserted flagstone passageway toward the approaching figure of his repulsive henchman. When he drew near, General Murdock silently stepped out of the concealing shadows to stand before him.

"I came as soon as I heard, Your Grace," he said in his impassive way.

"Well, it wasn't soon enough," snapped Mordesius, gesturing to the sticky splatter on his hands, face and robe. "As you can see, I was forced to take matters into my own hands."

Above his small mouth and weak chin, General Murdock's long, thin nose twitched as though he could smell the splatter, and was much drawn to it. "I am certain that Your Grace acquitted himself most admirably," he murmured. Tugging a brilliantly white silk handkerchief from the sleeve of his impeccably tailored black doublet, he offered it to his master.

Somewhat mollified, Mordesius accepted the proffered handkerchief, spat upon it and began matter-of-factly wiping the gore from his face and neck. "I *did* acquit myself most admirably, Murdock," he acknowledged with relish. "She thought she could best me, but she could not."

General Murdock smiled thinly, showing long, yellow teeth. "So the one who called herself Lady Bothwell is dead?" he asked.

"The one who called herself Lady Bothwell is the king's sister, elder by but a few minutes," said Mordesius, flinging the soiled handkerchief back at the General, "and no, she is not dead."

Appearing unfazed by the news that the king was not really the king because he had a living twin with a greater claim to the throne, General Murdock tucked the handkerchief back into his sleeve, nodded his small head and waited patiently for his master to continue.

"The night she was born, I ordered her removed from the palace and killed," explained Mordesius. Scowling, he added, "Obviously, my orders were only partially carried out."

Murdock, a military man through and through, frowned at the thought of such dereliction of duty but did not bother to ask if the one who'd failed Mordesius yet lived. He knew his master well enough to know that whoever had been told to dispose of the infant princess had been killed the instant he'd reported his task complete.

Instead, Murdock said, "And now the princess has returned to claim her birthright?"

"Hardly!" snorted Mordesius, smoothing back his thick, glossy hair. "Before this night, I do not believe she had any idea who she really was. And now that she knows, she does not appear to seek the crown."

"Even so, I assume you want her killed?"

"Of course," said Mordesius, who paused before adding, "eventually."

Murdock looked at him but said nothing.

Mordesius swallowed hard, trying to contain the sudden surge of excitement he felt at the prospect of being healed and lusted after. "As we already knew, the one who claimed to be her eunuch slave is actually a Methusian," he blurted. "But what we *didn't* know is that he's not just any Methusian, Murdock. He's Balthazar's bastard! And he said that before his father died, he gave him clues that, if followed, would lead to the healing Pool of Genezing!"

For a long moment, General Murdock stared at his master with an expression that might have been sympathy if he'd been capable of such an emotion. Then he licked his thin lips and carefully said, "Your Grace knows that the Methusian was lying, of course."

Though Mordesius had not really expected Murdock to greet his words with enthusiasm, he nevertheless despised him for his lack of it.

"I know that the cockroach was probably lying," muttered Mordesius, reaching up to massage his aching neck. "In fact, I would say that he was almost certainly lying. Regardless, I could not take the chance that he was not, and so I struck a deal with him—and with the princess, who goes by the name of Persephone. I will release them unharmed with a bag of gold and a promise to keep safe the king, and in return they will find the healing pool and advise me of its location."

"I . . . see," said General Murdock, his protuberant black eyes darting from side to side.

"No, I don't think you do," snapped Mordesius, thinking for the thousandth time what a repellent creature the General was. "I am not such a fool that I would trust the word of a Methusian and his whore, princess though she might be. Tomorrow when they leave the imperial capital, you will take a small contingent of men and follow them in secret. If they find the pool, you will kill them. If they do not appear to be looking for the pool, you will kill them. If they lead you to a Methusian nest, you will wait until the matter of the pool is settled one way or another, and then you will go back and kill every man, woman and child that inhabits the nest. Meantime, I *will* keep safe the king, but only so that I may bend him to my will in the furtherance of my own ambitions. Now, give me your cloak," ordered Mordesius, who was suddenly impatient to be away. "I must go to the king at once, and I do not wish to suffer his tiresome curiosity—or, indeed, any court gossip—as to how my beautiful robe came to be ruined."

"Of course, Your Grace," murmured General Murdock, unclasping his long, black velvet cloak and carefully draping it about his master's bony shoulders. "And what shall I do with those of my men who witnessed your exchange with the princess?"

"Have them clean up the mess they made," said Mordesius as he wrapped the cloak tightly around himself, "and then give them their reward."

General Murdock rocked forward on the toes of his shiny black boots. "And have you any particular reward in mind, Your Grace?" he asked, touching his unusually small hands together.

"Yes, as a matter of fact I do," replied Mordesius, his lips cinching into a tight little knot at the memory of how the brawny, sure-footed fools had gawked when the cockroach had mocked and toyed with him in front of the princess. "Cut off their ears for what they heard, put out their eyes for what they saw and then finish them off any way you like. And when you are done with them, there is something else I would have you do this night, Murdock. Something that will not only give me a great deal of personal satisfaction but will also encourage the king to set aside any thoughts he might have of refusing to bend to my will . . ."

Four

AFTER MORDESIUS LEFT THE CHAMBER, Persephone spent several breathless moments twisting and scratching in an effort to get her captor to let go of her hair. When he finally grunted with irritation, transferred his grip to her biceps and dragged her to her feet, she broke off her attack. The thought of obediently waiting for the Regent's most favored general to arrive galled her, but to struggle against the iron grip of the young soldier seemed a futile and foolish waste of energy she might need to get through the minutes and hours ahead.

In the charged stillness that followed, Persephone tossed aside the necklace bearing the amethyst pendant the Regent had gifted her, pushed her tangled hair out of her eyes and looked over at the still-kneeling Azriel. Though she was certain he could feel her eyes heavy upon him, he did not return or even acknowledge her gaze. So, with a half-hearted shrug of her shoulders, she looked away. As she did, her eyes fell upon the prone body of the soldier she'd impaled with her dagger. Without warning, a wave of nausea swept over her as it suddenly occurred to her that he was dead, his wife was widowed and his children were fatherless—all because of her.

The night she'd met Azriel she'd bragged that she'd killed dozens of men with her dagger, but the truth was that until now, she'd never killed anyone.

Not on purpose, anyway, she thought as her eyes leapt to the mutilated body of the pockmarked servant. The poor woman had risked her life for Persephone—once as a frightened child in the queen's birthing chamber and again on this night—and her reward had been a gruesome end. And, terrible truth be told, she was not the only one in the realm who'd lately met such an end because of Persephone.

And then there is the queen, thought Persephone. *The Regent accuses me of causing the death of my very own mother, and he says I will do the same to my brother, the king. Unless . . . unless . . .*

Unless Azriel really was the bastard son of Balthazar, unless he really did know of clues that would lead them to the healing pool, unless they really were able to find it . . .

Unless . . . unless . . . unless . . .

"Azriel!" whispered Persephone, unable to help herself.

At the sound of his name on her lips, Azriel slowly turned his head until he was gazing directly into her face. His jaw was set, his lips were slightly parted and the flickering orange glow from the dying fire was shining in his eyes.

"Yes, Your Highness?" he asked politely.

So politely, in fact, that Persephone felt her heart grow as cold as the ice in his eyes. She found herself torn between treating him with even icier disdain, pleading with him to forgive her and spitting at him. Before she could do any of these things, however, General Murdock entered the room, followed closely by two beefy soldiers. In a surprisingly gentle voice, the General ordered her and Azriel released. As though heartily relieved to receive the order, the young soldier holding Persephone sprang away from her. The one holding Azriel grunted and gave him a shove that sent him sprawling.

After picking up the amethyst pendant and tucking it into his pocket, the General gave Azriel a look of longing, as though he couldn't help thinking what a fine price his severed head would have fetched. Then he turned his blank, beady eyes upon Persephone.

"Highness," he murmured, bowing from the waist.

Feeling like a fool, and certain that the General was mocking her, Persephone cast a darting glance at Azriel to make sure he wasn't laughing at her, too. When she saw that he wasn't even looking at her, she looked away from him, squared her shoulders and lifted her chin.

"Yes, General?" she said briskly as Murdock straightened up from his bow. "What is it that you want?"

"If it pleases Your Highness, you are to be escorted to your rooms, there to bathe and dine as befits your royal station," he murmured. "As for your, hmm, *companion*, as it is now common knowledge that he is neither the eunuch slave you had claimed him to be nor your Master of the Bath but rather a Methusian outlaw in possession of all his . . . equipment, it would obviously be a scandal if he were to spend the night in your chamber. Therefore, I would like to suggest that he be taken—"

"No," said Persephone.

Azriel, who'd risen to his feet and was now standing close enough to touch, finally looked over at her.

She ignored him.

General Murdock's nostrils flared. "Highness," he said as his gaze drifted back to Azriel's head, "you haven't even heard my suggestion."

"I don't need to hear it," said Persephone. It mattered not that she could cheerfully have given Azriel a kick for his present aloofness; it mattered not that she suspected he could cheerfully have returned the favor for her having lied to him, run out on his love and snatched out from under his nose the destiny she'd allowed him to believe might belong to him. In a matter of minutes, her whole world had been turned upside down! She'd gone from a freedom-hungry nobody playing dress-up to save an orphan she'd never met to a princess who now held the life of her kind, sweet, long-lost brother in her hands. She needed to make sure that Azriel would be able to deliver that which he'd promised—but even more than that, she needed *him*, in a thousand ways she did not wish to examine too closely.

And so, with a decidedly un-royal toss of her head, she said, "I care not a whit for what scandal it may cause, General. This man will accompany me to my chamber, and there he will stay for as long as I so desire."

Beside her, Azriel made a noise that could have meant anything.

Long, thin nose twitching, General Murdock hesitated for just a moment before bowing low and murmuring, "As you wish, Your Highness."

A quarter of an hour later, a rumpled, exhausted and thoroughly wrung-out Persephone faced the four servants who'd been assigned to her the night she'd arrived at the palace disguised as the intrepid Lady Bothwell.

"Shall I prepare a bath, Your Highness?" asked Martha, the eldest and most proper of the four.

Persephone looked limply toward the claw-footed tub by the fireplace. Back when she'd been naught but a grubby little starveling, the very idea of soaking in a hot bath while a handful of attendants massaged and soaped her tired limbs and washed and brushed her tangled hair would have sent her into paroxysms of ecstasy. Now, though she could certainly have used a bath, all she really wanted was to be left alone. The walk to her chamber had been interminable. Not only had Azriel insisted upon silently walking several paces behind her (purportedly out of deference to her great station), but the multitudes that had trickled out of the Great Hall to line the corridors of the palace had gaped and whispered until she hadn't known what else to do but to play the part of the princess with such skill that, to her mortification, they'd positively tripped over themselves in their haste to make their obeisance to her. At least most of them had. Some of them—most notably Lord Bartok, the most powerful nobleman in the realm—had only stared in a manner that informed Persephone that if her life as a nobody had been fraught with danger and uncertainty, it was nothing compared to what her life as a princess was going to hold.

"Thank you, Martha," sighed Persephone, "but I don't think I'll take a bath—"

"SHALL WE ORDER UP SOME FOOD THEN, YOUR HIGHNESS?" shouted little Reeta, who was clearly beside herself with excitement at the revelation of her mistress's true identity.

In spite of the fact that she could not seem to stop trembling, Persephone found herself smiling. "Not just now, Reeta," she said, "though perhaps you could order up a feast for us to share upon the morrow."

Dazzled by the mind-boggling honor of being invited to eat from the table of an *actual princess*, Reeta clasped her little hands beneath her chin and sighed deeply. As she did so, Persephone turned to the shorter, plumper of Reeta's two older sisters and thanked her for hiding the little Methusian boy who'd been rescued from the dungeon that night.

"Well, when your man Azriel dashed in here with the Regent's New Men at his heels, he asked *very* nicely," purred Neeka, with a lingering smile at Azriel. "Besides, Methusian or not, we'd not have seen the child returned to the dungeon for all the diamonds in the Mines of Torodania."

Tall, angular Anya, the sister whose tongue had been cut out by the Regent when she'd been a child of only eight years, gave a heartfelt nod.

"Well, thank you," repeated Persephone, trying not to feel piqued by the way Neeka was smiling at Azriel. "You've all been good to me, and I shan't forget that you were loyal and kind even when you knew me for an imposter. Even so, I must ask more of you this night. First, I want you to fetch little Mateo to us, for though I know you'd be good to him, I suspect he'd feel more comfortable in the care of his clansman. Second, in the royal stables, you will find hiding a girl named Rachel who looks very much like me. Bring her to me without letting anyone see her face, for I do not think we need to add to the confusion of this night. If you see a dog wearing a tattered pink bow, you may bring him to me, as well, unless he tries to bite you. If he tries to bite you, it is his way of saying that he'd prefer to keep his own company a while longer yet."

At this, Azriel snorted derisively. Persephone ignored him.

"In addition to the girl and the dog, you will find a horse named Fleet in the vicinity of a sugarberry bush or a pile of turnips," she continued. "Earlier this evening he performed magnificent feats of bravery, and I would have you see to it that he is thoroughly rubbed down, fed, watered and given a clean stall a safe distance away from the ill-tempered mare called Lucifer."

"And shall we bring your man Azriel with us for protection?" asked Neeka, her bosom heaving at the prospect.

Azriel smiled at her.

"No," said Persephone shortly. "You shall not, for I would have words with him."

After casting Azriel a look of lust-tinged pity, Neeka followed her sisters and Martha out of the room, the wooden peg fastened to the stump at her right knee making a quiet *tap tap tap* as she went.

As soon as they were gone, Persephone turned toward Azriel. Before now, upon finding himself alone with her after they'd faced certain death together, Azriel would probably have stepped close enough to wrap his arms around her. And maybe he'd have lifted her off her feet and crushed her to him as though he could never hold her close enough, or maybe he'd have waited until the intoxicating nearness of his strength had turned her knees to water and she'd melted against him of her own accord.

Now, however, he took not one step toward her, only stood staring down at her with those eyes like river ice.

Persephone had no idea where to begin. If he'd shown his hurt, she'd have tried to soothe him; if he'd shown his anger, she'd definitely have fought with him. If he'd shown the least tenderness toward her, she knew for a certainty that she'd have collapsed into his arms.

But he showed nothing at all. Except for the shadows moving deep beneath the surface of the ice in his eyes, it was as though he'd gone to a place so far away that she could never hope to follow.

"I . . . I'm sorry that I lied and ran out on you, Azriel," she said at last.

"Oh?"

At the coolness of his tone, Persephone flinched and looked down at her hands. "I didn't want to hurt you," she said. "I was just . . . I was afraid for you. And for me," she added reluctantly, in the interest of complete honesty.

"Oh."

She waited for him to say something more. When he didn't, she lifted her head and looked at him. "Is that all you can say?" she asked, hazarding a tentative smile. "After everything we've been through together, all you can say is 'oh'?"

"What would you have me say, Your Highness?" he asked impassively.

Her smile vanished. "Don't call me that."

"As you wish, Princess," he intoned.

"Stop it!"

Scowling slightly, she eyed him askance, this chicken thief who'd bought her like a sow from market, embroiled her in a dangerous prophecy and was currently withholding from her the teasing warmth to which she'd become so accustomed. The teasing warmth that, truth be told, she'd never needed more desperately than she did at this moment.

Abruptly deciding to change tack, Persephone put her hands on her hips and said, "You know, you might do well to remember that you lied to me, too."

This brought a flush of indignation to Azriel's cheeks, thawing the ice in his eyes just a little. "What are you talking about?" he asked.

Gratified to have finally gotten *some* reaction out of him, Persephone swiftly stepped closer. "You told me you'd been abandoned to the Methusians as a child," she reminded him as she silently willed him to reach for her. "You said you had no memory of your early years."

Her words—or her sudden nearness—deepened the flush on Azriel's face so that his skin looked hot to the touch. "I never lied to *you*," he said, stepping away from her.

Persephone opened her mouth to protest, then closed it again as she thought about what he'd just said.

Then her heart began to pound.

"What are you saying?" she asked, pressing her hand against her throbbing chest. "Are you saying that you told me the truth, and you lied to the Regent? Are you saying that . . . that you are not Balthazar's bastard?"

"Yes, that is what I am saying, but—"

"So you do not know for a certainty that the healing Pool of Genezing exists?" she asked, her voice rising. "You have no knowledge of the clues that will lead us to it?"

"No, but—"

Persephone was so horrified by the implication that she thought she would fly at Azriel with her fists. Instead, her eyes rolled back into her head and her knees gave way without warning. Though she was not in a dead faint, she surely would have hit the floor if Azriel hadn't caught her first.

"Princess—Persephone—let me explain!" he exclaimed as he sank to his knees with her in his arms.

"You . . . you lied to save yourself from death, and your lies will cost the king his life," she gasped as she made a half-hearted attempt to push him away. "There is nothing to explain."

"Yes, there is something to explain," Azriel whispered, his grip on her easing ever so slightly. "Listen to me! Though I lied to save us *both* from death, my lies bought the king time as well, for I promise you that the Regent will not dare to harm him as long as he believes we may return to him with proof that the healing pool exists."

Struck by the soundness of this logic, Persephone immediately stopped struggling and lay limp as a child, reveling in the warmth of Azriel's shoulder against her cheek and the strength of his arms around her. "But how can we search for the pool if we don't know whether it exists and you haven't any clues?" she asked, craning her neck to look up at him.

Azriel stared down into her upturned face for so long that Persephone's heart began to pound again. Instead of leaning down to kiss her, however, he shook his head as though to clear it. Easing her off his lap, he helped her to her feet.

"I believe that the pool does exist, and my people have reason to believe that there are clues," he explained as he strode over to the long table by the shuttered windows and poured two goblets of mulled wine. "Over the years, a few have even gone in search of these clues."

"And have they found them?" asked Persephone, hoping she didn't sound as dismayed as she felt to find herself standing trembling and alone—again.

"Difficult to say, for none ever returned," said Azriel lightly. Walking back over, he handed one of the goblets to her before adding, "But that does not mean that we won't return, Princess."

Persephone gulped down some wine. "So you truly intend that we shall seek the pool?" she asked, wiping her mouth with the back of her hand.

"Yes."

"And . . . why would you take such risks for the life of an Erok king?" she asked, holding the stem of the goblet a little tighter.

"Since it sounds as though you do not seek the throne for yourself, keeping King Finnius alive and in power is the best hope my people have of seeing their persecution come to an end," explained Azriel with a shrug. "Besides, the healing pool is our sacred legacy, and I wish to see my people living in peace by its water's edge once more."

Persephone nodded and took another sip of wine. Just a few short hours earlier, she was sure that Azriel's response to that same question would have been to sidle close enough to take her breath away and to murmur in her ear that he would take such risks because he loved her desperately and knew that saving the life of this particular Erok king mattered more to her than almost anything.

But it was clear to her that things between them had changed. Or, more specifically, that his feelings toward her had changed. Though he was no longer as cold as he had been, neither was he quite as warm.

Even as Persephone was telling herself that this was probably just as well and that she had enough to worry about without worrying that she'd someday break the heart of this handsome rascal who'd once promised her the world, Azriel flashed his old pirate smile and raised his goblet to her.

"What are you doing?" she blurted, feeling distinctly unsettled by his sudden display of fondness.

"Toasting your health," he replied.

"Toasting my health?" she echoed in amazement. "But . . . but why?"

Azriel took a small step backward and smiled again. "Haven't you figured out what day it is, Persephone?"

Mutely, she shook her head.

"If it is the king's birthday today, then it is yours as well. And since we are about to venture forth together into gravest peril, and since I have made a solemn vow to protect your life with my own, and since I have a declared fondness for my own worthless hide, let me be the first to wish you a happy birthday, Your Highness—and to say that I sincerely hope that it will not be your last."

Five

AS MORDESIUS MADE HIS WAY through the crowded corridors toward the king's private chambers, he could tell by the way people stared and whispered that they'd guessed the truth: that the king and the woman known as "Lady Bothwell" were royal twins separated at birth, and that he, Mordesius, had had a hand in separating them.

Beyond enraging him, the stares and whispers made Mordesius more uneasy than he cared to admit. He was accustomed to nobodies treating him with painstaking courtesy borne of abject terror; he was used to noblemen treating him with frosty respect borne of an understanding that he had the power to raise and enrich—or break and impoverish.

Now, nobodies and nobility alike looked at him with morbid curiosity, as though they thought he was finished. As though they believed that when the come-of-age king learned of his past dark deeds he'd be transformed not from "the Great Regent Mordesius" to "Simply Mordesius" but from "the Great Regent Mordesius" to "Mordesius the Doomed."

Well, he snarled to himself as he came to a halt outside the king's heavily guarded chambers and barked to be announced to His Majesty, *we'll just see about that.*

The guard who'd hurried off to announce Mordesius returned in seconds.

"The king will see you at once, Your Grace!" he cried, rapping the butt of his poleax on the floor and clicking his heels together.

With a sour glance at the strong hand that clutched the poleax, Mordesius tugged General Murdock's black cloak more tightly around himself and slouched forward into the king's sumptuous, high-ceilinged inner chamber. The walls were hung with priceless tapestries and the polished floor gleamed in the light of many candles of such quality that they did not smoke or gutter in the least. A desk in one corner was strewn with the untidy evidence of neglected studies; across the room, a golden bowl of rare fruit glinted on a vast, ornately carved mahogany table. Next to the fruit bowl was one extremely small pile of white beans, one extremely large pile of white beans and a deck of playing cards that had been abandoned in apparent frustration. The insufferable cow who'd mothered King Finnius since infancy was sitting in a cushioned rocking chair near the fire with her feet propped up on the stuffed head of a great bear whose thick fur now served as a royal rug. In her lap lay one of the king's gem-encrusted velvet doublets. The sewing needle in her capable hand flew in and out of the fine material with such speed that it was almost a blur. She looked up when Mordesius entered the room but did not stop her mending or rise to her feet.

Mordesius resisted the urge to bare his teeth at her or even to indulge in visions of the skin flayed from her revoltingly sturdy peasant body. She would shortly be beyond the protection of her royal charge, in a location where he, Mordesius, would be able to personally assist her in finally coming to know her place in this world.

She could pay the price for her insolence then.

"Your Grace!" cried the lithe, dark-haired young king, striding forward with such purpose that it was hard to believe that only a short while earlier he'd been dancing in his shirt sleeves, smiling and bleary-eyed with drink. "What has happened? Where is Lady Bothwell? I tried to leave my chamber but the soldiers would not let me pass!"

"Your Majesty," murmured Mordesius in a voice oozing sympathy, "if you will recall, I ordered them to let no one pass, upon pain of death. It was for your own protection—"

"I don't care!" interrupted the king, jabbing his index finger into Mordesius's face so forcefully that the startled Regent took a stumbling step backward. "They should have obeyed my order, Your Grace. I am the king. I am of age to rule, and I *will* rule."

Out of the corner of his eye, Mordesius saw the cow placidly nod her bovine head.

Clenching the gnarled hands that yet held Murdock's black robe firmly in place, Mordesius willed himself to stay calm. "Of course the guards should have obeyed your order, Your Majesty," he said soothingly. "Only . . . perhaps they were unsure what to do seeing as how the power to rule the realm hasn't yet *officially* been transferred to you."

King Finnius coughed wetly into his sleeve. "I assure you that we will attend to that presently, Your Grace. At the moment, however, we have more pressing matters to discuss." Folding his arms across his slim chest, he said, "Back in the Great Hall, you claimed not to know why Lady Bothwell shared my scar. But Moira and I have come to the conclusion that there is only one possible way the scar on my arm and the one on the arm of Lady Bothwell could match so perfectly: we must have been scarred at the same time. And since Moira has been my nursemaid since I was handed to her at the threshold of the birthing chamber when I was but a few minutes old, and since the scar on my arm was yet raw when I was given into her care, it means that Lady Bothwell and I received our scars *inside the birthing chamber itself.* And the only way we could both have been inside the birthing chamber that night is if . . . is if . . ."

"Is if Queen Fey gave birth to both of them," said Moira blandly, when it became clear that the young king could not bring himself to complete the sentence that would at once bless him with a living sister and condemn him for having thought to marry her.

Mordesius bowed his head and breathed deeply, the smell of blood a calming reminder that in the end, vengeance was ever his. Then he lifted his head and said, "That is correct, Your Majesty."

"It is?" blinked King Finnius, who'd clearly expected his Regent to offer protest.

Even the cow looked surprised.

"Yes," said Mordesius. "Though I initially believed the erroneous reports that there was a plot afoot, after I had the opportunity to question Lady Bothwell in private and to more closely examine her scar, I knew that a miracle had taken place. I knew that your twin sister, the lost Erok princess, had finally come home to us."

At this, the king inhaled so sharply that he drove himself to a violent coughing fit. "It really is true, then?" he gasped as soon as he had the breath to do so.

"Yes, Your Majesty. And I would know because it was I who, at the request of the queen, gave you and the princess the wounds that scarred you," Mordesius explained in a voice thick with feigned emotion. "Your mother was dying of a raging fever brought on by the great strain of childbirth. She was ranting with fear that one of you would be stolen, and though I insisted that her fears were groundless, she insisted that I do as she bid, and so I did. Mere hours later, while I and the others were frantically tending to the dying queen, the unfathomable occurred: the infant princess was, in fact, stolen out of her cradle after her nursemaid succumbed to a powerful sleeping draught."

The king, who was still panting slightly, looked skeptical. "Even if all that you say is true, Your Grace, it does not explain why you did not immediately send out search parties. A royal princess had been kidnapped! She was marked as my twin—surely she might have been found!"

Mordesius pinched the bridge of his nose as though in an effort to hold back tears of regret. "I did not believe there was any hope that she'd be found alive, Your Majesty," he whispered. "That the nursemaid had succumbed to a sleeping draught led me to believe that Methusians were behind the kidnapping, and once I realized this, I could not believe they'd do other than murder the princess as retribution for the massacres perpetrated upon them by your father."

King Finnius turned away then and stayed with his back to Mordesius for so long that the Regent began to wonder if he'd gone too far pretending to cry.

Well, no matter if I did, thought Mordesius irritably. *There is more than one way to make a puppet dance, and very soon, this one will be dancing as though his life depended upon it.*

"Your Grace, why did you never tell me any of this?" asked King Finnius when he finally turned around again.

"Majesty, you'd already lost your mother and father," replied Mordesius, pretending not to notice the way the king was looking at him. "I saw no reason to burden you with yet another loss. Moreover, a kingdom headed by an orphaned boy king is a precarious thing at the best of times; I feared that if the nobility knew that a princess had been born first, they might question your right to the throne."

Mordesius hoped that the shocking news that he was not actually the rightful monarch might inspire the king to take a more sympathetic view of Mordesius's long-ago actions, and perhaps even to see the great advantage to himself of getting rid of the now grown-up princess.

Disappointingly, it did not appear to do either.

"The nobility might well have questioned my right to the throne—even as I, myself, must now do," frowned the king, "but they might also have accused you of killing the princess in order to protect your Regency."

"Yes," agreed Mordesius smoothly. "Either way, it would have been a disaster."

The king shrugged noncommittally. "And what is your explanation for why nearly all of those who attended my birth disappeared?" he asked.

Mordesius barely hesitated. "A princess had been kidnapped from a nursery that adjoined the birthing chamber. Someone from inside had to have arranged it."

"So you tortured them to find out who it was," said King Finnius, "just as you tortured poor Lord Pembleton's son."

"I did what I had to do," snapped Mordesius, loathing the other's holier-than-thou tone. "The only tragedy, Your Majesty, is that I never got the answers I sought."

"I see," said the king, stepping back from his Regent the way a nobleman might step back from a lowborn beggar stricken by the Great Sickness. "Well. Where is my sister now?"

"In her chamber," said Mordesius, resisting the urge to step forward and wrap his cold hands around the royal ingrate's throat. "She has asked that you not disturb her this night. I'm afraid . . . well, I'm afraid that she quite fell to pieces when she learned the truth about herself."

Smiling for the first time since the Regent had entered the room, the king said, "That does not sound like the Lady Bothwell I know."

You know nothing of Lady Bothwell, fool! shrieked Mordesius in his mind. Out loud he murmured, "Her real name is Persephone, Your Majesty, and I would be honored to make arrangements for the two of you to formally be reunited as brother and—"

"I'll make my own arrangements where my sister is concerned," interrupted the king. "However, I would have you send to me the servant who ran from the Great Hall—the one whose cries drew the attention of all to the matching scars. To have reacted as she did, the woman must have borne witness to the events in the birthing chamber, and since it would seem that she is the only living soul other than you to have done so, Your Grace, I am most eager to speak with her."

Mordesius sighed softly, recalling the delicious noise the drab had made when he'd first driven the blade into her belly. Then he cleared his throat and said, "Your Majesty, I am terribly sorry to have to inform you that the poor woman is dead."

Moira did not look the least surprised.

The king, on the other hand, looked utterly shocked. "Dead!" he blurted, his exclamation punctuated by yet another cough. "What do you mean 'dead'? Dead how?"

"Dead at the hands of the soldiers who sought to protect *you*," explained Mordesius mournfully. "Dead because they thought she meant to harm *you*."

Instead of flinching at the thought that a useless nobody had perished because of him as he once would have, the king grew very still.

"You ordered this?" he said.

Without taking his eyes off the boy, Mordesius slowly shook his head. "The deed was done by the time I arrived," he said. "And I can assure you that no one regrets it more than I, for that woman was the only one who could have confirmed all that I've told you. Had I only known that she existed—"

"You'd have long since had her tortured to death," said the king.

Mordesius opened his mouth to offer protest, then shut it again. Though he longed to fling open the shielding cloak and rub the king's squeaky-clean nose in the sticky mess clotted upon his robes, he'd have to be patient a while longer yet. He could not risk the open enmity of the fool until the princess *and* the cow were safely beyond anyone's ability to protect them. Then the peasant-hearted puppet would dance—or see those dearest to him pay the price.

It was this happy knowledge that allowed Mordesius to sound almost meek when he mumbled, "Majesty, if I have offended in thought or deed at any time during my long years of service to you, I stand ready to accept whatever punishment you see fit to mete out."

Out of the corner of his eye, he saw the nursemaid lean forward imperceptibly. The king said nothing for so long that Mordesius's cold heart began to pound out of fear that the fool was actually going to pass sentence and order him dragged away upon the moment.

But he did not. Instead, he said, "I do not seek to punish you, Mordesius. Though I confess that I find myself wondering at the tale you've told me this night, at present I've no proof of misdeed. And though I've lately come to realize that we do not share a vision of what a ruler should be, what is done is done. The past is behind us." He spread his hands wide, looking every inch the shining young king. "Tomorrow, a new day will dawn—and with it, a new era for the kingdom of Glyndoria!"

Though the cow by the fire looked disappointed, she nevertheless clapped heartily.

Reminding himself that he'd soon have the pleasure of mutilating the hands that so mocked him, Mordesius thanked the king for his munificence and cryptically suggested that he might be surprised by all that the following days would bring.

"Well," said the king with a weary chuckle, "I have always liked surprises."

"I know you have, Your Majesty," breathed Mordesius, bowing as low as his twisted back would permit. "Oh, I know you have."

Six

THE NEXT MORNING, Persephone awoke to the sound of little Reeta excitedly flinging back the plum-colored velvet bed curtains. While she was still blinking against the glare of the morning sun, tall, silent Anya opened the chamber door to a veritable army of kitchen servants bearing heavy platters of choice meats and cheeses, baskets brimming with breads, buns and pastries, bowls piled high with succulent fruits, pitchers of drink and dishes containing everything from clover honey and fresh butter to clotted cream, quails' eggs and a rainbow of quivering jellies. As usual, it was more food than Persephone could have eaten in half a lifetime, but she did not bother to ask why it should be so.

Clearly, the rumors of her prodigious appetite yet abounded.

After laying their burdens upon the long table beneath the open windows, every single one of the kitchen servants presented themselves at the foot of the great canopied bed to be dismissed. As they did so, each eyed the person-shaped lump beneath the covers next to Persephone with the electrified air of one who couldn't wait to share the tantalizing gossip that the long-lost princess had taken *another* lover besides the eunuch slave who was no eunuch at all but a handsome Methusian outlaw *who'd also spent the night in her chamber*!

In fact, the person-shaped lump in the bed was not "another" of Persephone's lovers. It was her doppelgänger, Rachel, the other girl the Methusians thought might be the key to seeing the prophecy of the Methusian king fulfilled at last.

The previous night, shortly after Azriel had toasted Persephone's health, Anya had returned to the room with little Mateo in her arms and Neeka at her heels. At Neeka's heels was Rachel, looking like a grubby ghoul on account of the smelly horse blanket she wore over her head to hide her startling likeness to the long-lost princess. Persephone had tugged off the blanket and tried to give her friend a hug, but Rachel had been quite unable to stop bobbing clumsy curtseys and babbling about what an honor it was to stand before Her *most* gracious Highness.

Persephone had been much dismayed by this behavior. Indeed, she did not know what she'd have done if Neeka had not come to the rescue by loudly whispering that although the court physicians would undoubtedly be eager to try to restore the girl's addled wits by drilling a hole in her skull, she, herself, felt that a very large goblet of wine might do the trick just as well.

Three very large goblets of wine later had seen Rachel bathed and comfortably curled up in a chair across from Persephone, laughing helplessly as Neeka solemnly imparted the happy, *happy* news that Azriel was not a eunuch after all.

Now, upon hearing the door shut behind the last of the deliciously scandalized kitchen servants, Rachel flung off the covers and sat up amid the mountain of feather pillows.

"I must say that being chased through the streets by a swarm of the Regent's horrid New Men, half-drowning in a filthy moat, coming within a hair of being stabbed, trampled and pitchforked to death and generally being terrified out of my wits was well worth a night's sleep in this bed," she announced as she yawned and stretched luxuriously.

"I know exactly what you mean," said Persephone, recalling her first night in the palace.

The two of them smiled at each other and then slid out of their respective sides of the bed in such unison that they looked more like one girl and her reflection than two separate girls. By the time they'd walked the ten paces to the table, Martha was already carving the roast pheasant, Anya was pouring tankards of mead and Reeta was breathlessly counting the honey buns to see if there were enough for each of them to have two. Neeka, meanwhile, was trying to feed a quail's egg to Azriel, who'd spent the night on the hard, cold floor without having made any attempt whatsoever to persuade Persephone that the bed was big enough for three, while little Mateo stood glued to his side watching the rest of them with the hooded eyes of a hunted child.

Persephone bade everyone good morning and was just about to point out to Neeka that Azriel could *probably* feed himself when there came a knock at the door. Martha immediately left off carving the pheasant to answer it. When she returned, she was carrying a folded, sealed piece of parchment.

"What is it?" asked Rachel as she sat down at the table, pulled the nearest large platter of meat toward her and began to eat.

Martha hesitated. "A letter," she said, "from the king."

Silence fell upon the room.

"What . . . what does it say?" asked Persephone.

Clearly pleased to have been granted the honor of opening the letter, Martha broke the wax seal and unfolded the creamy parchment. "It says only that the king wishes to see you as soon as may be."

Persephone took a deep breath. The king was so kind and sweet that she did not *think* he'd be angry with her for having pretended to be someone she was not and for having run out on him without a word of explanation or farewell after having shown him great affection. However, as she was rapidly discovering, some men could be funny about things like that. Moreover, her very existence threatened King Finnius's right to rule, and she had a fair idea that *all* kings could be funny about things like *that*.

"I suppose that means our feast will have to wait until after you're bathed and dressed," sighed Neeka as she reluctantly set the tiny quail's egg back in the bowl and took her hand off Azriel's thigh.

"Yes," said Persephone, trying not to sound pleased. "I suppose it does."

※

While Martha fetched the soaps and towels, Rachel picked out a gown and the sisters hauled buckets of steaming bathwater, Mateo left the chamber in the company of Azriel, who bid Persephone a polite goodbye without even *trying* to suggest that as her one-time Master of the Bath he ought to be the one to sponge her down.

An hour later, Persephone was freshly bathed and perfumed. Her hair was washed, brushed, oiled and piled atop her head in complicated twists and swirls, and she was exquisitely dressed in a full-skirted gown of forest-green velvet heavily embellished with gold brocade. She was halfway to the chamber door when she noticed lying on the floor the rusty key to the fetters she'd once worn. Azriel had pressed it into her hand the previous evening when he'd confessed that he'd ever been *her* slave; it had later slipped from her fingers when he'd swept her up in a passionate embrace. Flushing at the memory—and at the unexpected pang of regret the memory provoked—Persephone hastily snatched up the key, slipped it into her pocket and continued toward the chamber door.

Upon reaching it, she pulled it open, stepped into the hallway beyond and began hurriedly making her way toward the royal chambers in the southern wing of the palace. She kept her head down in the hope of not being noticed, but it was no use. As she swept past glittery-eyed nobles, hard-faced soldiers, clamoring petitioners and servants of all manner and station, it was nothing but curtseys and bows, whispers and stares. And she realized with a start that she'd forever lost the protection that went along with being beneath notice.

Henceforth, there will always be someone looking at me, considering me, wondering about me, plotting against me, she thought with a leap of anxiety as her fingers strayed through the torn pocket of her gown to the dagger at her thigh, which Azriel had been clever enough to palm the night before when he'd been shoved to the floor by his captor. *I will never be free to pursue my own destiny. I will ever be a slave to—*

A tiny, bright-eyed young noblewoman dressed in a gown of canary yellow hopped into the middle of the corridor so suddenly that Persephone, who still had her head down and who was practically running by this point, nearly tripped over her.

"Good day to you, Princess!" chirped Lord Bartok's daughter, Lady Aurelia, dropping into such a deep and respectful curtsey that it was hard to believe she'd recently tried to arrange to have Persephone thrown by a demented horse in the hope of seeing her neck broken.

"Good day," muttered Persephone, trying to step around her.

Lady Aurelia fluttered to one side, blocking her way without appearing to have done so on purpose. "I can only imagine what a shock it must have been to discover your true identity, Your Highness," she murmured in confidential tones. "It must be a great comfort to you to know that you already have at least one dear friend here at court."

Persephone, who knew of no such friend, looked puzzled.

"Me, Your Highness!" cried Lady Aurelia with all the false sincerity of a courtier born and bred. "I know my brother, Atticus, behaved like a bit of a cad last night—"

"Just before my horse kicked him in the head, your brother called me a whore, tore my gown, clouted me across the face and made clear his intention to use me for his 'entertainment'," said Persephone.

Those nearby gave scandalized gasps, but Lady Aurelia only laughed shrilly, as though her brother had meant to play the most marvelous prank. "Oh, men can be such beasts, can't they?" she giggled, clapping her small hands in delight. "Well, never mind him. It is our friendship—yours and mine!—that matters, Your Highness, and I hope that—"

"Excuse me," interrupted Persephone, pushing past Lady Aurelia with such determination that the flaxen-haired little noblewoman very nearly ended up on her backside.

"We will go riding again very soon, yes?" she trilled hopefully as Persephone hurried off down the corridor.

Persephone didn't bother to answer. Just ahead of her were the enormous gilt doors that opened into the echoing emptiness of the king's vast outer chamber. Shoving her way through them, she was about to call out to the guards on the far side of the chamber when a figure stepped out of the shadows behind her, startling her so badly that she'd drawn her dagger, hunkered down into a fighting stance and spun to face the threat before she realized what she was doing.

With a cry, one of the guards on the far side of the chamber bounded forward with his poleax poised to strike. The figure before Persephone impatiently waved him back, then stepped a bit farther out of the shadows. "You look much improved this morning, Highness," said Mordesius, his eyes gleaming at the sight of the blade he'd used to murder the pockmarked servant.

Slipping the dagger back into the scabbard at her thigh, Persephone rose up from her crouch and said, "What do you want?"

"I want many things," replied Mordesius huskily. "But what I want at this particular moment is to offer a suggestion."

Persephone did not ask what suggestion, but neither did she turn her back on him or walk away.

Mordesius smiled. "Last night I told the king that it was I who marked you and him as twins at the behest of your beloved mother, I who anguished after you were tragically kidnapped and I who joyfully recognized you for who you really were. I also told him that it was my overeager soldiers who killed the poor servant who'd borne witness to the events in the birthing chamber all those years ago," he explained. "I want to suggest that you say nothing that would cause the king to question this version of events."

Persephone nearly laughed aloud at his audacity. "And why do you suggest this?" she asked. "Is it because you fear that if the king were to learn the truth he would have you imprisoned—or worse?"

"I fear nothing," said Mordesius calmly. "I merely suggest that if the king was to hear your version of events, he might react in a way that would make it difficult for you and the cockroach to uphold your part of our little bargain. And that would make it *impossible* for me to uphold mine—an unfortunate thing given that you and those whose lives you would have me spare are yet within my grasp."

Curling her hands into fists, Persephone took an involuntary step toward him. "My companions—"

"Would be dead before you'd finished speaking the troublemaking words," confirmed Mordesius with a pointed glance at the poleax-wielding guards.

Persephone stepped back. "But the king—"

"Is one of those whose life you would have me spare," reminded Mordesius impatiently. "And if you think that I would allow you to see him without knowing for a certainty that you could not do or say anything to harm me, I encourage you to think again. Within the royal chambers, death waits beyond every wall, never more than a few paces away from His oblivious Majesty. Speak out of turn, Princess, and watch your dear brother promptly cut to pieces before your eyes."

Thinking to threaten him back, Persephone said, "The nobles—"

"Are loyal to no one but themselves," said Mordesius with a wave of his hand. "They bear me no love, but neither do they truly love the king, and his death—along with yours—would see the throne left vacant, waiting to be warmed by the pampered arse of the first noble fool who could fight his way to it."

"So I am well and truly trapped," said Persephone mutinously, "for to incite the king is to see him and my companions murdered and the kingdom torn apart by civil war."

"Exactly," beamed Mordesius, who had been so busy considering how his various threats would work to his personal advantage that he hadn't thought of it in precisely this way. "So enjoy your visit with the king, Princess. Give him whatever reason you think he'll accept to explain why you and the cockroach must leave the imperial city at once. And take comfort in the knowledge that before the great gates of Parthania close behind you, I will have given you a parting gift that will inspire you beyond your wildest imagination."

Seven

HAVING APPARENTLY SATISFIED HIMSELF that Persephone would behave, the Regent held out his bony arm and gallantly offered to escort her into the king's chambers. Though she was sorely tempted to grind the high, hard heel of her beaded slipper into his foot, her fear of him and of what he could do was too great for such an indulgence. Pushing past him without a word, she marched across the room and halted before the guards.

"I am here to see the king!" she declared, more loudly than she intended.

The nearest of the two guards, a wiry young man with an unusually shaped wine-colored birthmark on one cheek, bobbed his head and disappeared through the inner chamber door. A moment later, he reappeared and ushered her inside. After announcing her in a ringing voice, he vanished back through the door, leaving Persephone alone at the threshold of the king's inner chamber.

A movement by the window caught her eye.

The king!

Overcome by a sudden attack of nerves, Persephone gasped and dropped into a curtsey so low that her legs promptly gave way beneath her.

King Finnius strode over and stood before her. "It is good to see that some things never change," he said lightly as he extended his hand toward her.

"Yes, Your Majesty!" squeaked Persephone, who was so nervous that she ignored his proffered hand in favor of scrambling to her feet like a farm girl knocked off her milking stool.

"Henceforth, when we are alone together you must call me Finn," said the king, turning his head aside to cough.

"Yes, Your Majesty," agreed Persephone, even though she could no more imagine calling the king by his given name than she could imagine flying to the moon.

Except . . . except that he wasn't just the king. He was her brother, her twin, her *blood*.

Looking up into his eyes now, she realized that although they were blue and hers were violet, they were the same shape as hers and fringed just as thickly with dark lashes. And his hair was the color of hers, and his nose was the masculine version of her own, and—

"I cannot believe that you are my sister!" he burst.

"I know!" blurted Persephone, who hung her head before adding, "And, uh, I want you to know that I apologize for—"

"Entering my palace with the intent to cause mischief?" he suggested. "For enjoying my hospitality under false pretences? For allowing me to believe that you were bereft at the untimely death of your pretend husband? For attempting to run away without a word of farewell? For causing the son of the most powerful nobleman in the realm to be kicked in the head by a deranged horse?"

Persephone bit her lip against the urge to explain that brokendown old Fleet wasn't so much deranged as he was madly in love with her. "Yes, I apologize for all of those things," she mumbled, acutely embarrassed by the laundry list of her misdeeds.

Seeming equally embarrassed, the king mumbled, "I loved you, you know. I'd even intended to ask you to marry me."

Persephone was mortified beyond words, for although she'd always thought of King Finnius as handsome, sweet and kind, she'd never, ever, *ever* thought of him in "that" way. Even when Azriel had grumbled that the king was courting her, she'd never taken his accusations seriously. Indeed, she'd believed that Azriel's ridiculous comments were inspired by jealousy borne of the powerful attraction that existed—or at least *used* to exist—between the two of them.

Desperately, Persephone cast about now for the right thing to say to her smitten brother, but before she could think of anything cleverer than "uhhhh," the king's warm laughter rang out through the chamber.

"Lady Bothwell—I mean, Persephone—sister!" he said. "Do not fret. Like you, I grew up an orphan without kin, so it is a joyful thing to know that I am your brother. I realize now that I never truly had romantic feelings for you. It's just that when I came to see what a perfect queen you would make, I made myself *believe* that I did."

"But you did not," said Persephone, who wanted to be very clear on this point.

"No," agreed the king, who hesitated before asking, "Did . . . you ever believe you were in love with me?"

"Yes," lied Persephone at once, hoping that the lie would make Finn feel less foolish about his own feelings. "But I think it was the same for me—that I loved you but was not *in* love with you. Even more than this, I admired you, for I knew that you would one day be a great ruler."

"I like to think that I would have been," said Finn before clearing his throat and adding, "but, of course, we shall never know, for as the firstborn twin, the throne is yours by right of birth."

Persephone blinked at him. The previous twelve hours had been so crammed with staggering events and revelations that she'd not given even a passing thought as to what being firstborn might mean. Now that she did, her gut reaction was so powerful that it was almost violent.

"No!" she blurted.

"No?" said the king in surprise.

"No, I don't want the throne. No, I don't want to be queen."

"But you were born *first*."

"It doesn't matter."

"Doesn't matter!" exploded King Finnius, coughing so hard that he was forced to brace his hands against his thighs. "By the gods, of *course* it matters!"

"No, it doesn't!" insisted Persephone passionately. "You were raised a prince and groomed to be king. I have lived my whole life enslaved and yearning for freedom. Ruling a realm may be a great and grand thing, Your Majesty, but if you'll forgive me for saying so, it is naught but its own kind of enslavement, and I would not have it for anything!"

For a long time, the king remained hunched over, fighting to control his cough. At length, however, he raised himself up and regarded Persephone with slightly watery blue eyes. "Are you certain you'd not like . . . to take time . . . to ponder this matter further?" he panted.

"I've never been more certain of anything in my life," said Persephone. Then, concerned by his grayish pallor and the fact that he could not seem to catch his breath, she said, "Majesty, you do not look entirely well. Shall I fetch Moira?"

"No," he replied. "She sent word that she is unwell, and I would not have her disturbed."

"But—"

"I said no!" snapped the king, who was as contrite as could be the very next instant. "I'm so sorry! It's just . . . this cursèd cough makes me so wretchedly short-tempered at times. The court physicians concoct tonics and mix poultices and bleed me 'til I swear I've not a drop left in my veins, and *still* it persists. In truth," he dropped his voice a notch, "I cannot help but fear what will happen if it continues to get worse instead of better."

Forgetting that the trembling, dark-haired young man before her was the king, Persephone took a good grip of the front of his beautiful doublet. "Your cough will not get worse, do you hear?" she said, giving him a shake. "It will not get worse because I will not *let* it get worse."

"You are almost as convincing as the court physicians—and infinitely more terrifying," declared Finn with a breathless chuckle.

"Indeed, I would not be a bit surprised if your presence by my side in the coming months was enough to *frighten* my poor cough away."

Realizing that now was the time to explain to the king that she would not be by his side in the coming months, Persephone released her hold on his doublet and surreptitiously eyed the tapestry-covered walls for the spot from which death would come charging if she was to whisper troublemaking words to the king. *If* it would come charging, that is. Perhaps the Regent had been exaggerating or bluffing; perhaps the wisest and safest course of action would be to tell Finn the truth.

Even as she considered doing this, however, Persephone heard a sound behind the nearest wall. Heart pounding, she stepped away from Finn so fast that she snapped off the heel of her left slipper, lost her balance and would have fallen if Finn had not reached out and caught her hand.

"What you heard was only a rat. It seems there is ever one scuttling about in there," he confided as he steadied her. "Fortunately, they hardly ever manage to find their way into my chambers, so you needn't be afraid."

"I am . . . I am not afraid," gulped Persephone. "I just . . . I was startled and . . . and I suppose I was nervous about telling you that I must leave Parthania tomorrow."

"What?" said the king in amazement. "Why?"

It was on the tip of Persephone's tongue to concoct an elaborate lie. Then she thought about how kindly the king had forgiven her for her earlier falsehoods and how warmly he'd accepted her as kin, and she knew that she didn't want to lie to him any more than she absolutely had to.

And so, taking a deep breath, she said, "Do you remember my eunuch slave, Azriel?"

"Of course, though I am told that he is neither slave nor eunuch," replied the king in the carefully neutral voice of one who was trying very hard not to sound disapproving.

"That is true," said Persephone carelessly. "But the more important truth is that he intends to undertake a search for the healing Pool of Genezing, and I intend to go with him."

For a long moment, the king said nothing. Then, in the same neutral voice, he said, "The Pool of Genezing is a Methusian myth, Persephone."

"Azriel has reason to believe that it is real, and I made a promise that I'd help him find it," she replied, taking care not to mention that it was the Regent to whom she'd made the promise.

Finn looked genuinely alarmed. "You should not have made such a promise, Persephone, for even if Azriel is right and the pool is out there somewhere, I cannot see how the search for it could do other than put you in mortal danger! Let Azriel find the pool and be well rewarded for his efforts."

Certain that the Regent would not approve of the idea of Azriel going off on his own, Persephone shook her head. "I must go with him," she insisted. "I gave my word of honor, and besides, it is the only way I can be certain of learning the location of the pool. I trust Azriel, but I understand that he has no reason to trust me—or you, for that matter. For years his people have been persecuted in your name. They've been hunted and slaughtered; their infants have been bled like pigs for the healing power of their Methusian blood." The king's face had gone gray again, but Persephone pressed on. "If I were Azriel, I might think that the wisest and safest course of action for me to follow upon leaving the imperial city would be to get as far away as possible and to never return. And that is why we cannot send him on this quest by himself."

"I will send soldiers—"

"Soldiers committed the very atrocities of which I spoke!" exclaimed Persephone. "You cannot send soldiers, Your Majesty. It *must* be me who accompanies Azriel on his search for healing waters, and I am glad of it, for I cannot be certain of being able to frighten your cough away and now that I have found you, I could not abide losing you."

"I could not abide losing you, either," said Finn, with feeling. "That is why—"

"You will not lose me," interrupted Persephone with more confidence than she felt. "I've had an unusual upbringing for a princess and as a consequence I am unusually capable of taking care of myself. Moreover, Azriel has made a solemn vow to protect my life with his own, and while I must admit I've saved his life more times than he's saved mine, his vow ought to count for *something*."

"He's a good wrestler," acknowledged the king as he struggled to suppress a cough.

"I suppose," grimaced Persephone, recalling the lovely afternoon Azriel had ruined by foolishly provoking the king into a wrestling match.

"Even so—"

"And then there is this: if we find the healing pool, think of all the good you could do for your subjects," said Persephone enticingly. "Think of the pain and suffering that could be alleviated by even a thimbleful of healing water administered at your command. And you would not have a thimbleful at your disposal but an endless wellspring! If you will not let me go for the sake of allowing me to honor my word or for the sake of your own health, Your Majesty, you simply *must* let me go for the sake of your subjects!"

The king grimaced at her for saying the one thing he could not argue against. "Very well," he said, flinging his hands into the air. "Though you've not exactly asked for my permission to join Azriel on the quest for the healing pool, I grant it nonetheless—provided you come back to me in one piece."

Persephone nodded and tried not to think about the many reasons she might come back to him in *more* than one piece.

Or not at all.

Her imminent departure agreed upon, the king sent a note to Azriel asking him to make adequate preparations for the journey and granting him permission to freely requisition whatever he required in that regard. He then issued a royal command that Persephone spend the entire day with him. Smiling fondly, she solemnly declared herself the most loyal of subjects and vowed to obey him even unto death.

The two of them spent the rest of the morning lounging in the king's inner chamber sharing stories from their respective childhoods. Finn told of what it had been like to be raised by servants. He shared how it had felt to be a very small child dining alone in silence at the head of a table that could comfortably have seated forty. He described his first pony, the topiary maze a favorite gardener had once fashioned for his amusement and the stuffed rabbit named Sir Wabbity that Moira had made for him out of a handful of velvet scraps. With a faraway look in his eyes, he recounted the first time he'd stood alone upon the Grand Balcony to acknowledge the throngs of cheering lowborn subjects beyond the palace walls. He told of how he'd had to stand on his tiptoes to see over the stone balustrade, how his small neck had felt as though it would snap under the weight of the golden crown upon his head and how he'd later been scolded by Mordesius for waving too enthusiastically and smiling too much.

Persephone enjoyed Finn's stories very much, and though her own stories were bleak by comparison, she shared them with an uncharacteristically willing heart. She described years of waking each morning before dawn to haul water for the master's bath, and to polish silver and beat rugs and chop vegetables and wash floors and hang laundry and scrub out fire-blackened pots that were nearly as big as she was. She recalled collapsing exhausted into the warm ashes by the dying fire late each night only to lie awake for hours wondering about the parents she'd never known. She told of the terrible evening she'd been wagered by the master, who'd lost her to a tavern owner in a game of dice; she recounted how the tavern owner had been forced to drag her, kicking and screaming, away from her beloved Cookie and the only home she'd ever known. She told how the tavern owner had soon thereafter given her to the man who'd tried to stick his hand up her skirt and received a fork in the arm for his troubles, and how that man had turned around and sold her to a New Man overseer at the Mines of Torodania. She spoke of arriving at the mine to find herself brutally shorn, clothed in rags and driven down into a section of the mine so restricted that it was guarded not only by soldiers but also by huge, slavering dogs trained to tear out human throats. She told of working to the point of collapse and of never having enough to eat, of being too terrified to sleep and of befriending a clever rat named Faust. In a tremulous voice, she told how Faust had been eaten by one of the feral children who inhabited the darkness, how her grief had spurred her escape from the mines and how she'd eventually ended up on the owner's farm, where she'd labored until that fateful moonlit night when she'd surprised Azriel in the act of stealing a chicken.

Though plainly horrified by all that his lost twin had been forced to endure, Finn nevertheless abided by Persephone's request that they not allow the mood of the day to be ruined by sadness for things that could not be changed. Calling for a pair of slippers with intact heels, he gallantly got down on bended knee, slipped them onto Persephone's feet and then led her out to the beautiful royal garden. There, the two of them enjoyed a scrumptious picnic amid the blooms and the songbirds. Later, they made their way down to the harbor. Clambering down off the high, sturdy quay, they kicked off their shoes and spent a golden afternoon walking barefoot in the sand. They explored tidal pools, poked sticks at brilliantly colored snapping crabs and stuck their heads into the treacherous sea caves that dotted the cliff behind them until the roar of the incoming tide sent them scrambling to the safety of higher ground.

That evening, although a second night of feasting and entertainments had been planned in honor of the king's birthday, Finn was so enjoying his time alone with Persephone that he refused to attend. Instead, he ordered food and drink brought up to his private chambers. His handsome face shining with eagerness, he suggested to Persephone that they sup while sitting cross-legged upon the bearskin rug before the fire as they might have done when they were children, if they'd but had the chance.

Laughingly, she agreed.

And when they'd finally eaten their fill, and the first twinkling stars had begun to appear in the night sky beyond the open windows, and Finn was intently studying the playing cards in his hand in order to decide how many white beans to wager, Persephone could not help thinking what a very marvelous thing it was to have a brother, and what a very terrible thing it would be to lose him.

Again.

Eight

BY DAWN THE FOLLOWING DAY, Persephone was up and dressed like the princess she was, Rachel was swathed in the heavy linen bandages of a leper and little Mateo was garbed in the smart livery of a palace page boy. Azriel, who'd personally selected their traveling outfits, was himself dressed in a richly embroidered doublet of crimson velvet with sleeves puffed and fashionably slashed to reveal a white silk undershirt. To complement this, he'd selected matching velvet breeches, good black boots, a black traveling cloak and a gilded codpiece of such impressive size that Neeka simply could not stop smiling.

"You don't think it's too much, do you, Princess?" he asked anxiously, but with a gleam in his eye.

Vexed to find herself blushing, Persephone ignored his question in favor of asking him if it was really necessary for Rachel to dress as a leper.

"It is," he said as he casually planted his hands on his hips so that both index fingers just happened to be pointing directly at his gilded crotch. "Now, enough idle chatter and gawking at codpieces. Fetch your cloaks—it is time that we were on our way."

※

After an emotional farewell to Martha and the sisters, who vowed to say nothing to anyone of all they'd seen and heard within Persephone's chamber, Persephone peeled Neeka off Azriel and led him, Rachel and Mateo down to the palace courtyard. When they arrived, she was astounded and dismayed to see that Azriel had assembled a veritable entourage to accompany them on their travels: four lowborn men, eight women, four boys and fifteen identically caparisoned horses loaded down with packs and panniers.

"I don't think this is what my brother, the king, meant when he ordered you to make 'adequate' preparations, Azriel," said Persephone as she leaned down to give Cur a pat on his scruffy head.

"The king did not *order* me to make preparations, he *asked* me to do so," replied Azriel loftily. "He also granted me permission to freely requisition whatever I required in that regard, and that is what I have done. You are a princess, Your Highness. Not only are your comfort and safety of the greatest import, but you are a representative of the royal family about to embark upon a procession through the streets of the imperial capital. It would not be seemly for you to travel like a nobody."

"What he says is exactly true," came a familiar voice from behind them.

Persephone turned to see Finn dressed in one of his grandest ceremonial outfits. After embracing Persephone, patting Mateo on the head and uncertainly offering Rachel condolences on the matter of her hideous affliction, he complimented Azriel on his dashing ensemble.

"Thank you, Your Majesty," murmured Azriel with a graceful bow. "Please allow me to apologize for my earlier duplicity and to say that I hope you were not overly shocked when you learned that I was a Methusian outlaw."

"I was far more shocked when I learned that you were not a eunuch," admitted King Finnius, who seemed to be doing everything in his power to avoid looking at Azriel's ridiculous codpiece.

Smothering a smile, Azriel bowed again. As he did so, Finn put his arm around Persephone's shoulder and drew her aside.

"I received a great many gifts for our birthday, sister; it did not seem right that you should leave Parthania without getting any at all," he explained with a cough as he handed her something wrapped in blue velvet and tied with a silver ribbon.

Persephone, who hadn't received a birthday gift since she'd been dragged from the manor house all those years ago, reverently placed the package in the palm of her hand and tugged on the ribbon. Her breath caught as the folds of velvet fell away to reveal a linked bracelet hung with crude charms, an exquisitely crafted silver necklace and a heavy gold ring set with large rubies arranged in a perfect circle.

"The bracelet is an ancient piece said to confer protection, the ring bears the crest of the Erok royal family and will signal to all that we are as one, and the necklace belonged to our mother," explained Finn. He smiled before wistfully adding, "I am certain she'd have given it to you herself if she'd but had the chance."

Swallowing past the lump that had suddenly appeared in her throat, Persephone croaked, "They're . . . beautiful, Finn. Thank you. I just . . . I wish I had something to give you in return."

"Ah, but you do," said Finn, raising his index finger high in the air. "You can give me your word that while on this quest and ever afterward, you will run from danger, regardless of what quarter it comes from or who might suffer as a result of your actions."

Thoroughly warmed by this utterly unreasonable request, Persephone gave her twin a quick, impulsive hug and said, "You must know I cannot promise that. But I *can* promise that I will not run *toward* danger unless I have a very good reason to do so."

"That isn't really much of a promise," observed Finn ruefully as he coughed again, this time so violently that three tiny droplets of blood appeared on his lower lip.

"I'm afraid it's the best I can do," said Persephone, her heart clenching at the sight of the blood.

Casually, Finn ran his fingertip along his lip and the droplets disappeared. "Then let us hope you have more success finding the healing pool than you do acquiescing to the requests of your sovereign lord," he said lightly.

"Let us hope," replied Persephone, under her breath.

After helping Persephone don her new jewelry, Finn led her back to where the others were waiting and helped her into the saddle on Fleet's swayed back. As he did so, a reluctant groomsman helped the heavily bandaged Rachel and Mateo up onto a second horse, Azriel swung up onto a third, and the men, women and boys of the entourage all scrambled up onto theirs.

By the time everyone was ready to go, the king had likewise mounted his big, black hunter. Sitting straight and tall, he held his gloved hand out to Persephone. Side-by-side, they led the others through the watchtower passageway, through the gates of the imperial palace and out into the streets of Parthania. It was far too early for any member of the nobility to be up and about, but the streets were filled with those of low birth who'd turned out to see the beautiful, long-lost princess who'd spent most of her life enslaved, who knew what it was to empty chamber pots and who'd almost certainly known hunger and cold and pain. She was one of them, this princess, and she was a living testament to the fact that while there was breath, there was always hope that better days might come. And so they cheered her and threw flowers; little girls blew kisses and little boys threw their caps in the air. One awestruck woman reached out to touch the hem of Persephone's gown as she rode past; another got down on her knees and begged a royal blessing for her sick child. Young men hung from second-storey windows, happily risking life and limb for the merest glimpse of her.

At first, Persephone was so overwhelmed by the adulation that she sat rigid in the saddle, looking neither left nor right. At length, however, she began to feel the genuine warmth behind the display, and it was this, combined with Azriel's mocking whispers that she was behaving like a royal stick-in-the-mud, that finally got her smiling and waving. Seeing how this delighted both Finn and the crowd, she smiled and waved more enthusiastically. Indeed, she got so comfortable doing so that when they finally reached the great gates of the city and she heard a familiar voice calling her name, she almost smiled and waved in the direction of the caller.

Then she realized who the caller was.

"What is this?" demanded the king as he eyed the dozen mounted New Man soldiers with whom the Regent had arrived.

Mateo visibly trembled at the sight of the monster who'd imprisoned him.

"It is nothing of import, Majesty," called Mordesius with a cold look at the boy and an appraising look at the "leper" to whom he clung. "I only wondered if I might have a moment alone with the Princess."

Though Persephone could not imagine anything she wanted less than a moment alone with the Regent, she dared not deny him, and so she forced herself to cast a beseeching look at Finn. When he reluctantly nodded, she urged Fleet forward.

"What do you want?" she hissed at Mordesius, as soon as they were out of earshot of the king.

"I promised that before the great gates of Parthania closed behind you, I would give you a parting gift that would inspire you beyond your wildest imagination," he reminded.

"I had forgotten," said Persephone, hoping to give offense.

"No matter," said the Regent magnanimously. "You shall have your gift anyway. The idea for it came to me after we struck our bargain. It occurred to me that there was nothing to prevent you and the cockroach from wandering the realm indefinitely—always searching for the healing pool and conveniently never finding it. Feeling that this was not in keeping with the spirit of our agreement, I decided to provide you with an incentive to ensure that you promptly deliver what you have promised."

From his pannier, Mordesius removed a red glass jar stoppered with a cork. Carefully, he handed it to Persephone.

"This jar contains exactly one hundred of the white beans with which the king so enjoys gambling when he plays peasant games of chance with his insufferable nursemaid," he explained, wincing slightly as the horse beneath him moved unexpectedly. "Starting tomorrow, each day you will remove a single bean from the jar."

"And why will I do that?" asked Persephone, trying to sound haughty in spite of the sinking feeling in the pit of her stomach.

"To keep track of time," replied the Regent in a jolly voice. "Because you see, Princess, the day the last bean is removed from the jar, if you have not returned to Parthania with proof that the healing Pool of Genezing exists, your brother, the king, will die."

Nine

BEFORE PERSEPHONE COULD say anything in response to this new and terrible threat, Mordesius reined his horse around and cantered away, the hunched stiffness of his posture a testament to the pain caused him by the horse's bouncing gait. As the black-clad soldiers with whom he'd arrived clattered after him and the low-borns in their path scrambled to get out of the way, Azriel urged his horse close to Persephone's right side, and the king urged his horse close to her left.

"What did he want?" asked the king.

"Merely to wish me godspeed on my journey," replied Persephone as she surreptitiously slipped the jar of beans into the pack hanging over Fleet's bony right hip.

Azriel glanced in the direction of the disappearing jar but said nothing.

The king stared after the departing Regent. "When he asked me the reason for your hasty departure from the imperial capital, I told him the truth. He did not laugh in my face, but I could tell from his demeanor that he thought me a fool."

"I'm sorry, Your Majesty—" began Persephone.

"I'm not," coughed Finn. "I no longer care what Mordesius thinks about me or anything else. When I was a child, I saw only the side of him that he wished me to see, and those around me sheltered me from the truth about him. Perhaps they did so because they knew

I hadn't the power to stop him from doing what he pleased; perhaps they did so out of fear of retribution. Whatever the reason, I am a child no longer, and henceforth I mean to make it my business to see everything for what it really is that I may better see to the welfare of all people."

"Does that include the people who are not your people, Your Majesty?" asked Azriel, leaning forward so that he could see Finn on the other side of Persephone. "Does it include my people and the people belonging to the other three clans?"

"*Yes,*" said the king vehemently. "I know I have much to answer for in regards to how the clans of this realm have been treated by those who came before me, and I *will* answer for it. Though I cannot change the past, I shall do what I can to right past wrongs in the hope that someday, old wounds may be healed, and all people of this realm will be united in peace."

Azriel said nothing in response to this, only sat back in his saddle with a pensive expression on his face.

"Oh, Finn!" exclaimed Persephone, who could not resist leaning over to fling her arms about him. "You are going to be *such* a good ruler!"

At the sight of this impromptu display of affection between their shining young monarch and his beautiful, long-lost twin, the crowd cheered unrestrainedly. Glancing over his shoulder to investigate the cause of the outburst, Fleet was plainly shocked and dismayed to see his beloved Persephone exhibiting tenderness toward a creature other than himself. With an irate squeal, he lurched sideways away from the king's big hunter so suddenly that Persephone found herself embracing nothing but air. Dangerously off balance, she was half a heartbeat from tumbling headfirst onto the cobblestone road when Azriel leaned over, grabbed her around the waist and hauled her upright again.

"Take good care of my sister, Azriel," said Finn, who was unable to resist glancing at Azriel's hand, which yet lingered about Persephone's waist and which was clearly the cause of the sudden flush upon her cheeks. "Find the Pool of Genezing and, though you've not asked for it, I give you my word that I shall see to your people's protection should they choose to come out of hiding and settle by the pool as their ancestors of legend once did."

At these words, the pensive expression on Azriel's face deepened. Inclining his head toward the king in acknowledgment of both his request and his promise, he slipped his hand from Persephone's waist and motioned to Rachel and the others that it was time to go. Without thinking, Persephone twisted around in her saddle so that she could smile and wave to the humble people of Parthania one last time. Finn smiled at her as the crowd sent up a final heartfelt cry of affection, and she smiled back at him. Then, turning forward in her saddle once more, she led her traveling companions through the city gates, beyond the safety of the impenetrable city walls and out into the ofttimes treacherous Glyndorian countryside.

Half an hour later, a small group of riders pushed its way through the bustling throngs who'd begun streaming into the city intent upon the business of the new workday.

Half an hour after this, a nondescript figure cloaked in meanest homespun slipped through the gates after them.

Ten

One hundred white beans in the jar

INITIALLY, THE DIRT ROAD leading away from Parthania was two wagon widths wide. It rapidly narrowed, however, until at length it was wide enough for only two to ride abreast comfortably. At that point, Rachel cheerfully offered to rein in the horse that she and Mateo shared so that Persephone and Azriel might ride together at the head of the cavalcade.

As soon as Rachel's horse had fallen back, Persephone, who'd not wanted to further frighten Mateo by mentioning the Regent in front of him, showed Azriel the glass jar and explained its purpose.

"The Regent said he will kill the king if we do not return with proof that we've found the healing pool by the time we run out of beans!" she burst. Reaching out, she clutched the sleeve of Azriel's red velvet doublet and said, "You must tell me true—is there any hope at all that we will succeed? Because if there isn't, we ought to turn back at once!"

"And do what?" asked Azriel, glancing down at her clutching hand as though he wasn't quite sure what it was doing there.

Flushing with embarrassment, Persephone abruptly released her hold on him and made a silent vow to chop off her own hand if she *ever* found herself tempted to reach for him again.

"You told me that death awaits the king behind every wall," he continued. "Moreover, the Regent has a sizable army of New Men loyal to him alone. We haven't anywhere near the strength to oppose him, Persephone. To return as his enemies now would be to see the king cut down and us with him. That would leave the throne vacant—"

"And plunge the kingdom into civil war," she said irritably. "I know all that. I just . . . I hate the thought that I left without warning Finn that he is under a death sentence!"

"Your brother is no fool, Princess," said Azriel. "I am quite sure he knows that the Regent will attempt to hold onto power and that anyone who stands in his way will be at risk. Why else do you think he granted you permission to go traipsing around the realm in the company of a rogue such as myself?"

"Well . . . well, because I insisted," said Persephone, surprised by the question.

"No one knows better than I just how infernally persistent you can be when you want something," said Azriel with a smile that made her want to break her silent vow of a moment earlier. "However, I would suggest that King Finnius may also have sought to get you away from Parthania until he could be sure that it was safe for you to return."

Persephone looked toward the horizon as she silently considered the possibility that she may have underestimated her brother. Then she looked over at Azriel and said, "Even if you are right—even if Finn truly understands that he is in danger—it does not change the fact that one hundred days is not a lot of time to find something that may not exist."

"The pool does exist, and we do not need *a lot* of time," replied Azriel, reaching over to gently brush a few strands of hair from her face. "We only need *enough* time. And if the Fates are willing—and I am coming to believe that they are—we shall have it."

Despite the need for urgency, they were forced to travel at an almost leisurely pace because the escort included women and children who needed to ride slowly and rest often. The path they followed was a familiar one, for they were retracing the route they'd taken a week earlier when they'd journeyed to the imperial capital from the Methusian camp in the north. Though Persephone was not especially looking forward to returning to the bosom of the clan that had thought nothing of endangering her life once before, she'd agreed with Azriel and Rachel that the camp must be the first stop on the quest. There, they'd be able to reunite Mateo with his brother, collect provisions, review what was thought to be known about old Balthazar's discovery of the healing pool and solicit suggestions as to how they ought to go about finding it.

"And what if your clansmen do not think we should go about finding it?" asked Persephone with an impatient glance over her shoulder at the members of the unwieldy escort, many of whom were smiling and chatting away as though they were on some kind of pleasure outing. "What if they think that fulfilling the prophecy of the Methusian king is more important than finding the healing pool?"

"I think that when they have heard what I have to say, they will see that finding the pool and fulfilling the prophecy are intertwined," replied Azriel cryptically.

Before Persephone could ask him what he meant by this, there came a shout from across a nearby field. Recalling her harrowing encounter with the drunken Lord Atticus on the journey to Parthania, Persephone swung around in alarm.

Alarm gave way to surprise when instead of seeing half a dozen mischief-making noblemen, she saw several dozen lowborn field hands racing across the field toward her. They were all running as fast as they could through the gently swaying grain—the women holding their limp brown skirts high to avoid tripping over them, the men holding their caps in place to avoid losing them and the children zipping around them like so many little water beetles.

Bursting from the sea of grain, the men, women and children all skidded to a halt by the side of the road just ahead of Persephone and Azriel. Clearly delighted by the novelty of the approaching parade, they chattered and laughed as they drank in the sight of the identically caparisoned horses, the many attendants, the barking dogs, Persephone in her beautiful gown and Azriel in his velvet finery and massive codpiece. Even Rachel seemed to fascinate them—either because they'd never seen such a heavily bandaged leper or because if they had, they'd never seen one who waved so enthusiastically and called out such merry greetings.

Feeling every bit as self-conscious as she had at the beginning of the procession through the streets of Parthania, Persephone was just about to urge Fleet into a trot to get past the gawkers more quickly when Azriel stood up in his stirrups, grandly swept his arm toward her and shouted, "BEHOLD! THE KING'S LONG-LOST SISTER, THE PRINCESS PERSEPHONE!"

In a flurry of amazed excitement, the beaming women dipped curtseys, and the men snatched their caps off their heads and bowed. As they did so, Azriel reached into one of his panniers, withdrew a handful of gold coins and tossed them high into the air.

"What do you think you're doing?" hissed Persephone as the field workers noisily kissed the coins they'd caught and cried heartfelt blessings upon her. "And where did you get those coins?"

"I think I am making an investment," replied Azriel, jostling her arm to get her to wave. "A little goodwill shown toward the common folk can go a long way, and one never knows when the support of people such as these might come in handy. As for where I got the coins, the Regent promised me a sizable bag of gold, remember?"

"And he gave it to you?" asked Persephone, so surprised that she continued waving of her own volition.

"Not exactly," replied Azriel, grinning like a pirate.

Though stealing treasure from the Regent was obviously no joking matter, Persephone could not help laughing at how pleased Azriel was with himself for having done so. "Well," she said, smiling over at him, "I suppose he can't hate you any more than he already does."

"Oh," replied Azriel, with a casual glance into the distance behind them, "I wouldn't be too sure about that."

They showered gold and greetings upon untold numbers of delighted field hands, travelers and beggars that day before finally stopping for the night in the corner of a field near a gurgling brook and a small copse of trees. It was well before dusk, and the men, women and children of the escort immediately set to work tethering the horses, collecting firewood, refilling the waterskins, setting up the small, golden-tasseled royal tent and generally making the spot a camp fit for an esteemed royal princess.

Persephone sat off to one side with Rachel and Mateo, surveying the noisy, bustling scene with considerable concern.

"You're right to be worried about how little distance we covered today, of course," agreed Rachel quietly, her eyes on Mateo, who was sleeping with his head in her lap. "The problem is going to be getting Azriel to see reason. Though I'm sure he understands the need for haste, he is obviously having a difficult time reconciling this need with his concern that you travel in royal style."

"Don't worry," said Persephone as she leaned over to tuck a flapping piece of bandage behind Rachel's rather prominent ears. "I shall find a way to make him see reason."

"I'm sure you will," said Rachel, sucking in her cheeks to hide her smile.

Scowling at her doppelgänger's presumption, Persephone stood up, brushed off her dusty backside and looked around for Azriel that she might speak with him at once. Unfortunately, he was busy overseeing the final aspects of setting up camp. He continued to be busy throughout the evening—speaking at length with the men and women of the escort, teasing the boys, checking and rechecking the contents of the packs and panniers, ensuring that one and all had enough to eat.

Though Persephone probably could have issued a royal command that he set aside other tasks and speak with her, she'd have felt exceedingly awkward doing so and wasn't sure that he'd have obeyed in any event.

Long after the sun had set and the stars in the night sky had begun to twinkle in earnest, as the boys lay sleeping in their bedrolls and the men and women of the escort sat companionably chatting around the several fires that dotted the small camp, Azriel got up to check the horses one last time. Seeing her chance to corner him at last, Persephone jumped to her feet, grabbed Rachel by the hand and chased after him.

The two girls caught up with him as he was explaining to Fleet—for the umpteenth time, apparently—why he was not allowed to sleep in the royal tent. In response to these patient words of explanation, Fleet whinnied so abruptly and so shrilly that Azriel gave a startled shout. Biting back a smile, Persephone gave Fleet a kiss on the nose before turning to Azriel and saying, "We need to talk."

"All right," he murmured, stepping close to her at once.

Since being near him in the darkness had always made Persephone a little dizzy, and since she hadn't expected him to respond to her nearness the way he once would have, she hurriedly stepped back and stammered, "Azriel, this situation is intolerable—"

"Is it the leper?" he interrupted in a low voice. "Do you want me to get rid of her?"

Rachel smothered a laugh. After shooting her friend a look that said she ought not to encourage Azriel's silliness, Persephone turned back to him and said, "I am speaking of the escort. Not only are they hampering our progress to an alarming degree, but have you even considered what your clansmen are going to do when the lot of them come tramping through the secret tunnel beneath the waterfall? They nearly turned me into a bloody pincushion the first time I came through the tunnel, and I was but a lone intruder on a mission of mercy for one of their own!" Taking a deep breath, she clamped her hands around his sinewy biceps and gave him a little shake. "You must listen to me, Azriel," she said, trying not to notice the heat of his skin beneath her fingers. "I know that you are probably still coming to terms with the fact I am a princess rather than a nobody, and I appreciate that you are concerned for my comfort and safety, but I insist . . . no, I *beg* you to abandon the escort that we might proceed onward alone with all due haste."

"All right," murmured Azriel, slipping his hands to her waist in a way that suggested that he'd not only come to terms with the fact that she was a princess but had decided that he liked the idea very much indeed.

"What do you mean 'all right'?" she squeaked, her face in flames at the feel of his strong arms around her and his massive codpiece against her belly.

Behind her, Rachel smothered another laugh.

Azriel let go of Persephone as unexpectedly as he'd embraced her. Taking an even bigger step away from her than she'd earlier taken away from him, he said, "I mean, all right, tomorrow at dawn, you, Rachel, Mateo and I will proceed onward alone with all due haste."

Thrown by his suddenly conversational tone—as though he hadn't one instant earlier been holding her in his arms, whispering against her neck—Persephone swallowed hard and said, "But . . . but what about the escort?"

Azriel's smile flashed in the starlight, making her heart turn over.

"Wait and see about the escort," he said.

The next morning, Azriel roused Persephone well before dawn. Outside the tent, a chill wind whistled through the nearby trees.

"Time to rouse yourself, Princess," he sang, giving her blankets a sharp tug.

"Don't call me that," mumbled Persephone as she dragged the blankets back up over her head.

"Rachel is already up and changed into her new outfit," continued Azriel as he flipped over the blankets at the foot of the bed and gave her toe a tweak.

With a yelp, Persephone bolted upright. Hurriedly tucking her feet up beyond the risk of further attack, she said, "Rachel has a new outfit?"

"Fear not, Princess, I have a new outfit for you, too," assured Azriel as he deposited into her lap a limp pile of coarse cloth.

"What is this?" asked Persephone in dismay.

"Your new outfit," said Azriel with a smile in his voice. "Hurry and change, for we shall soon lose the cover of darkness. When you are dressed, leave your fine princess things on the bed and come join me by the fire."

Before Persephone could question his orders, he was gone, leaving her alone in the darkness to sort through the smelly pile, to wonder who he thought he was that he should give *her* orders and to wonder why on earth she was following them.

At length, she managed to fumble into her new "outfit." When she'd done so, she carefully transferred to the pocket of her shift the rusty fetters key, as well as the three treasures she kept with her always: the scrap of lace she'd torn from the hem of Cookie's apron the night she was dragged from the manor house, Faust's tail, which she'd hacked from his little corpse after the feral children of the mines had finished with him, and the auburn curl she'd cut from Azriel's head as he hung across Fleet's back dying of poison not so long ago. Then she tossed her fine princess things on the bed (all but the gifts that Finn had given her, which she had no intention of parting with whatever Azriel might presume to order) and ducked out of the tent.

Shivering, grumbling and hugging herself tight against the chill, Persephone hurried over to the nearest fire. A quick glance did not reveal Azriel; a second glance revealed him sitting practically at her feet. He was no longer wearing the embroidered velvet doublet and codpiece; instead, he was dressed like the other men, in plain breeches and a hooded cloak. Next to him sat Rachel. She was no longer dressed as a leper, but instead was dressed like Persephone and the other women, in a grubby shift and a knee-length robe with a long scarf that, in Rachel's case, was wrapped around her head to conceal every part of her face but her eyes. Mateo, who was sitting on Rachel's other side, was also wearing mean garments.

Nonplussed, Persephone plopped down beside Azriel. "Why are we dressed like this?" she asked as she accepted from him a pair of barely serviceable boots and a hunk of dark bread.

"So that we can proceed onward alone with all due haste," he replied.

After gingerly pulling on the boots, Persephone tore off a piece of bread and crammed it into her mouth. "I don't see how setting aside our beautiful clothes is going to allow us to proceed onward alone with all due haste," she said in a slightly garbled voice.

"Look around you, Princess," replied Azriel, his blue eyes glowing in the reflected light of the flames. "What do you see?"

As she chewed and swallowed her bite of bread, Persephone looked around. At first, she saw nothing of note.

Then it dawned on her.

"Five men, ten women, five boys, fifteen horses and five dogs," she said slowly. "All the men are dressed alike, all the women and boys are dressed alike. The horses are covered in identical hoods and long blankets; the dogs could be littermates. Split us into five groups, each containing one man, two women, one boy, three horses and one dog, and from a distance, it would be impossible to tell which group is which."

"Exactly," said Azriel with satisfaction. "In a moment, you, Rachel, Mateo and I will begin riding hard toward the Methusian camp. The other four groups will also begin riding hard, each in a different direction. The Regent is almost certainly having us followed, you see, and I intend to give his dogs the slip."

Instead of applauding Azriel's cleverness (as he rather appeared to expect her to do) Persephone gaped at him in horror. "And you thought that the best way to give his dogs the slip would be to use these people as decoys?" she exclaimed. "Azriel, have you even *considered* what is going to happen to them if—or, more likely, when—they get caught? The Regent despises lowborns almost as much as he despises Methusians, and I am quite certain that his soldiers will not appreciate being played for—"

"Princess?" murmured a voice at her other side.

"What?" she cried, whipping her head around.

The man was on one knee, hand over his heart. "All those you see before you knew the risks before we set out," he said with quiet dignity. "It would be wrong to look upon us as decoys, Your Highness, for in truth we are soldiers in your service. And while we are touched and humbled by your concern for our well-being, I assure you it is not necessary. Though Azriel has not told us the purpose of the journey that lies before you, he has assured us that it is for the good of the realm and for the promise of better days to come for all people. To play even a small role in the pursuit of such lofty ambitions is more than most of low birth could ever dream of. And that is why, even if Azriel had not given each of us gold enough to ensure that our families would hereafter be well provided for, there is not one among us who'd not have volunteered for this mission."

Just as he finished speaking, a blinding ray of sunlight burst over the horizon, heralding the arrival of dawn. Persephone blinked into the glory before looking back down into the face of the kneeling man at her side. She knew that to protest anything he'd said would be to insult him and all those who were about to risk their lives for her. Not for the first time, she thought that being a princess was going to be a thousand times harder than she could ever have imagined.

Reaching out, she laid a tentative hand upon the man's hooded head and said, "Then let me thank you for the service you will do for me this day and promise that it shall never be forgotten."

As the man bowed his head in gratitude and reverence, a screech from high overhead brought a smile to Persephone's lips. Squinting up into the early morning sky, she beheld Ivan, the proud and fearless hawk who'd followed her halfway across the realm, ever escaping those who sought to master him.

The hawk who chose that particular moment to deliver an excessively large splatter of droppings to the top of Azriel's head.

At the sight of Azriel hopping about in disgust while hawk droppings dripped down the sides of his hood like the contents of a cracked egg, the men, women and boys of the escort could not contain their hilarity. Rachel bowed her head to hide the mirth in her eyes, and Mateo laughed aloud for the first time since being rescued.

Somewhere nearby, Cur started barking.

"Azriel, if it is any comfort at all, I believe that deep down inside, Ivan is filled with remorse for what he just did," confided Persephone.

"Even if that were true, it would be no comfort at all!" huffed Azriel, grimacing as he accidentally smeared his fingers while trying to clean off his hood.

Taking a step backward so that he would not accidentally smear *her*, Persephone said, "Well, at least we'll always be able to cherish the thought that whatever befalls these brave soldiers in my service, we parted in merry spirits."

"Humph!" was the only reply.

Eleven

MORDESIUS LAY BACK in the finely upholstered leather chair and closed his eyes.

"Proceed," he ordered.

"Yes, Your Grace," whispered the terrified barber.

With infinite care, the stoop-shouldered man leaned forward and laid the straight blade against Mordesius's well-soaped cheek. He was the third member of his craft to tend to Mordesius in recent months, the first two having lost fingers as punishment for having allowed the blade to slip and mar the Regent's perfect complexion.

As he listened to the rasping sound the blade made as it scraped his cheek clean, Mordesius sighed deeply. Yesterday, after bidding the princess farewell, he'd ridden back to the imperial palace to await the return of the king that he might explain to him the way things now stood. Unfortunately, some interfering servant reached the fool first with the news that no one had seen his nursemaid Moira since the night before last. This had greatly alarmed the king, for he'd been under the impression that she'd been absent from her duties because of illness. After publicly berating himself for not having visited her sickbed personally even though any imbecile could have told him that it would have been irresponsible for him, a sickly king without a named heir, to knowingly expose himself to illness, he'd immediately canceled or postponed all business and festivities, and ordered that a search be undertaken.

Eager to tell the peasant-hearted fool what fate had *really* befallen the woman who'd ever treated Mordesius with such an appalling lack of respect, the Regent had proceeded to the king's chambers. He'd arrived only to find his way barred by one of the few guards in the imperial palace who'd been personally appointed by the king. Nervously, the young man had informed Mordesius that Lord Bartok had been put in charge of the search for the nursemaid and that the king had left orders that he wished to see no one unless the visitor had news of her whereabouts.

Mordesius's initial reaction had been to have the guard cut down where he stood, but as he'd opened his mouth to bark the order to the other guard, one of the many who'd been appointed by Mordesius and were loyal to him alone, it had suddenly occurred to him that perhaps the agony of knowing what had happened to his nursemaid could only be surpassed by the agony of *not* knowing what had happened to her.

Indeed, if King Finnius had not sent word late the previous evening that he intended to proceed this day with the ceremony that would see the power to rule the realm officially transferred to him, Mordesius might have been content to let the ingrate stew in his own juices for some time to come.

But alas, he *had* sent word and so—regrettably!—Mordesius was going to have to put an end to the sweet torture of not knowing.

As Mordesius mentally rehearsed how he planned to break the news to the king, the trembling barber wiped Mordesius's face with a lavender-scented towel, gingerly massaged a small dollop of reddish salve into his skin and held up a hand mirror so that the Regent could inspect the job he'd done.

"Hold the mirror steady, or I will have your hand removed," said Mordesius absently. Turning his head from side to side, he marveled at how handsome he still was and how wonderfully smooth and youthful looking his skin was.

The barber had done a magnificent job.

"You missed a spot," muttered Mordesius as he shoved the hand mirror away and awkwardly hauled himself up off the reclining chair.

At these words of dissatisfaction, the barber's eyes bulged. "Apologies, Your Grace!" he blubbered, falling to his knees.

Mordesius looked down his perfect nose at the man, despising him for his terror and wondering whether a close shave was worth letting such a pathetic wretch keep all his fingers.

At length he decided that it was—for now.

"Don't let it happen again," he said sourly. "Get out."

After the barber had fled, Mordesius looked at his reflection in the mirror one last time before departing himself. As he slouched through the corridors of the palace toward the king's chambers, he made careful note of all those who looked upon him with anything other than respect or fear. The stares of those who thought he was finished had made him uneasy the night Lady Bothwell had been revealed to be the king's twin, but they no longer did. Though he'd never been one to play peasant games of chance, it was an indisputable fact that he now held all the cards.

"Stand aside," he commanded the same young guard who'd barred his way the previous day.

Once again, the young man assumed the look of a cornered rabbit. With a darting glance at his fellow guard, who was studiously looking in the opposite direction, he cried, "Would that I could, Your Grace, but I fear that I cannot, for His Majesty has ordered that none but those having news of the nursemaid Moira's whereabouts should pass!"

"I have news," said Mordesius, mentally adding the rabbit to the long list of those who would someday pay for having offended him.

"*Oh*," said the young guard, heaving a great sigh of relief. "Well, in that case, I'll announce you at once."

"That won't be necessary," said Mordesius. "I'll announce myself."

For a moment, it looked as though the imbecile might actually insist upon following protocol. Then, as though suddenly realizing that to do so would be suicide, he reluctantly stepped aside.

How unfortunate for him that his change of heart will not save him from being racked until he cries for his mother, thought Mordesius as he shuffled into the king's inner chamber.

The door had barely shut behind him when the king was upon him. "You've found Moira?" he exclaimed.

"After a fashion," replied Mordesius carelessly.

"What do you mean 'after a fashion'?" demanded Finn, forgetting to turn his head or cover his mouth as he coughed. "Have you found her or not? Is she all right? Tell me what you know!"

Instead of answering the distraught young king, Mordesius pushed past him. Lurching over to the long, gleaming table that dominated the room, he plucked a golden pear from the fruit bowl that sat in the middle of the table and, after inspecting it carefully for bruises, took a large bite. As he noisily munched away, he casually made his way up to the head of the table and eased himself down into the chair in which the king himself always sat when dining in private.

King Finnius watched all of this with his mouth hanging open, too amazed to be indignant.

At last, when Mordesius was comfortably settled in the king's own chair, he waved the pear at the still-speechless monarch and said, "Majesty, the night we discovered that Lady Bothwell was actually your long-lost sister, do you recall me saying that you might be surprised by all that the following days would bring? And do you recall replying that you have always liked surprises?"

"Yes," said the king guardedly.

Leaning forward, Mordesius smiled broadly. "Well . . . surprise, Your Majesty!" he sang. "I have had your nursemaid imprisoned within my dungeon, in a cell so well hidden that none but I know the location of it."

"WHAT?"

"It is true," beamed Mordesius, taking another bite of the pear. "What's more, I have sent my most trusted general, Murdock, to follow the princess and the cockroach. He has orders to execute them instantly if he hears even the vaguest rumor that would suggest that my plans have not unfolded exactly as I intended. Oh, and I've also stationed battalions of my vast personal army of New Men throughout the realm and dispatched orders that if those in command do not hear from me at regular intervals, they are to begin slaughtering your lowborn subjects, starting with the women and children since they are the most useless."

Eyes flashing, Finn opened his mouth—

"I would not call for the guards if I were you, Your Majesty," advised Mordesius, who was enjoying himself immensely. "For one thing, they are almost all loyal to me, and for another thing, did you not hear what I just said? Everyone and everything you hold dear is within my power. And the real beauty of the situation is that you cannot harm me without putting them all in mortal peril. For you see, if anything should happen to me—indeed, if I should simply find myself so displeased by your behavior that I am incapable of visiting the dungeon or communicating with my minions—your insufferable nursemaid will starve alone in the darkness, your sister's pretty head will be parted from her body, and untold numbers of your weakest, most helpless subjects will be butchered without mercy."

Though King Finnius had grown deathly pale by this point, his voice was steady when he said, "Your Grace, why have you done these terrible things?"

Mordesius shook his heavy head. "Really, Majesty, you insult yourself by asking a question to which you already know the answer," he chided.

"You do not wish to give up the power to rule the realm," coughed Finn.

"I do not—but I will," lied Mordesius, who thought it prudent to sweeten his threats with the honey of hope, "but only if the princess and the Methusian return with proof that they have discovered the location of the healing Pool of Genezing."

"I thought you didn't believe in the pool."

"You thought wrong," said Mordesius, tossing the half-eaten pear to one side. "I have always believed that it is out there. That is why I allowed the cockroach and the princess to live—so that they might follow the clues and bring knowledge of the pool to me."

"So the promise she made to help Azriel find the pool was a promise made to *you*?" exclaimed the king.

"She didn't tell you?" said Mordesius, sticking out his lower lip in mock sympathy. "Well, I'm not surprised. She has ever been a lying—"

"She didn't lie, she just didn't tell the entire truth," interrupted Finn. "And from the sounds of it, she had little choice in the matter."

"Just as you have little choice now but to do as you're told," said Mordesius. Clapping his hands together as though in delight, he said, "Isn't it wonderful to know how much the two of you have in common?"

Finn ignored the taunt. "You've told me what will happen if my sister and Azriel return with proof that they've found the healing pool," he said tightly. "What will happen if they do not?"

Mordesius said nothing, only smiled.

The young king stared at his Regent. "You are a monster," he said softly. "You have always been a monster."

"And you are a peasant-hearted fool and always have been one," snapped Mordesius. "If you'd not been, you'd have long ago guessed what I was and taken measures to contain me."

"I was but a boy—"

"*I* was but a boy when I barricaded my father and brothers in my family's miserable lowborn hovel, set fire to the kindling I'd stacked against the walls and listened to the sounds of them being roasted alive!"

Horrified, the king dropped his gaze to the shiny pink scar tissue on Mordesius's hands. "So . . . the fire that caused your terrible injuries was not an accident . . ."

Mordesius emitted a sharp bark of laughter. "Of course not, imbecile. Ye gods, you are not fit to be king any more than your faithless whore of a sister is fit to be queen."

Finn flinched at the words, but all he said was, "Though the throne belongs to my sister by right of our birth order, she told me that she does not want to be queen."

"She told me much the same thing," said Mordesius, rising from his chair to wander over to the fireplace. "It is fortunate, really, for Lord Bartok's daughter Lady Aurelia desires the crown, and I would see it set upon her head."

"You would have that vicious little creature reign instead of me?" asked the king incredulously.

"No, I would have her reign *with* you—as your wife and queen," explained Mordesius as he planted his bony arse on the cushioned rocking chair in which the cow usually sat to do mending.

"And why would you want that?"

"As Regent, it is my duty to ensure that you make a suitable marriage and beget an heir," murmured Mordesius, as though there could be no other reason.

"Touched though I am by your concern for the succession," said the king scathingly, "I will not marry to please you."

Mordesius sighed and pressed the tips of his fingers against his brow in a gesture intended to convey to the king that he was nearing the end of his patience. "You will, or I will exact vengeance upon the insufferable cow in my dungeon."

The tall, handsome king walked over and looked down upon the man he'd once considered his most trusted adviser.

"Do not hurt Moira," he said steadily. "Bring me proof that she is alive, and I shall consider your proposal."

Mordesius thought for a moment before nodding his agreement.

After he'd done so, the king continued speaking in the same steady voice. "You know, the other night, when you said that if you'd offended in thought or deed at any time during your long years of service that you stood ready to accept whatever punishment I saw fit to mete out, I very nearly took you at your word. I'd begun to have grave misgivings about you, Mordesius, but in the end I decided that it would not be fair to punish you in the absence of proof. I did not wish my first act as the true, ruling king to be an unjust one. I see now that I should have had you imprisoned when I had the chance."

"Yes, you should have," agreed Mordesius. "But alas, you did not. Go to your bedchamber, Your Majesty. Take a moment to reflect upon all that we've discussed. Reconcile yourself to henceforth bending to my will in all things. Then don your finest doublet, and together, we shall go inform the great lords of the realm that the ceremony to transfer power will not take place as planned because it is your dearest wish that I continue to rule on your behalf." Mordesius leaned back in the cow's rocking chair and propped his feet up on the stuffed head of the great bear. "But before you go attend to all that," he added with a sigh of satisfaction, "pass me another pear, will you?"

Twelve

One hundred white beans in the jar

PERSEPHONE HUNKERED DOWN in the saddle, her fingers twined in Fleet's messy mane, her eyes squinted against the chill wind that whipped her face. Smiling fiercely, she imagined the dismay on the faces of the soldiers whom Azriel believed were lurking somewhere behind them. She knew that the trails being left by the galloping horses could be easily followed by tracking beasts and men alike, but between them and the men, women and children of the cavalcade, they were leaving five such trails. That meant that if the soldiers tracking them wanted to keep all five groups in sight, they were going to have to either split up or pick a single group to track and take their chances that they'd picked right. Either way, the likelihood that Persephone, Azriel, Rachel and Mateo were going to be able to reach the Methusian camp without being followed had just increased dramatically.

With this in mind, they rode hard all day, slowing to rest and water the horses only when absolutely necessary. Predictably, Azriel repeatedly attempted to lead them through shallow streams to eliminate their scent trail; equally predictably, Fleet panicked each time he did so. Though he'd recently exhibited tremendous courage swimming the deep and murky palace moat to rescue Persephone from certain death, the experience did not appear to have cured him of his pathological terror of getting his hooves wet. Luckily, the fact that Azriel could detect no signs of pursuit put him in such good humor that he only threatened to turn the neurotic nag into horse steaks half a dozen times.

It was dark by the time they finally stopped for the night. After tending to the horses, they supped on cheese and bread without starting a fire. Then, while Rachel was tucking Mateo into his bedroll and Azriel was settling in for a long night of watching over them all, Persephone groped in her pack for the glass jar the Regent had given her. Popping off the cork with the help of her dagger, she carefully stirred the cool white beans with her finger, taking solace in the fact that it felt as though there were too many to count.

But, of course, there weren't too many to count—there were exactly one hundred.

After a moment of stirring, Persephone plucked a single white bean from among the many, replaced the cork and tucked the jar back into the pack. Then, careful not to drop the bean, she lay down in the darkness to wait for sleep to come.

They traveled just as hard the following day and reached the Methusian camp on the evening of the day after that. The first to see them emerge from the tunnel beneath the waterfall was Tiny, the redheaded giant who'd held a knife to Persephone's throat the first time she'd visited the camp. By the time he'd finished giving Azriel a hug that would have crushed the rib cage of a lesser man, the rest of the Methusians had crowded around them, all chattering excitedly, shouting questions and laughing with joy and relief that their two clansmen and two prophecy girls were safe and come back to them at last.

After several moments of this noisy chaos, the boisterous crowd suddenly quieted and parted to allow their leader, Cairn, to step forward. It was she who'd unsealed the canister containing the words of the long-dead Seer—words that had set Persephone and Rachel on the road to Parthania in the first place.

Raising a fine, soot-colored eyebrow at Persephone, Cairn said, "When we last parted, I wasn't sure I'd ever see you again."

"Nor was I," admitted Persephone, recalling how consumed she'd been with thoughts of escape and freedom.

"When Rachel returned to us with little Raphael in tow and told how she'd last seen you riding astride behind the Regent Mordesius in the direction of the imperial palace, I could not imagine that you'd long be able to avoid discovery and death," continued Cairn. Looking beside Persephone to where Mateo was silently embracing his sobbing little brother, she asked, "How did you manage not only to avoid both of these fates but also to rescue a second Methusian orphan, this one from the depths of a dungeon from which none has ever emerged alive?"

Before Persephone could even begin trying to explain, Azriel said, "The short answer to your question is that we happened upon the rather interesting fact that Persephone is the elder twin of the Erok king. And while the Regent Mordesius initially expressed a rather alarming degree of concern regarding how this might affect his evil plans, in the end he agreed to release us all on the condition that we return to Parthania in less than one hundred days with proof that we'd found the healing Pool of Genezing."

For what seemed like an eternity, every Methusian in the clearing stared at Azriel as though he'd just announced that he was an elf king with a knack for spinning straw into gold.

At length, however, Cairn turned to Persephone and said, "You are an Erok princess?"

"Yes."

"How do you know this?"

"The scar she bears upon her arm matches perfectly a scar the king bears," Azriel answered for her. Reaching for Persephone's hand, he gently slid the loose sleeve of her shift up to her elbow and raised her arm so that all could see the scar. "Moreover," he continued, "we spoke with a servant who helped the dying queen give her newborns the burns that would forever mark them as twins. And the Regent himself admitted to having ordered a soldier to spirit the infant princess from the palace, there to murder her and dispose of her body."

"I see," said Cairn. "And why did you tell the Regent you would find the healing pool?"

Letting go of Persephone's hand, Azriel held his own hands wide and said, "The situation was desperate. I could think of no other way to save us but to promise that which I supposed the Regent desired above all else."

"But why would he believe such a promise?" asked Cairn.

"Because I told him that I was Balthazar's bastard," said Azriel with a cheeky grin. "And because I told him that before my 'father' died, he gave me clues to follow to find the pool."

Cairn looked puzzled. "It is not the dimmest story I have ever heard but neither is it the cleverest," she said frankly. "I am surprised the Regent believed it, and even more surprised that he let you go. How did it not occur to him that once you were safe there would be no reason to go searching for the pool, and *certainly* no reason to return to Parthania?"

"Because there is a reason," interjected Persephone. "Mordesius yet holds my brother, the king, captive, and if we do not return to the imperial capital with proof that we've found the pool, the Regent will kill him."

There was some murmuring at this. Then an unseen woman at the back of the crowd shouted, "What is it to us if the Erok king dies? There is not one among us who has not suffered at the hands of that monster who rules in his name!"

Persephone was astounded by the woman's words. "You cannot seriously think to blame my brother for the actions of the Regent," she protested. "He was naught but a powerless child up until his birthday five days ago!"

"Even so," muttered someone else, "his death—and yours—would leave the throne vacant."

At these words, Azriel casually unsheathed his sword and stepped forward until he was half-standing in front of Persephone.

"No one is going to hurt her, Azriel," murmured Cairn.

"I know it well," he replied, hefting the weapon so that the blade glinted in the fading sunlight.

Persephone drank in the intoxicating feel of his protective presence for a moment before deliberately stepping around him to face his people. "My brother's death and mine would not pave the way for any Methusian king, if that's what you're thinking," she said, her voice ringing through the clearing. "The Regent Mordesius would be the first to make a bid for the throne, and if he were to fail, it would come down to a fight among the Erok nobility. And I can assure you that there is not one among them who would treat your people with the decency and respect that my brother will if he lives to become a true ruling king. And *that* is why we must find the Pool of Genezing before it is too late!"

For a moment, none of the Methusians seemed to know what to say to this.

Then Cairn looked at Persephone and said, "I find it curious that you refused to believe in the prophecy of the Methusian king, and yet you appear to believe in the existence of a mythical healing pool that even we Methusians cannot be sure exists."

"I cannot afford to be skeptical," shrugged Persephone. "My brother's life depends upon the success of our quest."

"And yet the odds against success are incalculable."

Persephone could not have looked less daunted by these words. "As you, yourself, pointed out, I helped to rescue Mateo from the depths of a dungeon from which none has ever emerged alive," she said. "As far as I know, aside from a handful of Gorgishmen, I am the only person in the realm to have escaped from the Mines of Torodania. Most recently, after discovering that I was a royal princess who somehow survived a death sentence issued when I was mere hours old, I was welcomed with open arms by my brother, the king, even though my very existence could have toppled him from his throne. I have a habit of beating the odds, don't you think?"

"Without question," said Cairn, smiling faintly, "and yet I'm not certain I'd want you to beat them this time. As I'm sure you're aware, the healing Pool of Genezing is sacred to our people."

"My brother gave Azriel his word that he'd protect your people should you choose to come out of hiding and settle by the pool as your ancestors of legend once did."

"Even if we believed him, by your own admission he is the Regent's hostage," said Tiny in his booming voice. "To free him, you'll have to show the Regent where the pool is, and I'm guessing he didn't give our Azriel *his* word that he'd protect us if we sought to settle by our marvelous sacred pool."

"No, he didn't, though I must admit that I don't believe I'd have been entirely reassured if he had," confided Azriel, prompting a wave of mirthless laughter to ripple through the crowd. "In truth, I'd thought to cross that bridge when we come to it."

"But suppose you never come to it?" put in Fayla, the beautiful, brave, clever Methusian girl whom Persephone had once suspected of being Azriel's sweetheart. "Suppose Persephone dies on this quest of yours? If she is the one who is meant to bring about the coming of the Methusian king, all hope would be lost."

"She will not die, for I have made a vow to protect her with my life," said Azriel, so solemnly that Persephone nearly smiled. "What's more, I've come to believe that the search for the healing pool and the fulfillment of the prophecy are one and the same."

"How so?" asked Cairn, her eyes alert.

"Well . . . I think that the Erok king *is* the Methusian king," he said. Over the noisy exclamations and protests of his people, he continued, "Though I've not spent a great deal of time with King Finnius, I've spent enough to take his measure, and I can truthfully say that I've not found him wanting. Indeed, before we left the imperial capital, he told me that he means to make it his business to see to the welfare of *all* people—to answer for how the clans have been treated and to do what he can to right past wrongs in the hope that someday, all people of this realm may be united in peace."

"Even if that is true," said Fayla in a voice that indicated she had a hard time believing that it was, "the fact remains that the Erok king is not one of us and therefore cannot be the prophesied Methusian king."

"But what if he were to become a Methusian?" said Azriel.

"Became a Methusian?" spluttered Tiny. "Azriel, there is nothing to say that he'd want such a thing, and even assuming that he did, you know as well as I that we do not accept grown men as Methusians simply because they've been administered the oath and given the mark. And even assuming we did, if the Erok king is being held hostage by the Regent as you say he is, it would be suicide for one of us to attempt to reach him to do so!"

"I agree," said Azriel with the deeply satisfied tone of one who has led others to the exact place he wished them to go. "That is why I propose to *personally* make him a Methusian in the only other way possible under the circumstances."

"How?" asked Rachel in a mystified voice.

Turning to Persephone with a smile that set her heart pounding in her chest and alarm bells ringing in her ears, Azriel replied, "By marrying his sister, if she'll have me."

Thirteen

"READY, YOUR MAJESTY?" asked Mordesius, cutting another thin slice from the juicy apple in his hand.

"I am," said the pale young king, shakily tugging at the hem of his sombre black velvet doublet.

Two days had elapsed since Mordesius had gone to the royal chambers to explain to the king the way things now stood. After he'd done so, he'd sent the fool to the bedchamber to ready himself to go inform the great lords—in a convincing manner, if he knew what was good for him and all those he held dear—that it was his dearest wish that Mordesius continue to rule the kingdom in his stead.

Mordesius had initially been content to sit in the nursemaid's rocking chair eating the king's fruit and anticipating the reaction of the great lords to this tremendous news, but when the king had failed to reappear after half an hour, he'd grown impatient. Shoving open the bedchamber door without knocking, he'd been much dismayed to discover the king lying face down on the floor, breathing like a bellows. Knowing that he could not afford to let the fool die—yet—Mordesius had shouted for the guards to lift the gasping monarch onto his bed and thereafter to summon the court physicians. Those ghouls had spent an interminable while flapping about, sniffing the air and listening to the king's chest while muttering on about imbalanced humors and the ill effects of overexcitement. When they were done, their cadaverous, sparse-haired leader had plunged a filthy blade into the pale crook of the king's arm, bled him half-dry, dosed him with a vile-smelling tonic and ordered him to bed until further notice.

Though Mordesius had longed to drag the fool from the bed and set him dancing like the puppet he was, news of his infirmity had spread through the palace like wildfire. Mordesius knew that if he was seen to be anything other than solicitous of the king in his time of sickness, the great lords would be even more suspicious of the forthcoming announcement—and even more likely to balk at the idea of eventually naming Mordesius the king's heir.

And so, since ascending to the Erok throne was a dream second only to that of someday being hearty, hale and wholly healed, Mordesius had reluctantly decided to bide his time. The waiting had ended that morning when he'd entered the royal bedchamber unannounced to find the king not abed but standing straight and tall by an open window. If the puppet was well enough to want to look out upon the kingdom that no longer belonged to him, he was well enough to start dancing.

"Let us proceed to the Council chamber without further delay, then," declared Mordesius now. "The great lords have had a few anxious days wondering where the princess has gone to and when the ceremony officially transferring power to you is going to take place. Whilst I, personally, have taken great satisfaction in their discomfort, I think the time has come to set their minds at ease by explaining a few things, don't you?"

When King Finnius did not reply, Mordesius dropped the apple, picked up the rocking chair cushion and plunged the silver fruit knife into it. "I said, 'don't you?'" he repeated cheerfully as he ripped such a long, ragged hole in the fabric that the cushion disgorged nearly all of its stuffing.

"Yes," said King Finnius slowly, his eyes on the clumps of stuffing at his feet. "I do."

✳

Some minutes later, the king took his seat at the head of the long Council table. It had been Mordesius's idea for him to do so at the outset of the meeting so he could later stand and offer the seat to Mordesius in a gesture that would be as symbolically powerful as it would be satisfying.

As soon as the king was seated, the great lords likewise took their seats, looks of expectation bright upon their faces.

"My lords," said the king quietly.

When he said nothing more, only licked his pale lips, Mordesius tensed. Though he was *almost* certain he had the fool under his control, he was not *completely* certain. He knew that the king had long yearned for the day he would sit in the very seat he now occupied, that he might begin proving himself to these great men who'd been obligated to swear fealty to him when he was but an infant. To act the weakling before them by passing his kingdom into the hands of one whom he considered a monster would require, ironically enough, strength and resolve beyond that which most men possessed.

Before Mordesius could say anything to nudge the king toward his purpose, however, the greatest of the great lords, the powerful Lord Bartok, rose to his feet.

"Your Majesty, I am most relieved to see you looking so well," he said. "However, I am grieved to report that I have failed in my duty."

"Your duty?" said the king, coughing into a handkerchief.

"Your Majesty, I have found no trace of the woman called Moira," he explained in a tone so serious and respectful that Mordesius nearly laughed aloud, for he knew how galling it must have been for the great Lord Bartok to have been assigned the demeaning job of searching for the king's fat nursemaid. "No one has seen her since the night Lady Bothwell was revealed to be your sister, our long-lost princess," continued Lord Bartok. His pale eyes drifted to Mordesius, who was seated at the king's right hand, before drifting back to the king. "I am sorry, Your Majesty, but it appears that the woman has vanished into thin air."

The king sat up a little straighter in his ornately carved armchair. He'd been prepared by Mordesius as to what he should say if the subject of the cow arose.

Well, *warned* by Mordesius, was perhaps the more accurate way to put it.

"As it happens, my lord," King Finnius coughed, "I received word just this morning that, uh, in the middle of the night in question, Moira's cousin came to her with the message that her elderly father lay upon his deathbed, and so she departed the palace with all due haste, that she might attend to him in his hour of need."

"She did this without your permission?" asked Lord Bartok, affecting shock.

"Well, um, yes," said the king with obvious reluctance, "but only because she was so terribly worried about her father."

"Even so," rumbled Lord Belmont, clasping his hands over his ponderous belly, "it is not meet for a royal servant to treat her master, the king, in such an ill-considered manner."

The other noblemen at the table looked at one another and nodded in solemn agreement.

Mordesius saw the king bite his lower lip and nearly laughed aloud again, for he knew that the fool was struggling to stop himself from rushing to his nursemaid's defense. Leaning forward slightly so that he could see the faces of all those who sat around the table, Mordesius said, "My lords, His Majesty well understands the grave insult that has been done to him by that wretched woman, and you can rest assured that he intends to see her properly punished for it." Turning to the king, he smiled broadly and said, "Isn't that right, Your Majesty?"

"Yes," agreed King Finnius after a moment's hesitation.

Mordesius smiled again.

"Very good," said Lord Bartok approvingly. "Then perhaps, if it please Your Majesty, we can move on to the subject of the princess formerly known as Lady Bothwell."

"What about her?" asked King Finnius.

At this, many of the noblemen smothered chuckles. A flush stained the pale cheeks of the king; he stared at the chuckling noblemen until they fell silent and looked decidedly uncomfortable.

"Forgive me, Your Majesty," interjected Lord Bartok deferentially, "but though we've guessed by your matching scars that you and the princess are twins who were somehow separated at birth, we know nothing of how you came to be separated, where the princess has been all these years, what impact her presence will have on the realm nor why you allowed her to leave the imperial capital in the company of the Methusian outlaw who has been lewdly cavorting in her chamber since her arrival in Parthania."

Now the other noblemen shared deeply scandalized looks.

In spite of everything, King Finnius managed a smile. "I've never known Azriel to cavort," he said. "He is a good man, and he is taking my sister, the princess, to a private location to give her time to contemplate all that has happened these past days. You see, she did not come to Parthania in search of a great destiny—"

"Why did she come?" interrupted the minor nobleman who'd taken the Council seat of the fatally foolish Lord Pembleton after apoplexy rendered him incapable of doing much more than drooling.

Mordesius decided to answer on behalf of the king. "Having recently fallen upon hard times, our princess came to the imperial capital in the hope of securing a position in the employ of one of the great citizens of the realm. However, upon finding herself face-to-face with me on the night of her arrival, she was so overcome that she somehow found herself lying to impress me," he said, shrugging his uneven shoulders as if to say these things happened to him all the time. "Lie begat lie, until before she knew it, she was up to her pretty eyeballs in a dunghill of trouble."

"Except that she *wasn't* up to her eyeballs in trouble," rumbled Lord Belmont.

"No, of course not," agreed Mordesius smoothly. "I should have said that she *would* have been in trouble, had good fortune not blessed us all with the remarkable discovery that she was the lost twin, come home at last."

"And how is it that she came to be lost in the first place, Your Grace?" asked Lord Bartok guilelessly.

"That is a matter that shall remain between His Grace and me," said the king flatly, using the exact words that Mordesius had instructed him to use.

At this, a murmur of protest rose up among the noblemen.

King Finnius said not a word, but rose to his feet. Since they could not remain seated while their king was standing, all of them, even the high-and-mighty Lord Bartok, hastily stood up. Clenching his hands into fists, Finnius set his knuckles firmly upon the table and let his gaze fall upon one man after another. When he was finished, he sat down and casually motioned the now-silent noblemen to do the same.

Mordesius, who'd also stood when the king stood—but only to avoid having to make awkward explanations—gloated at the thought that while the peasant-hearted weakling actually appeared to have the strength to govern the great lords, he would never get to use it. Somehow, it made Mordesius's victory over the fool all the sweeter.

After a moment of silence, Lord Bartok cleared his throat and said, "You have corrected us, Your Majesty, and quite rightfully so. It is not our place to question your decisions; it is our place to do your will. To this end, I am pleased to report that all is in readiness for the ceremony that will officially transfer the power to rule the realm from the Regent Mordesius to your own esteemed self. The ceremony will, of course, be a most solemn occasion, but I thought to follow it with a feast the likes of which the realm has never seen and—"

"That won't be necessary, my lord," said King Finnius brusquely as he pressed his handkerchief to his lips.

"Majesty?"

The king shifted in his seat so that he could look up at the portrait of his powerful father, the great Octavio. "I said, 'that won't be necessary,'" he repeated, a little louder this time.

"What won't be necessary?" asked Lord Bartok.

"Any of it," said Finnius as he turned his attention back to the confused nobleman. "You see, for health reasons I have decided to indefinitely delay assuming my duties as true ruling king."

If a cannonball had crashed through the roof of the palace and smashed the Council table to splinters, it could not have caused a greater uproar than those few words. Some of the great lords leapt to their feet so suddenly that they knocked over their chairs; others let out involuntary cries of dismay. Still others covered their mouths as though speechless with horror.

The expectation that had so lit all their faces at the outset of the meeting had been abruptly extinguished, never to be rekindled.

Mordesius's dark heart sang.

"B-but, Your Majesty," stammered Lord Bartok, looking flustered for the first time in all the years that Mordesius had known him. "Much as I respect the Regent Mordesius, we and the rest of your subjects have waited these many years to be ruled by a *king* and—"

"As you, yourself, pointed out, my lord, it is not your place to question my decisions," interrupted King Finnius, stifling a wet cough with his handkerchief.

The arrogant, silver-haired patriarch of the Bartok dynasty said nothing, only opened and closed his mouth like a landed fish.

Mordesius placed his gnarled hands on his wasted thighs to keep from hugging himself with delight.

"And how are we to address His Grace henceforth?" asked the minor nobleman who'd taken Pembleton's seat.

"Even though I am, indeed, something far more than Regent owing to the fact that I now rule in place of a living adult king, I am so honored to have been asked to continue to serve on behalf of His most gracious Majesty that I need no fancy new title," said Mordesius in a voice dripping with false humility. "I am content to be called Regent still."

"Regent it is, then," wheezed Lord Belmont, who had yet to stop clutching his poor overworked heart.

As Lord Bartok and the rest of the noblemen nodded uncertainly and cast darting glances of alarm at one another, Mordesius fixed his beautiful dark eyes upon the king. As slowly as if he were swimming in a vat of molasses in the middle of January, King Finnius once more rose to his feet. This time, however, he stepped away from the chair at the head of the Council table and, after a moment's hesitation, gestured toward it. With a soft sigh, Mordesius stood. Nodding at the king as graciously as he could given the weight of his head upon his thin, aching neck, he shuffled forward, eased himself down into the seat of power and smiled out upon the great men who'd once mocked his ambitions but who now trembled before him.

The Council meeting did not last long after this—just long enough for Mordesius to make casual mention of his vast army of New Men for the benefit of any fools who might be contemplating rising up in protest of his appointment, and for him to suggest to Lord Bartok that though the ceremony transferring power would not take place, the feast could yet proceed as planned.

"In honor of your continued regency," said Lord Bartok coolly.

"Yes, exactly," replied Mordesius with pleasure.

He stood, then, and inwardly exulted at the sight of the great lords immediately rising to their feet as well. He let them stand in silence for a moment before dismissing them with the same casual gesture that the king so favored. As they were gathering their things, Mordesius turned to the king, who'd stood awkwardly by these last few minutes, a royal nobody with no seat at his own Council table, and suggested to him that he might want to return to his chambers and get some rest. Though his voice oozed concern, it was plain to all that the Something-Far-More-Than-Regent was dismissing the king as well.

After he'd sent the king packing, Mordesius lurched over, laid a hand upon Lord Bartok's sleeve and said, "I would speak with you."

Though the greatest of the great lords looked down at the lowborn hand upon his elegant, aristocratic arm with an expression of barely disguised distaste, his voice was impassive when he said, "Yes, Your Grace?"

Mordesius waited until everyone else had left the chamber. Then he said, "Can I assume that our . . . arrangement still stands?"

Lord Bartok went still as a statue. "Our arrangement?" he said cautiously.

Mordesius smiled. "You will see to it that the great lords name me the king's heir," he reminded. "In return, I will convince the king to become betrothed to your charming daughter, Lady Aurelia."

Lord Bartok stroked his trim silver beard as he considered how to respond.

Before he could decide, Mordesius added, "You should know that as a gesture of good faith, I have already broached the subject of betrothal with His Majesty."

"You have?" said Lord Bartok, his inborn lust for power surging in his pale eyes. "And how did he react? Was he agreeable to the proposed union?"

"I have reason to believe that he can be made to be so," said Mordesius coyly.

"But even if what you say is true," frowned Lord Bartok, "the king is of age now—surely he will expect to name his own heir."

"Do not trouble yourself with what the king does or does not expect," breathed Mordesius. "Now, more than ever before, he is content to take my counsel in all things."

Lord Bartok nodded his understanding of things best left unsaid. "Still," he pointed out, "there is the matter of the long-lost princess."

"She has no interest in the throne," said Mordesius dismissively. "Even if she did, she chose to venture forth beyond the protection of the great walls of Parthania in the company of a dangerous outlaw. Anything could happen to her out there."

"Indeed, it could," said Lord Bartok, the barest hint of a smile playing on his lips. "Still, we are not discussing the arrangement I originally envisioned, for the king does not hold the reins of power—you do."

"What of that?" snapped Mordesius, who was growing tired of the great lord's objections. "Your daughter will be queen. The children she bears will have the blood of kings coursing through their half-royal veins."

Lord Bartok's eyes gleamed at the prospect. "And when Aurelia does bear a child, you will give up your position in the line of succession?"

"Of course!" exclaimed Mordesius cheerfully, as though he would not dream of having it any other way. "Until then, however, I will expect to be acknowledged by all as heir apparent, and to have it known by all that I have the full support of the great Bartok dynasty behind me."

Though Lord Bartok was not a scrupulous man, and though Mordesius was dangling before him that which he desired above all else, he hesitated the way one might hesitate before striking a bargain with a snake—and a lowborn snake, at that.

Then he smiled his wintry smile and said, "Very well, Your Grace. A fortnight from the day the king and my daughter announce their betrothal, there shall be another announcement: that the great Regent Mordesius has been named heir to the Erok throne."

"Wonderful," beamed Mordesius, thinking how pleasant it was going to be when the king was finally dead and he was able to celebrate his own coronation by reducing the high-and-mighty bastard before him to a bucket of pulp. "Just . . . wonderful."

Fourteen

LATER THAT SAME NIGHT, Mordesius whistled as he slouched through the twisting maze of corridors in the dungeon that lay far beneath the palace. The damp stone walls glistened in the torchlight; screams echoed in the distance. Every so often, a well-fed rat materialized from the filthy straw at Mordesius's shuffling feet to scuttle away into the shadows. And, of course, the forgotten ones were forever shoving their clawlike hands through the tiny windows of their prison cells or pressing their ravaged faces hard against the bars to hoarsely beg for mercy—even the mercy of death. But if Mordesius thought about those wretches at all, it was only to think that they really ought to know better than to beg for mercy from him.

Reaching his destination at last, he withdrew a key from the pocket of his elegant, ermine-trimmed robe, inserted it into the heavy iron lock and twisted hard. The lock, which had recently been oiled, fell open at once. Grabbing the nearest torch off the wall, Mordesius pushed open the heavy door and peered inside.

The cell was dark and stifling, of course, with air foul enough to make one retch. On the other hand, it was reasonably dry and far larger than many cells, some of which were so tiny that on top of everything else, their occupants must suffer the torment of never being able to fully stretch out their painfully cramped muscles. This cell also boasted a comfortable chair, though the occupant of the cell, the king's beloved nursemaid Moira, was quite unable to enjoy sitting upon it since the short chains that shackled her to the wall did not reach that far. Instead, she sat on a fetid pile of straw on the cold, hard ground. In addition to her chains, the insufferable cow wore a ragged shift that she, herself, had been forced to strip from the fresh corpse of a toothless, gray-haired old woman one of the guards had discovered lying in an unlocked cell. The nursemaid also bore the marks of the beating General Murdock had personally bestowed upon her after abducting her and dragging her to this place. On the ground beside her were a nearly empty bucket of dirty water and a shiny silver platter heaped with wilted grass and clover—a little jest thought up by Mordesius, who'd not wanted the "cow" to think he'd forgotten to provide her with something to eat.

"Moo!" he called out now, by way of greeting.

With considerably more vigor than Mordesius thought she had any business having given that she'd not eaten human food since her abduction four days past, Moira turned her head and squinted up at him.

"You," she said.

"Yes, me," he agreed, trying not to feel piqued by her lack of terror. Shuffling forward into the room, he shoved the torch close to her face for the pleasure of seeing her jerk back from the flames. He then set the torch in a nearby bracket and settled himself upon the chair. Sighing to emphasize to the cow just how comfortable the chair was, Mordesius lifted a pair of rusted iron pliers off a nearby table of implements.

"I apologize for not coming to visit you earlier," he said. "I've been much occupied aboveground in the land of the living. After seeing the Methusian and the princess off on their quest for the healing Pool of Genezing, which they mean to find for me, that I may be restored to full vigor, I spent one day letting the king anguish over your mysterious disappearance and then another two days standing idly by while the fool convalesced—"

"His Majesty was ill?" asked Moira, her normally placid features animated by sudden loving concern. "Is he quite recovered?"

"Oh, he is well enough," said Mordesius with a flare of irritation.

"I am glad," murmured Moira with obvious relief. "I will pray that the Fates keep him so, and that they will keep the princess safe, as well. The king likes her, and so do I. She is kind and wise, and plays a clever game of cards."

If they'd been sitting in the king's chambers, such a deliberately provocative statement would have driven Mordesius into a blind rage. However, the sight of the cow chained to the wall, hungry and in pain, added to the knowledge that her ability to draw breath was a privilege that he could snatch away at any moment, miraculously enabled him to remain calm. Absently dragging the tip of his finger along the sharp edge of the pliers, he said, "Who and what you like are of no interest to me or anyone else—"

"They were always of interest to His Majesty," reminded Moira.

"Yes," snapped Mordesius, pressing his fingertip against the pliers' edge with such force that it began to bleed. "And look where your meddling has gotten him: this very afternoon, he was forced to advise the great lords of the realm that he wished me to continue to rule in his stead. Shortly, he shall be forced to announce his betrothal to Lord Bartok's daughter. A short while after that, he shall be forced to name me his heir. The Princess Persephone was given one hundred days to return to Parthania with proof that she and the cockroach have found the Pool of Genezing. If she accomplishes this unlikely feat, she and the king will both perish in unfortunate—and probably gruesome—accidents; if she fails to accomplish this feat, she and the king will likewise die in agony. And on that glorious day, I shall ascend to the throne. So you see, you thick-headed imbecile, the king's love of nobodies has made him a weakling, paving my path to glory and dooming him. Oh, and lest you start thinking too highly of yourself, it is not just you that he hopes to spare by bending to my will, it is also that whore of a sister of his and the vast herds of nameless, faceless lowborns whom he knows will be cut down if he does not do my bidding."

When the cow smiled at this, as though she was proud of the king's spineless behavior, the only thing that prevented Mordesius from driving the sharp tip of the pliers deep into her eye was the concern that he might accidentally pierce her brain and kill her. He'd waited so long for the pleasure of making her suffer that he would not risk ending her life too quickly.

"I wish there was some way I could tell His Majesty that I would gladly die to see him freed of your tyranny," she said now.

"Well, you can't, and even if you could, we both know he'd never accept your offer," said Mordesius impatiently. "However, you'll be happy to know that there *is* something you can do for him."

Holding the pliers out toward her, he opened and closed them several times, smiling at the delicious snipping sound they made.

"The king has requested proof that you are alive," he explained as he rose to his feet and shuffled toward her. "You can give him proof soft and warm enough to convince even the greatest skeptic that you yet breathe."

Moira gazed at him without fear. "Hold out your hand," he commanded.

After a moment's hesitation, she wordlessly did as he asked.

Smiling, Mordesius set the pliers at the base of her left index finger.

"Moo," he whispered as he slowly squeezed.

Fifteen

Ninety-seven white beans left in the jar

"MARRY ME?" BLURTED PERSEPHONE, who was finding it as hard to breathe as if she'd abruptly found herself in corsets laced up by a giant who knew not his own strength.

"Persephone—" began Azriel.

"No!" she cried, scurrying away from him, though he'd taken no step toward her. "No! The idea . . . the very notion is . . . is *preposterous*!"

"Actually, it isn't preposterous at all," said Cairn slowly. "You see, if one is adopted by our tribe as a child, as Azriel was, and later, upon coming of age, swears the oath and takes the mark, it is the same as blood to us. Though an adult cannot be adopted or, as Tiny pointed out, simply declare himself a Methusian, an adult *can* marry into the tribe, and if he or she does so, it is once again the same as blood to us. That means that if you were to marry Azriel, you would become a Methusian, and any who shared your blood would become Methusians by association."

"In other words, whether he wanted to or not, her brother, the king, would become a Methusian," said Rachel in a wondering voice.

"A Methusian king," said Tiny in an equally wondering voice.

"Oh, now, hold on a moment—"

"Azriel, you say that this Erok king Finnius told you that he means to see to the welfare of all people?" said Fayla, who did not seem to have noticed that Persephone was speaking.

"Yes," nodded Azriel. "He also said that he means to answer for how the clans have been treated and to do what he can to unite the realm."

"The prophecy said that there would be a Methusian king whose coming would unite the five clans of Glyndoria and set things to right for all people," said Cairn, her words coming more quickly now. "This Erok king vowed to do more or less the same thing!"

"I was struck by the same thought when I first heard His Majesty speak the words," said Azriel. "And as I mulled them over afterward, I began to wonder about recent events. Making our way to Parthania only to see Persephone swept off to the palace . . . descending into the dungeon only to stumble across the dying Methusian Seer . . . learning of a lost royal twin only to discover that Persephone is that twin . . . escaping execution at the hands of the Regent by promising to find the healing pool only to be told that if we do not do so, King Finnius will die. Finnius, the king who, unprompted, gave me his word that he'd protect us should we ever choose to come out of hiding and settle by the pool."

"Marry the girl . . . find the pool . . . save the king . . . fulfill the prophecy. It all fits," breathed Cairn, her eyes aglow with excitement. "Nay, it more than fits, for on that long-ago terrible night when the Seer spoke to me of the prophecy, I asked her why she could not have had a vision of the healing pool that we might once again have power over death itself. She reminded me that old Balthazar swore he'd found it and that it had brought Death to his very doorstep—and to ours. But she allowed that perhaps it would not ever be so, and that perhaps the coming king was meant to see our people safely settled on its shores once more. I think now that she'd already guessed that the pool and the prophecy were entwined but had not Seen exactly how they were entwined."

"But our Azriel has figured it out," boomed Tiny proudly, giving his friend such a wallop on the back that he nearly knocked him off his feet.

"And the truly remarkable thing," continued Cairn, "is that if he has figured correctly, and I can well believe that he has, not only will our people get that for which they have waited so long and suffered so much, but the princess will also see her dearest hope fulfilled."

Persephone, who'd been on the brink of offering vociferous protest to this mad talk, was brought up short by these last words. "What do you mean?" she asked guardedly.

Cairn spread her hands wide. "Only that if your brother is the prophesied Methusian king, it would be in my people's best interests to help you locate the pool, that he might be saved. But if he is not, we'd be foolish to allow you to risk your life venturing forth into the dangerous frontiers, for there can be little doubt in anyone's mind that you are the girl whose great destiny it is to help set a Methusian king upon the throne. You are an Erok princess—power, privilege and influence are yours by right of your royal birth. I cannot see why the Fates would have sent us you if they meant the great destiny to fall upon the shoulders of Rachel, a girl we found behind a fishmonger's stall."

Though this made more sense than Persephone cared to admit, she thought it an unkind thing to say in front of Rachel. So, after giving her doppelgänger's hand a sympathetic squeeze, she tossed her head at Cairn and said, "The Fates play tricks all the time."

"They do indeed," agreed the Methusian woman, whose dark eyes slid toward Azriel as she added, "and it appears that they've chosen to play their latest trick on *you*."

Persephone scowled as she suddenly realized that she could not argue this. For if she did not marry Azriel, Finn could not be the Methusian king. And if he could not be the Methusian king, the Methusians would attempt to stop her from looking for the healing pool. And even if they were unsuccessful in their attempt, she did not see how—alone, unaided and without the first clue where to start looking—she would possibly be able to find the pool and get back to Parthania before the beans in the jar ran out—and Finn's time with them.

Still.

It was no small matter, getting married. For one thing, it was forever. And for another thing, as her wedded husband, by law Azriel would have the right to tell her what to do and to beat her if she did not comply. It would be like being enslaved all over again! Worse even, because Azriel would have a right to expect her to fulfill certain marital . . . duties.

Duties that Persephone had no intention of being cornered into fulfilling.

And so, smiling at Azriel in a way that would have made a less oblivious man run for his life (or, at the very least, reach down to protect his manhood), Persephone took him by the elbow and propelled him back into the cool darkness of the tunnel so that they could share a few words in private.

"Careful how you grip," said the handsome rascal affably as he strode along before her. "For some reason, your fingers are pinching a little—"

Abruptly releasing his elbow, Persephone darted forward and spun around to face him. "You should have warned me that you were planning to *propose*," she hissed, reaching out to give him a real pinch.

Azriel let out a yelp of pain and surprise, but instead of jumping beyond the reach of her menacing digits, he gently caught her hands and pulled her close.

"I'm sorry I didn't warn you but I was worried that you wouldn't take me seriously," he murmured. "I hoped that if my proposal was immediately followed by the words of others who could see that our marriage had a higher purpose that you'd be more inclined to agree to be my bride."

Persephone felt her knees go weak at the word "bride" but all she said was, "I do not like being backed into corners, Azriel."

"This is no corner," he promised as he released her hands and slid his arms around her. "Our union would guarantee the help of my clan in the search for the healing pool, but you shall have my help either way."

"I shall?" she said, surprised and not surprised.

"Of course," he said easily. "And if you choose not to marry me, after it is all over one way or another, you shall be free to carry on alone in pursuit of a destiny that belongs to none but you. Myself, I will find a plot of land with a pretty little thatch-roofed cottage, a yard full of scratching chickens, a well-tended garden—"

"An apple orchard, a pond stocked with fish and an oak tree with a swing hung from a low branch so that on warm summer days you can push your clever wife and later, your babies," said Persephone in a rush, recalling the intoxicating description Azriel had once shared of the life he would choose. "You will have music and laughter each day, and the knowledge that it will all be there tomorrow, and for ten thousand tomorrows thereafter."

"That is exactly right," said Azriel, his gaze steady upon her.

Persephone's breath caught at a sudden vision of herself sitting on a swing, laughing and looking back at him as he pushed her ever higher.

"You could be the wife of my dreams, Persephone," he said softly.

"I . . . I doubt Finn would approve of his sister the princess living such a simple life," she heard herself croak.

"In that case, binding my fortunes to yours until death do us part would be a tremendous sacrifice on my part," murmured Azriel. "However, it is a sacrifice that I am willing to make."

"Then I am also willing to make a . . . sacrifice," she gulped before hurriedly adding, "For the sake of my brother, your people and all people."

For a long moment, Azriel just looked at her. Then, smiling slightly, he leaned so close that she could feel his breath on her lips. "Did you just agree to marry me, Persephone?"

"Yes," she breathed, leaning closer still.

The instant before her lips brushed against his, Azriel abruptly let go of her and stepped back. "And we're agreed then?" he asked.

"W-what?" stammered Persephone, who hadn't really heard the question.

"We're agreed?" said Azriel, a little louder. "We're only marrying for the sake of others?"

As his words slowly sunk in, Persephone was overcome by that same feeling of disappointment she'd had the night she'd realized that his willingness to undertake the quest had nothing to do with the fact that it mattered to her. This time, however, it was disappointment borne of the certainty that at another time and place, Azriel would never have agreed to marry her simply for the sake of others. Instead, he would have insisted that he was marrying her for the sake of his own heart, because it could not go on beating without her.

But of course, it was not another time and place.

Persephone cleared her throat. "Yes. Yes, of course—we're agreed," she said, striving to sound as matter-of-fact as he. "We're only marrying for the sake of others."

Azriel nodded crisply, then turned toward Rachel and the Methusians, whom Persephone was startled to see were crowded around the mouth of the tunnel wearing the rapt expressions of spectators watching an especially spellbinding play. When he gave a thumbs-up sign they all began cheering.

"Azriel?" said Persephone, touching his arm.

"Yes?" he said, turning back around so quickly that he nearly bumped into her.

"Since we're a-agreed that this will be more of a . . . an arrangement than a marriage," she mumbled, striving to sound nonchalant even as she felt her cheeks begin to burn with embarrassment, "can I assume that you'll not expect me to fulfill any marital, uh, duties?"

A shadow of something flickered across Azriel's face and was gone.

"Duties?" he said, sounding so absolutely perplexed that Persephone knew that he knew exactly what she was talking about.

Relieved to be back in familiar territory, Persephone dropped her hand to the dagger at her thigh and said, "You know—the kind of duties that would cause me to feel the need to slit you from bow to stern."

At this, Azriel smiled. "Oh, Princess," he said as he led her back out of the tunnel. "You needn't worry about *that*."

Perhaps because she and Azriel were only marrying for the sake of others, Persephone had just assumed that the wedding ceremony would be a rushed affair, to be gotten over with as quickly as possible so that they could get on with the business of finding the healing pool.

The instant she and Azriel emerged from the tunnel, however, it became clear to her that the Methusians had other ideas. For without warning, she found herself swallowed up by a crowd of women and girls who patted her back and pinched her cheeks and laughingly informed her that it was not meet for a bride to look upon her groom so close to the wedding. Then, singing at the top of their lungs, they all but carried her across the clearing to the same thatch-roofed hut into which she'd been unceremoniously tossed the first time she'd visited the Methusian camp. She was not tossed this time, however, but rather deposited with many promises that her upcoming "big day" would surpass her wildest dreams.

"But I have no such dreams!" she protested with a grimace at Rachel, who'd followed her into the hut. "I never imagined I'd get married at all—I never gave it the slightest thought! I just want to get this over with so that—"

"No dreams!" clucked a grandmotherly Methusian woman, reaching through the doorway to give her cheek another lusty pinch.

Fayla laughed as Persephone hastily retreated farther into the hut, beyond the reach of her well-wishers. "I'm sorry, Persephone, but we Methusians love a celebration, and there is no celebration we love more than a wedding," she explained. "I know you are eager to be on your way, but we cannot allow this joyous event to pass unremarked. Preparations for the ceremony will be completed by tomorrow sunset.

Until then, you must stay in here and promise that you won't try to sneak peeks at your betrothed."

Persephone swelled up with indignation. "I—"

Fayla was gone before Persephone could offer more protest than this. A short while later, Tiny arrived bearing two heavy blankets, a large brass pot full of hare stew, a loaf of dark bread, a jug of ale, a fat candle and the pack containing the jar of white beans. He was assisted in his task by Mateo's younger brother, Raphael, and also by Sabian, who flung his chubby arms about Persephone's neck and lisped in her ear that he had "mithed her motht grievouthly." When Persephone told Sabian that she'd missed him most grievously as well, he beamed at her and then trotted out the door after Tiny and Raphael.

As soon as he was gone, Persephone turned to Rachel and, in a low voice, said, "I just want you to know that I'm only marrying Azriel for the sake of others."

"Oh?" said Rachel as she tore off a hunk of bread and dunked it in the stew. "Are you sure about that?"

The question made Persephone almost as agitated as did the sidelong look Rachel was giving her. "What do you mean am I sure about that?" she spluttered. "Of course, I'm sure! Azriel and I agreed upon it."

"Really?" said Rachel innocently, taking a big bite of saucy bread. "Was that before or after you kissed?"

Persephone's heart missed a beat. "We didn't kiss," she said, her throat tightening at the memory of Azriel pulling away from her at the last second. "We only *almost* kissed and it didn't mean anything."

"Which is what your marriage vows will mean?" said Rachel, watching her closely.

"Exactly," said Persephone, lifting her chin. "Pass the ale."

Persephone spent most of the next day pacing inside the hut like a caged beast.

In the morning, Tiny and the boys came by with more food; in the afternoon, Fayla delivered a clean, pretty gown for Rachel. Somewhere in between, a gaggle of giggling girls showed up with a basin of cold water, a rag, a dish of slimy soap, a crude hairbrush and a handful of rusty hairpins. Persephone used the lot to attend to her toilette, all the while stubbornly telling herself that she was not such a princess that she *truly* yearned for her lovely claw-footed bathtub, her creamy speckled soaps and the soothing ministrations of Martha and the sisters.

It only *felt* like she did.

By the time sunset finally arrived, she and Rachel were as clean as they could be and their identical dark hair was brushed to a glossy shine. In addition, Persephone was as nervous as a cat and on the verge of throwing up.

Before she could do so, the door opened and three women entered the candlelit hut. The first carried an exquisitely crafted headpiece to which was attached a veil so sheer that it seemed hardly more than a mist. The second carried the most delicate pair of beaded slippers Persephone had ever seen in her life. And the third had a pair of silk stockings draped over one outstretched arm and a spectacular gown laid over the other. Exceedingly simple in its form, the material of the gown seemed more liquid than solid, and even in the dimness of the hut, it sparkled like sunlight on fast-running water.

"Oooooh," breathed Persephone, who'd temporarily forgotten that her wedding was naught but a transaction of necessity being undertaken for the sake of others.

"Where on earth did you get these things?" asked Rachel in amazement.

"Azriel says he 'borrowed' them from the Regent," explained the woman holding the dress.

"I hope they fit," said Rachel.

"Azriel says they're bound to," said the woman, "seeing how they were once worn by the princess's dead mother."

"They were *what?*" exclaimed Persephone and Rachel in unison. The woman chuckled at their reaction. "Worn by the princess's dead mother," she repeated. "It seems that while he was prowling about the Regent's bedchamber looking for gold, Azriel happened upon several large chests filled with the dead queen's finest clothing. Kept by the Regent for what purpose, I shudder to think, but anyway, Azriel decided to pick out a few things." The woman chuckled again— indulgently this time. "I'll warrant the scalawag had a mind to make you his bride even then, Princess, and thought to make your big day just as special as it could be."

Ignoring the look that Rachel was giving her, Persephone swallowed hard and stammered, "That was, uh, thoughtful of him, of course, but he really oughtn't to have taken such a risk."

"Oh, don't you worry about that," chortled the woman as she handed over the dress. "I'm sure you'll think of *some* way to make it up to him."

Persephone grimaced at this. Then, as soon as the three Methusian women left the hut, she nervously slipped out of the grubby shift she'd been wearing for days and stepped into her mother's gown. It fit perfectly, just as Azriel had anticipated it would. While Rachel laced up the back, Persephone pulled on the stockings, worked her feet into the beaded slippers and set the headpiece atop her head.

"You look perfect," sighed Rachel as she gave the veil one last twitch to ensure that it fell properly over Persephone's shoulders. "Why are you trembling? Are you nervous about the wedding night?"

"No," said Persephone, louder than she meant to. Reaching for her mug to moisten her suddenly dry mouth, she added, "Azriel said I needn't worry about that."

"Oh?" said Rachel as she crouched down to straighten the hem of Persephone's gown. "You mean because he intends to be a gentle lover?"

Her words jarred Persephone so badly that she nearly slopped ale down the front of the gown. "*What?*" she spluttered and coughed. "No! I mean because he doesn't expect me to . . . you know . . ."

"Are you sure?" asked Rachel doubtfully, looking up at her. "Because it seems to me that he might have meant something else entirely. For while he certainly seems the type to stay true to a wedded wife—which is what you will be, regardless of why you say you're marrying him— it is hard to imagine that he's the type who would be content to live the rest of his life without . . . you know."

Persephone flushed hotly at this shrewd and unsettling observation, but before she could offer protest, the sound of someone impatiently knocking on the door of the hut told her that it was time to go.

And so, with a hammering heart, Persephone lifted up the slippery, silvery-white skirt of her beautiful gown and stepped out of the hut—

And into a dream.

Sixteen

BACK IN THE IMPERIAL CAPITAL, the feast being held in honor of Mordesius's continued regency was proving every bit as magnificent as Lord Bartok had promised it would be. The dishes had been numerous and widely varied, and in the absence of the king, whom Mordesius had ordered not to attend, lest his royal presence prove a distraction, each dish had been presented to Mordesius by a servant on bended knee, for him to taste or not before sending onward to another table as he saw fit. Mordesius had made the most of this privilege, doling out the dishes with calculation and gloating inwardly at the dismayed (and often anxious) faces of those who received nothing to eat at all.

Later, after the meal was over, the head of every noble family in attendance had come forward with great ceremony to present him with a priceless gift of some sort—a golden chalice inlaid with gemstones, an exquisitely wrought tapestry, a dozen sable pelts, a pair of perfectly matched chestnut mares, a sword of finest steel.

Mordesius had not deluded himself into believing that these gifts had originally been meant for him, for he well knew that they'd been intended for the king, to celebrate his official coming to power, but it had not mattered. The only thing that had mattered was that like everything else that would once have belonged to the king, the gifts now belonged to him.

Yet in spite of the food and the gifts, as Mordesius sat alone on the royal dais listening to the music and watching the noblemen and noblewomen perform the traditional court dances for his entertainment, he could not help but feel that something was missing.

Drumming his fingers upon the purple-trimmed white linen that covered the long table before him, he allowed his gaze to drift to the table where the Princess Persephone had sat when she'd been Lady Bothwell, fresh to court and his personal guest at the execution of Lord Pembleton's son. She'd excited him, then—so much so that he'd gone to some trouble to have her so-called husband murdered that she might be free to wed again. Though he now knew her for a faithless whore of a princess who'd nearly destroyed him, Mordesius had to admit that he missed her. He missed the warm scent of her and the feel of her hand resting lightly upon his painfully thin arm; he missed the way she would smile at him and curtsey at his feet. Most of all, however, he missed her for never once having looked at him the way these dancing sows before him did: as infrequently and dartingly as common courtesy would allow, obviously revolted by the sight of him and terrified that he might crook his shiny pink finger toward them—or worse.

No, the gutter-reared princess had never looked at him like that. She had ever looked at him as though he was a man like any other. A man to be toyed with, amused, flattered, feared or even hated—but a man, nevertheless.

He wondered how she was faring now. He should know soon, for he'd ordered Murdock to send regular reports back to Parthania. Hopefully, his first report would also explain why four members of the princess's cavalcade—a man, two women and a boy—had been discovered supping in a tavern some leagues west of Parthania. A sharp-eyed New Man, suspicious of the quality of the horses the lowborns had been riding, had searched their panniers and discovered a small bag of gold and horse blankets edged in royal purple. When the thieving wretches had confessed to having deserted the princess, they'd been summarily executed, their heads stuck on pikes planted in the town square as a warning to others who would steal from their betters.

While he was satisfied with the fate the wretches had suffered, Mordesius had an uneasy feeling that there was more to the story, and he wanted to know what it was.

And may the gods help those headless corpses if it turns out that they caused some mischief that interfered with the princess's quest for the healing pool, he thought darkly, *for if they did, I shall see to it that every person who has ever known them dies screaming.*

His mood abruptly souring at the thought of a handful of useless nobodies ruining his chances of someday becoming well and whole, Mordesius folded his arms across his sunken chest, slumped down in his chair and glowered out at the twirling, tapping, leaping men and women. The ease with which they moved suddenly seemed more like a taunt than entertainment, and Mordesius was on the verge of falling into a genuine temper when he noticed a young woman in a shimmering gown of mint green standing at the edge of the dance floor.

She was looking at him.

On impulse, he sat up and crooked his finger at her. She froze like a startled fawn. When Mordesius impatiently crooked his finger again and nodded, she looked behind her to see if he'd been beckoning someone else. When she uncertainly turned back around, he jabbed his finger at her and crooked his finger for the last time.

Looking as though she might burst into tears, the panicked girl hastily scanned the crowd for her father, a lord so minor that Mordesius had not even bothered to learn his name. Unfortunately for her, instead of rushing forward to make some excuse as to why his daughter could not go to Mordesius, he glared at her and jerked his head toward the dais before turning to Mordesius and bowing low.

Mordesius's handsome face betrayed nothing, but he inwardly rejoiced at the incredible knowledge that his power had grown so great that a nobleman was willing to sacrifice his daughter to him.

The other noblemen and noblewomen in the Great Hall whispered and smothered unkind laughter behind their gloved hands as they watched the girl drag herself up the dais and miserably curtsey to Mordesius. Smiling broadly, he patted the seat next to him and then grandly gestured for the musicians to resume playing and the dancers to resume dancing. Feeling immeasurably better than he had a moment earlier and missing the Princess Persephone not at all, Mordesius laid his cold hand upon the trembling thigh of the young woman beside him.

One day very soon he would be a king.

He really ought to begin auditioning potential queens.

Seventeen

Ninety-six white beans left in the jar

THE NIGHT SKY WAS AWASH with twinkling stars and the air was perfumed with the smell of burning applewood. A haunting tune played upon a lone whistle pipe mingled most enchantingly with the sounds of the forest. Colored glass jars of every size and shape hung from the branches of the trees that surrounded the forest clearing; inside these jars, trapped fireflies flitted and pulsed. Directly in front of Persephone, pitch torches as tall as a man marked a path thickly strewn with the fragrant petals of wildflowers. On either side of the path stood the Methusians, all dressed in their colorful, layered finery, all smiling at her.

And waiting for her at the end of the path, looking wilder and more beautiful than ever:

Azriel.

"Move!" whispered Rachel, giving her a nudge from behind.

But Persephone didn't know if she *could* move. The very fact that it seemed like a dream made it seem all the more real. Fireflies, flower petals and gowns of liquid sunlight did not accompany transactions of necessity. And she and Azriel had agreed that this marriage must be a transaction of necessity because . . . because . . .

"You're not going to throw up, are you?" murmured Rachel.

Shaking her head so violently that she made herself dizzy, Persephone closed her eyes and forced herself to take several deep calming breaths, to focus on why she was doing this and to remember that it had nothing whatsoever to do with any feelings she might have for Azriel, whose very presence even now seemed to be tugging at something deep inside of her.

Then she opened her eyes and determinedly stepped onto the path.

The moment her beaded slipper touched the delicate petals, a soft sigh went up from the Methusians. Smiling in spite of her nervousness—or perhaps because of it—Persephone took another step, and another. She took strength from the knowledge that Rachel was right behind her; she trembled at the feel of Azriel's eyes upon her, drinking her in.

Indeed, it wasn't until she was standing by his side that she dared to look up at him.

As she did so, the rest of the world fell away.

"You are breathtaking," he said softly as he stared at her with eyes like ice on fire.

Persephone had never been as aware of him as she was in that moment. Though they weren't touching, it felt as though they were touching; though her eyes never left his face, she could see every part of him. Unbidden, images flashed through her mind—Azriel standing at the edge of the hot spring pool, bare-chested and about to unlace his breeches; Azriel describing the pretty little cottage he would share with a clever wife. Azriel risking his life to linger within the Regent's bedchamber that he might find her something beautiful to wear—something that would make this day just as special as it could be.

The images made Persephone feel helpless, like she was falling, falling with no way to stop herself and no knowledge of when or where the fall would end.

Or even *if* it would end.

When she finally managed to tear her gaze away from Azriel's face, Persephone noticed that Fleet and Cur were standing on his far side like a pair of freakish groomsmen—Cur looking mutinous with his freshly brushed fur and crisp new bow, Fleet torn between rolling his eyes with pleasure at the sight of her and contorting his big, horsey head in an effort to devour the gorgeous wreath of wildflowers that hung about his neck.

"You did this for me?" Persephone asked Azriel as the sensation of falling grew even more intense.

"Well, I certainly didn't do it for me," he smiled, gesturing to a couple of fresh scratches she hadn't noticed before.

Cairn started to speak then. At first, Persephone could hardly see or hear her. All she could see was Azriel; all she could hear was the pounding of her own heart. Then the pounding faded and Azriel was promising to love and cherish none but her. To be the wings that lifted her higher in times of joy and the rock upon which she might stand in times of trouble. To respect and honor her, to devote himself entirely to her happiness and contentment, to be fearless in his protection of her and any children the Fates might see fit to bless them with. To commit his soul so completely to hers that not even Death itself would be able to part them, that their union might last beyond this mortal world and into the next world and into the next after that, unto forever.

Then Persephone heard herself vowing the same in a voice that hardly sounded like her own, and then Cairn was smiling and saying, "Azriel, you may kiss your bride."

Persephone's breath caught at these words, and caught again as Azriel reached for her. He moved so slowly that she could easily have stepped back or ducked away, but she did neither of these things. Instead, she closed her eyes and leaned into his kiss.

As their lips met, Rachel sighed rapturously, Cur snarled menacingly, Fleet neighed with indignation and the Methusians sent up a tremendous cheer. Though Azriel's lips were yet pressed against hers, Persephone could not help laughing at the odd confluence of sounds. At her laughter, Azriel abruptly pulled away from her and gave a loud cheer of his own. Then, spinning her in his arms, he dipped her so far back that her veil and hair swept the ground. As they resumed kissing, the Methusians cheered again, Fayla grabbed Fleet's bridle to prevent him from trying to trample the passion out of Azriel, and Tiny stepped forward just in time to block Cur, who'd launched himself into the air, clearly intent upon taking a juicy chunk out of the amorous groom's backside.

At the feel of Azriel's strong arms about her, his kiss deeper than the deepest ocean, Persephone gave up trying to stay focused on why she was doing this and instead allowed herself to get lost in the dream. Reaching up, she twined her arms about his neck and pulled him closer still.

Cairn let them indulge themselves for an almost indecent length of time before conspicuously clearing her throat. When the newlyweds gave no sign of having heard her, little Sabian trundled forward, propped his hands upon his chubby knees and bellowed in Azriel's ear that it was time to "THTOP KITHING!" Startled, Persephone gasped and clung to Azriel so fiercely that it threw them both off balance.

Lunging one leg forward so that he was half-kneeling with her yet in his arms, Azriel beamed down at her. "Fear not, wife, for I will never let you fall."

She laughed, and the next instant Rachel was dragging Persephone out of Azriel's arms, hugging her and sniffling that it had been *such* a romantic ceremony. And then someone was shoving a brimming goblet into her hand, and several dozen wildly excited Methusian children were herding her and Azriel past a nearby bonfire to a raised dais. The dais was just large enough to accommodate a small, rough-hewn table and a bench for two, and it was covered by an arch fashioned out of young branches bent, tied together and hung with yet more wildflowers and more captive fireflies.

"It's lovely," said Persephone in a wondering voice.

"You're lovely," murmured Azriel, catching her about the waist with his strong hands.

At his touch, Persephone inhaled sharply, but instead of pulling her close and kissing her again as she'd expected him to, he hoisted her so high into the air that she shrieked and dropped her goblet, drenching several children with wine. As the Methusians roared with laughter, Azriel flashed them his wickedest pirate smile. Then, setting his scowling bride down upon the dais with exaggerated care, he jumped up after her and called for more wine.

The feast that followed was nothing like the feasts at the imperial palace had been, with their rare delicacies, cunning pastries and innumerable platters of artfully presented fish and fowl. But the bread was hearty, the butter creamy, the cheeses well aged, the meat succulent and the wine plentiful. Moreover, unlike palace feasts where Persephone had ever felt on edge—never knowing from which direction danger might spring next, always feeling many pairs of cold, speculative eyes upon her—she could not help but enjoy the Methusian feast. The good food was followed by music, dancing and more drinking. As the night deepened, the air grew brisker, the stars brighter, the laughter louder and the merrymaking more boisterous. Children with big eyes, sticky fingers and mouths crammed with pilfered sweetmeats darted about in pursuit of Cur and the other barking dogs; beautiful girls with bare feet and bells at their ankles lifted their skirts and danced until the young men watching them broke into spontaneous, and often comical, displays of drunken virility. Near the spot where Fleet stood with his horsey head eyeball-deep in a giant tub of cut turnips, Tiny sat gazing at Fayla with mute, bleary-eyed adoration while she chatted with Rachel and pretended not to notice.

Indeed, Persephone was enjoying herself so much that she'd quite forgotten about her earlier conversation with Rachel about "you know."

It was well after midnight when Cairn, who looked as though she'd been celebrating quite as hard as anyone else, stepped up to the dais and raised her hands high in the air. As soon as the Methusians noticed her standing there, they began snickering good-naturedly, elbowing one another in the ribs and grinning up at Persephone in a way that caused her to feel a tiny prickle of alarm.

Turning to Azriel, who was wearing an expression of such angelic innocence that the tiny prickle instantly turned into a full-fledged stab of alarm, Persephone was about to ask him what was going on when Cairn's voice rang out across the clearing.

"My good people!" she cried. "The time has come for us to put the newlyweds to bed!"

This announcement was followed by several cymbal crashes and a chorus of drunken cheers.

"What?" gasped Persephone, leaping to her feet so fast that she lost her balance and would have toppled backward off the dais if Azriel hadn't reached out to steady her.

Cairn took a deep breath. "I said, THE TIME HAS COME FOR—"

"I heard what you *said*," blurted Persephone, flapping her hands in agitation. "I just . . . I think there's been some kind of mistake—"

"There's no mistake, Princess," interrupted Cairn, hiccupping into her fist. "As Azriel is well aware, it is not enough for you to be wedded. You must be wedded *and* bedded."

Whipping around, Persephone reached out to give her ne'er-do-well groom a fearsome pinch only to find that he was being carted off on the shoulders of his stumbling, still-cheering comrades.

"Where are they taking him?" she demanded, trying to sound fierce in spite of her badly knocking knees.

"To change out of his wedding clothes and into his consummation robe," explained Cairn with another hiccup.

"His *consummation robe*?" wailed Persephone, forgetting to sound fierce.

Cairn grinned and nodded as Fayla and the other Methusian women tugged Persephone off the dais and laughingly propelled her across the clearing to a small hut set well apart from the others. "So you needn't be concerned about keeping the rest of us awake all night with your lovemaking noises," confided the grandmotherly woman with the cheek-pinching compulsion.

"Remind him you're doing this for the sake of others," advised a suspiciously solemn-faced Rachel.

Before Persephone could say anything to this *useless* piece of advice, the door of the hut was thrown open to reveal a bed so enormous that it took up most of the hut's candlelit interior.

"But . . . but there's no table!" she spluttered. "There's not even a chair!"

Fayla chuckled as she pushed Persephone into the hut and swiftly unlaced her gown. "You don't need help getting into your consummation shift, do you?" she asked, gesturing to a simple white shift at the foot of the bed.

"What? No!" blurted Persephone, clutching her loosened gown to her chest to keep it from slipping down to her ankles. "But—"

She broke off at the sound of drunken singing and lewd male laughter approaching fast.

"Here he comes!" cried Fayla, clapping her hands together in apparent delight.

And then she was gone.

For half a heartbeat, Persephone just stood in the narrow gap between the bed and the wall, staring at the closed hut door and trying to decide if it would be worse to greet Azriel wearing her "consummation shift" or to greet him half-dressed. Deciding that the latter would be worse, she hastily slipped out of her mother's liquid sunlight gown and tugged the shift down over her head. Seconds later, the door of the hut burst open to reveal Azriel upon its threshold. Besides a robe that gaped to reveal his powerful chest and hard, flat stomach, the only other thing he appeared to be wearing was an expression that set her heart pounding.

Desperately, she tried to clear her head, but it was impossible. Stomach fluttering and every inch of her tingling, Persephone watched helplessly as Tiny and the other men whispered a few last suggestions into Azriel's ear before guffawing loudly at their own cleverness and shoving him forward into the hut.

As the door slammed behind him, Azriel stumbled toward Persephone in a display of clumsiness that didn't fool her for an instant. Nevertheless, she was forced to scurry backward to avoid his ridiculously windmilling arms. After half a dozen steps, she felt her back bump up against the wall, and the next minute Azriel was so close that she couldn't even *breathe* without some part of her touching some part of him. Without taking his eyes off hers, Azriel eased one forearm against the wall above her head and leaned even closer.

"Persephone?" he whispered as he slowly traced the length of her bottom lip with the index finger of his free hand.

"Yes?" she replied breathlessly.

"I just want to say that you mustn't think you can have me just because we're married," he murmured in a voice so seductive that it took Persephone a moment to process what he'd said.

"W-what?" she asked confusedly.

"We married for the sake of others, remember?" continued Azriel in the same seductive voice as he slowly planted a light kiss near her right ear. "This marriage has a higher purpose, remember?" He planted another kiss near her left ear and did not pull away. "I think that if I asked, you would claim that the vows we spoke and the kisses we shared meant nothing at all."

"O-ohh," stammered Persephone, who could not help closing her eyes. "Well, uh—"

"I have my pride, you know," interrupted Azriel, his warm breath tickling her neck, "and my honor, as well. I cannot allow you to take advantage of me just because you now call me husband. Though it is true that I once professed my love for you and swore that I could not live without you, we've agreed that our marriage will be a platonic one. And even though the sight of you standing in the candlelight tousled, barefoot and completely naked beneath your shift is enough to make a man weep tears of blood, I cannot allow you to entice me into compromising myself." Azriel sighed deeply and brushed a strand of hair from her face. "Does that make sense to you?" he murmured. "Or . . . do you think that perhaps this marriage of ours might be something more than a transaction of necessity?"

For a fleeting moment, nothing in the world made sense to Persephone but the lingering feel of Azriel's fingers brushing against her skin, and she could think of no reason why their marriage shouldn't be something *much* more than a transaction of necessity. Then she remembered Finn and the Regent and the jar of white beans and the quest for the healing pool. She thought of the Methusians who, for all their jolly laughter and good-natured ribbing, would have thwarted her plans to seek the pool if this marriage to Azriel had not fit into their own plans. She recalled how she'd ever been at the mercy of someone else's whims and how she had ever hungered for the freedom to be her own master. And it occurred to her that if it was true that this hunger for freedom did not seem to gnaw at her in quite the same way as it used to, it was also true that it had been a part of her for so long that she did not know if she'd ever be able to entirely cast it aside.

As she pondered all of these things, the mad fever that had consumed her since she'd first stepped into the dream earlier that evening slowly began to recede.

When it had receded completely, Persephone reluctantly looked up at Azriel and saw at once that there was no need to explain any of this to him. The ice in his eyes told her that he already knew the spell had been broken and that he'd already begun to retreat to that faraway place where she could never hope to follow.

"A transaction of necessity it is, then," he said easily, nodding as he stepped away from her.

For some reason, Persephone felt a flutter of panic. "Azriel—"

"You understand, of course, that tomorrow we shall have to act as though I bedded you well and often this night," he interrupted in conversational tones.

"O-oh," she stammered, flushing. "Yes, of . . . of course—"

"Good," nodded Azriel. "Now that we've settled that, shall we try to get some sleep?"

"All right," mumbled Persephone. Casting a darting glance at the enormous bed, she hesitantly asked Azriel where he was going to sleep.

"What do you mean where am I going to sleep?" he asked in a puzzled voice. "I am going to sleep in the bed. Where else would I sleep?"

"I don't know," said Persephone lamely. "On the floor, perhaps?"

"I am not your eunuch slave anymore, Your Highness."

Though Azriel sounded almost like his old self when he said this, Persephone did not rise to the bait. She could not spar with him—not here, not now. For though it was she who'd closed the door on making their marriage something more than a transaction for the sake of others and she who'd put the ice back into his eyes, it grieved her nonetheless.

And so, in response to his teasing comment, she merely nodded stiffly, picked up a pillow and tried to edge past him so that she could lie down on the floor by the door.

"Wait," said Azriel, moving to block her way. Sounding almost exasperated, he said, "There is room enough in the bed for both of us, Persephone."

Clutching the pillow to her breast, she shrugged and bit her trembling lower lip.

"We will be expected to bed down together from now on," pointed out Azriel, who seemed visibly moved by the sight of her trembling lip. "Do you intend to spend the rest of your life sleeping on the floor?"

Persephone shrugged again and looked away.

Azriel slid his finger under her chin and tilted her head up so that she could not help but look at him. "You are far and away the most maddening woman I've ever met in my life," he said gently. "I'm sorry for teasing you—I didn't mean to hurt your feelings. How could I have? I've vowed to devote myself entirely to your happiness and contentment, remember? This, on top of everything else I've vowed on your behalf!" Smiling down at her with a warmth that made Persephone want to burst into tears or fling her arms around him or both, he said, "Blow out the candles, wife. Remove your dagger and lie down on your side of the bed. I promise I'll behave myself until the very day you beg me to do otherwise."

Persephone was so relieved that Azriel had come back to her from his faraway place that she willingly did as he bade. For what seemed like an eternity, she lay in the darkness unable to sleep for the nearness of him in bed beside her.

"Azriel?" she whispered at length.

"Yes?" he said, sounding quite as wide awake as she.

"I . . . I'm sorry, too."

"I know."

And later still: "Azriel?"

"Yes?"

"You are very kind to me."

"You are worth it."

Eighteen

GENERAL MURDOCK'S beady eyes gleamed in the darkness.

Though his soldiers had been much dismayed three dawns past when the identical groups of riders had galloped off in different directions from the princess's camp, General Murdock had not been dismayed. A military man did not *get* dismayed, just as he did not get angry or panic or act impulsively. Rather, he planned as well as he could, calmly assessed new facts as they emerged and adjusted his plans accordingly. That is why General Murdock had been able to remain calm while his panicked soldiers had dashed around trying to break camp and get the horses saddled as quickly as possible. Stroking his weak chin, he'd carefully considered all that he'd observed through his spyglass in the moments leading up to the abrupt departure of the galloping riders. In particular, he'd considered the fact that one of the men had gotten down on bended knee before one of the women, and that she'd responded by laying a hand upon his hooded head. The gesture had been a fleeting one, for another man had immediately leapt to his feet and begun hopping about for reasons unknown, but it'd had the unmistakable look of a royal blessing.

With this in mind, rather than weakening his tracking force by sending a soldier or two chasing after each group, as the princess and the Methusian had obviously hoped he'd do, General Murdock had decided to keep his force together and follow only the group that included the woman who'd bestowed the blessing. His soldiers had been visibly surprised by this decision. Indeed, one of them—an excited, gangly-limbed boy who was a prime example of the poor quality of recruits that had lately poured in to swell the ranks of the Regent's already mighty army of New Men—had even questioned the wisdom of putting all their eggs in one basket.

General Murdock had responded by impassively explaining to the youth that a military man took risks. Then, ordering him and the other soldiers to their horses, he'd led them all in such a careful pursuit of their quarry that the two women, the man and the boy had had no idea they were being followed.

Now, as he crouched in the shadows of the hidden tunnel beneath the waterfall watching the laughing Methusians trickle back into the clearing after having delivered the princess and her new husband to the hut in the woods, General Murdock thought how handsomely that particular risk had paid off. Not only had he discovered a Methusian nest bigger than any he'd discovered in many years, but in four-and-twenty hours of watching and listening, he'd gathered much vital intelligence. He'd seen the face of the princess's friend. He'd heard the Methusian called Azriel admit to having lied to the Regent about being Balthazar's bastard. He'd seen the liar joined in matrimony to the woman whom the Regent both desired and despised beyond all reason, a crime for which he would someday suffer most exquisitely.

And he'd learned that the Methusians believed in a king whose prophesied coming would unite the five clans of Glyndoria. The treasonous nature of the prophecy offended General Murdock deeply. And while he'd never been one to believe in anything that smacked of fancy and could not see how his master's plans to become king could possibly be thwarted by a handful of outlaws, he could not help feeling vaguely uneasy at the thought that by marrying the liar, the princess had made the doomed King Finnius a Methusian.

As General Murdock nibbled on an immaculate fingernail and absently wondered if this meant that he was now lawfully entitled—or even duty-bound—to murder the young king, the Methusian music started up once more, drawing his attention back to the nest. He did not see yawning children and pretty girls with jingling bells at their ankles as much as he saw prey animals, and his long, thin nose twitched as his gaze flicked from one to the next. He could hardly contain himself and yet, he did. For he had orders not to attack until the princess and the Methusian had either found the healing pool or given up looking for it, and a military man always followed orders. The nest would be purged in due course, and when it was, he would be guaranteed a handsome reward.

With this satisfying thought, General Murdock drew farther back into the shadows, turned and slunk back the way he'd come so many hours earlier. In the morning, he would send one of his men back to the Regent in Parthania with news of all that he'd seen and heard. Then he would issue a belated order to have gagged and flogged to death the boy who'd questioned the wisdom of putting all their eggs in one basket. Under normal circumstances, General Murdock wouldn't necessarily have had him flogged to *death* for questioning a decision, but with the princess and the Methusian about to embark upon their quest, he could not afford to have a man crippled by the whip slowing them down. And he certainly could not afford to let the infraction go unpunished. Small breakdowns in discipline and order invariably led to larger breakdowns in discipline and order, and General Murdock prided himself on setting an example for the entire army by maintaining the highest possible standards of behavior among the troops under his direct command.

For now, though, he wished only to retire to his camp tent for a few well-deserved hours of rest upon a cot made up with sheets bleached white as snow and scented with lavender. The sheets were an extravagance, but one of many that General Murdock forgave himself for indulging in.

He was a military man, after all, not an animal.

Nineteen

FROM HIS PERCH high in the tree, the man in meanest homespun watched the General emerge from behind the waterfall. The man was exhausted from three days of hard travel followed by four-and-twenty hours of alternately watching for the General and watching his men, who were camped yonder. But he was also exhilarated, for he knew that he was doing a great service for the realm. It was true that not everyone would think so, but *he* certainly thought so. And that was why, beyond the obvious reason, that he'd hardly batted an eye when he'd heard what he was being asked to do.

The first part of his mission was simple enough: to secretly follow whoever had been sent to follow the princess and to take whatever actions were necessary to ensure that this individual was unable to send reports back to Parthania. Though the man had not been told in so many words that he was to kill the messengers, he knew it was expected of him. And while he was not looking forward to the killing, he'd killed out of necessity before, and he understood that small acts of evil must sometimes be committed for the sake of the greater good.

He was content that his conscience would be clear on the matter of the dead messengers.

It was the second part of his mission that gave the man pause, for he'd seen the princess in action, and he did not think she'd take kindly to what he'd been asked to do to her. Moreover, he wasn't sure he entirely understood why doing such a thing would be for the good of the realm. The way he saw it, just the opposite would be true.

Still.

If someone from an infinitely greater station than he felt it was so, then it must be so.

And so he would continue to secretly follow the General, he would kill the messengers and he would try not to think too much about the second part of his orders.

With luck, it would never come to that.

Twenty

Ninety-five white beans left in the jar

THE MORNING AFTER HER WEDDING, Persephone awoke as she'd learned to do during her nightmare months of enslavement deep within the Mines of Torodania: without altering her breathing pattern or succumbing to the twitches that gave others away, with every fiber of her being alert to lurking danger and every muscle tensed to spring into defensive action.

Of course, she was no longer a half-dead little starveling curled up in a dirty ball; she was a married princess. And the lurking danger was not some feral child with glittering eyes; it was her new husband. And while it was true that he'd not done anything especially dangerous the previous night (besides lie next to her breathing softly, occasionally shifting in his sleep and generally making it impossible for her to forget that he was there), there was every chance that he was still lying barely dressed in the bed beside her, and she did not know if she could bear the intimacy of opening her eyes to the sight of his warm and sleepy smile.

After some moments spent lying tense and unmoving, however, Persephone began to feel a bit foolish, so she opened one eye the barest of cracks. To her surprise, Azriel was *not* in bed beside her. Opening both eyes, she sat up, looked around and was dismayed to see that he wasn't even in the hut.

Before she could begin to wonder where he'd gone to, there came a knock at the door. Pulling the blanket up to her chin, Persephone invited the caller inside. The next instant, the door opened to reveal Azriel with a familiar-looking pile of coarse cloth tucked under one arm.

"A good morning to you, wife," he said.

"A good morning to you . . . ," she replied awkwardly, the word "husband" sticking in her throat.

Azriel smiled. Handing her the pile of cloth—which was, as she'd suspected, the lowborn disguise she'd worn before changing into her beautiful gown of liquid sunlight—he said, "You must dress and come out at once. Everyone is waiting for you."

Persephone pressed the smelly bundle to her chest. "Why are they waiting for me?" she asked suspiciously, thinking of the Methusians' fondness for springing things like marriage and consummation on a person.

As though he'd read her thoughts, Azriel laughed aloud. "They are waiting to see you take the Methusian mark, for until you do so you cannot be considered a full member of the clan, and neither can your brother, the king."

"Oh," said Persephone, relaxing slightly.

"After that, we'll break our fast while we go over what is known about old Balthazar's discovery of the healing pool," he continued. "And after *that*, we'll gather the necessary supplies and begin our quest in earnest."

Satisfied with the morning's plan, Persephone shooed Azriel out of the hut, then quickly dressed and made her way through the woods to the clearing where the tribe was assembled. As soon as she came into view, half the Methusians started clapping and cheering, while the other half—the bleary-eyed, greenish-faced ones who'd had too much wedding wine to drink the night before—clutched their heads and groaned loudly. Not wanting to think about why people were clapping and cheering, Persephone ducked her head to hide her burning cheeks and hurried to stand beside Rachel, who was beaming at her most vexingly. She was almost there when she remembered what Azriel had said about the need to act as though she'd been bedded "well and often." Realizing that a *true* wife would probably want to stand by her new husband's side, she pivoted on one heel and slowly walked over to Azriel, who tenderly wrapped his arms around her.

"Wife," he murmured, smiling down at her.

"Husband," she muttered, feeling her cheeks burn hotter still.

At this display of newlywed affection, Rachel beamed harder, and many of the Methusians chuckled and nudged one another. After a moment, Cairn, who was looking only a *little* greenish, called for quiet. Then she spread her hands wide and began to speak.

"When the world was young, we Methusians were many, and we all lived as one in a corner of the realm that belonged to none but us. We thrived as no others in Glyndoria thrived, for the land upon which we lived was fertile beyond measure, and at its heart there existed a miraculous pool whose waters could cure any ill. For untold generations we lived in health and happiness, until the day one of our own spilled the blood of a trusted companion at the water's edge. The blood tainted the pool, the pool dried up and the once-fertile lands were as dust in the wind. To stay was to starve, so we moved on. We have been a wandering people ever since—an echo of the healing power of the pool coursing through our veins, the belief that the pool will someday reappear burning in our hearts. That is why our mark takes the form of a droplet of water—to remind each of us who we are, where we came from and where we hope to return to one day. To take the mark is to pledge allegiance to a clan that will love and protect you as one of their own, and to willingly accept the peril that goes along with joining the ranks of a hunted people. Tell us now, Persephone, wife of Azriel," said Cairn in a voice trembling with emotion, "do you willingly pledge such allegiance and accept such peril?"

For a long moment, Persephone said nothing. Though she knew that her answer must be "yes" for Finn's sake, the word stuck in her throat. She was not overly concerned with the notion of accepting peril, but to pledge allegiance under false pretenses, even for the right reasons, just felt wrong.

"Wife?" murmured Azriel. Drawing her even closer, he slid a forefinger under her chin and tilted her head so that she was looking up at him.

He is a Methusian, she thought suddenly. *I could pledge allegiance to him and mean it.*

"Yes, Cairn," she said, though she was yet looking at Azriel. "I willingly do as you ask."

As had become custom in these dangerous times, Persephone took the mark of the Methusians on a patch of skin that none but she—and, in his dreams, her husband—would ever see. After she'd done so, the whole clan sat down at the long tables to eat and go over what they knew about Balthazar's discovery of the healing pool.

"*Supposed* discovery," said Fayla, who was sitting across from where Persephone was wedged between Azriel and Rachel.

"Supposed discovery," conceded Cairn from her spot beside Fayla and Tiny, who still smelled of wine and who was slumped over, unmoving, with his head buried in his folded arms.

"The fact is that no Methusian ever heard the story of the discovery first-hand," said Fayla.

"Why not?" asked Persephone in surprise as she piled her platter with thick slices of meat and wedges of cheese, sausages, boiled eggs, fried potatoes, leftover wedding cake and bread smeared with sugarberry jam.

"As the Methusian ambassador to Parthania, it would not have been appropriate for Balthazar to have a contingent of his clansmen living within the walls of the imperial palace," said Fayla, eyeing Persephone's platter with amusement, as though she had a fair notion how the freshly minted Methusian had worked up such an appetite.

"It would have been seen as an act of aggression," explained Azriel, as he poured his famished bride a mug of ale.

"Exactly," said Cairn, smiling at his gallantry. "Besides, what need had Balthazar for his clansmen? As ambassador, it was his job to establish relationships with those outside the clan, and by all accounts he did this well. Indeed, he and King Octavio were said to have been good friends for many years. As dear to each other as brothers, it was said. In fact, after Balthazar disappeared and was given up for dead, it was the Erok king himself who arranged for the private funeral service that Balthazar ruined by showing up alive and well—"

"And boasting of having discovered the reborn Pool of Genezing," finished Fayla.

Cairn nodded.

Persephone gestured for Rachel to pass the steaming porridge. As she served herself up several hefty ladlefuls of the stuff, she said, "Did he offer any proof of his discovery?"

"Proof?" said Azriel, slipping his arm around her as naturally as any man would around his wife. Brushing his lips against her suddenly scarlet cheek, he said, "No. But they say he had scars suggestive of a mishap that ought to have killed him, scars that looked many years healed even though he'd only been gone from Parthania for a matter of weeks."

"'They' say he had scars? Who are 'they,' Azriel?" asked Rachel, drizzling honey over her own sticky pile of porridge before handing the honey pot to Persephone, who could not help herself leaning into Azriel as she passed it on down the table.

"That's just it: we don't know who 'they' are," said Fayla. "Because no Methusian had a chance to speak with Balthazar before his arrest, all we know is rumor. Tittle-tattle whispered by servants who happened to peep through the right keyholes."

"Not everything servants say is 'tittle-tattle,' Fayla," said Persephone pointedly.

"That is true," agreed the beautiful Methusian girl as she cast a sidelong glance at Tiny, who'd just moaned softly. "But it is also true that a story told a thousand times over is likely to change completely over the course of the telling."

"All right, then," interjected Rachel. "What do you *think* you know about the discovery of the pool?"

"We think that Balthazar discovered it after a long sea journey," said Fayla. "We think he was shipwrecked and that he made it to shore only to soon after find himself chased by a frothing beast into a place of nightmares."

"How soon after he reached shore was he chased?" asked Persephone.

"Impossible to say. It could have been minutes, hours or even days," put in Cairn. "Balthazar was a known storyteller with a reputation for not allowing facts to hinder the telling of a good tale. In the case of this particular tale, it is reasonable to assume that he might also have been being purposely vague to prevent anyone from guessing the whereabouts of the pool."

"And the frothing beast? And the place of nightmares?" said Persephone as Azriel casually took his arm from around her.

"Again, impossible to say," said Cairn. "Though I can tell you that those exact phrases—'frothing beast' and 'place of nightmares'—were heard over and over again in the reports we managed to collect."

"Anything else?" asked Persephone, frustrated both by how little valuable information they had to offer and by how much she missed the feel of Azriel's arm around her.

Slumped beside Fayla, Tiny stirred for the first time since sitting down at the table. "We think old Balthazar found the pool at night—" he began hoarsely, wincing at the sound of his own voice.

"Then perhaps the beast he mentioned was a ravenous night creature of some kind," said Rachel with a shiver. "Like a bear or a wolf—something you might find prowling around the darkest part of the Great Forest after the sun goes down."

When Fayla allowed that it was possible, Rachel shivered again and reached for more sausages.

"There are only two other things we *think* we know," said Cairn. "The first is that while he was running away from the beast in the darkness, Balthazar fell far enough to be mortally wounded. And the second is that he spoke privately to the ambassadors of each of the other three outlying clans in the hours before his arrest."

"Do you know why Balthazar sailed away from Parthania in the first place?" asked Persephone, inhaling sharply at the sudden feel of Azriel's hand upon her knee. "Because if we knew where he was headed—"

"We don't," said Fayla flatly. "That is why approaching the Panoraki, Marinese and Gorgish to find out what he might have told their ambassadors is our best hope of narrowing down the search area."

"*Our* best hope?" said Persephone in surprise.

"Tiny and I thought to join you on the quest," said Fayla with a hint of defiance, as though she rather resented the fact that her participation hadn't been assumed or even requested.

Persephone glanced at Tiny, who currently looked as though he'd have to be transported by sledge, spoon-fed mush and administered fluids by dropper to survive a trip to the backhouse.

Seeing Persephone's glance, Fayla stiffened and said, "Of course, if you'd rather undertake the quest by yourselves—"

"No, no," said Persephone hurriedly. "Your assistance would be greatly appreciated."

"All right," said Fayla, somewhat mollified. "Then the only question that remains is: Who should we approach first?"

"In spite of the great dangers associated with doing so, it must be the Panoraki," declared Cairn. "Their various clans live high upon the mountains in the north. To reach them, you will have to risk crippling falls, bitter cold and deadly snow beasts. You will also have to risk being butchered without warning. The Panoraki are fierce fighters and powerful beyond imagining. Moreover, years of having their clansmen kidnapped and their beloved woolly sheep stolen and slaughtered—often by slave hunters posing as Methusian outlaws—have instilled in them a tendency to attack first and ask questions later."

"And these are the people you suggest we approach first?" said Persephone, sounding so dismayed that Cairn actually laughed.

"Yes," she said, "because old Balthazar was said to have been closer to the Panoraki Barka than to the ambassadors of either of the other two outlying clans. If he told anyone anything meaningful about his discovery, it would have been Barka. And though Barka and the other two ambassadors were later arrested and imprisoned, never to be seen again, unlike Balthazar, all three of them would have had time to get a message to their people."

Something in Cairn's words niggled at the back of Persephone's mind, but she set it aside to think about later. "And if Balthazar told this Barka nothing, or if this Barka didn't manage to get a message to his people?" she asked.

"You'll have to approach the Marinese and the Gorgishmen. I suggest you try the Marinese first. Though the artisan tribe is notoriously puritanical and rigid in their ways, they are not known to be a warring people. Indeed, time and again over the years they've shown a willingness to do almost anything to avoid conflict with outsiders. In approaching them, the most significant danger you're likely to face is the channel crossing you'll need to make to reach their settlement on the Island of Ru, where they fled to in the early years of Mordesius's regency."

"And if the Marinese can tell us nothing?" asked Fayla.

"Then you'll have to travel westward across Glyndoria to the Valley of Gorg, where the last of the free Gorgishmen reside," said Cairn grimly. "Even before the bad times came, the Gorgish . . . well, let's just say that they were not renowned for their forthright and welcoming attitudes. Even now, only the very boldest of slave hunters will go after them, and it is said that more than half of these disappear without a trace."

"No great loss," quipped Fayla.

"Agreed," grunted Tiny, shakily lifting his head three inches before dropping it back into his folded arms.

Frowning at the picture Cairn had painted of the westernmost people, Rachel said, "If the Gorgish ambassador was anything like you describe, why would your kinsman Balthazar have confided in him?"

"I do not think he would have," said Cairn frankly. "That is why I do not think you ought to approach the Gorgish until you've exhausted all other avenues for finding the pool."

"And what dangers can we expect to encounter in the Valley of Gorg?" asked Persephone, hoping that she sounded like a brave adventurer and not like a suddenly apprehensive girl.

"Besides crude traps and cruder insults? None at all," said Tiny gruffly, finally lifting his head all the way up. Squinting and shielding his eyes, he said, "The Valley of Gorg is said to be beautiful beyond description, a paradise on earth fit for the gods themselves."

Persephone laughed shortly and without much mirth. "That is good," she said, "for it means that if we do not freeze, starve, fall to our deaths, drown, get torn to pieces by beasts, get clubbed, speared, eaten or otherwise perish most gruesomely, we shall have something to look forward to."

"And so we shall," agreed Azriel, Fayla, Tiny and Rachel with varying degrees of enthusiasm.

"And so you shall," said Cairn softly.

Twenty-One

MANY MILES TO THE SOUTH, Mordesius entered the king's private chambers unannounced as had become his habit over these past few days. Whistling cheerily, he shuffled across the polished floor to the long table where the royal fool sat alone, listlessly picking at his morning meal. The king did not stand when Mordesius entered the room and did not look up as he approached. Under normal circumstances, Mordesius would have been much insulted by such treatment, but such was his eagerness to give the king his latest surprise that he hardly noticed.

Coming to a halt beside the fool's ornately carved, velvet-cushioned armchair, Mordesius peeled back the corners of the white silk handkerchief he held in his left hand. Gingerly picking up the stinking thing that lay nestled within, he set it down next to a plate of greasy sausages.

At the sight of the decomposing finger, the king let out a bellow of shock, leapt to his feet and scrambled away from the table as fast as he could.

"It is not as fresh as it was a few days ago," sighed Mordesius, "but I can get you another if you like."

"What . . . what is this?" stammered Finn, breathing hard.

"This?" said Mordesius, using one of the sausages to give the finger a poke. "This is a finger, Your Majesty, one that used to be attached to the peasant hand of your insufferable nursemaid."

"No!" gasped Finn, his pale face growing even paler.

"Yes!" mocked Mordesius, waving his hands in the air. "Yes!"

The king coughed then, so suddenly and so violently that when he wiped his mouth with the back of his hand it came away smeared with red. "I . . . I have done everything you've asked of me," he wheezed, pressing his hand against his chest as though this might aid in the drawing of breath. "Why would you do such a thing to Moira?"

Wrinkling his nose in distaste at the sight of the king's bloodied hand, Mordesius said, "Beyond the fact that it gave me great pleasure to watch her writhe in agony, I did it because you asked me to do it, Your Majesty."

The king's blue eyes bulged in outrage. "That is a lie!"

Mordesius smiled. "Back when I first explained to you the way things were, do you recall saying that you'd consider my proposal that you marry Lord Bartok's daughter if I brought you proof that your nursemaid was still alive?" he asked slyly. "Well, here is your proof. Please accept my apologies for the delay in delivering it. You might think that it would be impossible for a man to forget that he had a severed finger tucked away in his desk drawer, but you know what it is like to be consumed by the responsibilities of running a kingdom." Mordesius stopped suddenly, opened his eyes wide and covered his mouth as though he'd just made an embarrassing slip of the tongue. "Oh, wait," he whispered through his fingers. "You do *not* know what it is like to be consumed by the responsibilities of running a kingdom."

Smiling broadly, he searched the young king's face for some sign that these taunts, along with the knowledge that his beloved cow had been tortured at his unwitting behest, had finally broken him.

But Finnius was a king in more than name. He was a king at heart, a true prince of the blood to his very marrow. Biting his lower lip to keep from coughing, he drew himself up to his full height, looked down into the handsome face of the monster who'd once been his most trusted adviser and said, "Very well."

"Very well?" said Mordesius uncomprehendingly.

"Very well, I will marry Lady Aurelia," said Finn. "Will there be anything else, Your Grace?"

Mordesius stared up at him, despising him for his courage and dignity almost as much as for the height, strength and grace that afforded him such a regal bearing—one that Mordesius, with his twisted back and uneven legs, knew he would never in a thousand years be able to copy.

Unless the princess and cockroach found the healing pool, that is. If they found the pool, then he, Mordesius, would become as tall, strong and graceful as any man in the kingdom—and far more so than this young fool, who would soon thereafter be as corrupt and stinking as the thing that now lay on the table before him.

"Yes, there will be something else," muttered Mordesius, feeling sour in spite of the ever-comforting vision of the king dead at his feet. "This afternoon I want you to go out onto the Grand Balcony and present yourself to the common people. The lords of the realm have had the opportunity to observe you dining in state on several occasions over these past few days and to convince themselves of that which is in their best interests to believe: namely, that you acted of your own free will when you announced that you wished me to continue to rule in your stead. The merchants and tradesmen seem willing to accept the new reality for the same reason, but the low-born masses are having a more difficult time reconciling themselves to your actions. Touchingly, it seems as though they are convinced that their beloved young king would not have abandoned them except under extreme duress. You will convince them otherwise. You will don your golden crown and most festive doublet, rouge those pasty cheeks of yours, march out onto the Grand Balcony and smile and wave like a ninny as you have always done, that the fears of the nobodies may be calmed."

"I've never known you to concern yourself with the fears of the least of my subjects," observed King Finnius coolly.

"Nor do I concern myself with them now," said Mordesius. "But such rumblings encourage your so-called subjects to avoid embracing their fate, and I would not have it so. For just this very day I've given orders that all lowborn slums in Parthania are to be burned to the ground, their occupants to be sent to wherever they can be of most use to the realm. Able-bodied men shall be given the opportunity to join my personal army. Along with the infirm, ancients, women and children, those who refuse will be relocated to frontier settlements in need of cheap, expendable labor. All except the very smallest of the children, of course. They will be sent onward to the Mines of Torodania, where my New Men overseers are ever in need of fresh recruits to toil within the deepest, darkest, narrowest, most treacherous of the tunnels."

"You cannot—" began Finn.

"I can, and I will, and if you speak against me or my plans to anyone, the streets of Parthania will run red with lowborn blood," said Mordesius matter-of-factly. "At least if you behave, *some* of the slum dwellers will have *some* hope of surviving, as will your nine-fingered nursemaid."

When the king said nothing, Mordesius knew he had won—again. "Very good," he said in an upbeat voice. "Now, I must—"

"You know," murmured the king as he gazed at the cushionless chair upon which the cow used to plant her rump, "Moira would sooner see herself dead than see such evils committed in the name of saving her."

Mordesius threw his heavy head back so far that pain shot through his thin stalk of a neck, twisting his jolly laugh into a scream of pain.

"Dead!" he panted when he'd recovered enough to speak. "Your Majesty, if you fail to cooperate, do you honestly think that I will show that cow such mercy as to simply kill her? I hope you do not—because I will not! I will see her long for death and never be granted it. And believe me when I say that I have the talent and experience required to keep the nearly dead alive for years. Now, if we're quite through here, I must take my leave of you, for *I* have important matters of state to attend to—not the least of which includes making arrangements for your betrothal ceremony."

Finn opened his mouth as though he meant to ask a question but abruptly seemed to think better of it. "Fine," he said instead. "Only, what am I to do with Moira's . . . with the finger?"

"Keep it," urged Mordesius as he picked up a greasy sausage with his bare fingers and took a lusty bite. "I brought it as a surprise for you, after all. And I can get another for myself any time I like."

"As if I would want one of your fingers for myself!" chortled Mordesius that night as he sat in the comfortable chair in the fetid cell where the nursemaid yet resided, shackled to the glistening wall, wallowing in her own filth, her stringy hair hanging in rat's tails.

It was disgusting, really, the way she kept herself. Seeing it, and seeing that she'd hardly touched the fresh grass and clover that were being delivered daily, Mordesius might have been tempted to say that she was more like a hog than a cow except that she'd grown too thin to be properly compared to a hog. She was not nearly as thin as she'd eventually be, of course, and not nearly as thin as she'd have been if Mordesius, fearful that she'd starve to death before he'd finished having his fun with her, had not reluctantly ordered that she be allowed to receive a share of moldy bread every two days. But she was definitely thinner than a hog.

"You should have seen the king's face when I told him that he was the reason I'd cut off your finger," said Mordesius now, smiling broadly at the memory. "He was almost as distraught then as he was when I told him that you'd writhed in agony when I'd done the deed."

"But I did not writhe in agony," said Moira.

"No," agreed Mordesius with a flicker of irritation. "No, you did not. But you will." Then, abruptly changing the subject to one he knew would cause her pain even if cutting off her fingers did not, he said, "His Majesty's health appears to be worsening, by the way. He gasps for breath all the time, and I have even seen him cough up blood."

"Blood!" exclaimed Moira, who was so alarmed by this news that she leaned forward, unconsciously straining against her shackles.

"Yes, blood!" cried Mordesius, pleased by her reaction, and by the fact that her sudden movement had opened the dirty scab of her finger stump, causing it to ooze fresh blood.

Moira did not seem to have noticed that her wound had reopened. "This is not good, not good at all," she murmured. "You're not preventing His Majesty from being tended by his physicians or from being bled and dosed with his tonics, are you? You're not causing him to suffer from hunger or cold or any other hardship?"

"Don't be stupid," snapped Mordesius, annoyed by her concern for the king. "He is no good to me dead—at least, not at the moment, he isn't. I need him healthy enough to do my bidding."

Mordesius waited for the cow to start mooing that she was sure the king would sooner die than do his bidding.

Instead, she said, "And how fares the Princess Persephone?"

At the mention of the princess, Mordesius's mood shifted again. She'd been on his mind again of late. The young woman from the banquet—the one who'd been served up by her noble father like a platter of tender sweetmeats for Mordesius to sample as he would— had shown no enthusiasm whatsoever during her audition. As soon as his bedchamber door had slammed shut behind her, Mordesius had found his thoughts drifting back to the Princess Persephone who, he was quite certain, would never have wept in such an undignified manner. He smiled now at the thought of the princess, faithless whore though she was.

"Do you know that the king has not once asked me how his beloved sister fares?" he told the nursemaid. "I think he almost asked this morning but changed his mind at the last moment. Perhaps he hopes that keeping me from thinking about her will somehow protect her. Silly, isn't it, when he should know that she is never far from my thoughts and that she could not be in greater danger if she were stripped, soaked in beef broth and staked down in a pit of starving weasels?"

Moira gazed up at him impassively, as though waiting for him to get to the point.

Mordesius stopped smiling at once. "In truth, I do not know how the princess fares for I've yet to receive a report from my man who is following her," he muttered.

"Perhaps she and her Methusian lover have evaded your man."

Mordesius's eyes bulged in outrage. "The cockroach is not her *lover*!" he half-shrieked.

Gripping the arms of the chair, he twisted in his seat and was about to bellow for a guard to come rip the cow's filthy tongue out of her head when it occurred to him that such an act would not only deprive him of the pleasure of one day hearing her beg for mercy but, perhaps more importantly, it would give her the pleasure of knowing how grievously her disgusting insinuation had upset him.

And so he turned back around, slapped the arms of his chair and laughed loudly to show her that her words had no power over him. When he was done, he leaned forward and asked her if she liked surprises. As she warily shook her head, he reached into the pocket of his robe and said, "Be that as it may, I have one for you."

Obviously believing that her surprise would be something akin to the stinking one he'd given to the king that morning, the nursemaid recoiled. Laughing again, Mordesius paused for dramatic effect before withdrawing his hand with a flourish and holding up a perfect golden pear.

Moira sighed audibly and licked her cracked lips.

Mordesius dangled the piece of fruit under her lowborn nose for a few seconds before snatching it away, saying, "This is not for you. Miserable wretches like you do not eat the fruit of kings. However, I thought you might enjoy watching me eat it, that you might be reminded of the life you once led and all the things you once knew."

As the cow swallowed the saliva that had filled her mouth at the sight of the pear, Mordesius slowly bit into the succulent fruit.

"It is funny, really," he mused as he chewed, "I've always despised you, and yet down here I find myself chatting with you as though we are old friends. I suppose there are times when even I can find a measure of comfort in having someone to talk to."

Moira watched him through her curtain of stringy hair. Mordesius took another bite of the pear, this time taking care to let the cool, sweet juice of the fruit run down his chin.

"And by 'someone,'" he said as he wiped his mouth with the back of his hand and set the barely eaten pear down onto the floor just beyond Moira's reach, "I mean, of course, someone who will never leave this dungeon alive."

Twenty-Two

Ninety white beans left in the jar

"WHAT WAS THAT?" asked Rachel in a hushed voice.

"Nothing," said Fayla shortly.

From deep within the Great Forest at their backs, the "nothing" roared again.

As Fayla casually notched an arrow into her bow, Persephone, who seemed to be feeling the cold more than the others, shivered violently and hugged her knees tighter. Since departing the Methusian camp five days past, they'd been hiking north along the western edge of the forest with the river at their left side, never far from sight. They'd have saved a full day if they'd cut straight through the forest, but Azriel had convinced them that it was not worth the risk. The forest was unimaginably vast and, in many places, so thickly treed that no sunlight at all penetrated the canopy, making it nigh impossible to determine direction. According to Azriel, a lost man might wander in circles for days until he finally perished of thirst, starvation or madness borne of the endless gloom. That is, if he wasn't first attacked by one of the lowborn rebel bands rumored to hide among the trees or eaten by one of the many large, fearsome "nothings" that called the forest home.

They'd have saved another full day, not to mention a good deal of exhaustion, if they'd traveled by horseback instead of by foot. However, since no horse (not even the indomitable Fleet) could be expected to climb up the side of a snow-covered mountain, they'd decided to forgo the luxury of mounts to avoid having to abandon them in the foothills to the mercies of the first hungry "nothing" that came looking for an easy meal.

Though Fleet had been visibly distraught when he'd realized that he was being left behind, as Persephone sat on the cold, hard ground listening to the sound of the distant roars, she was glad that she'd stood her ground with him. She was also glad that Cur had been far more interested in chasing after the silver-furred, half-wolf female he'd discovered running with the Methusian dog pack than he had been in pursuing Persephone to parts unknown.

Knowing her faithful friends were safe with the Methusians gave Persephone at least one comforting thought to cling to at times like this.

"Pay no mind to the roaring," said Azriel easily as he fed another branch into the campfire that was doing little to dispel the cold. "It is only a bear."

"Big bear," gulped Rachel, whose prominent ears seemed to be quivering with the strain of listening for danger.

"Not as big as them that live upon the mountains," offered Tiny, taking a surreptitious nip out of his hip flask. "They say those beasts can weigh as much as ten horses, with claws and teeth to rip a man apart as easily as if he were a piece of wet parchment."

"Tales to frighten children," sniffed Fayla, even as she drew her bowstring tighter.

"That's not what I heard—" began Tiny.

"Either way, the only bear we need to concern ourselves with right now is a long way off in the forest and therefore of no concern at all," interrupted Azriel cheerfully. "So why don't you all go to your tents and try to get some rest? Before tomorrow midday we should finally be north of the forest and into the mountain foothills; a few hours after that, I expect we'll be climbing in earnest and in need of every ounce of strength we can call upon."

"Rest would be a good idea, Azriel, but, uh, I'm not sure you ought to take the first watch," said Fayla with uncharacteristic delicacy.

"But—"

"Your wife looks cold," said Tiny bluntly. "Be a good husband and go warm her up. I'll wake you, or, ahem, interrupt you, when it's your turn to stand watch and not a minute earlier."

After removing another white bean from the Regent's jar and stiffly informing a grinning Tiny that he could henceforth keep his lascivious suggestions to himself thank you very much, Persephone crawled into the tent with Azriel. On the first day after leaving the Methusian camp, she'd told Rachel what had happened on her wedding night. Rachel had not said much when she learned that Persephone had refused to consummate the marriage. However, she *had* given Persephone that same speculative look she'd given her when she'd declared that she was only marrying Azriel for the sake of others—the look that said she had knowledge of some greater truth and was content to wait for Persephone to discover it for herself.

Much aggravated by Rachel's attitude, Persephone had not deigned to speak of the matter with her again. She had, however, continued to play the part of a new bride to keep up appearances for the sake of Fayla and Tiny. That included sharing an extremely small tent with Azriel—if an old blanket thrown over bent branches and pegged to the ground at the corners with sharpened twigs *could* be called a tent. The first night after leaving the Methusian camp, she'd initially lain on her back with her arms pressed against her sides to ensure that no part of her touched any part of her new husband. Unfortunately, the tent was so narrow and Azriel's shoulders were so broad that this had required her to lie with half of her rigidly held body poking out of the tent. Not only had Persephone worried that this might seem odd behavior on the part of a loving young wife, but after only a short while she'd begun shivering uncontrollably. Recalling another night when she'd been unable to keep her teeth from chattering and Azriel had tucked his cloak about her and offered to join her beneath it, she'd waited for him to reach for her. But he had not reached for her, and eventually she'd been forced to wriggle back into the tent and give him a poke to get him to lie on his side so that there'd be room enough for both of them. He'd wordlessly complied. After she'd likewise rolled onto her side, he'd encircled her with his powerful arm and drawn her back against him. As they'd lain there unspeaking, close as a pair of nestled spoons, Persephone had hardly been able to breathe for wondering what might happen next. But the only thing that had happened next was that Azriel had started murmuring and smacking his lips softly as though in sleep. Warmed to the point of feeling decidedly over-heated, Persephone had done her best to quell the unwelcome urges that Azriel's closeness was provoking and force herself to sleep.

It had been the same every night since, except for those times when Azriel undertook an activity that he solemnly insisted was *crucial* to maintaining the charade that they were truly married: namely, knock-ing about the tiny tent emitting muffled grunts and moans suggestive of a pair of lust-filled newlyweds trying to conceal their passionate lovemaking. Though this ridiculous theater—and the enthusiasm with which Azriel performed it—had mortified Persephone almost beyond the point of reason, she had forced herself to endure it in pained silence.

Until now.

"Not tonight," she whispered the instant she heard Azriel take the deep breath that always seemed to precede the first moan.

Azriel, who'd crawled into the tent on his stomach and was yet propped up on his elbows, leaned close and reminded her that Tiny and Fayla were expecting him to be a good husband and warm her up.

Persephone swallowed hard at the sight of his broad-shouldered silhouette looming above her. "Be that as it may," she whispered, "between listening to the sounds of the night beasts and knowing all that tomorrow may bring, I am not in the mood."

"Spoken like a true wedded wife," murmured Azriel, chuckling so seductively that Persephone almost reached for him.

But she did not reach for him, and after a long moment he rolled onto his side and pulled her close to warm her. And while she knew she ought to be grateful, she could not help feeling dissatisfied in a way that she was quite sure other methods of warming would have taken care of completely.

The next morning, Persephone emerged from the tent to find the ground covered with snow.

"It snowed during the night," Tiny gruffly informed her as he tromped past carrying the freshly filled waterskins.

"Yes, I can see that," she said as she leaned over to brush snow off the knees of her fringed breeches, which Fayla had said would be most practical upon the mountains.

Following Tiny over to the meager fire, Persephone joined him and the others in a meal of cold roast grouse left over from the previous evening, washed down with a swig of icy water from the nearby river. When they were done, they broke camp and shouldered their various packs and bundles. Each carried his or her own bedroll, weapons, waterskins, extra clothing, flint pouch, small purse of gold, dried meat and cheese enough to last one person several days and whatever personal effects they'd seen fit to bring along. In addition, the men carried the tents, the cooking pot, several goodly lengths of rope, two sturdy axes, trade goods and an assortment of Methusian concoctions ranging from sleeping potions to poisons.

Loaded down as they all were, the going had been hard ever since they'd left the Methusian camp. On this day it seemed especially so to Persephone, who could not seem to get warm no matter how briskly she moved, and whose breathing felt more labored with each step she took. She pushed herself hard and kept her complaints to herself, however, and by the time the sun had climbed high enough to melt the snow that had fallen during the night, they'd reached the foothills of the Mountains of Pan.

Leaning up against the nearest boulder, Persephone gingerly eased the pack off her back and took a small sip from her waterskin. Relieved though she was to be beyond the gloom of the forest's edge, she was filled with trepidation at the sight of the mountains. Though she'd caught glimpses of their snow-capped peaks from time to time over the last two days, the trees had mostly shielded them from view. Now they rose up before her, monoliths of ice and rock and snow, some of such great height that their peaks pierced the clouds. Indeed, the tallest seemed to stretch to the very heavens themselves.

"The mountains are so vast, Azriel," said Persephone, feeling decidedly small and insignificant by comparison. "How will we ever find the Panoraki?"

"I am counting on them finding us," he replied as he scanned the nearest peaks using the little brass spyglass he'd thought to bring along.

Looking as though she wasn't altogether sure that getting caught trespassing upon the mountains by the Panoraki would be a good thing, Rachel said, "And if they don't find us? If we end up caught on the mountains at night without shelter?"

Azriel slid the spyglass back into the leather canister slung across his chest. "If we haven't made contact by suppertime, I say we come back down, spend the night in the foothills and go up again tomorrow. I don't think that's going to be necessary, though, for I saw movement upon yonder mountain," he said, pointing to one of the nearer, smaller, less intimidating peaks. "And unless I am very much mistaken, it was a pair of woolly sheep. And wherever there are woolly sheep, there are sure to be Panoraki."

"And Panoraki traps," said Fayla grimly.

"And Panoraki warriors carrying Panoraki battle-axes," added Tiny with a growl.

"Yes," agreed Azriel cheerfully. "Shall we proceed?"

Twenty-Three

Eighty-nine white beans left in the jar

THOUGH THE PEAK IN QUESTION had looked to Persephone to be only a short hike away, it was midafternoon before they reached the base of it, distances apparently being difficult to judge in the shadow of the mountains that dwarfed everything in sight. Glad that no one seemed to have noticed how hard she was shivering or the fact that she could not seem to get enough air into her lungs no matter how deeply she inhaled, Persephone scrambled up the mountainside after the others. To her dismay, it was so steep in places that she had to use her hands to climb. Worse, it was covered with loose rock that was ever causing one of them to lose their footing, slide half a dozen hard-earned paces and crash into the climber directly below.

Persephone had just been thusly knocked off her feet for the third time when she heard a familiar scream.

Intensely grateful for the excuse to try to catch her breath, she looked down to the place in the foothills where the last of the old trees stood.

There, forlornly perched on the highest branch of the tallest tree, was Ivan.

Smiling fondly at the sight of the feathered friend who'd followed her so well and so far, Persephone lifted her tired arm in salute. "I'll be back soon, Ivan!" she called, her voice echoing over and over until it faded to nothingness.

In response, the hawk screeched once and burst into flight.

"Coming, Mrs. Azriel?" inquired Tiny, peering down at her from his place directly above her on the slope.

Just barely managing not to scowl at him, Persephone nodded once, dragged herself to her feet and resumed climbing.

In due course, they climbed high enough to trade the treacherous scree-covered slopes for the wintry world of the high mountain. There, the cold was as sharp as knives and the sun shone blindingly in a sky more brilliantly blue than any Persephone had ever seen in her life. Here a rock face or crevasse barred their upward path; there, a river of ice shifted, groaning in the eerie silence.

After what seemed like an eternity, Fayla finally stopped to ask Azriel if they were close to the place he thought he'd seen the woolly sheep. As she listened to him reply that he thought they were, Persephone suffered a sudden attack of dizziness. Not wanting to make a fool of herself by toppling off the edge of the snow precipice along which they'd been climbing, she hastily leaned over to brace her hands against her knees and was dully amazed to see two droplets of blood appear in the snow. Mesmerized, she watched as a third droplet appeared, ruby red and beautiful against the pure whiteness.

Even as it dawned on her that the blood was hers and that she ought to cover it up before somebody decided to make a silly fuss out of nothing, Rachel drew everyone's attention to it by crying out, "Persephone, you're bleeding!"

Squinting over at her friend, Persephone wiped her dripping nose with the back of her gloved hand and mumbled, "It's just a nosebleed."

Moving toward her with surprising swiftness given the depth of the snow, Azriel cradled her head in his hands and tilted it upward so that he could get a closer look at her face.

The glare of direct sunlight was like having red-hot, four-inch nails driven into Persephone's brain via her eyeballs. Gasping at the pain, she squeezed her eyes shut and jerked her head out of Azriel's grasp.

"You're sick," he said, his voice sharp with alarm.

"I'm fine," she retorted. Staggering to her feet, she took three great sucking gulps of air, lifted her chin and said, "See?"

"You're standing lopsided," whispered Rachel in an embarrassed voice as she gently pressed her finger against Persephone's shoulder to guide her into an upright position.

Muttering under his breath that she should have *told* him she wasn't feeling well, Azriel grabbed Persephone by the hand and pulled her as far away from the edge of the precipice as he could. Then, using his ax to sever a ten-foot length from the coiled rope that had been slung over his shoulder, he tied one end snugly about her waist.

"What . . . what do you think you're doing?" spluttered Persephone.

"Preventing you from falling off the side of the mountain," he replied tersely as he tied the other end around his own waist. "We'll head down immediately—"

"No!" she protested as she tried in vain to untie or wriggle loose of the humiliating rope.

"Yes," said Azriel, picking up his ax. "It's almost suppertime anyway, and we agreed we'd descend by then if we'd not made contact with the Panoraki, and we haven't done so. Do you think you can walk?"

"Of course I can *walk*," huffed Persephone as she slowly began to list to one side again.

"Good," said Azriel, pushing her upright once more, "because we've nothing out of which to fashion a sledge or a sled, and while I would most gladly carry you down in my arms, I suspect that I am going to need the use of them to keep us both from tumbling headfirst down the mountain and dashing our brains out on the rocks below. Let's go."

Turning around before she had a chance to offer further protest, Azriel motioned for Tiny, Fayla and Rachel to start back the way they'd come. Unwell though she was, Persephone was so put off by her husband's bossy behavior that she folded her arms across her heaving chest and dug her heels into the snow. Almost immediately, however, she was yanked forward by the short rope that now joined them. Thereafter, she had no choice but to stumble along in Azriel's footsteps—or be dragged along behind him.

The companions soon left the lip of the precipice and struck out back across a great snowy bowl littered with chunks of rock and ice shed by the sheer slopes that loomed above it. Up until now there'd been no more than the odd whisper of wind; now there was not even that. For some reason, the stillness made Persephone uneasy and heightened her feeling that they were being watched by unfriendly eyes.

Like unwelcome fish in a barrel.

Knowing that they were in the very heart of Panoraki territory— and knowing the fate that generally befell fish in a barrel—Persephone was about to ask if anyone else shared her uneasy feeling when she saw movement out of the corner of her eye.

"Azriel," she called breathlessly as she whipped her head around for a better look. "I think I see a woolly—"

"Bear!" bleated Rachel.

Rachel was right. It wasn't a woolly sheep, as Persephone had assumed, but a bear.

And it was charging straight at them.

Persephone fumbled for her dagger even though it seemed a ridiculously puny weapon with which to face such a beast. As she did so, Tiny and Azriel raised their axes, and Fayla notched an arrow in her bow. Rachel, meanwhile, floundered forward to put herself between Persephone and the bear, as though allowing herself to be eaten first was the only contribution she could think to make under the circumstances.

Surprisingly, the great white mountain bear came to a skidding halt some twenty paces away from where Rachel stood trembling.

The beast was big, all right, though not nearly as big as Persephone would have expected it to be given Tiny's description. Moreover, it did not seem ferocious in the least. On the contrary, as it sat on its haunches examining them with its big head cocked to one side and its black eyes alive with curiosity, it almost seemed friendly.

"Claws and teeth to rip a man apart as easily as if he were a piece of wet parchment," chuckled Fayla softly without lowering her bow. "I told you they were tales to frighten children, Tiny."

"I don't think they were," said Azriel in a voice so strained that it made the hair on the back of Persephone's neck stand on end. "Look at how downy his fur is, Fayla, and how big his paws are. This is no full-grown bear—*this is a baby!*"

Even as Azriel said this, there came a roar so fierce that it shook the earth and turned Persephone's knees to water. Looking across the bowl, she was horrified to see the baby's much, MUCH larger mother charging toward them with frightening speed. Her lips were peeled back to reveal her vicious teeth, and her six-inch black claws were tearing at the snow crust beneath her huge, padded paws. Persephone, who could not imagine a blade or bow on earth that would not have seemed a ridiculously puny weapon with which to face such a beast, was about to turn and run when she heard a loud *crack* from somewhere high above them.

It sounded like a thunderclap, and for an instant after she heard it, Persephone heard nothing else—not the sound of her own pounding heart, not even the sound of the approaching mother bear.

Then she heard the distant rumble. Looking up, she saw that an enormous ledge of snow had broken away and was slowly beginning to slide down the sheer slope above them.

"AVALANCHE!" bellowed Tiny. "RUN!"

As if heeding Tiny's advice, the suddenly frightened baby bear gave a plaintive wail, turned and began galloping toward its mother. Tiny, evidently believing that his best chance would be to make it to shelter at the far side of the bowl, grabbed Fayla's hand and charged forward like a man possessed. Certain that she, Azriel and Rachel were too far behind to make it across the bowl in time, Persephone turned and began stumbling back toward the precipice. That the rope at her waist was slack told her that Azriel was close behind her; a glance over her shoulder revealed that Rachel was close behind him.

The charging mother bear, who had her bawling baby by the scruff of the neck, was rapidly gaining on Rachel, and the roaring avalanche was hurtling toward them all.

Her eyes focused on the shelter of the rock face twenty paces away, Persephone tried not to give in to panic as she urged her leaden legs to move faster.

Now she was sixteen paces away . . . now twelve . . . now seven . . .

Suddenly, the ground beneath her feet gave way and she plunged downward so fast that her heart shot into her throat. She had no time to scream, however, because almost immediately her body jerked to a halt as the rope at her waist went taut. For half a heartbeat she dangled in midair with her head thrown back and her arms thrown wide. Then, before she could even begin to wonder how she was going to get herself out of this predicament, she started to slip. Over the roar of the approaching avalanche, she heard Rachel screaming; she saw the mother bear bound over the narrow opening of the hidden crevasse through which she'd fallen.

Then she saw Azriel's boots. He was desperately trying to dig his heels into the icy snow, but it was no use.

Her weight was going to drag him in after her. Wildly, Persephone looked over her left shoulder.

When she saw nothing but nothing, she realized that she wasn't just going to drag him in—she was going to drag him to his *death*.

This knowledge caused her to give in to the panic she'd managed to keep at bay when she'd only had a snarling bear and a deadly avalanche bearing down on her. With a sudden surge of energy and without the slightest thought for her own fate, she lifted the dagger that she yet clutched in her hand and began frantically sawing at the rope that connected her to Azriel.

Unfortunately for the handsome Methusian—and to Persephone's complete and utter horror—she'd hardly severed more than a few threads of the thick, sturdy rope before Azriel's heels slipped and he came tumbling into the abyss after her.

Twenty-Four

GENERAL MURDOCK SIGHED contentedly and dabbed his mouth with a white napkin. As a rule, he did not enjoy dining on horseflesh, but he'd been some days without a meal of fresh liver, and a military man always made do in a pinch. Besides, the animal whose soft parts currently graced his platter had no longer been needed because his rider had lately been punished to death, and why should some beast of the forest have the pleasure of an easy meal when he, General Murdock, desired one?

Belching softly, he took a nibble of stale bread, accidentally sprinkling the linen tablecloth before him with crumbs as he did so. Frowning slightly, he set the bread at the edge of his bloody platter and carefully brushed the crumbs to the ground. Only then did he begin to chew. While he chewed, he gazed absently at the slopes of the mountain that the princess and her companions had ascended. How pleased he was to be down here in the foothills instead of up there on the mountain! Though it was not warm down here, and though the spot he'd chosen to make camp was far from comfortable, it was infinitely warmer and more comfortable down here than it was up there, where a man's chances of survival ranged from slim to none. General Murdock would not have hesitated to follow the princess to the very top of the world if it had been necessary, of course, but it had not been necessary. He knew these mountains well from his early days as a slave hunter, and he knew that the path his quarry had taken up this particular peak was the only safe path down again.

The princess and her companions could trudge around up there suffering cold and discomfort all they liked; he would be waiting for them when they came down again.

If they came down again.

As if on cue, a soldier clutching a brass spyglass appeared some twenty paces away. He was the one who'd been assigned to visually track the progress of the princess and her companions, and though he was clearly bursting to report some news he believed to be of great moment, he said not a word.

To test him, General Murdock took another bite of bread, two more dainty bites of liver and a sip of fine claret before acknowledging his presence.

"Yes?" he finally said as he wiped a wayward dribble of liver juice off his chin.

The soldier opened his mouth slightly then clamped it shut again and took a hesitant step backward. General Murdock permitted himself a small smile. Clearly, the message he'd hoped to convey by lashing the man's comrade to death had been received: obey orders promptly and do so without questioning.

That, of course, included the standing order not to interrupt the General while he was enjoying his evening meal.

"Do not be frightened, son," he said now, beckoning the young man forward. "You have something to say, and I would hear what it is."

For an instant, the soldier didn't seem to want to draw closer. Then, as though abruptly realizing that to fail to do so would be tantamount to failing to promptly obey an order, he bounded forward and blurted, "There's been an avalanche upon the mountain, sir!"

"A Panoraki trap?" asked General Murdock, who was all too familiar with such things, having nearly perished in such a trap during a slave hunting expedition many years ago.

"Difficult to say, sir," replied the soldier.

"And what of the princess and her companions?"

"I can report with certainty that more than one was swept off the mountain."

"And the others?"

"Possibly escaped and sheltering undetected, possibly buried alive, possibly eaten."

General Murdock's beady eyes gleamed. "Eaten?" he breathed, licking his lips.

The soldier recoiled imperceptibly at this reaction but recovered almost at once. "Just before the avalanche struck, it looked as though they were being chased by a mountain bear . . ."

"Ah."

"It . . . it all happened very fast, sir," said the soldier nervously.

"I understand," murmured General Murdock, touching his steepled fingers to his thin lips.

The thought that the princess and her companions may be dead did not alarm him. Though such an outcome so early in the game had the potential to enrage the Regent to such a degree that he might well unleash his wrath upon his most favored general, a military man did not jump to conclusions based on idle speculation. A military man gathered what facts he could and drew his conclusions accordingly.

And since it was impossible to gather facts about what had happened upon the high slope from down here in the foothills, he was going to have to send an expedition up the mountain for a closer look. Though a necessary decision, it was not a welcome one. He'd left Parthania with seven men; having lost one to punishment and having sent one back to the Regent to deliver his first report, he had only five left. If he sent two up the mountain—which he would have to do, since sending a man up there alone would be folly—and if they were both to perish, he would be down to just three soldiers until such time as the messenger returned from Parthania with the requested replacements.

Given the high attrition rate of his small troop thus far, it was a risk.

Still, a military man took the risks. And so General Murdock fixed his eyes upon the soldier and said, "Take one of your comrades and venture up to the place where these events occurred. If you find the frozen bodies of the princess and her companions, bring back some proof of your findings. If you find no sign of the princess and her companions, we will have to assume that they are dead and that their bodies lie buried beneath the snow. If one or more of them is not dead, watch them but do not allow yourselves to be seen unless the princess or the Methusian is in mortal peril. The lives of the others do not concern me, but those two cannot be allowed to perish because my Lord Regent believes they are the key to finding something he desires above all else."

The soldier looked as though he very much wanted to ask what that something was, but wisely, he did not. Instead, he said, "So if the princess or the Methusian are in danger, we are to do what we can to save them?"

"Yes."

The soldier nodded once. "Very well, sir. And . . . when shall we begin our ascent?" he asked in a voice that told General Murdock that the boy already knew the answer—and dreaded it.

General Murdock permitted himself another small smile. "You will ascend at once, of course, that you might gather the facts before a sudden storm or another avalanche buries them forever," he said, giving his long, twitching nose a dainty scratch. "I appreciate that you may have concerns about spending the night on the mountain unsheltered, but I have survived a night on such a mountain; it is always possible that you will, too. And if you do not—well, the price you will have paid for a chance to elevate yourself beyond your humble beginnings will have been a 'steep' one, indeed."

"Yes, sir," said the soldier, smiling weakly at his general's play on words.

Feeling pleased with his own cleverness, the orders he'd issued and his bellyful of horse liver, General Murdock sighed with renewed contentment. He then ordered the soldier to send someone to take away his platter and bring the dessert cheeses he so enjoyed at the end of his evening meal.

The soldier nodded, but before he could hurry off to promptly do as he'd been ordered, General Murdock called him back.

"There is one other thing I would like you to do," he said.

"Sir?"

"As you make your way toward the base of the mountain, undertake another search for any sign of this 'Ivan' fellow to whom the princess called. If you find him, do what you must to extract information as to his purpose in following the princess. Then slit his throat and leave him where he lies, that some lucky beast of the forest might have the pleasure of an easy meal, too."

Twenty-Five

THE MAN IN MEANEST HOMESPUN watched without much concern as the two soldiers stopped to tuck several small sticks of firewood into their packs before unenthusiastically continuing to trudge toward the mountain along a path that would lead them right past the tree in which he sat. He, too, had a spyglass; he, too, had seen the mountain bear and the avalanche and was wondering what fate had befallen the princess and her companions.

Unlike the approaching soldiers, however, the man had no intention of ascending the mountain to find out. The princess and her companions would come down or they wouldn't. The man was almost certain that his master in this matter would want him to find out why they hadn't come down if they didn't, and to intervene if the princess was in danger, that she might later play her part in his grand plans. Yet "almost certain" wasn't the same thing as "absolutely certain," and it was not the man's place to make judgment calls. It was his place to follow orders, and for now his orders were to follow whoever was following the princess and to ensure that this individual was unable to send reports back to Parthania.

Just south of the Methusian camp, the body of a soldier lay rotting in the bushes—a testament to the diligence with which the man in homespun followed orders.

Turning his thoughts from the dead soldier and his never-to-be-delivered report, the man harkened back to the strange incident that had taken place earlier that day. Having decided that the tall tree in which he currently sat offered the perfect vantage point from which to watch both the General's camp and the princess and her companions, he'd climbed to the very top and was just settling in when a hawk alighted at the end of a branch above him. Peering down at the man as though incensed by his presence, the creature had ruffled its feathers and screeched loudly. Annoyed, the man had plucked a pine cone from the nearest branch and had been about to fling it at the bird when the princess had suddenly begun shouting to somebody called "Ivan." Looking up at the mountain, the man had nearly jumped out of his skin when he'd seen that the princess was not only staring right at him *but was also smiling and waving*!

The man's first wild thought was that she'd somehow spotted him hidden among the branches and had mistaken him for an acquaintance by the name of "Ivan." His second, steadier thought was that he was too well hidden to have been spotted and that if the princess *had* noticed an acquaintance perched in a tree at the edge of nowhere, she'd probably have acted just a bit more surprised. With this in mind, he'd hastily looked around for whomever it was that she'd actually been waving to.

But he'd seen no one at all. The princess had eventually resumed climbing, the hawk had flown away and since then the man had done nothing but watch and wait.

And listen.

Crunch . . . crunch . . . crunch . . .

The soldiers were so close now that the man could hear the crunch of old pine needles beneath their boots and hear snatches of their conversation. They seemed to be arguing—something about their orders and Methusian trinkets and the rights of New Men.

Interesting.

But not important to the man in meanest homespun. What was important to him was that he follow his orders for the greater good of the realm. Tugging his cloak more tightly about his shoulders, he recalled what his master in this matter had told him: that there would come a day when poets would write verses praising his heroism and minstrels would sing of how he'd singlehandedly changed the course of Glyndorian history.

It was a very grand thing for one whom the midwife had wanted to drown at birth for being marked by the devil.

But that was not important, either.

What was important was that the man do the job he'd been sent to do, and that he do it without letting his conscience be troubled by who might get hurt along the way.

Twenty-Six

Eighty-nine white beans left in the jar

PERSEPHONE BARELY HAD TIME to register the fact that Azriel was hurtling through the crevasse toward her before she slammed onto the icy ledge she'd have noticed if she'd looked over her right shoulder while she'd been dangling in midair. Without thinking, she immediately drove her dagger deep into the ice at her side and grabbed onto it with both hands. The next instant, the rope at her waist snapped taut. Though the lower half of her body was jerked off the ledge, by some miracle her dagger stayed anchored and her hold on it stayed true.

And then the avalanche was roaring over the crack through which she and Azriel had fallen, burying all but a sliver at the far end.

And then it was over and the world was plunged into deafening silence.

It was into this silence that Azriel called, "Cut the rope, wife! Save yourself!"

Persephone's arms were beginning to tremble so violently with the effort of holding both herself and Azriel up that she was barely able to gasp out, "Do . . . do you still have your ax and your knife?"

There was a pause, as though the handsome Methusian believed she was about to tell him to cut the rope himself and was much dismayed by how readily she was agreeing to save herself at his expense. Then, cautiously, he said, "Y-y-yes, I still have my ax and knife . . ."

"WELL, THEN, YOU GREAT USELESS OAF, USE THEM . . . TO CLIMB UP HERE . . . BEFORE MY DAGGER SLIPS . . . AND WE BOTH . . . GO PLUMMETING . . . TO OUR DEATHS!" hollered Persephone in between gasps and grunts.

From somewhere below her dangling feet there came an offended huff. Then came the sound of metal biting into ice and then—mercifully!—the feel of the rope slackening. Without Azriel's dead weight dragging her down, Persephone was able to wriggle forward on her elbows, throw one leg up onto the narrow ledge and drag the rest of her body up after it. As she lay on her side gasping and trying to blink away the black spots that danced before her eyes, Azriel's knife hand rose up above the edge of the ledge and drove downward, half-burying the blade in the ice. There was a pause in which Persephone could hear Azriel breathing heavily. Then the top of his head appeared, then his blue eyes. There was another pause and then, with a final grunt of effort, he heaved himself onto his elbows and scrambled up onto the ledge beside her. As he did so, his foot knocked a loose chunk of ice over the edge.

While Persephone struggled into a sitting position to make room for him, she listened intently for the sound of the ice chunk hitting the bottom of the crevasse.

It never came.

"I had thought that binding my fortunes to yours would be a sacrifice on my part, but it would appear that being bound to you has saved me in very truth," said Azriel lightly, having obviously noted the lack of sound as well. When Persephone didn't reply, he tilted his head toward hers and murmured, "This is where you say that being bound to me saved you, as well, and that this knowledge, combined with the heightened physical awareness you are feeling on account of your most recent near-death experience, compels you to confess that when we get out of here you will finally be ready to beg me not to behave myself."

Persephone smiled weakly but didn't say anything in response to this teasing reference to the words he'd spoken on their wedding night. Instead, she looked around the eerie blue dimness, trying not to think about how very unlikely it was that they *would* get out of there. The narrow ledge on which they sat was twenty feet below the opening of the crevasse. The walls above it angled out over the bottomless abyss. The first fifteen feet were sheer ice; the last five were packed snow in which a climber might bury a knife or ax blade only to have it come away without warning.

And even if she or Azriel somehow managed to make it to the top of the crevasse without falling, the opening was entirely buried in snow except for a tiny crack at the far end that was all but unreachable from their current position.

Rescue was clearly their only hope—if, indeed, there was anyone left to rescue them.

Even as this occurred to her, Azriel cupped his gloved hands around his mouth and bellowed for Rachel, Fayla and Tiny. The sound of his voice ricocheted off the walls of the crevasse before eventually fading to silence, and although Persephone held her breath and listened with all her might, she heard no reply.

Indeed, from the world above she heard nothing at all. Unwilling to consider the dread possibility that their companions had all perished in the avalanche—or had afterward been turned into mincemeat by the panicked mother bear—Persephone turned her attention to her and Azriel's immediate survival. Their supplies were meager. They had flints with which to start a fire but no fuel to feed it; they were surrounded by ice, but without a fire to melt it to water, it would not quench their thirst. They had food enough for two or three days—longer if they rationed carefully—but without a fire to keep them warm, they would most likely freeze to death long before they starved to death.

Or at least, *she* most likely would. For although she'd somehow found the strength to survive her "most recent near-death experience," the sickness that had been steadily worsening since that morning had taken its toll. And Persephone knew from her time in the mines that the weak were always the first to go.

As if to punctuate this bleak thought, she felt something warm trickle out of her left nostril.

"I think my nose is bleeding again," she said.

"Lie down," said Azriel, shifting to make room for her to stretch out.

"No, that's okay," she wheezed. "I'm—"

"Fine," interrupted Azriel briskly. "Yes, I know, I can tell by the way you've been gasping, shivering, squinting, stumbling and bleeding without cause. Believe me, wife, I ask you to lie down not for your sake but for mine, for my lap is feeling uncomfortably chilled and I think that your head would be the very thing to warm it up."

Though Persephone felt she ought to protest, her body was crashing so hard that she was unable to put forth more than a token effort. "Well, all right," she mumbled. "But I feel it is my duty to warn you that this situation has the potential to cause irreparable harm to my womanly pride."

"And if that happens, the consequences could be truly dire?" guessed Azriel with a smile.

"Exactly," she said, with a smile of her own.

Neither of them said anything more as Azriel gently helped her remove her pack. Lying down, she put her head in his lap. Almost immediately after she'd done so, she was struck by a wave of exhaustion so powerful that she was unable to summon the energy required to swat away Azriel's hand when he insisted upon pinching her nostrils shut to stop the bleeding. Feeling helpless as a child, she simply lay there with her eyes closed and her head swimming. The warmth of Azriel's strong thigh beneath her neck was inexpressibly comforting, and when he stopped pinching her nostrils and began tenderly stroking her hair, she could not keep from sighing aloud. As she hovered in that shimmery in-between place between wakefulness and sleep, the thought that a near-death experience really *did* heighten one's physical awareness had just flitted through her mind when—

"IS THERE ANYONE ALIVE DOWN THERE?"

Heart leaping so hard that it took what was left of her breath away, Persephone's eyes flew open to the sight of Rachel's face peering down at her from the tiny crack that had escaped being buried in snow.

"You're *both* alive?" cried Rachel. "Oh, thank the gods!"

As she said this, a bit of snow fell from the spot directly beneath where she was standing.

"Careful!" panted Persephone as she laboriously maneuvered herself into a sitting position. "For your own sake as well as for ours, you must be—"

"Rachel!" interrupted Azriel in a voice that was almost harsh. "Where are Tiny and Fayla?"

The joy that had thus far lighted up Rachel's face fled instantly, leaving only troubled shadows behind. After a pause that spoke louder than words ever could, she swallowed hard and called, "I'm sorry, Azriel."

There was another pause, this one of stunned disbelief. Then, in an incredulous voice, Azriel said, "What are you saying? Are you saying that they are *dead*?"

"I am saying that they are . . . nowhere," replied Rachel quietly.

Persephone felt ill when she realized what her friend was too softhearted to say aloud: namely, that Fayla and Tiny had been swept away or buried alive. That they were dead, their bodies forever lost to the mountain.

"Oh, Azriel," she murmured, tentatively touching his shoulder.

The grief-stricken Methusian did not shrug off her comforting hand, but neither did he acknowledge it. Instead, in a painfully businesslike manner, he asked Rachel if she had any rope.

"No," she replied.

"Neither do I—it slipped off my shoulder when I fell into the crevasse," said Azriel. And then: "This is a problem."

"It is, but don't worry," said Rachel bravely. "I'll go for help."

Azriel didn't say anything in response to this, and neither did Persephone. For all intents and purposes, Rachel was alone high on the mountain and night was falling fast. Even if she somehow made it down to the foothills in the darkness, she was miles from the nearest settlement. Even if she somehow reached it, it was unlikely that she'd be able to convince a complete stranger that a long-lost Erok princess was trapped in the heart of Panoraki territory and that he ought to risk his life to rescue her. And even if she managed to do so, the chances were slim that Persephone, sick as she was, would be alive by the time help arrived.

Still, it was their only hope, and Persephone knew there was nothing whatsoever to be gained by giving voice to her doubts. Therefore, instead of doing so, she merely suggested to Rachel that before leaving she mark the crevasse in some way, since shouting from below could not be relied upon as a means to guide would-be rescuers to the proper location.

"I'll mark it to be safe, but you needn't worry," said Rachel. "Earlier, when Azriel was shouting, I heard him clear as a bell."

"You did?" said Persephone in surprise. "Why didn't you call back?"

"The mother bear appeared to be trying to decide whether to take her baby back to her den or to eat me, and I thought it best not to start yelling just in case it annoyed her and tipped the balance in favor of eating me."

Rachel sounded so earnest when she said this that in almost any other circumstance, Persephone would have smiled.

"A wise choice, I think," was all she said now. "You'd better make haste, now, Rachel. Godspeed and good luck, and . . . if for some reason you don't return—"

"I will return."

"I know you will, but if you don't—"

"Goodbye, Princess. Be kind to your husband in his time of grief, and I will be back before you know it."

After Rachel left, Persephone sat next to Azriel in awkward silence, wondering what she should do. She'd experienced the profound grief of sudden, catastrophic loss several times in her life, but she'd never known what it was to be comforted. All she knew for a certainty was that words and wishes could not bring back the lost and the dead.

At length, she did the only thing she could think to do, which was to reach out and touch his shoulder again. This time he briefly pressed his lips together in polite acknowledgment. Instead of making Persephone feel as though she'd done the right thing, his reaction made her feel as though her gesture had been woefully inadequate. And so, taking her courage into her hands, she unsteadily climbed over his outstretched legs, planted one knee on either side of them, sat down on his lap and, after a moment's hesitation, tentatively wrapped both arms around him. As soon as she did this, Azriel heaved a shuddering sigh and pulled her so close that as she lay against his chest feeling the beat of his heart against hers, she had a fair idea that she'd done the right thing, after all.

They survived the long, cold night by staying locked in this embrace that somehow felt more intimate than passion. When the thin light of dawn at last began to pervade the gloom of the crevasse, Azriel lightly brushed his lips against Persephone's forehead.

"Good morning, wife," he whispered. "How do you feel?"

"Well enough," she lied, hoping he wouldn't notice how much more labored her breathing had become.

If he did notice, he didn't say anything. Instead, he leaned forward as though he meant to kiss her. Without thinking, Persephone tilted her head to meet him halfway. Before their lips could meet, however, the crevasse darkened abruptly.

Frowning slightly, Persephone looked around to see Rachel's head in the crack above, half-blotting out the sunlight. Her heart sank at the sight, for though she was pleased to know that her friend yet lived, she was much disappointed by the fact that she'd not yet left to find help.

Before she could ask why she'd not yet done so, Rachel called out, "Well, I have good news and bad news."

Azriel sat up from his reclining position so fast that it made Persephone dizzy. "What is the good news?" he demanded, the hope that it concerned Fayla and Tiny fierce upon his handsome face.

"The good news is that I've found a way to get you out of there," replied Rachel.

Azriel said nothing, only nodded as he slowly leaned back against the wall of the crevasse.

Wishing there was something she could do to ease his pain and disappointment but knowing there was not, Persephone took a great gulp of air and called, "What . . . what is the bad news, Rachel?"

As if in response, a big, hairy head abruptly appeared in the crack next to Rachel's.

"The bad news," faltered Rachel, "is that it seems that the Panoraki do not care for trespassers."

Twenty-Seven

MORDESIUS HAD BEEN BUSY.

So busy, in fact, that he'd not met with the king for several days. Well, why would he have? The king was a royal nobody whose opinions mattered not at all, and Mordesius saw no need, nor had he time in his hectic schedule, to coddle the fool by pretending otherwise.

As he lurched toward the king's chambers now, Mordesius reflected upon all that he'd accomplished in just a few short days. The most satisfying bit of business by far, of course, had been overseeing the routing of the Parthanian slums. It had not gone as smoothly as he would have liked, for the slums' lowborn inhabitants had not been entirely soothed by the sight of their smiling, waving ninny of a king, but the wretches had paid dearly for the trouble they'd caused. The only thing left to do now was to haul away what little remained of the charred hovels and those who'd burned to death inside them, and to scrub clean the many paving stones that had been stained with the blood of those who'd resisted their destinies.

With a smile that made a passing pageboy shrink back in terror, Mordesius moved on to consider the other items he'd crossed off his "to-do" list. In addition to having conducted another Council meeting, he'd ignored two summonses sent by the king and issued a precautionary arrest warrant for the father of the girl he'd auditioned and then banished on account of her now ruined reputation. He'd also suffered through several wardrobe fittings and visited the cow in the dungeon twice—once to chat of inconsequential things, and once to fling a cup of beef broth at her to ensure that she smelled especially appetizing to the legions of glittery-eyed vermin that ever lurked just beyond the torchlight. Best of all, he'd managed to hammer out the details concerning the betrothal ceremony that would soon take place between the king and Lord Bartok's daughter. Admittedly, Mordesius was not best pleased by the outcome of these particular discussions. He'd wanted the ceremony to be a private affair with just two witnesses who could later be disposed of in the event that it someday became advantageous for him to claim that the ceremony had never taken place at all. Whether Lord Bartok had understood and feared this very possibility, or whether he'd simply wanted to rub his fellow noblemen's noses in his own family's tremendous good fortune, he'd absolutely insisted that the betrothal ceremony be treated as a grand affair of state. Mordesius had trembled with outrage that the high-and-mighty silver-haired bastard had thought that he could insist upon *anything*, but in the end, he'd gritted his teeth and acquiesced with a show of good grace. The unfortunate truth was that until the Council named him heir, Mordesius needed Lord Bartok.

Fortunately, there was a pleasanter truth: that in due course, Lord Bartok's insolence would be paid back a hundredfold. Nay, a *thousandfold* . . .

"Open the door," muttered Mordesius now, as he approached the New Men standing guard outside the king's inner chamber.

Rather than leaping to obey as quickly as possible, the soldier to whom he'd given the order cast an uncertain glance toward his fellow soldier and stammered, "Uh, well, the thing is, Your Grace—"

The imbecile's next words were choked off by a single scathing look from Mordesius, and with the fumbling clumsiness of a walking dead man (which, indeed, he now was), the soldier hastened to open the door. Mordesius slouched across the threshold of the king's inner chamber and then stopped abruptly. He'd thought to find the windows shuttered tight and the room smelling of sickness and despair; he'd hoped to find the pale, coughing king propped up in bed, wrapped in blankets by the fire or huddled in a corner somewhere.

Instead, every shutter in the chamber was thrown wide. Specks of dust danced in the thick wedges of warm yellow sunlight that streamed through the open windows; the air was perfumed with the scent of the honeysuckles, lilacs and lilies that grew in the royal garden below.

As for the king, he was, indeed, sitting by the fire, and he was, indeed, pale and coughing. However, he was not wrapped in blankets. On the contrary, he was fully dressed in a splendid doublet of forest-green velvet with puffed sleeves slashed to show off a cloth-of-silver undershirt that matched perfectly the silver buckles on his polished black shoes. And far from huddling, he was sitting comfortably—not in his own high-backed chair, but in the chair upon which his nurse-maid used to plant her once-fat arse. Most galling of all, *the fool was holding half a dozen playing cards in his hand!*

Mordesius jammed his scarred hands upon his hips. "What is the meaning of this?" he demanded irritably.

At these words, there came a tiny shriek and a little head piled high with flaxen curls peeped out from behind the king's high-backed chair.

Mordesius was so shocked that he dropped his hands from his skinny hips and staggered backward. "Lady Aurelia!" he blurted.

"Good day, Your Grace!" she chirped as she started to her feet.

"Sit, Lady Aurelia, sit," bade the king, nonchalantly waving her back into her seat. Coughing into his sleeve, he said, "As you can see from the way my Lord Regent greets me, we do not stand upon ceremony within my inner chamber. Isn't that right, Your Grace?"

Mordesius nodded wordlessly, but his mind was whirling. What in the name of the gods was Bartok's daughter doing here?

As if in response to this unspoken question, King Finnius coughed again and said, "After our last discussion in which we agreed that Lady Aurelia and I ought to wed for the sake of the realm, I decided to send for her, that we might get to know one another a little better."

"His Majesty has been teaching me how to play cards!" trilled the lady in question as she playfully fanned her face with the cards she had clutched in her bony little hand.

"Has he," said Mordesius faintly.

"Yes, though he is *so* much cleverer than I am that I'm afraid he has won every single hand!" twittered Lady Aurelia, gazing at the king with such admiration that even though Mordesius knew it was the false coin of a grasping courtier, he felt a sharp stab of envy.

"Well," he said brusquely, "I've come here to share with His Majesty the details of your upcoming betrothal ceremony. It will take place—"

"Here at the palace in three days' time," said the king absently as he nudged three white beans into the center of the small mahogany table before him. "Yes, I know. Lady Aurelia has told me everything."

"My father has promised me that the feast that follows the ceremony shall be the most spectacular the realm has ever seen," she breathed, her bright eyes glittering.

"And he has promised me that our wedding feast shall make the betrothal feast look like a lowborn corn roast," added the king.

At these words, Mordesius felt the blood drain from his face. "What . . . what do you mean 'he has promised you'?" he spluttered. "Lord Bartok has been *here*? To see *you*?"

Seized by a sudden coughing fit, the king could only nod in reply. When the fit was over, he shakily wiped the blood from his pale lips and drained the wine goblet that was sitting next to his pile of white beans. The instant he set the goblet back down, a one-legged servant stepped forward to refill it.

"Thank you, Neeka," gasped the king with a wan smile. Under other circumstances, Mordesius would have been much affronted that the slattern who'd replaced the cow had failed to offer *him* wine. However, at present he was too affronted by the fact that the king had dared to meet with Lord Bartok in secret to be affronted by anything else.

He needed to speak privately with the king at once to find out just how much damage had been done by this secret meeting, and just how brutal a punishment would have to be meted out to ensure that another one never took place.

"Your Majesty," said Mordesius, his voice strained with the effort of trying not to snarl, "though I do not like to intrude, I'm afraid there is business we need to attend to."

"What business?" asked the king.

"Business of the realm," replied Mordesius, with a pointed look at Bartok's spawn.

The king smiled across the pile of beans at his birdlike soon-to-be betrothed. "Whatever you have to say to me you can say in front of Lady Aurelia," he said.

"I think not, Your Majesty," said Mordesius, through his teeth.

"But Lady Aurelia will be my wife, Your Grace," frowned the king. *"But she is not your wife yet!"*

"A formality," said the king mildly, after a moment of awkward silence. Then, laying his cards face down on the table, he smiled at Lady Aurelia again and said, "Still, if my Lord Regent wishes to speak with me alone, I suppose I ought to accommodate him. After all he has done for me and my realm these many years, I would say it is the least I can do for him, wouldn't you, Lady Aurelia?"

"Oh, yes, Your Majesty!" she cried.

Knowing that Lady Aurelia would have agreed just as enthusiastically if the king had suggested beheading him on the spot, Mordesius nodded as graciously as he could given that he was a heartbeat away from gouging out both their eyes.

"Very well," said the king amiably, rising to his feet. "Then I bid you good day, Lady Aurelia."

"And a good day to you, Your Majesty," she trilled, hopping to her feet and dipping him a curtsey. "I shall look forward to our next meeting."

"As shall I," he said with an elegant bow.

✳

The instant Lady Aurelia was gone the king dropped back down onto the nursemaid's chair. Clearly, he'd been working hard at looking effortlessly comfortable.

Though the knowledge pleased Mordesius, he did not smile.

"Is something the matter, Your Grace?" asked the king, slumping forward with his elbows on his knees.

"Yes, something is the matter!" snarled Mordesius, sweeping the white beans off the mahogany table with the back of his hand. "What do you mean meeting with that little shrew behind my back? Not to mention meeting with her conniving father?"

The king appeared genuinely shocked. "But . . . but I thought you'd approve!" he stammered.

"You thought I'd approve?" barked Mordesius with a startling burst of high-pitched laughter. "You thought I'd *approve*?"

"Yes!" exclaimed the king, gesturing with his hands. "You spend your days running the kingdom; I have nothing to do but think! And the more I thought about our last conversation, the more I came to see how strange it would seem if I, a king come of age, did not show an interest in the matter of my own marriage. And I began to worry that if I did not make some effort to better acquaint myself with my betrothed-to-be and her family, people might start to think that I did not truly support the marriage. Or worse, that I was being coerced into it! And I realized that if they started to think *that*, they'd soon wonder what else I was being coerced into. And after your recent heartless treatment of the city's lowborn inhabitants, not to mention the terrible injury you inflicted upon poor Moira, I feared what you'd do if such rumors were to interfere with your plans!"

Lips curled in disdain at the blubbering blue blood before him, Mordesius sneered, "I am *touched* that you care so deeply for my plans."

"I care nothing for your plans," coughed the king. "I care only for the fates of those I would see kept safe from harm."

"If you care so deeply," said Mordesius with a chilling smile, "you really ought to have consulted with me before meeting with Bartok and his spawn."

"I tried to consult with you!" burst King Finnius, who immediately winced and pressed his hand against his chest as though pained by the effort of forceful speech. "I sent you two summonses, but you never came," he gasped. "What else would you have had me do?"

Mordesius did not reply at once. Though he was loath to be reminded of it, the royal nobody *had* sent two summonses—summonses that he, Mordesius, had taken great pleasure in ignoring. Moreover, the fool had a point about the wisdom of showing an interest in his own marriage, and the potential consequences of failing to do so.

Snapping his fingers at the slattern, Mordesius called for wine. As she bustled off to fetch another goblet, he eased himself down into the king's high-backed chair and said, "I had *obviously* intended for you to play the part of the eager, involved bridegroom-to-be. My only concern was that you'd done so without my express permission. Do something like that again, and I will surprise you not with a fat finger but instead with a nose and two ears. Do you understand?"

"I do," said King Finnius quietly.

"Good," smiled Mordesius. "Now tell me: What did you and Lady Aurelia speak about?"

"Nothing."

Mordesius stopped smiling at once. "Nothing?" he snapped.

"Nothing of import," clarified King Finnius. "She giggled and told me I was handsome and clever; I told her she was beautiful and promised her expensive gifts."

Feeling a pang at the knowledge that no young noblewoman had ever called *him* handsome and clever, Mordesius moodily asked the king what he and Lord Bartok had spoken about.

"Nothing beyond what you'd expect," he replied. "He said his daughter had been desperately in love with me for years and would have agreed to marry me if I'd been a lowborn beggar living in a gutter;

I said that no woman in the realm was more charming or better suited to be my wife and queen."

"Are you certain that is all you said?" asked Mordesius suspiciously before taking a sip from the wine goblet that had appeared on the table in front of him.

"What else would I have said, Your Grace?" asked the king wearily. "Given all that I've thus far sacrificed to save my sister, my nursemaid and the most vulnerable of my subjects, do you honestly believe that I'd have confided anything of import in a courtier who has never put anything before his own best interests?"

"No," said Mordesius, inwardly chuckling at how dismayed the high-and-mighty lord must have been when he'd realized that the king was utterly beyond his influence. He would have assumed that it was simply because the royal fool had another, shrewder master; how amusing to know that it was also because his measure had been taken and found wanting.

Not for the first time, Mordesius thought how ironic it was that the sickly boy king who sat wheezing in his imprisoned nursemaid's chair actually seemed to have what it would have taken to command the great lords of the kingdom.

Well, life was full of ironies.

"Your Grace," the king was saying now, "if I have set your mind at ease in the matter of my dealings with Lord Bartok and Lady Aurelia, may I ask if you've had any news of my sister and her quest for the healing pool?"

"I have," lied Mordesius, who was, in truth, growing increasingly concerned that he'd yet to receive a single report from General Murdock. "However, I've had no news that I care to share with *you*."

"I see," said King Finnius, nodding as though he'd expected as much. "And . . . did you truly have business of the realm that you wished to discuss with me?"

Mordesius laughed so explosively that he sprayed the fool's pale face with spittle. "No, Your Majesty," he chortled when he was finally able. "No, I did not truly have business of the realm that I wished to discuss with you, nor will I ever have. There is a thing I would ask of you, though," he added, sounding almost mischievous.

"Oh?" said the king guardedly. "And what is that?"

"I would ask you to beg forgiveness for the way you treated me in front of Lady Aurelia."

The king sighed. "Your Grace, when we are in the company of others, I cannot treat you with deference," he said, coughing into his velvet sleeve. "As we've just now discussed, I must continue to behave as your king, else people will suspect that something is amiss."

"Be that as it may, I did not care for your condescending behavior, and you *will* beg forgiveness for it."

For a moment, it looked as though the king might actually protest. Then, with a shrug that said this particular battle was not worth fighting, he rose to his feet, drew himself up to his full height and said, "Very well. My Lord Regent, I beg forgiveness for—"

"No," smirked Mordesius. "Get down on your knees and beg for it."

After the briefest of hesitations, King Finnius got down on his knees. "Your Grace," he said quietly and with a dignity that made Mordesius want to slap him, "I beg your forgiveness for the way I spoke to you in front of Lady Aurelia."

Mordesius stared down at the bowed head of the kneeling king, his cold heart crying out at the irony of the fact that a fool as sick and subjugated as the one before him could yet look as shining and golden as a strapping young god.

Then, sourly muttering that he was not in a particularly forgiving mood, he turned and shuffled from the room.

Twenty-Eight

Eighty-eight white beans left in the jar

THE HUGE, HAIRY HEAD of the Panoraki warrior abruptly disappeared from the crack in the snow above Persephone and Azriel. The next minute, one end of a thick, swinging rope was fed down into the crevasse. It was a development that would have been considerably more comforting had the end of the rope not been tied in a noose.

Persephone shivered violently at the sight of it.

"I don't believe it is meant for our necks, Princess," said Azriel under his breath as he eased her off his lap, got to his feet and leaned out over the abyss to reach for the rope.

"Send the wench up first," called the Panoraki gruffly.

"She is no wench," Azriel called back, "she is my wedded wife and you will treat her—"

"ANY WAY I PLEASE!" shouted the Panoraki, shoving his hairy head back into the crack, "For she is a criminal and my prisoner, and so are you. So send her up at once or I'll leave you both to your deaths. And if you think I won't, think again, little man, for I tell you there is nothing the mother goddess of the mountain enjoys so much as a meal of frozen corpses. And there is nothing that I, Ghengor, enjoy so much as being the one to feed it to her!"

"Oh," muttered Azriel. "Well, since you put it that way . . ."

Dropping to his knees beside Persephone, he sliced the rope that tied them together, then slipped the noose of the rope over her head and under her arms. After checking the knot to make sure that it was properly tied, he cinched the noose tight under her armpits and helped her stand.

"My . . . pack," panted Persephone.

"I'll bring it up," he whispered. "Do you still have your dagger?"

"Yes," she mumbled as she swayed on her frozen feet, "but . . . I really don't know what good it will do me, Azriel. I . . . I can't seem to feel my—"

Without warning, the Panoraki Ghengor gave the rope a sharp tug, wrenching Persephone away from Azriel's steadying touch and pulling her off the ice ledge. Her heart lurched horribly, and the next instant she was dangling over the abyss. Feeling as helpless as a rag doll, she dimly hoped that the man on the other end of the rope wasn't reconsidering his decision not to feed her to his mountain goddess. Then she was ascending, farther and farther from where Azriel stood watching with his gloved hands clenched into fists.

Before she knew it, she was being pulled from the womb of darkness and ice into a world of overly brilliant sunlight. Wordlessly, the Panoraki man, who smelled of wet wool, dung fires and too few baths, deposited her into the snow beside the crevasse. Then he bent over her limp body, stripped her of weapons and was halfway through wrestling the noose up over her head when he noticed something that made him gasp aloud.

"Gods' blood, you're the very image of the villain who startled my poor sheep!"

"As I've already explained, I didn't mean to startle them," said Rachel with exaggerated patience as she tried to edge past the man's great bulk to get to Persephone. "And she is not actually the very image of me. Her features are finer than mine, you see, and my ears stick out more than hers, and—"

Giving Rachel a sudden, one-armed shove that sent her sprawling, the Panoraki yanked the rope free of Persephone at last. Gesturing toward the battle-ax that hung at his waist, he advised her and Rachel not to move—advice that was really not necessary in the case of Persephone, who wasn't sure she'd ever be able to move again. Then he turned and fed the noose back down into the darkness. Moments later, Azriel emerged from the crevasse.

Upon seeing Persephone shivering and gasping in the arms of Rachel (who'd ignored the advice about not moving), he threw down his ax and his knife, shrugged off both packs and the rope and started toward her.

The one named Ghengor immediately stepped sideways to block his way. "Where do you think you're going?" he growled as he plucked the battle-ax from his belt.

Azriel stepped back and held up his hands to show that he carried no weapon. "I'm going to tend to my wife," he said evenly. "She's sick."

"Aye, she's sick," agreed the man without sympathy. "'Tis the mountain that's made her so. Sometimes it pleases the goddess to wreak vengeance upon those who do not belong here. Warmth and nourishment can improve the symptoms, but the only cure is to descend to the foothills at once."

"Then we will descend to the foothills at once," said Azriel.

"Not until you've answered for your crimes, you won't."

Before Azriel could argue, lunge for his blade or suggest that they settle their differences by wrestling (a heroic and manly challenge that would absolutely have resulted in Azriel being mangled beyond recognition), Rachel slapped the snow beside her.

"Oh, enough with your talk of crimes and villains!" she cried. "For the last time, *I did not mean to startle your herd.* It was dark, and I lost my footing. It's not my fault that you and your infernal sheep were sleeping at the bottom of the snowdrift I happened to tumble down!"

"MY SHEEP ARE NOT INFERNAL!" bellowed Ghengor, shaking his battle-ax at her. "And your heartless treatment of them is only one of your crimes, villain! There is also the matter of your criminal companions having violated the goddess of the mountain by having penetrated one of her private places!"

Rachel and Persephone could not help grimacing at these indelicate words, but Azriel only cleared his throat and said, "If you're referring to the crevasse, I can assure you that my wife and I never intended to 'penetrate' it. We were running from an avalanche and a bear when we fell in—"

"A thing that would not have happened if you'd not trespassed upon the mountain in the first place," concluded Ghengor triumphantly as he stomped over and snatched up Azriel's knife and ax.

"You . . . are right," wheezed Persephone, holding one frozen, trembling hand out to him. "But . . . I can explain—"

"You'd better hope for your sakes that you can and that the prince of my people likes what you have to say," he grunted as he shoved his handful of weapons into his belt, "or the mother goddess of the mountain shall have her meal, after all."

With that, Ghengor turned and began striding up the mountain as briskly and easily as if he was taking a pleasure stroll in the royal garden. He did not bother to look back to see if the "criminals" were following, and why would he? Even if Persephone had not been gravely ill, for her, Azriel and Rachel to even attempt to flee would have been a folly bordering on the ridiculous. There was nothing for them to do but to follow the silent, fur-clad figure ahead of them, and to hope that they were not following it to their doom.

Since Persephone could barely stand, let alone walk, Azriel, in addition to carrying both their packs on his back, carried her in his arms. As strong, sure-footed and determined as he was, however, he was no match for the mountain. When he slipped on a hidden patch of ice and fell for the third time—not letting go of Persephone but very nearly sending them both hurtling down a rock face—Ghengor had had enough. Stomping back to the spot where Azriel was struggling to get to his feet without jostling his barely conscious wife too badly, the giant ripped Persephone from his arms and flung her over his shoulder with almost as much care and tenderness as one might show toward a sack of bad potatoes.

"Don't do anything stupid, little man," growled the Panoraki as he turned and continued up the mountain.

Feeling sick unto death and reeling with the shock of having been torn from the relative warmth and comfort of Azriel's protective embrace, Persephone could not find the strength to warn him against reckless heroics. All she could do was wince at the smell of the giant's dirty furs against her face, and at the feel of his meaty hand gripping her leg tight, and at the pounding pain in her upside-down head. She couldn't feel her gloved hands, but she could see them dangling just past the ends of her dark hair, which had come loose from its messy plait. Vaguely, she felt droplets of warm liquid shivering at the tip of her nose before falling away; turning her head slightly, she saw a trail of crimson spots in the snow next to Rachel's footprints, and she realized that her nose must be bleeding again.

That's not good, she thought dully.

"Isn't ascending farther up the mountain going to make Persephone sicker?" came Rachel's anxious voice then, so faintly that Persephone found herself wondering how her friend could be so far away and so close, all at the same time.

"Probably," the Panoraki grunted in response.

As Persephone hung limply over the man's shoulder, dimly pondering the fact that this answer ought to have made her feel angry or scared but instead made her feel nothing at all, she felt a sudden, searing pain behind her eyes.

Then a darkness as seductive and inviting as Death abruptly stole over her, and she knew no more.

Twenty-Nine

Eighty-eight white beans left in the jar

PERSEPHONE AWOKE SLOWLY in a place that sounded and smelled like an overcrowded barn, and to an agony worse than any she'd ever known. Worse than hunger, cold or thirst, worse than being whipped or beaten, it felt as though her hands and feet had been pounded with a mallet, stuck with pins and set ablaze. The pain was so bad, in fact, that it was all she could do to lie unmoving instead of groaning aloud or vomiting or—

My hands and feet! she thought with a jolt. *I can feel my hands and feet!*

Hard on the heels of this most welcome knowledge was the realization that she was thinking more clearly and breathing more easily than she had in days and that she was no longer shivering with cold. On the contrary, she seemed to be sweating profusely. Without opening her eyes, she shifted imperceptibly and felt a weight upon her. It was a poorly cured fur, judging by the odor, and it seemed that there was another beneath her. Relieved that her captors were clearly trying to warm her up (encouraging news in view of the fact that the goddess of the mountain preferred *frozen* corpses), Persephone had just begun to listen in earnest for some indication that Azriel and Rachel were near and well when she sensed a large presence right in front of her face. Heart in her throat, she lay unmoving and tense, wishing that she still had her dagger and waiting to see what the presence would do. When the presence did nothing but breathe on her, she slowly opened one eye the merest of cracks . . .

And jerked her head back in surprise when she discovered that she was nose to nose with an enormous sheep. The beast sported mighty curling horns and a magnificent coat of flowing, white wool that looked as though it had been washed, combed, oiled and trimmed on a regular basis. At Persephone's sudden movement, it baaed noisily, turned and bolted away from her.

Realizing that there was no longer any point trying to maintain the pretense of sleep, Persephone opened both eyes. The first person she saw was Ghengor, the Panoraki warrior who'd carried her to this place. He was standing nearby with his feet shoulder width apart and his battle-ax clutched tight in one hairy hand.

"Did you enjoy startling the great lord ram of our herd, villain?" he demanded in a voice quivering with outrage.

"I didn't mean to startle it," croaked Persephone. "I just—"

"I am not interested in your excuses!" bellowed Ghengor, shaking his battle-ax at her. "And my prince will not be interested in them, either!"

Heart hammering hard, Persephone gingerly placed her throbbing hands against the ratty fur upon which she was lying and pushed herself into a sitting position. "Where is your prince?" she asked, blinking at the pain in her head. "And . . . and where are my companions?"

Instead of answering her, Ghengor stalked off after the startled ram. Persephone watched him go. Then, seeing that there were no other enraged, battle-ax-wielding warriors within gutting distance, she took a few tentative sips of warm, nourishing broth from the horn mug someone had set by her side. As she did so, she surreptitiously surveyed her surroundings.

The Panoraki dwelling was a vast, high-ceilinged cavern, presumably somewhere deep in the high mountain. It was meagerly lit by dung fires and crude candelabra crammed with dripping tallow candles. These guttered and smoked so badly that Persephone was surprised she was breathing at all, let alone breathing better than before. Most of the rocky floor was strewn with ragged furs and straw so ancient that it hardly looked like straw at all. At the very center of the cavern, however, a perfect circle had been swept bare and ringed with sheep skulls, each of which had a candle jammed into the hole that had been drilled into its polished top. In addition to the many fur-clad men, women and children, there were sheep everywhere, including upon every single one of the many rock ledges that jutted out from the cavern walls. Even as Persephone wondered how on earth one got up to the ledges near the ceiling, the baaing, bolting great lord ram scrambled up onto a lower ledge and began gracefully making his way upward, the disgruntled warrior right behind him, leaping effortlessly from ledge to ledge in spite of his great bulk.

As she watched the sheep and the warrior scatter the other occupants of the ledges as they climbed ever higher, a voice directly behind her whispered,

"Pssst!"

Turning around so fast that she knocked over the half-full horn mug of broth, Persephone saw a sight that truly took her breath away. It was not that Azriel and Rachel were lying trussed up on the ground, it was that *on the ground next to them were Fayla and Tiny!*

Without thinking, Persephone threw her handsome, hog-tied husband a smile to show that she shared his joy that sometimes words and wishes could bring back the lost and the dead, after all. Then she cast a cautious glance over her shoulder. Upon seeing that her outraged captor was still busy trying to catch and calm his precious ram, she unsteadily got to her hot, stinging feet and hobbled over to get a better look at Tiny, who, worrisomely, was not tied up at all but was instead lying on his back. Fayla, whose wrists were bound in front of her but whose ankles were unbound, was sitting at his side.

"Thank the gods you're both alive," said Persephone, grunting as she ungracefully maneuvered herself into a kneeling position. "How badly are you hurt?"

"I'm fine," said Fayla, whose left eye was swollen shut and whose beautiful hair was tangled and matted with blood and dirt. "It's Tiny who's hurt."

"Not much hurt," gasped the big redheaded Methusian.

"Both of your legs are broken," said Fayla tightly.

"Not much broken," groaned Tiny, biting his lip.

Nodding, Fayla wordlessly leaned forward to wipe the sweat from his brow with a rag held in her bound hands.

Persephone shared a tense look with Azriel, the knowledge that a man with two broken legs could not travel, let alone descend a treacherous mountain, hanging in the air between them. Then she turned back to Fayla and said, "What happened? How did you survive the avalanche?"

"Turns out it was man-made—a Panoraki trap," replied Fayla. "We were all supposed to be swept over the edge to our deaths or into the arms of the waiting warriors, whichever fate the 'mother goddess of the mountain' saw fit to grant us. Unfortunately for the Panoraki who sprung the trap, the bear showed up, and things didn't quite go according to plan. But I guess it doesn't really matter since they got us all the same. Worse still, they know we're Methusians because one of them spotted the mark on Tiny's hip through a tear in his breeches."

"And do they know why we've come?" asked Persephone in a low voice.

Fayla shook her head. "They said it was for their prince to hear our explanation and to decide what's to be done with us," she murmured as she leaned forward to tenderly wipe Tiny's brow again.

Persephone nodded. She still felt weak—as Ghengor had warned, warmth and nourishment had allayed her symptoms but had not cured her of the mountain sickness that had caused them. However, she felt considerably stronger than she had earlier, and with the return of her strength had come the return of her determination and sense of purpose. The situation appeared desperate, but in truth it was not desperate at all. She and her companions had wanted the Panoraki to find them. Indeed, they had been counting on it. And though they'd not exactly been welcomed with open arms, Persephone had to believe that the Panoraki would see reason once she had a chance to explain that they were seeking the healing pool for the good of *all* people. Once that happened, surely they would be convinced to tell what they knew about Balthazar's discovery and to do what they could to help Tiny.

Unconsciously straightening her spine and lifting her chin, Persephone laid a comforting hand upon Fayla's shoulder and said, "Don't worry, Fayla. It's going to be—"

Before she could say "all right," there came a shout from outside the cavern. Upon hearing it, three powerful-looking women hurried to heave open the stout wooden door at the mouth of the cavern. The next instant, two heavily cloaked figures wearing the horned helmets of warriors stomped inside in a flurry of swirling snow.

At their appearance, there arose a sudden, anxious murmur.

"What happened?" bellowed Ghengor as he leapt down to the floor of the cavern with the now-placid great lord ram at his heels. "Where are the others?"

The slightly smaller of the two snow-encrusted warriors removed her helmet and shook out her long, stringy hair. "The others went after Dax and Xanther," she announced.

"What do you mean they went after Dax and Xanther?" Ghengor was demanding now. "What happened to Dax and Xanther?"

"It appears that they were taken," she replied grimly.

"No!" cried Ghengor, flinging up his hands in horror. "Taken by whom?"

Extending her arm, the woman warrior opened her large hand to reveal a shred of brightly colored cloth and a small piece of colored glass that might have come from a potion jar.

"Taken by Methusians."

Thirty

THE MAN IN MEANEST HOMESPUN lowered the spyglass to his lap and rubbed his aching eye. In the waking hours since the princess had gotten swallowed up by the avalanche, there'd been so much to see that his poor eye had hardly had a rest at all.

The previous evening, in addition to regularly observing the General's camp to ensure that no messengers were being dispatched, the man had alternated between following the upward progress of the two soldiers and watching the site of the avalanche for some sign of the princess. He'd seen no sign of her, but shortly after the avalanche had ended, he'd seen one of her companions emerge from behind a rock face and linger for a few moments before starting back down the mountain on a path that would lead her directly into the arms of the ascending soldiers. Shortly thereafter, he'd watched as mountain men who looked more like bears than men had appeared out of nowhere to dig out and drag away two more of the princess's companions, one of whom looked to be injured. By the time they'd disappeared into the mists of the high mountain, it had grown too dark to see anything more, anyway. So the man had carefully stowed his spyglass, chewed on a piece of dried venison to ease the gnawing hunger in his stomach, sipped sparingly from his waterskin and lashed himself to the tree to get some much-needed sleep.

Shortly after dawn this morning, some instinct had caused him to awaken with a start. He'd gotten the spyglass to his eye just in time to see the princess pulled from the bowels of the mountain. As he'd nodded with satisfaction at the certainty that the one who'd sent him would be pleased that she yet lived, he'd caught a movement at the lower edge of his field of vision. Shifting the spyglass so that he could focus his full attention on the movement, the man in homespun had been amazed to see that the two soldiers had not only managed to survive the night but had survived with enough strength left to attack a herd of Panoraki sheep. Having heard that the Panoraki were huge and mighty warriors, the man had not been especially impressed with the shepherd's size or battle skills, but he'd been tremendously impressed by his willingness to place himself between the soldiers and the sheep, that his herd might have a chance to flee to higher ground. By this feat of bravery, he'd managed to save the entire herd but one. And while trying to rescue this one, he, himself, had been captured.

The man in homespun realized now what the soldiers who'd passed beneath his tree the night before had been arguing about. They'd been arguing about whether they ought to take advantage of their foray onto the mountain to enrich themselves with plunder and slaves, as was their so-called right as New Men. The man could have told them that they'd be fools to do so. Deviating from orders almost always caused unforeseen complications, and unforeseen complications almost always got people killed.

The man could only hope, for the sake of his own mission, that in this particular case, the princess and her companions would not be the people who paid the price for the soldiers' foolishness.

Thirty-One

Eighty-eight white beans left in the jar

UPON HEARING THAT METHUSIANS had taken his tribesmen, Ghengor was upon Persephone almost before she knew what
was happening. Ignoring Rachel's pleading protests and Azriel's
furious bellows, the warrior snatched up a handful of Persephone's
hair, dragged her through the suddenly hostile crowd to the circle of
polished sheep skulls and forced her to her knees.

As the Panoraki who'd been sitting upon the high rock ledges
nimbly leapt down to the ground to join those already gathered around
the circle of skulls, Ghengor shoved his hairy face in Persephone's and
shouted, "Tell me where your tribesmen have taken Dax and Xanther,
villain, and I shall show you the mercy of using the sharp edge of my
battle-ax to remove your filthy Methusian head instead of using the
hammer edge to smash it to a pulp, bit by bloody bit!"

"I don't know where your two tribesmen are—"began Persephone,
who could all but feel the hair pulling away from her scalp.

"Liar!" shouted Ghengor, giving her head a vicious shake. "You and
your lot are the decoys sent to distract us so that your other tribesmen
could make mischief upon the mighty Panoraki!"

"No," protested Persephone, scowling so that the brute would not
have the satisfaction of seeing her wince. "I and my lot came to the
mountain alone, in peace, to ask you about—"

"LIAR!" bellowed Ghengor again, giving her head another shake.

All at once, Persephone had had enough. She was sick of being sick and in pain, and she was *especially* sick of being manhandled, threatened and shouted at by this perpetually outraged buffoon. And so, taking as deep a breath as she could manage, she shouted, "I am *not* a liar! Use your tiny brain, you great hairy imbecile! In the entire realm, there are hardly enough Methusians left to help a one-handed man tie his shoes. Why on earth would we risk half a dozen of us to kidnap two of you? And why would Methusians leave behind evidence that Methusians were the kidnappers when such evidence would surely mean the deaths of the Methusians in your keeping? *Obviously*, the kidnapping was the work of slave catchers who wanted you to believe that it was the work of Methusians!"

"Aha!" cried Ghengor. "So you are slave catchers!"

"No!" said Persephone, who was beginning to wonder if the fool had any brain at all. "In the name of the gods, will you just listen to me?"

"I will not," decided Ghengor. "You are a lying, trespassing, sheep-startling, mountain-penetrating Methusian villain, and it is my right as your captor to do with you what I wish. And what I wish to do is to turn you into a meal for my beloved goddess!"

Having heretofore been under the impression that she was going to have an opportunity to explain herself to a Panoraki prince at some point, Persephone hurriedly twisted around to talk Ghengor out of doing anything rash.

Most unfortunately, he'd already raised his battle-ax to deliver the killing blow.

Without a moment's hesitation or, indeed, any thought as to what she might accomplish by her own rash actions, Persephone flung her hand out. Through the soft leather of Ghengor's baggy pants, she caught a piece of scrotum flesh between her fingernails and pinched as hard as she possibly could. Without letting go of her hair, Ghengor leapt several feet into the air, emitting a rather horrible high-pitched scream as he did so. When he came back down to earth (panting hard) he snarled, flipped the battle-ax in his hand so that the hammer edge was now pointing toward Persephone's temple and, with a blood-curdling battle cry, drove the ax downward with all his might.

An instant before Persephone's brains were splattered all over the gleaming sheep skulls, the larger of the two warriors who'd blown in with the snow growled, "Stop."

Ghengor managed to stop mid-swing, but he did not lower his battle-ax, and he did not let go of Persephone's hair.

The other Panoraki stepped forward. "I am Prince Barka," he said gruffly as he eased off his great horned helmet. "And unless I am very much mistaken—and I am not, for we Panoraki never are—you are one of the dungeon servants who helped me escape the Regent and his little games."

While the rest of the Panoraki in the cavern rumbled among themselves at this remarkable utterance, Persephone felt a leap of excitement as she recognized the big man who'd been chained to the dungeon wall back in Parthania. His skin had lost its sickly pallor, and he'd gained some much-needed weight since she'd last seen him, but his hair and his beard were every bit as matted and messy (more matted and messier, even), and his presence was just as imposing.

"Yes!" she exclaimed, even as something important niggled at the back of her mind. "Yes, I was one of those who helped you escape! Only I'm not really a dungeon servant—"

"As I recall, you are not really a Methusian, either, and yet here you are in the company of Methusians," said Barka, who jerked his head toward Fayla and Tiny before handing his helmet to the grubby, long-haired child who'd come forward to reverently receive it.

"Well, uh, as it happens, I *am* a Methusian—"

"And yet that night in the dungeon you claimed not to be one," recalled Barka, scratching at something burrowed deep within his bushy beard.

"I *told* you she was a liar," muttered Ghengor.

"Shut up," said Persephone, who was feeling considerably more confident now that she knew that she and Azriel had saved the life of the prince who had the power to free them. Looking up at Barka, she said, "I am not a liar. I wasn't a Methusian back in the dungeon, but I am one now on account of having recently married one of their own. In fact, I married the very Methusian who released you from your shackles. His name is Azriel. That's him on the floor over there, wriggling like a landed fish—"

"I am not *wriggling*," called Azriel in a crabby voice.

Persephone and Barka shared a look that said they both knew that he was *so* wriggling. "I didn't lie about being a dungeon servant, either," continued Persephone in confidential tones. "It is true that when you saw me last, I was disguised as one, but that was because it was the only way Azriel and I could think to rescue his little clansman."

Barka's dark, deep-set eyes lit up at the mention of his former fellow dungeon dweller. "And how fares Mateo?" he asked, clutching his battle-ax tighter as though fearful of the response.

"He is safe and well and reunited with his brother," replied Persephone, smiling as she recalled listening through the dungeon door to the sound of the tone-deaf Panoraki prince giving singing tips to the Methusian boy with the voice of an angel.

"Good!" cried Barka, beaming through his copious facial hair. "That is very good. Mateo was a brave little lad. Nearly as brave as old Balthazar himself."

At the name of the Methusian who'd discovered the healing pool, the niggling something at the back of Persephone's mind burst into the forefront of her consciousness. "You're Barka!" she gasped. "You're *the* Barka!"

"Yes," agreed Barka proudly, as though it did not occur to him that Persephone might be excited for any reason other than the fact that he was who he was. "I am a prince," he said, in case she'd missed it the first time.

"You were also the Panoraki ambassador to Parthania back before it all went bad," breathed Persephone. "Cairn said that Balthazar was closer to you than either of the other two ambassadors. She said that if Balthazar had told anyone anything about his discovery, it would have been you."

"His discovery?" said Barka, stiffening at once.

Persephone was so excited that she did not notice the prince's sudden change in demeanor. "The healing Pool of Genezing," she said enthusiastically. "My companions and I are seeking it—that is why we came to the mountains to find you. We wanted to ask you—"

"Fetch her companions to me, Ghengor," ordered Barka.

Muttering under his breath, Ghengor reluctantly released Persephone's hair, turned and stomped toward Azriel, Rachel, Fayla and Tiny.

Rubbing her aching scalp, Persephone staggered to her swollen feet. As she did so, she called after Ghengor that he was not to move Tiny. This instruction was given further weight by Fayla, who informed Ghengor that she'd do considerably more than *pinch* his scrotum if he so much as looked sideways at her injured clansman. Scowling, Ghengor looked over his meaty shoulder at Barka, who impatiently told him to leave be both the broken-legged Methusian and his ill-tempered nursemaid.

A moment later, after having untied the ropes at their ankles, the still-scowling warrior returned to the circle of skulls, prodding Azriel and Rachel before him like a couple of wayward sheep.

Persephone flashed them both a tentative smile. Rachel smiled back at once, but Azriel gave her a warning look she didn't understand.

Then Barka was speaking.

"You came to the mountains to find us," he said.

"To find you, actually," said Persephone, who was still smiling. "As I said, my companions and I are seeking—"

"So Ghengor's accusations are true, then?" said Barka.

"What?" said Persephone, her smile fading just a little.

"You *did* trespass on our mountain?" said Barka.

"Well, yes, but—"

"And did you also startle our wonderful woolly sheep?"

"Not . . . not on purpose," stammered Persephone. "And before you ask, we didn't, uh, penetrate the mountain on purpose, either."

"But you *did* penetrate it?" said Barka.

Persephone felt a droplet of sweat trickle down her back. "Yes, but—"

"And did your clansmen take Dax and Xanther?"

"No!" blurted Persephone with a jolt of panic, for she had a sense that this particular crime must surely carry the greatest consequence. "No, I swear to you—"

"Why do you seek the healing pool?" barked the suddenly ferocious prince.

Caught off guard, Persephone cried, "To save my brother, the Erok king!"

Over the crowd's deafening guffaws of unpleasant laughter, Ghengor jeered, "The Erok king has no Methusian sister, liar!"

"He does, and I am she!" insisted Persephone, clenching her hands into fists so the Panoraki would not see her trembling. "I was stolen at birth by order of the Regent Mordesius and was only recently reunited with my twin. I promise you that I speak the truth—I even wear a ring that bears the crest of the Erok royal family. And see this scar I bear upon my arm?" she asked as she pushed up her sleeve and raised her arm above her head. "King Finnius bears its match."

"LIES!" shouted Ghengor, shaking his battle-ax at Persephone.

"Perhaps not," said Barka thoughtfully as he thrust his hand into his beard to give his face another vigorous scratch. "After my escape from the dungeon, I heard strange rumors on the roads outside Parthania. I even met a bandit who showed me a gold coin that had supposedly been tossed to him by some peacock in the long-lost princess's cavalcade."

"That was you, Azriel!" whispered Rachel eagerly, giving the scowling Methusian a nudge with her elbow.

Persephone extended her hands toward Barka in a gesture of supplication. "The Regent holds my brother hostage and will kill him if my companions and I do not return to Parthania in less than a hundred days with proof that we've found the healing pool," she said in a quiet but steady voice. "You do not know Finn, but I know that he will be a good and just king to all people if he gets the chance—"

"THE MIGHTY PANORAKI WILL NEVER BOW TO AN EROK KING!" bellowed Ghengor, throwing his arms wide so unexpectedly that he nearly decapitated his prince with the battle-ax he yet clutched in his hand.

At his words, the warriors all shouted and pounded the ground with their own battle-axes. Several sheep baaed anxiously.

"He is not just an Erok king!" Persephone called over the din. Fixing her gaze upon Barka, she said, "By virtue of my marriage to Azriel, Finn is also a Methusian. Just as Mateo is a Methusian—just as your dead friend Balthazar was a Methusian."

"THE MIGHTY PANORAKI WILL NEVER BOW TO A METHUSIAN KING!" bellowed Ghengor.

More shouting and pounding and baaing.

"I do not believe my brother would ask such a thing of you!" shouted Persephone, who could happily have picked up one of the gleaming sheep skulls at her feet and knocked the loud-mouthed Ghengor over the head with it. "Finn does not mean to conquer, he wishes merely to unite all people of the realm in peace. But he won't get the chance unless—"

"Unless I betray my dead friend and tell you what I know of the healing pool," said Barka bluntly. Folding his massive arms across his chest, he looked down at Persephone and said, "If you are who you say you are, and I've a mind to believe that you are, the Erok King Octavio was your sire. Tell me, lass, why would I trust the word of one sprung from the loins of the man who ordered me imprisoned—a man whose minion stole eighteen years of my life?"

Persephone answered from her heart, the words falling from her lips almost before she knew what she was saying. "Because I know what it is to have eighteen years of your life stolen," she said passionately, her voice ringing throughout the high-ceilinged cavern. "And because I am not my father *or* his minion. And because whatever Balthazar told you about his discovery of the healing pool does not belong to you. It belongs to his people. To *my* people," she said fiercely, glancing over at Azriel. "And do you know why else?"

"Why else?" asked Barka, sounding almost curious.

Persephone lifted her chin, pointed her trembling forefinger at the big Panoraki's face and said, "Because you owe us for releasing you from that dungeon when the safer course of action by far would have been for Azriel to slit your hairy throat."

For a long moment after she said this, it seemed as though everybody in the cavern—even the sheep, even Barka himself—was holding their breath, waiting to see what he would say.

"It is true that I am indebted to you and that whatever knowledge I have of the healing Pool of Genezing belongs to your people," he finally said with a deliberateness that told Persephone he was choosing his words with great care. "However, it is also true that you have freely admitted to crimes against my people and that those crimes cannot go unpunished."

Nodding with satisfaction at this last bit, Ghengor hoisted his battle-ax onto his shoulder and briskly stepped forward to bash Persephone's brains out.

Barka stopped him with a raised hand. "We are a civilized people, Ghengor," he admonished solemnly. "You shall not slaughter her as you would a diseased ewe."

"*Thank you*," said Persephone, heaving a great sigh of relief.

"Instead, you shall face her in a fight to the death," decided Barka to the raucous hoots and cheers of the Panoraki. "If she wins, the crimes committed by her and her companions will be freely forgiven, and they shall have the everlasting friendship of our people and all that implies."

"And if she loses," temporized Ghengor, "I get to feed her *and* her companions to the mother goddess of the mountains?"

"That sounds fair," agreed Barka.

Before a thoroughly alarmed Persephone could offer her opinion that this sounded anything *but* fair, Azriel, whose hands were yet tied behind his back, shoved his way forward to stand by her side.

"My wife is a mighty warrior, but she is much weakened by sickness," he said loudly. "Forcing her into a fight to the death in her current state would be tantamount to executing her. If you are, indeed, a civilized people, you must allow her to choose a champion to fight in her stead! Otherwise—"

"Very well, very well," interrupted Barka, flapping his hand at Azriel to shush him. "If she wishes, the princess may choose a champion."

Persephone, who knew for a certainty that she would die if she had to face Ghengor herself, turned and looked up into Azriel's beautiful blue eyes. He nodded without fear and then, giving her the little lopsided smile he lately seemed to reserve for such dire situations, he leaned forward and gave her a deep, lingering kiss on the mouth.

When she finally pulled away, Persephone sighed softly, turned back to Barka and said, "I choose *you* as my champion."

"Me?" he blurted, seeming every bit as surprised and dismayed by this request as Azriel and Ghengor did.

"That's right," said Persephone serenely, ignoring Azriel's fierce whispers of protest. "As the leader of a civilized people, surely you see the great honor to be had in standing champion for one who saved your life."

Barka glared down at her for only an instant before irritably gesturing for her and Azriel to step outside the circle of sheep skulls. He then turned, snapped his fingers at Ghengor and grunted, "Ready, then, brother?"

Ghengor responded by giving a mighty roar and trying to chop off his prince's right leg. From that moment on, the fight was swift and brutal. Persephone could not believe how fast the two warriors could swing their heavy battle-axes, nor how fast they could duck, jump and twirl in an effort to avoid having their limbs or heads hacked off.

Unfortunately, though Barka was the bigger of the two, it soon became clear that he was far from fully recovered from his years in captivity. As his evasive movements grew clumsier and his breathing grew more labored, it occurred to Persephone that she'd made a terrible blunder. Namely, she'd forced the only Panoraki who'd ever spoken personally with Balthazar about the healing pool into a fight to the death that he was probably going to lose.

Even as this thought crossed her mind, one of Barka's ax swings went wide. Jumping back to avoid being disemboweled, Persephone accidentally bumped into the great lord ram of the herd. The high-strung beast immediately baaed in such noisy distress that Ghengor couldn't help but cast a darting glance over to see what was wrong. The instant he did so, Barka kicked his legs out from under him and leapt forward to stand over top of his prone body. Eyes glittering with bloodlust, the great Panoraki prince wrapped both hands around the handle of his battle-ax and raised it high above his head.

"NO!" cried Persephone, who realized with a jolt that this would be yet another senseless death upon her conscience. "No—please! Don't kill him!"

For three thudding heartbeats, Barka did not move a muscle. Then, slowly, he nodded at Persephone, lowered his battle-ax and stepped away from his defeated clansman.

Rolling to his knees, Ghengor looked up at Persephone from behind his curtain of tangled hair. "You . . . you . . ."

Persephone was about to tell him that he need not thank her for her timely intervention when he bellowed, "How could you, villain! A warrior does not allow a weakling from another tribe to beg for mercy for him! You have shamed me before my people! How will my pride ever recover? How will I ever be able to—"

"Hit him," said Persephone.

Without a word, Barka raised his battle-ax and smashed his tribesman across the side of the head with the dull edge. Ghengor dropped like a rock.

"He's . . . he's not dead, is he?" asked Persephone with a dubious glance at the fallen warrior.

"Not at all," replied Barka shortly, "but ye can rest assured that when he wakes up, Ghengor here will have a headache to be proud of."

Thirty-Two

Eighty-eight white beans left in the jar

ALTHOUGH THE FIGHT between Barka and Ghengor had not ended in death as had been promised, the Panoraki evidently felt that justice had been served, because even before Ghengor's inert body had been dragged away, Azriel, Rachel and Fayla were being untied and offered horn mugs of warm broth, and Tiny's poor legs were being splinted as only mountain men well used to tending broken limbs could splint them.

In due course, the Panoraki warriors who'd gone after Dax and Xanther returned to the cavern. They'd managed to rescue the young shepherd named Dax and to feed the two New Men who'd kidnapped him to the mother goddess of the mountain, but they'd been too late to save Xanther. Like the Panoraki, Persephone was filled with horror when the warriors grimly explained that by the time they'd tracked the New Men to their sorry camp on the lower slopes of the mountain, Xanther had already been murdered and partway eaten. Unlike the Panoraki, however, her horror abated considerably when the bereft warriors unwrapped the piece of burlap in which they'd wrapped poor Xanther's body and she saw that Xanther had been a ram, and a nice fat ram, at that.

Barka offered up a few gruff words of comfort for the living and a blessing for the dead. Then, after the last of the Panoraki had filed past Xanther's woolly body to pay their final respects, a whistling warrior sawed off his horns, skinned and spit what was left of him and set him to cook over a stoked dung fire. As the ram began to sizzle in earnest, Barka strode up to Persephone, the ram's bloody heart cradled in his cupped hands.

"For *you*, Princess," he said reverently, holding it out to her.

Like most people in Parthania, Persephone knew almost nothing of the ways of the Panoraki, so she tried not to look completely revolted as she gingerly took the heart from him. "Oh, uh, thank you," she said with as polite a smile as she could muster under the circumstances.

"You're welcome," beamed Barka.

A moment of awkward silence followed in which Persephone became aware of the fact that everybody in the cavern was watching her intently. Swallowing hard, she gestured to the heart in her hands and said, "I . . . I don't mean to sound rude, but, um, what am I supposed to do with it?"

"What are you supposed to do with it? You're supposed to eat it, of course!" cried Barka, who leaned forward before adding in an urgent whisper, "'Tis a great honor being afforded you, lass! You must not insult my people by refusing to partake!"

Though her own heart sank and her gorge rose at the prospect, Persephone nodded, for she knew that she could not afford to insult these people. Casting a despairing glance at Azriel—who shrugged—and at Rachel—who grimaced—she closed her eyes, opened her mouth, lifted the cold, slimy organ to her lips and was about to take a bite when she heard a noise that made her freeze.

Opening one eye, she saw that the great Panoraki prince was jiggling with silent laughter.

Lowering her hands, Persephone pursed her lips at him. "Eating a raw ram heart isn't really a great honor among your people, is it?" she asked stiffly.

As Barka shook his head, the rest of the Panoraki and, indeed, her own faithless companions, exploded with laughter.

"That wasn't funny," scowled Persephone as she flung the contents of her hands at Barka's head.

"It most certainly was funny," chortled Barka as he wiped a smear of heart slime off his forehead. "It was also payback for naming me your champion and nearly getting me killed by my own bloody clansman. Now, my feisty princess and other honored guests, let us fill your mugs with something stronger than broth and find somewhere private to sit that we may comfortably speak of things long past."

Barka led them to a nook near the back of the cavern. It was so small that there'd not have been room for them all if Azriel had not suggested that his lovely bride snuggle in between his legs. Though Persephone had been utterly mortified when he'd said these lewd-sounding words in front of *everybody*, she'd not known how to reject his proposed seating arrangement without appearing suspiciously unaffectionate. Now, as she leaned back against his chest with her head resting against his shoulder and his strong arms loosely encircling her, she had to admit that she was secretly glad to be sitting right where she was. The mountain sickness that yet afflicted her and the excitement of the past hours had caught up with her at last. Eager as she was to hear what Barka had to say about the Pool of Genezing, she was also exhausted and in need of the kind of comfort that only Azriel's nearness seemed able to provide.

"So Balthazar *did* speak to you of the healing pool, then?" Persephone asked Barka as she took an infinitesimally small sip of the eye-watering liquid fire that was "something stronger than broth."

"Speak to me of the healing pool?" snorted Barka as he topped up Tiny's mug for the third time. "I couldn't get him to shut up about it, could I? I tell you, I knew there'd be trouble the minute he showed up at his own funeral babbling on about how the legendary healing pool had sprung up once more and how he alone knew its secret location."

Barka smiled ruefully and shook his head. "He was a wonderful story-teller, your Balthazar—always waving his arms around and rolling his eyes at the good bits—but I must admit I wasn't watching him while he was telling that particular story. I was watching our friend the Regent, and I knew by the look in those cold, black eyes of his that he believed every word your fool of a clansman was saying, and that Balthazar's big mouth was going to cost him dearer than he could possibly imagine. Too bad I was too thick-headed to imagine just how dearly it was going to cost *me*."

Persephone waited for Barka to continue. When he didn't, she touched his sleeve and gently said, "So . . . what did he tell you? Balthazar, I mean."

Starting a little at her touch, Barka cleared his throat as though embarrassed. "The night before the big-headed imbecile was taken up by the old king's guards, Balthazar came to my chamber," he recounted. "He was even drunker than usual and in high spirits. Over a game of dice in which he lost four gold coins to me—a debt that remains unpaid to this day, incidentally—he blathered on about how, despite us being the greatest of friends and him loving me like a brother, he couldn't *possibly* tell me anything about his wondrous discovery. I told the buffoon that I wasn't the least interested in his stupid discovery and that I'd thank him to keep his ugly gob shut about it. Of course, this put him in a great lather to confide in me. Whispering like a drunkard—which is to say extremely loudly and with a considerable amount of flying spittle—he told me he'd been shipwrecked after a long sea journey and that sometime after making it to shore, he'd been chased into a place of nightmares by a frothing monster."

"We know that already," said Fayla, a trifle impatiently.

Barka drank deeply from his horned mug, wiped his mouth with the back of his hand and said, "Then I suppose you also know why Balthazar sailed away from Parthania in the first place?"

"No!" said Persephone quickly. "That is one of the things we don't know."

Barka nodded in a pleased sort of way. "Well, one night when he was very drunk—"

"Sounds to me like Balthazar was often very drunk," observed Tiny in a disapproving voice as he held out his mug for another refill.

"He was," agreed Barka, chuckling as he poured. "Anyhow, one night when he was very drunk, on a whim he commandeered a ship to take him north to inspect a small estate he'd won off King Octavio during an all-night game of cards some weeks earlier. If memory serves, the estate was located in the Nicene prefecture. Just north of the Mines of Torodania, I believe, about two days' ride from the coast."

Azriel, who was not drinking, leaned forward so that his warm chest pressed more firmly against Persephone's back. "So, if the healing pool exists," he said, unconsciously tightening his arms around her in his excitement, "it is likely on or near the realm's western seaboard, somewhere between Parthania and the northernmost tip of Glyndoria."

"That has always been my guess," said Barka. "But remember, Methusian, you speak of an area that is many leagues of mostly untamed wilderness. Searching for an itty-bitty pool in all that would be like looking for a runty tick in a mountain of wool. And what do you mean 'if' the healing pool exists? It does exist. Balthazar brought back proof that it does."

"Are you talking about the scars that some believed bore out his claim that he'd suffered and survived a near-fatal injury?" said Fayla skeptically.

"No, my prickly little nursemaid, I am not talking about his scars," replied Barka. "Most everyone I spoke to assumed that the scars were just a clever trick. No, I am talking about the gift that Balthazar gave to Fey."

"Who was Fey?" asked Rachel, stifling a yawn that reminded Persephone that her poor friend had not slept in almost two days.

"She was the daughter of the Marinese ambassador," said Barka. "She later became queen of the old Erok king and mother of the new."

Stifling another yawn, Rachel leaned over and tapped Persephone on the shoulder. "That means she was your mother, too," she whispered, just in case her friend had failed to make the connection.

Persephone, whose heart had begun to pound at the mention of the mother she'd never known, nodded.

"Fey was more than just a beauty," continued Barka in a reminiscent tone. "She was a rare spirit, Fey was. Every man at court was half in love with her, and Balthazar was no exception. That last night we played dice together, he told me that he'd given her a gift. Something he'd brought back from the pool with him—a thing that proved beyond a doubt that the pool existed."

"What was it?" asked Persephone, unconsciously clutching Azriel's thigh in *her* excitement.

"I don't know," said Barka. "Balthazar wouldn't tell me. He said it was a private matter between him and a beautiful girl who wouldn't look twice at me if I was tap-dancing naked on top of my own fat head." He chuckled at the memory. "Whatever it was, though, there's a chance that her people are in possession of it. Though her father was imprisoned at the same time I was and perished soon thereafter, Fey herself was never imprisoned. The Regent told me she made it all the way back to Syon only to be ordered to return to Parthania and marry the old king," he said in disgust. "The Marinese Elders had promised her to him, you see, in exchange for his promise that their people would be left in peace."

"A promise that wasn't kept," observed Azriel.

"No," agreed Barka shortly. "Mordesius forced the Marinese from their beautiful seaside village to the Island of Ru mere months later. He used to laugh about the elders' gullibility when he was playing his little games with me. Anyhow, the point is that Fey may have taken Balthazar's gift with her when she returned to her people and that they may yet have it."

Persephone frowned. "Even assuming they do have it and are willing to show it to us, finding proof that the pool exists won't necessarily get us any closer to finding the pool itself," she observed. Cocking her head at Barka, she said, "Do you think it's possible that Balthazar gave Fey . . . I mean, my mother . . . more than the gift? Do you think he might have given her a clue as to where the pool was located?"

"Seeing as how we're talking about Balthazar and a beautiful woman, I'd have to say that anything is possible," snorted Barka, draining his mug.

"Then I think it makes sense for us to stick with the original plan and approach the Marinese next," decided Persephone, whose gaze drifted to Tiny before she delicately added, "only . . ."

"Only you'll have to do so without the benefit of my company," acknowledged Tiny gruffly.

"And without the benefit of mine," added Fayla as she tenderly brushed a lock of fiery hair off his forehead.

"Now, Fayla—" began the big Methusian.

"I'm not leaving you!" she interrupted fiercely.

Though Tiny blustered and grumbled and offered several feeble clucks of protest, it was obvious to all that he was enormously pleased by her devotion.

Smiling, Persephone asked Barka if Fayla and Tiny could stay with the Panoraki until Tiny's legs had healed enough to make travel possible.

"Of course!" said Barka magnanimously. "This day you've won the friendship of my great people, and the mighty Panoraki always stand by their friends in times of trouble."

"That is good to know," murmured Azriel under his breath.

Persephone thought she detected a hidden meaning in his words, but before she could ask him about it, a little girl trotted up and informed them that Xanther would either be overcooked or cold if they didn't come soon to sup. Appearing thoroughly alarmed, Barka immediately started to rise, but Persephone put out a hand to stop him.

"There is just one more thing I would ask," she said.

With a longing glance in the direction of his supper, Barka slowly sat back down and gestured for her to hurry up and ask her question.

"The Gorgishman who was imprisoned with you in the dungeon," said Persephone. "Was he the ambassador to Parthania for his people back when you were ambassador for the Panoraki?"

"He was, but you'll learn nothing useful about the healing pool from him for three reasons, Princess," said Barka. "First, Balthazar never liked the self-important, double-crossing pissant, so I hardly think it likely that he told him anything about anything. Second, even if Balthazar did tell him something, the surly, conniving little sneak was imprisoned even before I was, and he went stark raving mad within weeks of being crammed into that hanging cage. Third, the greedy, toe-sucking weasel is dead."

"Dead!" exclaimed Persephone in shock and dismay. "But I thought you were going to take him with you when you fled the dungeon!"

"I *did* take him with me," flared Barka. "But apparently Gorgishmen don't much care for water, because no sooner had we jumped through the trapdoor into the river below our cell than the ingrate tried to climb *right up on top of my head*. By the time I finally managed to peel him off me, I was half-drowned and in no mood to worry if the little shite knew how to dog-paddle. I flung him as far away from me as I could and that was the last I saw of him!"

"Well," said Persephone in a subdued voice, after a moment of uncomfortable silence. "It is unfortunate that he is dead, but it sounds as though his death isn't a particular loss where our quest for the healing pool is concerned."

"You're right on one count, anyway," sniffed Barka, rising to his feet. "Now, come. Let us go get a share of meat before that pack of jackals I call my beloved clansmen pick poor Xanther's bones clean."

The meat was delicious, though the ewe milk with which it was served was a little rancid and the cheese had a few too many hairs for Persephone's liking. Afterward, the Panoraki spent several hours acting out cherished tales of daring and bravery and singing a selection of clan favorites (Barka's voice was the best of the lot) before finally allowing their exhausted guests to collapse upon the ancient, smelly straw and go to sleep.

The next morning, Persephone awoke to the sight of Ghengor sitting on a rock not far from where she was lying in Azriel's arms. The Panoraki warrior had a very broad smile upon his hairy face.

"Look!" he said proudly, pointing to a purple goose-egg-sized lump on the side of his head.

"It is, uh, impressive," said Persephone uncertainly as she felt Azriel stir beside her.

"I'll probably never see straight again," bragged Ghengor.

After the woozy warrior tottered off, Azriel sleepily pulled Persephone back into his arms, called her "wife" and nuzzled her neck so enticingly that she didn't think to pull away from him until he'd already pulled away from her. Feeling a pang of longing, she went to wake Rachel. The two girls joined Azriel in choking down more rancid milk and hairy cheese, then the three of them collected their packs, reclaimed their confiscated weapons and went to bid farewell to the two they were leaving behind.

"As soon as you're able, make for the Methusian camp," Azriel advised Fayla and Tiny. "Let Cairn and the others know that the quest is proceeding better than we could have hoped. Tell them we'll rejoin the clan as soon as we've found the healing pool, settled things with the Regent and saved the king."

If it struck Fayla and Tiny, as it struck Persephone, that the list of tasks that yet lay before her, Azriel and Rachel sounded almost ridiculously impossible, their expressions did not betray it. Instead, an emotional Tiny gave each of them as powerful a wallop on the back as he could manage from his reclining position, and Fayla hugged Azriel hard and gave the girls an only half-joking order to take good care of him since he was only a man, after all.

After they'd said their goodbyes, Barka walked the three who were carrying onward to the mouth of the cavern.

"Are you certain you don't need an escort down to the foothills?" he asked.

"We're certain," said Persephone firmly. "I'm feeling much improved, and you've already done so much for us. Besides, we got up the mountain well enough—I'm sure we'll be able to get safely down provided your warriors don't decide to bring another avalanche down on our heads."

Barka chuckled at this. "I'll bash in their brains if they do," he promised as he stepped aside to allow the three women to heave open the stout wooden door at the cavern's entrance. "Now, before you set out, may I offer a piece of advice, Princess?" Without waiting for an answer, he said, "Get to the coastal town of Syon as quickly as you possibly can. Crossing the channel that separates the mainland from the Island of Ru is a treacherous journey at the best of times; during storm season it is a veritable death trap."

"And I'm guessing that storm season is almost upon us?" said Persephone, blinking as the door opened to reveal the sudden, blinding glare of sun on snow.

"Yes! The storm season is almost upon us!" exclaimed Barka, who seemed amazed by her powers of deduction. "It may even have begun. Being so far from the sea, it is hard to say. But what is *not* hard to say is that if you do not make the crossing before the storms hit, you'll not be able to make it until after they end. And that will delay your meeting with the Marinese by at least a couple of months."

"But we don't have a couple of months," said Persephone in alarm. "My brother does not have a couple of months!"

"Then you'd best make haste, Princess," shrugged Barka, extending his arm into the swirling cold as though to usher them onward.

Nodding, Persephone and Rachel stepped outside and began trudging through the knee-deep snow. Azriel also stepped outside and started walking, but after just a few paces, he stopped and began ostentatiously digging for something in the pocket of his breeches. When he found what he was looking for, he threw Persephone a rakish grin and then tossed the glinting contents of his hand to Barka.

The Panoraki prince managed to catch all four gold coins in midair. "Much obliged, peacock!" he called, the roar of his laughter spilling out of the cavern and echoing throughout the mountain. "Good luck to you all!"

Thirty-Three

GENERAL MURDOCK STARED impassively at the headless bodies that lay at his feet.

Well, to be precise, they weren't *headless*—the heads were there, more or less. They just weren't shaped much like heads anymore, and their contents had been splattered halfway up the rock face against which the bodies had been propped.

General Murdock shook his own small head. If he'd been another kind of man, he might have become enraged by the foolishness that had cost him two more soldiers, for it was clear to him that foolishness had been behind their deaths. Their foolishness, to be precise. The pile of frozen animal entrails next to the half-burnt sticks told him that his soldiers had stolen a Panoraki sheep and tried to make a meal of it; that they'd had their skulls caved in and their bodies ritualistically positioned told him that the Panoraki had discovered the theft and had retaliated by turning his soldiers into a sacrifice for their mountain goddess.

Truly, if he'd been another kind of man, General Murdock might have become enraged.

But he was not another kind of man. He was a military man, and military men did not get enraged. They assessed the advantages and disadvantages of every situation, and one of the advantages of this particular situation was that the recklessly foolish soldiers were dead. That meant that he, General Murdock, was not going to have to waste even a single moment of his valuable time punishing them in a manner that would instruct their fellow soldiers as to the perils of deviating from orders.

Of course, that the two men were dead also meant that he was now down to just the three soldiers and would be until such time as the requested replacements arrived from Parthania. This was one of the reasons he'd decided to personally climb the mountain to investigate after the soldier who was now in charge of the spyglass had nervously informed him that there seemed to be something amiss upon the lower mountain. General Murdock's instincts had told him that something like this had happened, and he'd decided that he and the mission could not afford to see another pair of fools perish.

Not yet, anyway.

Furrowing his high, narrow brow ever so slightly, General Murdock turned away from the bodies at his feet and began creeping about the makeshift camp looking for some evidence that the dead soldiers had done more than come up here and eat stolen mutton. They'd been sent up the mountain with orders to assist the princess if they discovered that she was alive and in mortal peril, or to bring back some proof that she was dead if they discovered her frozen body. General Murdock could see nothing that would indicate that the soldiers had found her alive *or* dead. Did this mean they'd not bothered to look for her, or did it mean that they *had* looked for her but had not found her?

As he daintily tapped a fingernail against his long, yellow teeth and pondered this mystery, General Murdock suddenly heard voices approaching from above. Luckily, like any military man worth his salt, the first thing the General had done upon arriving at the makeshift camp was to scope out a hiding place. In this instance, the place was a crack in the rock face that was deep enough to cast a dark shadow and just wide enough to accommodate one gifted with the ability to squeeze into remarkably small spaces. Moving with the speed and silence that had spelled doom for so many, General Murdock scurried into his hiding place and fell still.

The next minute, the princess, her Methusian lover (no, her Methusian *husband*) and the girl who resembled the princess trudged into sight. Upon spying the bodies of General Murdock's soldiers, the girl who bore the princess's likeness did not scream or faint, but she did bend over and vomit copiously. Impressively, the princess did not scream, faint *or* vomit. Instead, she made a tight-lipped comment to her husband about slave hunters getting what they deserved. Then she walked forward to get a closer look at what was left of his men.

She came to a halt almost directly in front of the crack in the rock face. General Murdock knew that if she looked to her right, she would see his beady eyes gleaming out at her from the shadows. Some people, upon seeing such a thing in such an unexpected place, would *not* see it because their minds would not allow them to see it. But General Murdock had an idea that the princess would see it, because he had an idea that she'd seen beady eyes gleaming out at her from the shadows before.

The thought filled him with tension. He did not doubt for a moment that he'd be able to kill the princess, her Methusian husband and the other girl—with his hands and teeth, if he had to—but such action would be in direct violation of his orders.

And so, since General Murdock could not abide the idea of violating his orders, he squeezed a little farther into the crack and waited with bated breath. The princess, who was so close that his long, thin nose quivered with the scent of her, now looked over her left shoulder, to the place where the other girl was wiping vomit off her mouth and breathlessly apologizing for having vomited. The princess chuckled and waved away her apology. She then asked her husband if he truly thought it would be wise for them to take the risk of cutting through the Great Forest. He replied that he thought it would be, on account of their urgent need to reach Syon in advance of the coming storm season. After saying that she was of a similar mind, the princess started to say something else then froze abruptly, like a deer that had just heard a twig snap.

General Murdock froze, too—his thin lips slightly parted, his thin fingers curled as into claws, his heart beating at its usual slow, steady pace even though he knew that he might be just seconds away from being forced to violate his orders.

Fortunately for him, however, the princess did not look right or do anything else that would have necessitated such a regrettable course of action. Instead, she shrugged violently as if to throw off the unwelcome feeling that had come over her. Then she announced that she did not wish to linger further and suggested to the other two that they move on and leave the mother goddess of the mountain to her meal.

The other two readily agreed, and within seconds the princess had stepped beyond General Murdock's line of vision. He listened intently to the fading sounds of her and her companions' downward progress, and when he judged it safe to do so, he wriggled out of the crack in the rock face and permitted himself a small smile.

By his quick-thinking actions, he'd managed not only to preserve the integrity of his mission but also to gather vital intelligence. For if the princess and her companions were in such a rush to reach the coast before the storms hit that they would risk the dangers of the Great Forest, it could only mean that they intended to journey to the Island of Ru to seek out the Marinese.

And that told General Murdock two important things that he would order one of his three remaining men to relay to Mordesius at once.

First, it told him where he and his last two men would be able to pick up their quarry's trail again in the not-so-unlikely event that they lost it in the dark and unpredictable Great Forest. Second, it told him that the princess and her companions were yet in pursuit of their objective.

And therefore, so was he.

Thirty-Four

"WHAT DO YOU MEAN he's not back from the garden yet?" snapped Mordesius as he impatiently daubed at the nick on his chin that had yet to stop bleeding. "What is he doing in the garden? Gods' blood, the betrothal ceremony was set to begin half an hour ago! The great lords and ladies of the kingdom are all assembled and waiting for him in the chapel!"

The one-legged slattern who'd taken the nursemaid's place bowed her head. "I'm sorry, Your Grace," she said in a voice that could have meant she was truly sorry or else could have meant that she was not sorry at all. "Perhaps the king feels that because he is the king it is for others to wait on his pleasure and not the other way around."

"What do you know about the feelings of kings, you stupid, low-born trollop!" snarled Mordesius, flinging the bloodied handkerchief at her. "Send someone to fetch the king *at once* or I will have you—"

Before he could finish uttering his threat, the door behind him opened and the pale, disheveled king strode in with his brother-in-law-to-be close upon his heels. Evidently, the king had just said something vastly amusing because the perpetually inebriated Lord Atticus was laughing like a hyena with its testicles caught in a steel trap.

"Good afternoon, Your Grace," said the king, who was more than a little out of breath.

Mordesius tilted his head in the smallest possible show of deference he thought he could get away with in front of Lord Bartok's ne'er-do-well son. "Good afternoon, Your Majesty," he said tightly. "Have you by chance forgotten what day it is?"

"No, indeed," said the fool, daring to sound sheepish, "though I suspect from your unhappy countenance that Lord Atticus and I may have lost track of the time. Forgive me, Your Grace, I *beg* of you."

Mordesius looked at the king sharply when he said this, wondering if he was making a sly reference to having been forced to beg forgiveness at their last meeting, but the king was seized by a coughing fit so sudden and violent that he did not appear to notice.

When his fit was over, he gave Mordesius a wan smile and said, "Lord Atticus surprised me with a hawk to replace the one I recently freed on account of its attitude problem. Afterward, he suggested that we wrestle awhile."

"So while poor Lady Aurelia was pacing the floor of her chamber, fretting that you'd forsaken her, you were *wrestling*?" breathed Mordesius, who could not believe that the fool had kept him waiting that he might roll around getting grass stains on his breeches.

"We were," grinned Lord Atticus, whose watery, red eyes kept sliding to the slattern's ample chest. "And I dare say that my future brother-in-law, the king, must be the finest wrestler in all the realm, for I'd thought myself unbeatable and yet he beat me every match!"

Mordesius felt a familiar flare of irritation as he listened to these words of fawning praise—praise of a kind that no courtier ever seemed to feel the need to heap upon *him*. Praise that was obviously a lie, for though his soft belly and legs hardly recommended Lord Atticus as a champion, he was healthy and probably outweighed the king by forty pounds. The notion that the pale, sickly king had repeatedly bested him was utterly ludicrous.

"Take comfort in the knowledge that my charming bride-to-be need fret no more, Your Grace," the royal fool was saying now. "Nor shall she be kept waiting much longer, for I suspect that my bath has already been prepared and my betrothal outfit laid out. Am I correct, Neeka?"

"You are, Your Majesty," she replied with a smile that bordered on coquettish and a curtsey so brisk that it set her bosom bobbing and Lord Atticus's head with it.

"Very well," said Mordesius through his teeth. "I shall return to the chapel and announce your *imminent* arrival."

"Good," nodded the king, as though Mordesius had just agreed to obey a command instead of having subtly given one. "Lord Atticus, I would ask something of you, as well."

"Anything, Your Majesty," said Atticus, puffing out his chest and stepping past Mordesius with all the swagger of one whose family's star was on the ascendancy.

The king coughed violently again, this time into a handkerchief, which told Mordesius that there'd probably been blood. Then he pulled a diamond-encrusted sapphire ring from the little finger of his left hand and held it out to the young lord. "Please go at once to your sister's chamber and give to her this token of my esteem, along with my apologies for my thoughtlessness," he panted, wincing as he pressed an elegant hand against his rib cage.

Licking his fleshy lips, Lord Atticus stared greedily at the exquisite bauble before plucking it from the king's grasp. Then, with a bow to the king, a nod to Mordesius and a final leer at the servant girl, he turned and strode out of the room as smartly as was possible for a half-drunk laggard.

After he was gone, Mordesius longed to scream at the king for . . . well, for *everything*. But he resisted the urge, for the betrothal ceremony was too important a part of his own personal plans to risk further delay. So, choking down his fury, he tersely ordered the king to get ready. King Finnius, whose shoulders had begun to slump the minute Atticus was gone, nodded wearily and wordlessly made for his waiting bath.

The instant the bedchamber door closed behind him, Mordesius fixed his cold, dark gaze upon the slattern.

"I despise servants who do not know their place," he informed her.

"Smile at the king like that again, and I will have your face slashed. Offer me your thoughts regarding his feelings again, and I will have your tongue cut out. Do you understand?"

For a long moment, the slattern only stared at Mordesius so expressionlessly that he began to wonder if she'd heard him.

Then she dipped him a curtsey so perfect that as he turned and began slouching out of the room, it fleetingly occurred to him that he might actually have to stop thinking of her as "the slattern."

When he thought of her at all, that is.

Less than an hour later, Mordesius stood at the front of the chapel beside the kneeling king. Struggling to hold his heavy head high, he strived for a fatherly countenance so that none of the watching nobles might suspect that their king had reason to feel anything but affection for the trusted counselor who'd guided him since infancy.

Mordesius looked from the bowed head of the king to that of Lady Aurelia, who was wearing the sapphire ring, a gown of brilliant blue and the unmistakable air of a bright-eyed little bird who'd just caught the juiciest worm in the garden. He was torn between gloating that he'd brought his plans this far and worrying that they might yet come to naught. Even setting aside the certainty that Lord Bartok would attempt a double-cross now that he had what he wanted—an attempt that Mordesius would just as certainly thwart—there was the matter of the king. Mordesius had been more disturbed than he cared to admit by the scene that had played out earlier in the royal chambers. For though the king had thus far done all that he'd been commanded to do, there was something about the manner in which he was doing things these days that was making Mordesius feel vaguely uneasy. Moreover, there were moments when Mordesius thought he detected a fleeting look of rebellion in the fool's eyes. Or, even more dangerous than rebellion: kingliness. Those moments never failed to leave Mordesius with the disconcerting feeling that he'd peered into the eyes of a caged lion biding its time, and he liked that feeling not at all.

Still, he was not *certain* that he saw these things in the king's eyes. And even if he did, as long as he had the coughing fool and those he cared for under his thumb, Mordesius knew there was no real harm the king could do to him or his plans.

The same could not be said for General Murdock, from whom he'd yet to receive a single report. For as much as Mordesius longed to be king, he longed even more fiercely to have his terrible injuries healed. And this could only come to pass if the princess and the Methusian found the healing pool before they realized they were being followed—and if, after killing them, Murdock returned to Parthania to tell Mordesius the location of the pool.

Though he knew there could be many reasonable explanations for why he'd not yet heard from his most trusted general, Mordesius could not keep suspicious thoughts from creeping in at the edges of his mind. What if the reason Murdock had sent no reports was that he'd followed the princess and the Methusian to the pool only to find himself overcome by a sudden lust for its power? Not to cure any illness or injury in himself, of course, but rather to be able to hold out the hope of healing to those willing and able to pay exorbitantly for it. Such a thing would surely make Murdock the richest, most powerful man in the kingdom. True, Mordesius had never seen Murdock lust after anything. And true, the General had never sought riches or power and instead had always seemed to desire only to be allowed to continue to serve, but *still*. Mordesius knew how he himself would think if he were the only person alive who knew the location of the Pool of Genezing, and it was almost impossible for him to believe that anyone else could think differently.

As the minister presiding over the betrothal ceremony droned on and the pain in Mordesius's neck grew steadily worse, he made an impromptu decision to dispatch orders to the commanders of every

New Man outpost in the kingdom to be on the lookout for General Murdock and to secretly send word if he was spotted. Mordesius wasn't yet sure what he'd do with this information when he received it—much would depend on how much further into his mind his suspicions had crept. However, his cold heart already felt lighter knowing that he'd soon be casting a net that would enable him to catch and destroy Murdock if it turned out that the General was deceiving him.

Or perhaps even if it turned out that he wasn't deceiving him.

After all, if Murdock followed the princess and the Methusian to the healing pool, he would know its location. And upon reflection, Mordesius thought it would really be rather pleasant to be the only person alive to know such a thing.

The betrothal ceremony lasted so long that by the time the minister finally bade the betrothed couple to rise, Mordesius had decided that the smiling wretch would shortly follow the recently fumble-fingered (now fingerless) barber to the dungeon that he might never again plague anyone with his endless oratory. This happy decision gave Mordesius the strength to continue to hold his head high all the long way from the front of the chapel, through the garden, across the courtyard and into the Great Hall where the betrothal feast awaited.

As Lord Bartok had promised, it was the most spectacular the realm had ever seen. The wine and ale were plentiful and of best quality; four-and-twenty meat dishes were followed by twice as many dishes of fish and fowl. Half of these turned out to be two or more creatures cunningly cooked one inside the other; each was accompanied by a sauce, jelly or gravy that perfectly complemented its particular texture and flavor. Supplementing these marvelous dishes were breads and pies and soups and greens and a host of sublime delicacies, some of which were so unusual that Mordesius himself could not guess their origin. Artfully presented cheese and fruit platters were followed by sweetmeats and pastries and marchpane confections of stunning creativity. The grandest of these was a perfect miniature of the imperial palace that was so detailed that the tiny king and his even tinier betrothed could clearly be seen waving from the miniature Grand Balcony. Indeed, this final confection was so elaborate that it had to be carried into the Great Hall on a litter borne by eight kitchen servants, and everyone but Mordesius cried out in genuine delight at the sight of it.

Truly, the betrothal feast was such a spectacle that it was hard to imagine how the coming wedding feast would ever be able to outdo it. As he sat staring out at the delighted noble gluttons before him, Mordesius sourly thought to himself that if there was anyone who could see it done, it would be the high-and-mighty bastard Bartok.

"Would you care for a piece of cake, Your Grace?" chirped Lady Aurelia, who'd taken Mordesius's usual seat at the king's right hand, and who now looked like a little bird who'd just *eaten* the juiciest worm in the garden.

"No," said Mordesius shortly, even though he'd have liked nothing better than to grind between his beautiful teeth the two almond-paste figurines from the miniature Grand Balcony.

Lady Aurelia's prim little mouth tightened with displeasure at this curt reply, but Mordesius took no notice. Instead, he looked past her to the king, whom he'd noted had eaten little of the bounty that had been placed before him during the last few hours. As he watched the coughing fool compliment the beaming pastry chef on the genius of his creations, Mordesius was struck again by a thought that had occurred to him when he'd earlier sized the king up against Lord Atticus: namely, that he appeared to have lost a good deal of weight in a very short time. Though the sharpness of his features and the almost ethereal glow of his pale skin rendered him handsomer than ever, there was no denying that he looked desperately ill.

Ill unto death, even.

"Y-you look pleased, Your Grace," offered the young woman seated at Mordesius's right side.

Swiveling the head that sat so heavy upon the thin, aching stalk of his neck, Mordesius regarded her without pleasure. Though her figure was pleasing enough, and she was dressed richly enough and came from sufficiently noble stock, he did not favor her. She was plain as dirt, and she stared at her platter when she spoke, which was infrequently. Though it was possible she feared being auditioned and banished—a reasonable fear, as it happened—Mordesius suspected she behaved this way because she believed it gave her the appearance of being a proper Erok maiden.

Mordesius did not think it gave her the appearance of a proper Erok maiden. He thought it gave her the appearance of an idiot. He gave his head a rueful shake. As so often happened these days when he was in the company of some hapless female who'd been thrust at him by her minor noble family in the hope of gaining some minuscule advantage, he found himself thinking of the Princess Persephone. He smiled now at the memory of her on the floor at his feet—struggling futilely, begging him not to kill the cockroach, promising him that she'd do *anything*. The princess was not plain, and she was anything but an idiot. Still smiling faintly as the memory of her on her knees slowly faded from his mind's eye, Mordesius noticed that the plain-faced thing at his side was smiling tentatively at her plate.

"Why are *you* smiling?" he snapped.

She stopped smiling at once.

"Eat your cake," he muttered. "It is almost time for the king and his betrothed to step out onto the Grand Balcony to present them-selves to the rabble beyond the palace walls. After they have done so, I shall retire for the evening."

"And . . . and I?" she gulped, looking at him directly for the first time.

Mordesius moodily shrugged his narrow, crooked shoulders. She was no princess, but she was noble and as willing as he was likely to find in his present condition.

"You shall retire with me."

✳

Shortly after this tiresome exchange, the lords and ladies in the Great Hall toasted the betrothed couple one final time before rising to their pampered feet. Most made their way out of doors to find a spot in the courtyard below the Grand Balcony. The king, Lady Aurelia, her father, her brother and a select group of courtiers made their way upstairs to the balcony itself. Mordesius was, of course, part of this group.

He waited until the celebratory fireworks had begun and the king was about to step onto the balcony to draw him aside and inform him that within the next fortnight, the Council would come to him recommending that he, Mordesius, be named heir to the Erok throne.

"And when they do," said Mordesius, "you shall give royal assent and thereafter present me to one and all as your successor."

The king, who was so exhausted that he had large, dark circles under his thickly lashed blue eyes, went very still at these words. "My father-in-law-to-be is . . . an influential member of Council, Your Grace," he said, his breath coming in short gasps. "I do not think . . . he will support your bid to be named heir."

"On the contrary, I have his word of honor that he will support it," replied Mordesius with a meaningful glance at Lady Aurelia, who was standing at the threshold of the balcony crying out in ostentatious delight at the fireworks and reveling in the sycophantic attentions of those young noblewomen who'd managed to choke down their jealousy in order to curry favor with she who would shortly become queen.

Smiling slightly and with only a trace of bitterness, King Finnius nodded his dawning understanding of the new and far more dangerous situation in which he found himself. "May I ask . . . why you are telling me this now, Your Grace?"

"In the admittedly unlikely event that Lord Bartok decides to make the Council aware of his support for me sooner rather than later, I did not want you to be so surprised by the forthcoming suggestion that you failed to act exactly as I would wish," explained Mordesius.

"For as I am sure you can imagine, anything less than your full support in this matter will result in severe consequences for those you care most about."

"And what of the consequences for my sister if I give you my support in this matter—what of the consequences for me?" said the king as he raised a finger to his impatient betrothed to indicate that he'd be with her momentarily.

Mordesius thought he saw a flicker of something in the fool's unwavering gaze, but it was gone before he could be sure. "The consequences for you and your sister, Your Majesty?" he said in an utterly baffled voice. "I'm sure I don't know what you mean. What possible consequence for the two of you could come from me being named heir to the Erok throne?"

Thirty-Five

"HE'S NOT AS STUPID as he looks, apparently," chuckled Mordesius late the following evening as he lounged in his comfortable chair looking down at the cow.

"The king does not look stupid," mooed the one named Moira, who was lounging in a most unpleasant mixture of rat droppings, rotting straw and her own disgusting filth.

"He does," insisted Mordesius. "Not as stupid as you, of course. But stupid all the same."

Mordesius smiled. He did not really think that the king looked stupid, but he knew that saying so would upset the fool's former nursemaid.

Unfortunately, she did not look the least upset. "I expect that His Majesty looked very fine in his betrothal outfit," she said with a smile of genuine pleasure. "Tall and handsome."

"He looked well enough—for a walking invalid," snapped Mordesius, his own smile vanishing.

The cow's brow furrowed slightly at this, but all she said was, "Knowing the great Lord Bartok, I'll warrant it was a magnificent betrothal feast."

Leaning forward in his chair, Mordesius was about to snarl that the feast had been as magnificent as a puddle of piss in a chamber pot when it occurred to him that this was perhaps the very reaction she was trying to provoke. So instead, he leaned back in his chair, patted his nonexistent belly and sighed, "It was such a feast that I confess I am yet feeling the effects of having overindulged in all that rich food and fine wine. Moreover, I'm still so tired that I cannot wait to slip on my silken nightshirt and climb into my luxurious bed." He affected a petulant pout before adding, "You do not know what it is like to have to attend feasts and fireworks and festivities in addition to ruling a kingdom. You get to sit around here all day doing nothing!"

The cow's only response was to smile faintly as she used the back of her four-fingered hand to scratch her peasant nose. The chains that shackled her to the glistening stone wall clinked softly as she did so.

"The king never mentions you, you know," confided Mordesius, jerking his crumpled foot away from a rat that had silently scuttled out of the shadows to investigate. "Strange, isn't it?" When the nursemaid did not respond to this taunt, Mordesius continued. "I think perhaps it is because you've been replaced. For years I tried to get the king to see that servants are replaced as easily as smashed dinner plates, and it seems I've succeeded at last. He's taken a real fancy to the one-legged slattern who has taken your place. Indeed, at the risk of hurting your feelings, I'd say he appears to care for her even more than he cared for you!"

"I am pleased to hear that His Majesty has a servant for whom he cares," murmured Moira.

"I wouldn't be too glad if I were you," snapped Mordesius, "for I've a feeling she'll not be serving him for long. Why, only yesterday she behaved in such an unseemly manner that I found myself seriously considering slashing her face and cutting out her tongue. But perhaps I'll do neither of those things. Perhaps I'll cut off her fingers instead. Just as I cut off one of yours—just as I cut off those of the idiot barber who gave me this cut." Mordesius pointed to the nick on his chin. "Well, to be fair, I didn't cut off *all* of the barber's fingers. He cut off most of them—with his own razor. I only cut off the last few, since he hadn't fingers enough left to do it himself."

Moira did not shudder or cringe upon hearing Mordesius's juicy description of the fate that had befallen the poor barber. Instead, she said, "Are you going to murder the king once you've been named heir?"

Pleased to have come back round to this most satisfying topic, Mordesius smiled. "Murder is such an ugly word," he said with a philosophical wave of his shiny pink hand. "I prefer to think of it as helping along the natural course of events. For, as it happens, the king grows sicker by the day."

"Sicker?" echoed the nursemaid, anxiety plain upon her gaunt, dirty face.

"Oh, yes," said Mordesius with relish. "He's lost a great deal of weight and the cough that ever plagues him could only be worse if the blood he spit up with each wracking fit were to choke off his ability to breathe altogether—"

"The princess and her Methusian lover will find the Pool of Genezing!" burst Moira, straining against her bonds as though she'd be able to do something more heroic than fall face-first into the muck if she somehow managed to break free of them. "They will return to Parthania to lead His Majesty to the healing waters, and he will be cured!"

Mordesius gritted his teeth against the urge to shriek that the cockroach was *not* the princess's lover! "Even if they find the pool and are foolish enough to return to Parthania, it will do the king no good at all. I cannot risk killing him any time soon for fear that word of his death would reach the princess, inspiring her to abandon her quest for the pool," he said, his heart clenching at the thought. "But you may rest assured that your beloved Majesty will be dead within days—nay, within hours!—of the princess's return."

"Lord Bartok will be anticipating such treachery," said Moira. "He will take steps to prevent you from harming the king."

"He will, but only until his daughter gives birth and he's able to get himself named the royal child's Lord Regent," said Mordesius, smiling at her feeble attempt to cause him distress. "At such time, he'll want the king dead every bit as much as I will, and he'll want me dead along with him. Most unfortunately for Lord Bartok, however, such a time shall never come because the king will never have the chance to get a child upon Lady Aurelia. Regrettably, the much-anticipated royal wedding will suffer setback after setback until, on the very eve of the grand event, when the long-lost princess has returned and all seems to be in readiness, the poor sick king shall die in his sleep, suffocated by his own bloody phlegm."

The nursemaid could not help drawing back in horror. "You will smother him," she gasped.

"I will slip a powerful sleeping draught into his evening wine," explained Mordesius. "Then, after I have sent the alarmed servants running for the court physicians that they might examine the cause of the king's inexplicable loss of consciousness, I will hold a pillow over his face until he breathes no more."

"Everyone will suspect."

"But no one will know," said Mordesius. "And even if they did, what could they do? I will be a king ascended to the throne with the declared approval of the great lords and the support of a vast army of New Men loyal to none but me."

"And what will happen to the princess?"

"If she failed to find the healing pool, one day very soon after the king's tragic demise, while she is out riding in a vain effort to find respite from her terrible grief, she shall be waylaid by brigands, relieved of that little dagger she is so fond of carrying around and stabbed in her own faithless heart with it."

"And if she succeeded?" asked Moira in a low voice. "If she found the healing pool?"

Mordesius smiled broadly. "The same, I think."

For a long moment the cow said nothing. Then she said, "Your Grace, I beg you not to do these terrible things." Laboriously maneuvering herself up onto her now-bony old knees, she bowed so low that her stringy gray hair brushed the muck. "Spare the king and the princess and I . . . I will willingly die the most agonizing death you can possibly conceive of."

Though Mordesius longed to laugh aloud at the suggestion that her miserable lowborn life was worth the lives of not one but *two* royals, he did not. Instead, he cocked his head to one side and tapped his chin as though contemplating her offer.

"You will do that anyway," he said at last.

Then he rose to his feet, took the torch from the wall bracket and slowly lurched out of the cell, leaving her in darkness.

And, hopefully, despair.

Thirty-Six

Eighty-four white beans left in the jar

"I'M BEGINNING TO THINK we should not have cut through the forest," croaked Persephone, trying to sound lighthearted in spite of the fact that her throat was so parched she was finding it difficult to swallow.

Rachel nodded unhappily as she reached up to scratch at an insect bite upon her grimy neck.

"Cutting through the forest was a risk we agreed we ought to take given our urgent need to reach the coast in advance of the coming storm season," reminded Azriel as he stopped for the hundredth time to scan the vast, endless sameness of the forest for some sign that they were yet traveling east.

In a normal forest they'd have easily been able to tell direction from the growth of the moss on the tree trunks, since in a normal forest moss grew thickest on the shaded north side of the trees, particularly the young trees. But this was not a normal forest. This was the Great Forest. Here, moss grew evenly on all sides of the trees because the canopy overhead was so thick there was nothing *but* shade. And here, there were no young trees because any saplings that managed to take root soon withered and died in the shadow of their mighty, ancient brethren. Since entering the forest four days past, every so often Azriel had climbed to the top of the tallest tree in the vicinity to determine direction from the position of the sun. Try as they might to thereafter stay upon an easterly course, however, each time he'd climbed up to check their position again he'd discovered that they'd drifted off course, sometimes so far off course that they'd somehow ended up traveling *west*.

Though none of them wanted to say it, the truth was that they were hopelessly lost—as lost as Finn was going to be if they didn't find the eastern edge of the forest very soon.

To make matters worse, the last of the Xanther meat had spoiled three days past, the hunting and foraging had been disappointing, and they'd not seen water in two days. Even that had been nothing but a tepid puddle covered in a skin of green slime. It had tasted of dirt and bitterness, and Persephone would gladly have given all the diamonds in the Mines of Torodania to have a mugful of it now, for her share of the dewdrops they'd managed to painstakingly collect these past mornings had done nothing whatsoever to slake her growing thirst.

Yet there were bright spots in the gloom. For one thing, Persephone had fully recovered from the sickness that had so debilitated her while she was upon the mountain. For another thing, Ivan had returned. Shortly after dusk the previous evening, he'd swooped down out of nowhere to present Persephone with the gift of a dead hare and to ruffle his feathers so menacingly at Azriel that, hungry as he was, the offended Methusian had only grudgingly agreed to partake of the hare after it had been skinned and roasted.

A third bright spot was that in four days of walking in circles, though they'd heard many roars and snarls and growls—some from frighteningly close by—they'd not encountered a single ferocious beast intent upon tearing them to pieces. Azriel could not understand why this should be so, for he believed that the scent of them and the sounds of their progress should long ago have drawn every large predator for miles around. He'd been so certain of this, in fact, that on their first night in the forest, he'd herded Persephone and Rachel into a hollow at the base of a giant tree, drawn his sword and spent the entire night on his feet, guarding the entrance and waiting for the attack he was sure would come.

But it had not come—not that night, nor on any night that had followed. Even so, Persephone could not help glancing over her shoulder from time to time as they trudged along. Though she never detected a whisper of movement or a telltale glint of eyes peering back at her from the misty gloom, she could not shake the feeling that they were being followed.

No, not being followed.

Being *stalked.*

"I suppose I ought to go up and check our direction again," said Azriel now, reaching for the lowest branch of the tree before him.

The instant his hand touched the branch, Ivan alighted upon it and began opening and closing his sharp little beak to show that he couldn't wait to jab it into Azriel's hand—or better yet, bury it in his eyeball.

Azriel scowled and snatched back his hand. Rachel laughed.

"I'll check our position," offered Persephone, smiling as she shrugged off her pack. "Ivan will tolerate my intrusion better than yours, and besides, I've hardly seen the sun in four days. Even a glimpse of it would be welcome."

"Well, all right," muttered Azriel, eyeing Ivan askance, "but be careful."

"I'm a good climber," reminded Persephone, thinking back to the night she'd climbed a tree in an attempt to escape from him.

Azriel's grumble told her that he was remembering the same thing. Smiling again, she jumped for the branch on which Ivan was yet perched. Hauling herself up onto it, she paused to blow a kiss to her feathered friend. The gesture caused him to screech with embarrassment and explode into flight. After he was gone, Persephone reached for the next branch. Thereafter, she climbed quickly and easily, for though she was hungry and thirsty, she wasn't yet weak with hunger and thirst.

And even if I should become so, I will never lie down and wait for Death to claim me, she vowed as she carefully rose up onto her tiptoes in an effort to reach the next sturdy branch. *Death will have to cut me down in my tracks. It will have to—*

A sudden, human scream from somewhere below and far behind her startled Persephone so badly that her body gave a violent spasm and she lurched forward. With a cry, she jerked back in an effort to regain her balance, overcompensated and nearly toppled backward off the branch. Forward and backward she wobbled wildly for several heart-stopping seconds before finally managing to fling her arms around the tree trunk. As her badly trembling knees gave way beneath her and she sat on the branch hugging the tree for all she was worth, she heard another scream. This one was cut short with chilling abruptness and was followed by the sound of men crashing through the forest toward the very tree in which she was sitting.

Her trembling knees abruptly forgotten, Persephone snatched her dagger from the scabbard on her thigh, clamped it between her teeth and began shimmying down the tree as fast as she could. There was no doubt in her mind that it was her cry that had brought the men currently running toward Azriel and Rachel, and Persephone did not intend to see the two of them stand alone against the approaching menace.

Unfortunately, before she was able to get all the way down, a dozen masked men materialized out of the greenish shadows. Most wielded crude clubs or farm implements such as pitchforks and axes and the like. However, one wielded a sword that was even bigger than Azriel's sword, and one—a surly-looking dwarf who stood close by the swordsman's side—wielded nothing more impressive than two stones connected by a long string.

"Lay down your sword," commanded the swordsman in an accent that was unmistakably lowborn.

"If it is all the same to you," said Azriel lightly, "I think I'd prefer to keep it with me."

Persephone knew he was playing for time—sizing up the situation, trying to gauge his chances of cutting them all down before taking a mortal wound himself, should it come to that. Shifting her dagger from her teeth to her hand, she bit her lip against the urge to bellow down to him that his chances of doing so were approximately *zero*.

"It is not all the same to me," said the swordsman. "Lay down your sword or face the consequences."

Azriel casually shifted into a fighting stance. "You look like reasonable men," he said with a winning smile at the nearest pitchfork-wielding masked ruffian. "Perhaps we could discuss the situation over a mug of—"

Without warning, the smaller man lifted his strange rock-and-string contraption over his head. After giving it several rapid twirls, he flung it at Azriel's legs, which quickly became so entangled that when the man charged and slammed into him, Azriel went sprawling. Though he managed to hold onto his sword, this didn't do him much good, because by the time his face hit the forest floor, the man had plopped down onto his back. And struggle and heave though he might, Azriel was utterly unable to budge the villain, let alone throw him.

"Give me one good reason why I shouldn't cut out your heart for having brought danger to our very doorstep," said the swordsman.

"I can give you several," said Azriel even as Persephone puzzled over the ruffian's accusation. "First, I happen to be quite as attached to my heart as it is to me. Second, my companion and I are but innocent travelers—"

"That is not true," interrupted the swordsman, wagging a finger at him. "Innocent travelers are not pursued by soldiers from the Regent's army of New Men."

Rachel, who was standing with her back pressed against the tree in which Persephone was perched, gasped at this.

"We're being pursued?" asked Azriel in alarm.

"Not anymore," grunted the pitchfork-wielding ruffian, shoving the bloody tines of his pitchfork under Azriel's nose.

Up in the tree, Persephone shuddered for all sorts of reasons.

"Innocent travelers are not pursued by soldiers, but wanted criminals often are," continued the swordsman as he idly ran his thumb along his sword blade. "Ofttimes, wanted criminals also have sizable bounties placed on their heads." Looking over at Rachel, he smiled. "Tell me, sweetheart," he said in an almost-friendly voice, "do you have a bounty on that pretty head of yours?"

Without waiting to see if the bandit's next move would be to remove Rachel's pretty head and without even *trying* to gauge her chances of cutting down all the bandits before taking a mortal wound herself, Persephone dropped out of the tree. As intended, she landed squarely on the back of the startled swordsman. With a loud "OOF," he slammed to the ground. He didn't lie where he fell, though. Instead, he reared up onto his knees so fast that Persephone, who'd had the wind knocked out of her, nearly lost her hold on him.

She managed to hold on, however, and the next moment the masked swordsman felt the tip of her dagger at his throat.

"Lay down your sword!" she commanded. "And have your men lay down their weapons, as well!"

"If it is all the same to you—" began the swordsman.

"Now!" cried Persephone, digging the point of the dagger a little deeper into the flesh of his throat.

To her surprise, without another word of protest the swordsman tossed his sword to one side and indicated to his men that they should follow suit. As soon as they'd done so, a petrified-looking Rachel darted forward and gathered up the weapons. After ordering all the other ruffians to lie on their bellies with their hands where she could see them, Persephone ordered the swordsman's surly sidekick to get off Azriel. When the man told her to piss off, she decided not to press the issue for the moment. Instead, she eased her dagger away from the now-swordless swordsman's throat and stepped back. Slowly, as though half-expecting her to plunge her blade into his back at any moment, he got to his feet and turned around.

Without taking his eyes off Persephone, he slyly called to his sidekick, "The one you're sitting on is too damn handsome to be low-born and too damn brave to be highborn. Peel down his breeches and see if he bears the mark of the Methusians on his pretty arse, will you?"

Though Persephone managed not to cry out in protest, the flash of alarm that swept across her face apparently told the swordsman all he needed to know.

Chuckling at how easily he'd managed to trick the truth out of her, he raised his hand to stop his companion from ripping off Azriel's breeches—a task the man had already enthusiastically cracked his big knuckles in preparation of undertaking. Then he said, "So, you're not just wanted criminals, then, but wanted *Methusian* criminals."

Persephone knew it was too late to deny it and that a denial would almost certainly result in Azriel suffering a thorough body exam at the hands of his vanquisher, who would eventually find the mark anyway. So, clutching her dagger a little tighter, she licked her dry lips and said, "The one with the pretty arse and I are Methusians, yes. But criminals? No."

The swordsman laughed mirthlessly. "In this realm, all Methusians are criminals," he reminded her, "though I can assure you that I would not have it so, for to be compared to bonny infants and strutting pea-cocks is an insult to us real criminals."

At the mention of strutting peacocks, Rachel glanced down at Azriel, who pretended not to notice that she was looking at him.

"Is that what you are?" Persephone asked the swordsman warily. "Real criminals?"

"That depends on your definition," he replied. "Do you consider real criminals to be those who steal from their betters, set fires, cause riots and generally do what they can to cause unrest in all corners of the kingdom?"

"I do."

"Then we are real criminals, Methusian girl," he said with a nod of satisfaction. "You've nothing to fear from us, though. Our only quarrel is with the Regent Mordesius and all those who dance to his hateful tune. You and your companions do not count yourselves among that lot, do you?"

It was clear that he'd asked the question in jest, and it was on the tip of Persephone's tongue to tell him that they most certainly did not count themselves among "that lot." At the last second, however, she changed her mind. For the truth was that in a twisted way, she, Azriel and Rachel *were* dancing to the Regent's hateful tune. And some instinct told her that if she lied to or misled this man now, she'd someday have cause to regret it.

And so, casually dropping into a fighting stance just in case he lunged at her when he learned the truth, Persephone took a deep breath and said, "We do not count ourselves among 'that lot,' but neither are we exactly what we appear to be." Slowly, she extended the hand upon which she wore the ring that bore the crest of the Erok royal family and added, "For you see, though I am a Methusian, I am also sister to the Erok king, Finnius."

In response to these words and the sight of the ring, the man dropped to one knee so fast he probably would have shattered his kneecap if he'd been standing on stone.

"Princess," he breathed, pressing his clasped hands to his breast. "Tales of you, your beauty and the generosity you've shown to the lowest in this realm come before you. Let me be the first to say that it is an *honor* to meet you."

The other ruffians, who were still lying face down on the ground, all murmured and nodded without lifting their heads.

"Really?" said Persephone, casting a rather nonplussed glance at Azriel, who managed a grin in spite of the extremely heavy dwarf upon his back. "Oh! Well, uh, that's . . . that's good to know." She stopped then and waited for the kneeling man to say or do something. When he didn't, she cleared her throat and, feeling rather foolish, said, "Rise and, um, tell me your name."

The swordsman leapt to his feet at once. "Your Highness, some call me Robert the Champion and some call me Robert the Rascal."

Persephone smiled. "And what shall I call you?" she asked.

"Your most humble servant," he purred, bowing with a lack of grace no nobleman in the realm would have been shown and a sincerity that no nobleman in the realm could have matched. "Indeed, Your Highness, if there is ever anything I or any of my men can do for you, you need only ask."

Persephone smiled again, this time with gratitude. "I thank you kindly for the offer, Robert, and would take you up on it at once," she said. "For you see, in addition to being in rather desperate need of food and drink, my companions and I require help getting out of the forest, for we have urgent business on the coast. Oh, and I'd be much obliged if you'd ask your companion to get off my . . . my . . ."

"HUSBAND!" called Azriel irritably as he made yet another futile attempt to throw off his vanquisher.

"Ah! The prince consort," said Robert reverently as he leaned over to brush a moldy leaf off Azriel's face. Snapping his fingers at the dwarf (who used Azriel's head to help push himself to his feet), Robert said, "Big Ben is not just my companion, Your Highness. He is one of the fiercest resistance fighters in the kingdom."

Rachel gave Big Ben a tentative smile. "We have a very large friend who goes by the name of Tiny," she whispered.

"So?" grunted the man rudely.

Robert laughed.

"Come," he said. "It is too late to safely lead you to the forest's edge now, so if it pleases Your Highness, you may sup and stay with us this night. Upon the morrow we shall take you where you seek to go that you may continue on your way."

In addition to several stout storage sheds containing items ranging from weapons and coils of rope to purses of gold and women's undergarments, the rebel camp consisted of at least three dozen sturdy shelters nestled high among the trees and cunningly connected by a series of narrow swinging bridges. As they supped, Robert explained that they'd not always lived thusly. Years earlier, when he and the first of his band had initially sought refuge in the Great Forest, they'd lived on the ground in huts. However, after having lost one man too many to attacks by the night beasts of the forest, they'd given up and climbed into the trees.

At the mention of the night beasts, Azriel commented on the remarkable good fortune that he, Persephone and Rachel had had to have passed four whole nights in the forest without being attacked by one.

"'Twas not all good fortune," said Robert as he wiped his greasy mouth with one of the white linen napkins that had belonged to the soldiers that he and his men had earlier slain. "The three soldiers that were following you killed at least two timber wolves and one very large cat—it was the discovery of their carcasses that first alerted us to intruders in the forest. If I didn't know better, I'd say those soldiers were trying to keep you alive. Mayhap we'll find out for certain when my brothers return with the one that got away." Robert paused to pop a pilfered sweetmeat into his mouth before adding, "If the wretch is still breathing by then, that is."

Persephone nodded as she sank her teeth into one of the remarkably perfect pears that had been found in the same pack as the linen napkins and the sweetmeats. She was not as surprised as Robert that the soldiers had tried to keep them alive. Dead slaves were of little worth to slave hunters, and Persephone would have bet a small fortune that the soldiers killed by Robert's men had been comrades of the slave hunters who'd met their grisly end upon the mountain. Obviously, the thought that one had got away made her almost as uneasy as the idea that she'd been hunted unawares, but whatever threat the soldiers had posed had ended with them.

Much as she yearned to confront the wretch who yet lived—well, *maybe* lived—she, Azriel and Rachel agreed that they must press on at first light whether Robert's brothers had returned or not.

Despite these plans for an early start the following day, everybody sat up late visiting by the light of the moon, the stars and the torches that flickered all around them. While Rachel basked in the glory of being the only unmarried female in a camp full of men who could not do enough for her, Robert spoke at length to Persephone and Azriel about the wrongs he and his men sought to right by their sedition. The Erok lowborns did not seek to supplant their betters, he explained earnestly. They sought only to be allowed to live in peace and to work hard as their forebears had ever done. It was not fair, Robert insisted, that hundreds should be turned off their land so that a single noble-man might put in a garden or a deer park. It was not right, he said, that families should be torn apart, mothers never to see daughters again, fathers never to know the fates of sons.

Much moved, Persephone promised Robert that she would carry his words to her brother, the king, and do all that she could to help him set these wrongs to right. Then, feeling that she ought to give something more than words to this man who'd had so much taken from him by those of high station, she sealed her promise with a gift.

"It is an ancient piece said to confer protection," she said as she handed him the charm bracelet that Finn had given her. "I would like you to have it."

"Your Highness is . . . most generous," said Robert gruffly. Turning to Azriel, he added, "You are a very lucky man to be wed to such a woman, my prince."

"Yes," murmured Azriel, giving Persephone the same look that she'd given her first mug of water in two days—one that sent a ripple of pure desire shooting straight through her belly, "I am."

Eventually, Rachel retired alone to the tree shelter belonging to the man who'd won the shoving match granting him the honor of offering it to her. Persephone and Azriel, meanwhile, retired to the "royal chamber," which, judging by the way Big Ben stomped and glowered, was more commonly known as his chamber.

Upon finding herself alone with Azriel for the first time since being trapped in the crevasse, Persephone rather expected him to use teasing whispers, gentle kisses and fluttery touches to try to entice her into allowing him to quench the thirst that had earlier seemed to rage in him so fiercely. To her surprise, he did none of these things. And though Persephone clung fiercely to the image of just how coldly she'd have spurned him if he *had* done them, it did nothing whatsoever to distract her from her traitorous body's response to the feel of him lying so close to her in the darkness.

The next morning, they all awoke early. By dawn Robert and Big Ben had led them to the eastern edge of the forest. At the sight of the rising sun and of Ivan flying loop-the-loops over the wide-open space before her, Persephone felt her spirits soar higher than they had in many days.

They may not have saved any time cutting through the Great Forest, but they'd made it through alive and, according to Robert, if they hurried, they'd reach the coastal village of Syon as early as midday tomorrow.

Even more encouraging, judging by the appearance of the sky at the distant horizon, the storm season had not yet begun. That meant there was still a chance they'd be able to find a ship willing to take them across the channel to the Island of Ru where the Marinese now resided.

And *that* meant the race to find the pool and save Finn's life might still be won.

Thirty-Seven

HIS SMALL HANDS trembling violently, General Murdock pushed the protruding coil of intestine back into the bloody gash in his belly. If he'd not been a military man drilled in the acceptance of cold hard facts, he'd have found it difficult to believe that his mission could have gone so badly, so quickly.

For four days, he and his two remaining soldiers had tracked the princess and her companions through the Great Forest. It had been easy, for the misty gloom of the forest had provided ample cover, and as it had evidently not occurred to the princess's Methusian husband that anything but a dumb animal might be stalking them, he'd made no effort to conceal their trail. General Murdock had not been so careless, for he knew that some of the most notorious lowborn rebel bands in the realm dwelled within the Great Forest. These included the band that had instigated the recent riots in which he'd been forced to sacrifice two of his finest lieutenants in order to lure the rebel leaders to their deaths. When he'd thought about how he'd thereafter nearly been roasted alive in his own tent by Methusians intent upon rescuing their little clansman, a small, primordial part of General Murdock had wanted to hunt down these rebels and tear out their throats. However, the military man in him had understood that any such confrontation would have been detrimental to his mission. He'd therefore steered his men well clear of the Methusian's clumsy trail and taken all necessary steps to conceal his own.

That is why the rebel attack had come as such a shock. They'd come out of nowhere, and the only thing that had saved him from being instantly pitchforked to death alongside his men was that he'd happened to be a dozen paces away enjoying a quiet moment of reflection when the attack occurred. Upon hearing the shrill screams of his men, he'd immediately stepped behind the nearest tree, turned and started silently slinking away from the sounds of the screams. Cowardice had not caused him to act thusly, of course, but rather the thought that he would fail in his duty if he was to be murdered alongside his men.

Unfortunately, two of the rebels had spotted him and given chase. By casting terrified glances over his shoulder and pretending to falter, he'd lured them onward. And when he'd been certain that they were far enough away from their companions that their screams would not be heard, he'd turned abruptly and attacked.

As it happened, they'd not even had time to scream.

However, one of them had had time to slit his belly.

Wiping his clammy forehead with the back of his bloody hand, General Murdock leaned against the nearest tree, understanding that if he sat now, he might never get up again. He needed to decide what he was going to do, and he needed to decide quickly. Could he continue to follow the princess? Difficult to say. The rebel's blade did not appear to have pierced the intestine itself; if he'd had his pack, he'd probably have been able to stitch up the wound with catgut and fashion some sort of bandage to keep out the dirt. But he did not have his pack.

General Murdock's long nose twitched. Had the wound already begun to fester or was the odor he detected only a figment of a fevered imagination?

If it had not yet begun to fester, it soon would. And when it did, death would quickly follow. Death, and duty unfulfilled.

It was this prospect of duty unfulfilled that spurred General Murdock to decide to break off his pursuit of the princess in favor of making for the New Man training camp northeast of the Great

Forest. Upon reaching it, he'd have his wound tended and take all steps necessary to recover his strength as quickly as possible. While convalescing, he'd select a new company of soldiers to accompany him once he resumed pursuit. He'd also send a carefully worded message to the Regent explaining the situation and assuring him that he knew where to find the princess and would do so as soon as he was able.

How fortunate that he'd happened to overhear where the princess and her companions were headed next.

Indeed, if he'd been the kind of man who believed in fate, General Murdock might have been tempted to believe that finding the healing pool was the princess's destiny and that killing her was his.

But he was not the kind of man who believed in fate. He was the kind of man who believed in cold hard facts.

And so, keeping one hand firmly pressed against the gash in his belly, General Murdock pushed away from the tree and forced himself to begin staggering in what that small, primordial part of his brain told him was a northeast direction.

Because the fact was, even if he somehow survived the night in the forest, if he didn't reach the training camp by the next day, it would almost certainly be too late.

Thirty-Eight

WHEN THE LOWBORN REBELS attacked General Murdock, the man in meanest homespun had been caught quite as off guard as the General had been.

It was he who'd killed the two timber wolves and the big cat. He hadn't enjoyed killing such proud beasts any more than he'd enjoyed killing the second messenger, but the alternative would have been to allow them to eat him, and he was quite sure that he'd have enjoyed *that* even less.

The man had, of course, understood why the beasts had come after him instead of going after either of the two groups ahead of him. He was traveling alone behind the others, and in the world of a large predator, this marked him as a weakling that had become separated from its herd—an easy meal, as it were.

Well, he'd shown them who was a weakling. A miserable childhood spent defending himself against the taunts and threats of bigger children had taught the man to wield a slingshot almost as well as a Gorgishman. In the case of all three beasts, the rocks they'd taken to the head had so stunned them that he'd been able to slit their throats before they recovered.

Unfortunately, it had not occurred to the man that their carcasses might alert the forest dwellers to the presence of intruders. Well, to be more precise, the man hadn't realized that there *were* any forest dwellers. That is probably why he'd nearly had an apoplexy when they'd appeared out of nowhere, stabbing with their pitchforks and chopping with their axes.

Luckily, he'd been far enough back not to be noticed, but not so far back that he hadn't noticed the General fleeing with two of the forest dwellers in hot pursuit. Surreptitiously, he'd followed these three until without warning he'd come across the bodies of the two pursuers. Their injuries had been so horrific that they'd actually made the man's gorge rise. He'd been about to turn away when he'd noticed that one of them had bloodied his knife. Cautiously, then, the man had proceeded onward only to come across General Murdock shoving his guts back into his belly. From his hiding place, the man had watched the General sweat and tremble briefly before appearing to come to some decision that prompted him to stagger off—not toward the place where he'd last seen the princess, but *away* from it!

The man in homespun had been aghast.

The one who'd set him to this task had said that he needed to fulfill his orders for the greater good of the realm. However, if he was to fulfill the first part of his orders, which required him to follow the General, he would not be able to execute the second part of them, which involved the princess.

Worriedly, the man realized that he was not going to be able to simply follow orders.

He was going to have to *think*.

After a long hard moment of thinking, he decided that he ought to retrace his steps and pick up the princess's trail. One of the reasons he thought this was that since the General's soldiers were all dead, he could not send any more reports to Parthania. The other reason was that alone and wounded as he was, the beasts of the forest wouldn't just mark the General as a weakling, they would mark him as an injured, dying weakling.

And in the world of a large predator, there was no easier meal to be had.

Thirty-Nine

Eighty-two white beans left in the jar

AS ANTICIPATED, PERSEPHONE, Azriel and Rachel arrived in the coastal town of Syon the day after they'd said goodbye to Robert and Big Ben at the edge of the Great Forest.

Anxious though she was to find a ship and cross the channel to the Island of Ru while the weather held, Persephone could not help pausing to marvel at the inexpressible beauty of the town that had once belonged to the Marinese. Streets cobbled even more cunningly than those in the imperial capital were lined with tall, closely set buildings that looked as though they'd been carved from blocks of pure salt. Wrapped in narrow, curving stone staircases and topped with twisting spires, these buildings were like works of art. Indeed, evidence of the artistry of the Marinese could be seen in everything from the imposing statues of the Marinese sea gods to the elaborate public fountains to the intricately carved stone benches and stalls of the bustling market.

As Persephone felt the sea breeze tug at the skirt she'd changed into before entering town, she breathed deeply of the salty air and thought of Dane, the sad, old Marinese craftsman from the manor house where she'd lived with her Cookie until that terrible night the master had lost her in a game of dice. Dane had grown up in this beautiful town at a time when it had still belonged to his people; he'd apprenticed for many years at his father's knee that he might one day become a great craftsman himself. How awful, then, to have been sacrificed by his own people and handed over to a man like the master. To have been forced to live in a town like Wickendale, with its slums and slave markets and muck-filled streets, where the stomach-churning miasma of rot and waste ever hung heavy in the air.

When we've found the healing pool and rid the realm of the Regent, I will ask Finn to give Syon back to the Marinese, thought Persephone suddenly. *I will return to Wickendale and free Dane—and Cookie, too!*

Smiling as she imagined the expression on Cookie's face at the news that the poor, overworked little orphan girl she'd loved so well was actually a princess, Persephone followed Azriel and Rachel down to the harbor. It was humming with activity. Servants and others were busy unloading the holds of docked vessels; rowboats were conducting notable persons between the shore and the dozens of large ships anchored in the harbor's deeper waters. Dubious-looking characters in rickety flats bobbed from ship to ship trying to tempt those left aboard into handing over hard-earned coin for exorbitantly priced fresh fruit, red meat and liquor. Merchants hurried along in search of the next lucrative shipping contract; darting street urchins picked pockets and threw rocks at the crying seagulls. Sailors too long at sea roamed the wharf in search of strong drink and welcoming women.

There was so much activity, in fact, that Persephone was quite sure they'd have no trouble at all finding passage to the Island of Ru. To her dismay, however, it soon became clear that few captains were willing to risk a channel crossing so close to the storm season, and *none* were willing to risk undertaking such a journey with women on board.

Women, apparently, were bad luck.

"Don't worry," said Azriel, chuckling as he held Persephone's wrists to keep her from shaking her fists at the swarthy specimen who'd most recently brought this tidbit of valuable information to their attention. "I have an idea."

Turning to Rachel, who'd lived friendless and alone on the streets of Syon before being discovered by Fayla, he asked her to lead them to an inn. She found a modest one situated not far from the market. After paying for the last available room, Azriel extracted a promise from Persephone that she'd stay put and a promise from Rachel that she'd see to it that Persephone stayed put, then he ducked back out into the street.

He was not gone long.

"I've found passage to and from the Island of Ru for two men aboard the only ship in the harbor willing to make a channel crossing," he announced triumphantly as he stepped sideways into the room, the door frame being too narrow to accommodate the breadth of his shoulders. Persephone and Rachel stared at him blankly.

"Only one of you will be able to accompany me to the island," he explained in a slightly exasperated voice, "and she will have to be disguised as a man."

Without realizing what she was doing, Persephone reached up and touched her hair. As surely as she knew that it must be her who accompanied Azriel to the island, she knew that to pass for a man, she was going to have to cut her hair. The thought filled her with dismay. From the start she'd known that she might have to sacrifice her life on this quest of theirs, but she'd never *dreamt* that she'd have to sacrifice her hair! Thick, dark and glossy, it had not been shorn since the night she'd arrived at the Mines of Torodania. She shuddered now as she recalled huddling in the darkness of the mine shaft running her fingers back and forth over her scabby, bristly scalp. She did not know if she could cut her hair now. She supposed she'd have to but—

The sudden feel of Azriel's fingers gently gathering up her hair caused all further thought to fly out of her head. Piling her tresses upon her head, he leaned down, gave her neck a lingering kiss, then laid his lips beside her ear and whispered, "I would not have you cut your beautiful hair, wife."

Breathless at the undercurrent of want in his voice and having completely forgotten that Rachel was still in the room, Persephone languorously turned her face toward his. As she did so, Azriel plopped a boyish cap down onto her head.

"No need to cut your hair if we can conceal it under a cap," he murmured, his lips so close to hers that she could almost feel them—almost.

Persephone trembled, wondering why he tormented her like this, wondering why she allowed it.

"We leave in an hour," said Azriel, turning from her abruptly. "I'll be back for you then."

As soon as he was gone, Persephone changed into her fringed breeches, bound her breasts with a length of sturdy linen and plaited her hair that it might be more neatly concealed beneath the cap. When she was done, Rachel spent a few moments coaching her on the fine art of walking and talking like a man.

"Swing your arms!" instructed Rachel as she watched Persephone swagger back and forth across the tiny room. "Stomp your feet! Scratch your armpits! Snort and spit! May I ask you a question?"

"Of course," grunted Persephone, scratching like a baboon with body lice.

"Why will you not lie with him?" asked Rachel.

Persephone froze mid-scratch.

"He is a good man and your wedded husband," continued Rachel matter-of-factly. "And it is clear that you want him as desperately as he wants you. Is the reason you've not yet consummated your marriage that you do not consider it a true marriage? You know—because it was not a royal ceremony and because you spoke your silly vows under duress?"

"No," said Persephone stiffly, unable to recall ever having referred to her wedding vows as *silly*.

"Is it that you intend to have the marriage set aside once Azriel has helped you find the healing pool?" asked Rachel. "You know—that you may select a consort more befitting one of your great station?"

"No!" spluttered Persephone, offended by the very suggestion.

"Well, then, is it because you do not believe that Azriel truly cares for you as a person but only seeks to satisfy his voracious carnal appetites at the expense of your maidenhood?"

"NO!"

Smiling in a way that told Persephone she'd never believed any of these was the reason, Rachel murmured, "'No' can be a hard habit to break, Princess."

"Saying 'no' to Azriel is not a habit," said Persephone, surprised to find her throat tightening at the memory of the night in the rebel camp when he hadn't even given her the *chance* to say no.

Rachel reached out and tucked a stray strand of hair up under her friend's boyish cap. "I am glad to hear it," she said gently, "for it means that come what may, you shall never have cause to regret the things you did not do."

Azriel returned sooner than expected to breathlessly report that the captain of the ship upon which he'd arranged passage was threatening to set sail without them if they weren't aboard in a matter of minutes.

Throwing her arms around Rachel, whom she loved dearly in spite of her unwelcome habit of making shrewd observations, Persephone promised her friend that they'd be back in two days—three at the most! Then, hurriedly pressing into Rachel's hand the few coins they had left between the three of them, she followed Azriel out the door.

They ran all the way to the harbor and down the wharf to a ship with a poorly patched mainsail and a faded hull encrusted with barnacles. Persephone would've liked to ask Azriel if he was certain that the vessel was seaworthy, but as he was already pounding up the gangplank, she had no choice but to follow. The instant her feet hit the deck, she heard someone bellow an order to cast off.

"Azriel—" she began in a deliberately deeper voice.

"Go stand by the starboard rail, boy, while I settle up with the captain," he interrupted, giving her a hearty shove in the right direction.

Resisting the urge to scowl at his retreating back, Persephone swaggered across the deck and leaned against the starboard rail. Almost immediately, a leering sailor with a face like old leather sidled up to her.

"My, but yer a *very* pretty boy," he said, giving her a broad, gap-toothed grin.

"Oh," said Persephone gruffly. "Well, uh, thank you."

Nodding, the sailor leaned back so that he could get a good rear view. Then he licked his peeling lips and said, "I suppose ya belong to that big fella what's talkin' to the cap'n?"

It was on the tip of Persephone's tongue to tell the boor that she didn't belong to *anybody* when it occurred to her that a pretty boy on a ship full of sex-starved sailors could do worse than belong to a "big fella" like Azriel. So instead of proudly proclaiming her freedom, she growled, "Yes, that's right. I belong to him—so you'd better shove off before he comes over here and turns you into shark bait!"

Muttering darkly, the sailor stomped away.

Though the channel crossing had been known to take days in stormy conditions, the conditions that day were so ideal that by early evening the Island of Ru appeared on the horizon. From a distance it looked like nothing but a large, forbidding mass of dark, jagged rock shrouded in mist; as the ship drew nearer, it looked like nothing but a large, forbidding mass of dark, jagged rock shrouded in mist. Persephone could only imagine the despair the Marinese must have felt being driven from a town as beautiful as Syon to a place as desolate as this.

At length, the captain announced that he'd taken the ship in as close to the reef as he dared, and that Azriel and "Percy" (as Azriel had cheerfully introduced Persephone) would have to row themselves to shore. If they did not return to the ship by noon the following day, the captain would sail away and leave them to their fate. If it looked like a storm was brewing, he would sail away and leave them to their fate. If he saw a single Marinese ship put to water, he would sail away and leave them to their fate . . .

As the captain continued to list the many and varied reasons he would sail away and leave them to their fate, a sudden gust of wind caught the brim of Persephone's cap. With a gasp, she reached up to keep it from flying off her head.

Like her cry in the Great Forest, the gasp was neither loud nor long. Under the circumstances, however, it was something infinitely worse:

It was *girlish*.

A collective gasp went up among the sailors. Before Persephone could spit or scratch her armpits to prove that she was a real man just like them, the nearest soldier snatched off her cap. As her glossy braid tumbled free, he fell back in superstitious terror.

"There's a woman aboard!" he shrieked. "There's a woman aboard! Oh, may the gods of the sea have mercy—there's a woman aboard!"

The leering sailor with the face like old leather was upon Persephone before her dagger was halfway out of the scabbard. While half a dozen of his shipmates held Azriel down, the sailor hoisted her, kicking and squirming and scratching like a madwoman, into his sweaty arms and held her out over the starboard railing.

"Who's shark bait now, pretty boy?" he sneered.

And without further ado, he opened his arms and dumped her into the sea.

Forty

THE KING WAS GONE.

Worse, no one could tell Mordesius where he'd gone *to*. The Regent had questioned the royal guards, the body servants, the chambermaids, the serving wenches and the physicians. He'd have happily tortured the information out of the slattern if he could have found her, but she was gone, too. Upon learning this, the possibility that she and the king had run away together had flitted through Mordesius's mind, but he'd dismissed it at once. Though the king was a fool, he was a *royal* fool, and the thought of him lying with that mouthy, one-legged trollop was too repulsive to bear contemplating.

As he lurched toward the Council chamber now, Mordesius cursed himself for not having considered that something like this might happen. He should have spent less energy worrying about Murdock and his lack of reports, and paid more attention to that rebellious look in the king's eye. He should have realized that a boy who had the blood of kings coursing through his veins would never give up his kingdom without a fight. He should have warned the New Men posted outside the royal chambers that they'd be boiled alive if they allowed the king to escape.

Well, they knew now.

Unfortunately, they'd been unable to give him even a shred of useful information before they'd been poached into the afterlife. And now Mordesius was going to have to face Lord Bartok and the rest of the great lords with the humiliating news that he'd temporarily misplaced the king. This was going to make him look like an incompetent imbecile! It was also going to give Lord Bartok an excuse not to uphold his side of their little bargain.

And how long would it be before some ambitious lord idly wondered whether a man appointed by the king to rule in the king's stead ought to be allowed to continue to do so when the king was not available to confirm that these were yet his wishes?

Truly, this was a disaster.

Mordesius would've preferred to have bluffed his way through the situation by telling Bartok and the rest of them that the king had been stricken by some illness that was going to require complete isolation for an indefinite period of time, but it was too late for that. Too many servants knew that the king was missing; it was only a matter of time before their lowborn tittle-tattle reached the ears of their betters.

No.

Mordesius's only hope was to announce the news first and hope that he and his plans would be able to survive.

As luck would have it, he arrived at the Council chamber to find Lord Bartok lingering in the corridor outside chatting with several minor lords who were obviously eager to ingratiate themselves with the future father-in-law of the king. Though Mordesius was certain that Lord Bartok saw him waiting there, the high-and-mighty bastard continued chatting with the minor lords for several minutes more before indicating with an elegant gesture that they should proceed onward into the Council chamber. Only then did he approach Mordesius.

Mordesius forced himself to nod politely. Lord Bartok did not return the courtesy.

"Can I help you, Your Grace?" he asked, his pale blue eyes drifting to the beads of sweat on Mordesius's brow.

Resisting the urge to wipe his brow and then claw out the eyes that were regarding it with such distaste, Mordesius took a deep breath and said, "My lord . . . the king is gone."

Instead of gasping in shock or demanding details or insisting that they immediately raise the alarm, Lord Bartok smiled indulgently and said, "Yes, I know."

Mordesius felt as though a giant hand had just squeezed all the air out of his lungs.

"What . . . what do you mean you *know*?" he asked breathlessly.

Lord Bartok smiled again. "The king and Aurelia have gone on a short progress, Your Grace, their intended final stop being my country estate near the town of Wickendale," he explained. "They thought it might be nice for the country people to get a glimpse of the royal-couple-to-be. They also felt that time alone beyond the prying eyes of the court would give them an opportunity to get to know one another a little better. His Majesty was reluctant at first—for some strange reason, he thought you'd disapprove—but I pointed out to him that he is the king and must therefore do as he pleases."

"He should have informed me of his plans," snapped Mordesius.

Wrinkling his patrician nose at Mordesius's uncouth tone, Lord Bartok reached into his doublet, withdrew a piece of rolled parchment and handed it over. Breaking the seal, which was unquestionably the king's own, Mordesius immediately noted that the letter had been written in the king's hand and dated the previous day.

"Why did I not receive this earlier?" he demanded.

"An unfortunate oversight, Your Grace," said Lord Bartok with an elegant shrug.

Mordesius could feel the blood pounding hot and hard at his temple. "And why is it that no one in attendance to the king knew where he'd gone?" he asked, biting off each word.

"That was my idea," confided Lord Bartok. "I feared that if certain members of the court knew that King Finnius and Aurelia were going on a progress, they'd beg to be allowed to accompany them, and the poor children would have no peace at all. So I convinced the king to disguise himself until he was beyond the city walls."

Clenching his clawlike hands into fists, Mordesius struggled to control himself. He'd known that Bartok would move against him, of course, but he'd never imagined that he'd *dare* to kidnap the king. Oh, he'd done it so cleverly that no one would ever be able to accuse him of treason, but he'd done it all the same, and now Bartok controlled the royal fool. It was a staggering blow to Mordesius, for if he did not have the king, he could not threaten him into doing his bidding. Bartok wouldn't care if the nursemaid was left to starve and ten thousand lowborn infants were butchered, and he'd have every reason to be *pleased* if the princess was beheaded.

"Your Grace, you appear distressed by this news," murmured Lord Bartok, frowning slightly as his eyes once again drifted to Mordesius's sweaty brow. "I assure you that you've no cause to be. Our bargain still stands; my only thought in this matter was the happiness of the king and my daughter. In due course, they shall reach my estate, and if Your Grace wishes, we can always ride forth and meet them there."

Mordesius longed to shriek an order to have the king returned to the imperial palace at once. However, he could not be certain that Bartok would comply, and he did not wish to clash openly with the man while there was yet a chance he intended to uphold his end of their bargain.

And so, instead of shrieking, Mordesius bared his beautiful teeth and said, "My lord, a visit to your northern estate would be a welcome respite from my many duties."

Smiling faintly, Lord Bartok nodded and, using the same gesture he'd used on the minor lords, he indicated that Mordesius should proceed into the Council chamber. Deciding that being reduced to pulp was too kind a fate for the smug, silver-haired bastard, Mordesius nodded tersely, lifted his heavy head and shuffled forward to greet the waiting noblemen.

✳

After announcing that the king and Lady Aurelia had gone on a short progress in a manner that implied that the progress not only had his blessing but had been his idea, Mordesius brought up the subject of succession to test Lord Bartok.

To his astonishment, the nobleman immediately rose to his feet, nodded respectfully toward the head of the table and proceeded to speak eloquently and at great length about the need to settle the issue as soon as may be. With rising excitement, Mordesius waited for him to get to the point: to tell Council that they ought to do what the king had (purportedly) wanted them to do all along and name Mordesius heir.

Unfortunately, having Lord Bartok champion his cause backfired in a way that Mordesius had not seen coming. Because while the great lords would never have dared to speak freely if it had been Mordesius who'd raised the issue of succession, they apparently felt entirely comfortable doing so when it was one of their own who'd raised it. Nothing was as it once was, they said. Wasn't the king betrothed now? Wouldn't the royal wedding soon take place? Wouldn't a royal infant follow shortly thereafter? And what about the Princess Persephone? Even if something were to happen to the king before he was able to get a child upon his queen, there was always his long-lost sister, wasn't there? Where *was* the Princess Persephone, by the way? Have you had any word from her, Your Grace?

"I have," lied Mordesius, who was white-lipped and trembling with rage. "The princess is well, but as I have told you before, she has no interest in the throne."

"Yes, as *you* have told us, Your Grace . . . ," said Lord Bartok, half to himself.

Mordesius stiffened at once. "Do you have something you wish to say, my lord?" he asked coldly.

Lord Bartok made a great show of hesitating. "I . . . only wonder if my fellow noblemen would be more comfortable addressing the issue of succession if they were able to hear the *princess* say that she has no interest in the throne," he said in a voice that suggested he was deeply embarrassed by his fellow noblemen's lack of faith in the words of their Lord Regent.

A murmur of consternation went up around the table.

Mordesius stared at Bartok, trying to figure out what he was up to. "Very well," he said after a long moment. "I shall write to the princess with a request that she send a letter to Council confirming—"

"Forgive me, Your Grace," interrupted Lord Bartok with an apologetic shrug, "but no one knows what the princess's handwriting looks like—if, indeed, she even knows how to write at all. I daresay the only thing that would assuage the concerns of my fellow noblemen would be if the princess were to come to Parthania and address Council in person. Isn't that right, my lords?"

It was clear from the alarmed expressions on the faces of most of Bartok's fellow noblemen that they understood they'd just been tossed into the middle of something dangerous and that they weren't sure which way to jump. To agree with the powerful Lord Bartok was to make an enemy of the most feared man in the kingdom; to disagree with Lord Bartok was to make an enemy of the future father-in-law of the king.

And so the noblemen neither agreed nor disagreed with Lord Bartok. Instead, they stared at the tabletop and prayed they'd not be singled out to speak.

Breathing hard, Mordesius wondered for the thousandth time how it was that the Fates could have given health and high birth to this contemptible collection of worms while withholding both from someone like him. Indeed, the only one among them that wasn't a worm was Bartok—and he was a snake.

But he was a snake who held many cards at the moment. He was in possession of the king, he had a daughter destined to be queen and he held sway over nearly every great lord in the realm.

And that is why, although Mordesius longed to see him torn to pieces for daring to blindside him with this troublesome delay tactic, he merely shrugged as though the issue was of minor importance and said, "I suppose there'd be no harm in writing to the princess to ask if she'd be willing to address Council."

"Thank you, Your Grace," murmured Lord Bartok with a wintry smile.

Mordesius smiled back.

However many cards Bartok held, the game was not over yet.

Forty-One

Eighty-two white beans left in the jar

PERSEPHONE SCREAMED the whole long way down from the sweaty arms of the leering sailor to the surface of the sea. Plunging deep into the brisk, salty water, she twisted and wriggled like a confused mermaid for what seemed like an eternity before finally managing to orient herself in the direction of the light. Swimming hard toward it, she surfaced just in time to see Azriel running along the starboard railing with the grace of an acrobat. He made one final sword lunge at the sailors from whom he'd somehow broken free, then he turned and launched himself overboard, flinging his sword seaward as he did so.

Even before he hit the water, Persephone heard the captain bellow an order to lift anchor. The sailors jumped to obey so quickly that by the time Azriel surfaced next to her, the ship was already moving.

For a long, silent moment the two of them just floated upon the gently rising and falling swells, watching their passage back to the mainland sail away without them.

Then, in a mild voice, Azriel said, "I don't recall the captain saying he'd sail away and leave us to our fate if he discovered that one of us was a beautiful woman, do you, Percy?"

Too anxious to even think about smiling, Persephone shook her head and said, "Azriel, what are we going to do now?"

"Now?" he replied, squinting against the reflected sunlight that was making his eyes sparkle like sapphires. "Now, we are going to swim."

Though they struck out strongly and swam for what seemed like a very long time, the island that had appeared so close from the ship deck did not seem to be getting any closer. More concerning still, the swells that had been so gentle at first were getting bigger and more powerful with each passing moment.

"How . . . how much . . . farther, do you think?" panted Persephone, rolling onto her back to rest and catch her breath.

"I don't know," said Azriel, eyeing her exhausted form with obvious trepidation.

Swimming hard, he caught the next big wave and rode it to its zenith that he might get a better view of what lay before them. Persephone felt a flutter of apprehension as another wave rolled between them, blocking her view of him. When the wave passed, she saw that although Azriel had been carried almost fifteen feet away from her, he was grinning with relief.

"The waves all seem to be cresting up ahead. That must mean we're almost at the reef!" he shouted as he started swimming back toward her. "It looks a little, uh, challenging, but if we can get past it safely, we'll be in a lagoon and after that—"

He stopped talking abruptly as something powerful appeared to catch hold of him.

Shark! thought Persephone with a jolt of primal terror.

But it wasn't a shark.

"I'm caught in some sort of current," called Azriel, sounding almost surprised.

"Well, get out of it!" shouted Persephone, who was almost as terrified by the speed with which the strange current was sweeping him back out to sea as she would have been by the sight of a dorsal fin cutting through the water.

"I don't know if I can!" shouted Azriel, whose powerful arms were pulling hard through the water to no apparent avail.

"Well, try!"

"I *am* trying!"

Persephone didn't waste her breath shouting for him to try harder because she didn't want him to waste his breath replying. Moreover, she knew from her intermittent glimpses of his swiftly receding form that he was trying as hard as he possibly could.

Forgetting her own exhaustion and refusing to acknowledge the fact that if Azriel could not free himself from the current, there was not even the slightest chance she'd be able to free them both, Persephone took a deep breath and kicked to bring herself around that she might start swimming toward him. As she kicked, however, her left shin scraped against something hard and sharp as a razor. Gasping in pain and surprise, she accidentally inhaled some briny spray and began to cough.

Before she could fully clear her lungs, the water in front of her was sucked backward in a rush, revealing the beautiful and deadly reef. Then the shadow of a huge, cresting wave reared up behind her, and she was violently tumbled into oblivion.

Persephone opened her stinging eyes slowly and with great difficulty to find that she was lying on her stomach with her face turned toward the sun of a dying day. Water lapped gently at her legs; her mouth tasted of salt and sand.

Gingerly, she pushed herself onto her hands and knees. She coughed and spit several times. When a cursory examination revealed several scrapes and bruises but no real injuries beyond a slightly shredded left shin, she staggered to her feet. Shielding her eyes, she carefully scanned the black sand beach for Azriel. When she saw no sign of him, she cupped her hands around her mouth and shouted his name. When he didn't answer, she shouted louder, bellowing that if this was his idea of a joke, it wasn't funny in the least.

The distant sound of waves crashing against the reef was the only reply.

Clasping her suddenly trembling hands together, Persephone forced herself to look seaward—past the lagoon, past the reef, to the place beyond where she'd last seen Azriel fighting to free himself from the current that had been dragging him ever farther from shore.

It'll be a real blow to his manly pride if I have to swim out there and save his life, she told herself edgily as her eyes swept back and forth across the distant water looking for the speck that could be him—still fighting, still floating, still breathing.

But there was no speck.

She searched the beach again.

For nearly an hour she searched, only this time she didn't just scan, she ran, all the way to one end of the beach and then all the way to the other. Then all the way back again, this time bellowing into the nooks and crannies formed by the jagged black rocks that ringed the long beach and rose up into the mists that hovered above it. Her thought was that after reaching shore, Azriel had crawled into some sheltered spot before falling unconscious. For Persephone knew that he *must* be unconscious, otherwise he'd have answered her by now. Indeed, his handsome face would have been the first thing she'd have seen upon opening her eyes.

But yours are the only footprints in the sand, whispered a voice in her head.

"So?" said Persephone aloud as she fought to keep from shaking.

So Azriel did not reach shore, whispered the voice.

"You are wrong," said Persephone, louder than before.

Azriel never fought his way free of the current, whispered the voice, full of sorrow. *Exhaustion overtook him.*

He drowned.

Persephone's knees buckled without warning at the sudden vision of her husband's eyes fixed in death, his body floating in eerie silence just beneath the rippling sunlit surface before slowly sinking toward the cold, black depths.

Though she knew in her heart that it had probably happened this way, she also knew that it couldn't have. It just *couldn't* have! Azriel had made a solemn vow to protect her with his life! Indeed, he was more alive than anyone Persephone had ever met in *her* life! Feeling as though she could hardly breathe, Persephone tried to imagine a world without Azriel's slow smile, fast hands and eyes like blue flames; without his ready wit and dauntless courage; without his tendency to huff when things didn't go his way. She tried to believe that she would never again lay her cheek against his warm chest, would never again feel his strong arms around her, would never again feel him lying so close to her in the darkness.

So close, but not touching.

Hugging her knees tightly to her suddenly aching chest, Persephone remembered the conversation she'd had with Rachel about never having cause to regret the things she had not done. And she knew for a bitter certainty that if she lived for a thousand years, she'd never cease to regret not having reached for Azriel when she'd had the chance to do so.

Saying no to him *had* become a habit, just as wishing for a destiny that belonged to none but her had become a habit.

At the terrible thought that she was going to end up getting exactly what she'd always wished for, Persephone choked back a sob and pressed her forehead hard against her knees. She'd lost those close to her before, but it had never felt quite like this. Like a piece of her had been torn away, leaving a wound that would never heal.

Like she would never be whole again.

For what seemed like an eternity, Persephone sat unmoving on the sand, too drained by shock and grief to think. Then she wearily lifted her head . . .

And nearly dropped dead of a heart attack at the sight of Azriel walking down the beach toward her.

Broad shouldered and barefoot, with his auburn hair dripping wet and the red-gold rays of the setting sun at his bare back, he looked more beautiful than Persephone had thought it was possible for a human being to look.

Upon seeing that she'd finally noticed him, Azriel raised his hand in casual greeting and gave her one of his little lopsided smiles.

Persephone did not stop to think but was on her feet in one instant and running toward him in the next. No, not running—flying. She closed the distance between them in a trice and hurled herself into his arms with such force that Azriel—that unmoveable monolith, that all-powerful Methusian—fell backward onto the sand with a grunt.

"Why, hello, Percy—" he began.

Persephone shut him up with a kiss that would have taken away the breath of the north wind itself. Twining her fingers in his short, auburn curls, she kissed him deeper and deeper until, without warning, he grabbed her wrists, wrenched himself away from her kiss and growled, "*Stop!*"

Persephone froze.

Azriel gazed at her warily, searchingly. She tingled at the feel of his hungry eyes upon her, at the feel of her small wrists trapped in his powerful grip, at the feel of him lying so strong and lean and shirtless beneath her.

"You, uh, seem to be feeling a heightened physical awareness on account of *my* most recent near-death experience, wife," he observed at length.

Though his tone was determinedly light, Persephone could feel his chest heaving beneath hers. Feeling that familiar dizziness that his nearness so often provoked, she nodded impatiently and leaned in for another kiss.

Releasing her wrists, Azriel slid his hands up to her shoulders. Roughly, he halted her progress the instant before their lips met.

"Are you sure?" he asked huskily. "I need you to be very sure, for I would not have you do something you'll regret."

Persephone nodded again, even more impatiently. All she wanted was for him to stop talking and—

Swiftly, Azriel slid his arms around her and rolled them both over so that she was lying on her back and he was propped on one elbow leaning over her.

"Do you truly wish to be a wife to me in every way?" he demanded, his voice ragged with pent-up longing.

Persephone's heart was hammering so hard she could barely hear him. But that was a good thing, because she didn't want to hear him, didn't want to answer him, didn't want to think. All she wanted was to say the one word that would ensure she'd never have cause to regret the things she had not done.

And so she said it:

"Yes."

Forty-Two

BY THE TIME AZRIEL and Persephone were finally spent and the world around them had begun to exist again, the air had grown chilly and a bank of dark clouds had begun rolling across the dusky sky toward them, blotting out the early evening starlight as it came.

As she lay on her back feeling Azriel's bare thigh pressed against hers and listening to him struggle to slow his breathing even as she struggled to slow hers, Persephone was intensely grateful for the encroaching darkness. Having followed through on her "yes" with an abandon that had driven them both to ever-more dizzying heights of passion, she suddenly felt more than a little embarrassed by her display of unbridled enthusiasm . . . and by the fact that she was wearing nothing but the scabbard strapped to her thigh . . . and by the fact that this was considerably more than Azriel was wearing.

What Persephone needed at that moment was for Azriel to roll onto his side and pull her closer than close. To intoxicate her all over again; to whisper and tease and do whatever else he could think of to get her good and comfortable with the idea of being his wife in every way.

Unfortunately, before he could do any of those things—indeed, before either of them had fully caught their breath—Azriel grabbed his breeches, rolled to his feet and hissed, "*Someone is coming!*"

Knowing that under the circumstances she ought not to feel stung by the lack of warmth in his voice (but feeling stung nonetheless), Persephone scrambled to cover her nakedness, a task that somehow seemed infinitely more pressing than drawing her dagger. She'd just managed to pull on her own damp breeches and yank her shirt down over her head when three men with white-blond hair filed out from between two large rocks at the edge of the beach. The first man carried a torch, the second carried three spears and the last had a stringer of fat fish slung over one shoulder.

As Persephone would have expected, having learned from the Marinese artisan Dane of the passive nature of most of his people, the three men approached diffidently and without any aggressive posturing. Even so, she inhaled sharply when they drew close enough to see clearly. Not because they'd done anything at all threatening, but because the acutely discomfited expressions on their faces told Persephone that they'd . . . seen . . . everything. And as mortifying as this would have been under normal circumstances, it was a thousand times worse under the present circumstances.

For Dane had *also* told Persephone that the Marinese were a painfully modest people who lived in strict accordance with a rigid moral code. And she was fairly certain that this code did *not* include tearing off one's clothes and making wild, passionate love on a beach in plain view of anyone who might happen to saunter by.

"I am Roark," said the man carrying the torch.

He was looking at Azriel when he said this, but a furiously blushing Persephone forced herself to speak first. "I am Persephone, and this is my *husband*, Azriel," she said, emphasizing the word "husband" in the hope that it would make her seem more like a dutiful wife and less like a complete strumpet.

Roark nodded uncomfortably without looking at her. "We've never welcomed strangers to our island because too often strangers are New Men seeking slaves. Yet you do not look like New Men, and I see no ship anchored beyond the reef," he said to Azriel.

"How did you and your . . . wife come to find yourselves on our island?"

"We swam to shore several hours ago after having been tossed off the ship upon which we'd been sailing," began Azriel.

"But your island was ever our intended destination," put in Persephone, who was torn between feeling royally irked by the way Roark was ignoring her and utterly mortified by what he must think of her. Pushing back her thick dark hair, she tugged open the collar of her shirt in a way that made the man holding the stringer of fish squeak like a startled mouse. Gesturing to the exquisitely crafted silver necklace Finn had given to her before leaving Parthania, she said, "I would not expect you to recognize this, but it was given to my mother—"

"Ambassador Dakkar's daughter Fey," said Roark in surprise, casting his first darting glance at Persephone's face.

Persephone felt a leap of excitement. "Yes!" she exclaimed, stepping forward in her eagerness to tell him more.

Roark took such a hasty step backward that he nearly tripped over the man holding the spears. "Though you are the very picture of Fey, you cannot possibly be her daughter," said Roark uncertainly. "All know that Fey endured the travails of childbirth only once and that was to bring forth the boy king, Finnius, in whose name the Regent Mordesius has ruled these many years."

Pushing aside the thrill she felt upon hearing that she resembled her mother—and resisting the urge to pepper this man who appeared to have known Fey with questions about her—Persephone said, "The night my mother gave birth to the king, she gave birth to me, as well."

Roark's fair eyebrows flew up in surprise at this, but Persephone pressed on. "Royal twins did not fit into the Regent's plans, so he ordered me disposed of at once. The Fates spared me and later reunited me with my brother. It is for his sake, and for the sakes of all people in Glyndoria, that my husband and I are here. For you see, Mordesius holds King Finnius captive against our return with knowledge of the healing Pool of Genezing. Years ago, the Methusian ambassador, Balthazar, claimed to have found it, and we have reason to believe that he gave my mother a gift that proved its existence. Our hope is that he also told her something of its whereabouts, and that before she died, she passed this information along to one of your people."

The man with the spears started to say something, but Roark cut him off with a raised hand. "If Fey told anyone anything, it would have been the Elders," he said impassively. "And before they'll consider telling *you* anything, the Elders are going to want to know what possessed the Regent to set a half-Marinese, half-Erok princess and her husband upon a quest for the healing pool of Methusian lore. What made him believe that the two of you would even know where to begin?"

It was a reasonable question, but one that made Persephone's heart start pounding, for the only answer was—

"Because I am a Methusian," said Azriel, fearlessly in spite of having no weapon to defend himself in the admittedly unlikely event that they tried to murder him on the spot. "And because I told the Regent that I was Balthazar's bastard."

None of the Marinese attacked upon hearing that Azriel was Methusian, but the man holding the stringer of fish did recoil in horror.

"You're a bastard?" he gasped.

"No," replied Azriel, flashing him a grin. "I'm a liar."

After giving Azriel the kind of look one might give a dinner guest who'd just broken wind in the middle of grace, Roark excused himself to confer in private with the other two men. As soon as they'd stepped away, Azriel reached for Persephone's hand. She sighed with pleasure at his touch but snatched her hand away when she saw the man holding the stringer of fish cast a furtive glance in her direction.

"What's wrong?" murmured Azriel, sliding his arm around her and pulling her close.

"Nothing!" whispered Persephone. "It's just . . ."

Too embarrassed to spell out she'd rather not give her dead mother's people more reason to think her an utter trollop—and feeling that Azriel really ought to have been able to figure that much out for himself—Persephone settled for trying to wriggle away from him.

"Ahem."

Azriel let go of Persephone so abruptly that she staggered slightly as she turned to face Roark, whose lips were pressed together into a painfully thin line of disapproval.

"As I told you," he said, "we have never welcomed strangers to this island."

Persephone began to protest, "But—"

"But you are not a stranger," continued Roark without looking at her. "You are the daughter of a daughter of the clan and therefore kin. We will take you and your Methusian husband to our village on the other side of the island. There, it will be for the Elders to decide what you are or are not told, and what is to be done with you until such time as you can find passage back to the mainland."

The hike across the island took several hours, and Persephone's heart was in her throat every step of the way. Not only had the bank of dark clouds blotted out the moonlight and a good deal of the starlight by the time they set out, but the uneven, rocky trail took them up jagged cliff faces, down steep ravines, along crumbling ridges and over fissures at least a dozen hands wide.

By the time they reached the village, Persephone was exhausted. Still, she could not help exclaiming in delight at the sight of it. Set in a vast clearing sheltered from the nearby restless sea by bushy trees growing in such neat rows that they must have been deliberately planted, the village consisted of a surprising number of circular huts with pointy, shingled roofs. The huts were set on either side of spiraling pathways paved with flat, black stones. Outside the door of each hut hung a set of chimes that tinkled prettily in the breeze that was growing brisker with each passing moment. Some huts were smaller and some were larger; the largest of all were found in the center of the village, clustered around what Persephone assumed was the village square. As the hour was late, the square was deserted. Even so, it was ringed with glowing lanterns that hung from what looked to be intricately carved ivory tusks. "How is it that your lanterns shine so bright and steady?" asked Persephone in amazement. "And where on earth did you get the ivory?"

"It is not ivory, it is whalebone," explained Roark shortly after sending the man with the spears running off with a whispered word. "The lanterns shine so because they are filled with oil rendered from whale blubber. This island is nowhere near as rich as the lands surrounding Syon were. We are able to harvest timber enough to build our domiciles, but the wooded areas are too sparse to provide fuel for cooking and heating, and we've no adequate sources of wax or tallow for light. Luckily, soon after we were relocated, we discovered that once a year, whales return to breed off the northern tip of the island. The hunting of them is dangerous beyond measure, but they provide oil for our lamps and stoves, meat for our plates and bone for sculpting."

By the time Roark had finished speaking, the man with the spears was hurrying back toward them. In his wake was a girl. She was wearing a plainly cut white shift that covered her from neck to toe, and she looked to be about three years younger than Persephone. "This is Ekatarina," said Roark, gesturing toward the girl.

The girl said nothing, only dipped a demure curtsey.

"Ekatarina shall be your wife's companion for the duration of your stay in our village," Roark informed Azriel. Turning to the girl, he said, "Ekatarina, this is Persephone, daughter of Ambassador Dakkar's daughter Fey, sister of the Erok king, Finnius, wife of the Methusian Azriel. After finding her something *suitable* to wear, see that she receives food and drink, then take her to your domicile and let her share your sleeping pallet. Tomorrow morning—"

"Wait!" interrupted Persephone and Azriel at the exact same time. Roark looked at Azriel. Azriel looked at Persephone. Pleased that Azriel had noticed the irksome way Roark tended to treat her and was sensitive enough not to fall in with it, she gave him a quick smile. Then she turned to Roark and said, "I thought we were going to see the Elders."

Roark pressed his lips together again. "The Elders meet when the Elders meet, and they do not meet now," he said. "When they are ready to grant you an audience, Daughter of Fey, you shall be summoned."

Though this was not the answer Persephone had been hoping for, she nodded reluctantly before gesturing toward Azriel that it was his turn to give voice to whatever it was he wished to say.

Azriel smiled in a way that made Persephone's breath catch. Then, with all the sensitivity of a thick wooden post, he said, "I was rather hoping that the princess might share *my* sleeping pallet, Roark. She is my wedded wife, after all, and it has been many days since we've enjoyed the comfort of lying together in a real bed."

At these words, Persephone's mouth dropped open, and her face felt as though it had burst into flames.

Roark looked like he'd swallowed his lips.

"Among our people, men and women are housed separately and only come together to couple for the sake of making children," he said stiffly. "Do you . . . seek to couple with your wife this night?"

Though Roark was too polite to say "do you wish to couple with your wife *again*," Persephone knew that this was what he was thinking. And she knew what Azriel's answer to the question would surely be. Indeed, she could tell by the way he was holding his hands that it was all he could do to keep from reaching for her on the spot. And though the very thought made her knees weak, she could not bear the scandalized look on Roark's face and so she hurriedly said,

"Of course my husband does not seek to, uh, couple with me this night." Then, before Azriel could offer protest (or rip off her clothes right there and then to prove that he did *so* wish to couple with her this night), Persephone turned to Ekatarina and rather breathlessly said, "Let's go."

The girl immediately bowed her blond head in acquiescence, turned and started walking. With her hands modestly clasped before her and a gait that made it seem almost as though she were floating, she silently led Persephone to a very large domicile not far from the village square. Lifting the glowing lantern that hung next to the chimes outside this particular domicile, she pushed open the door and stepped inside. Persephone followed and was immediately surprised—not only by the steamy warmth but also by the peculiar sound.

"What is that?" she asked, cocking her head to one side. "It sounds like . . . chewing."

"It *is* chewing," replied Ekatarina with a bright eagerness that did not seem to fit with her heretofore diffident comportment. Pointing to leafy trays that lined the vast shelves that took up at least half of the domicile, she said, "When we left Syon, our Elders ordered silkworms brought along in the hope of establishing a healthy colony."

"It looks as though you succeeded," commented Persephone as she followed the girl across the domicile.

"Day and night the worms feed upon mulberry leaves and our looms are ever busy," agreed Ekatarina contentedly as she set down the lantern and began carefully rummaging through a trunk on the floor. At length, she held up a shift that looked exactly like the one she was wearing. "This is a kjole, the traditional garment of the women of my people." She cleared her throat and bowed her head before continuing in an embarrassed mumble, "Your, um, gaping shirt and tight breeches are, uh, very fine and lovely, the perfect outfit for an Erok princess as beautiful as you, I'm sure, but, uh, Roark said . . . that is to say I think the Elders and, indeed, everyone would be, um, more comfortable if . . . if—"

"If, during my stay in your village, I was to dress as a modest young woman instead of a harlot—or a man?" suggested Persephone dryly.

"Yes!" cried Ekatarina, looking up with such a relieved smile that Persephone had to smile back.

"Well," she said, reaching for the long, shapeless kjole, "I've played a noblewoman, a dungeon servant and a pretty boy. Let us see if I have it in me to play an ordinary girl."

After she'd changed and brushed out her hair, Persephone followed Ekatarina to another of the large domiciles. Here, the girl gave her a goblet of watery wine and a bowl of cold stew swimming with fish heads, seaweed and chunks of a bitter, whitish tuber that Persephone had never seen before. If it was far from being the most palatable dish she'd ever been served, it was also far from being the least. Famished as she was, she ate every last fish head.

When she was done, she followed Ekatarina through the sleeping village to a small domicile near the outskirts. Putting her index finger to her lips to show Persephone that she must be quiet, Ekatarina extinguished the lantern, set it down outside the hut and tiptoed inside. Trying not to trip on her kjole, which was slightly too long for her, Persephone tiptoed after her. By the meager light of the few stars that had not yet been consumed by the bank of clouds, Persephone saw that the hut was full of sleeping young blond girls. Their pallets were arranged in a pretty ring, with the heads all pointed toward the outer wall of the domicile and feet all pointed toward the center.

"You will sleep with me," whispered Ekatarina, pointing to the lone empty pallet.

The pallet was narrow but deliciously comfortable, having been constructed of thick silk bands woven tightly together and strung across a sturdy wooden frame. The comforter Ekatarina tucked around the two of them was comfortable, too, though its vaguely fishy smell led Persephone to believe that it had been stuffed with the feathers of seabirds.

As she lay next to Ekatarina, listening to the sounds of the rising wind, the crashing sea and the tinkling chimes, Persephone tried not to think about the things she could do nothing about at the present moment. Things like not knowing when or even if the Marinese Elders would see her and Azriel and what they could or would tell them about the healing pool if they did; things like not knowing how she and Azriel would get back to the mainland, how long it would take them to do so and what Rachel would do in the meantime.

Though she had some success keeping these thoughts at bay, try though she might, Persephone simply could not stop thinking about Azriel. She could not stop thinking about what had happened between them on the beach—how incredible it had been, and how it probably would have happened again this night if he'd been allowed to share a bed with her. Sighing softly, she'd just given herself over to wondering where her handsome husband was at that moment when a sudden vision of him squashed in beside Roark on a similar pallet in the men's domicile caused her to start giggling.

"What's wrong?" whispered Ekatarina drowsily.

"N-nothing!" choked Persephone, struggling to control her laughter at the thought of Azriel glaring and huffing at the unfairness of a world that would see him bedded down with a disapproving, fishy-smelling man instead of with an agreeable young wife.

"A decent young girl does not trouble herself with unsuitable thoughts, Princess," admonished Ekatarina gently.

"I know, I know," said Persephone, who was yet jiggling with barely contained mirth. "I'm sorry, Ekatarina. Good night."

Hours later, Persephone was jarred awake by a crack of thunder so loud it shook the entire island. A second crack of thunder caused her to spasm with such violence that she nearly knocked Ekatarina off the pallet.

"Don't be afraid," murmured Ekatarina, snuggling closer. "It is just a storm."

Though the girl's words were clearly intended to comfort, they had the exact opposite effect.

For as she stared through the window of the domicile at the flashes of green-tinged sheet lightning that were lighting up the night sky, Persephone knew that it was not *just* a storm—it was the first storm of a storm season that could last months.

And she and Azriel, who had only eighty-one days left to find the healing pool and save Finn's life, were trapped on the wrong side of the channel.

Forty-Three

MORDESIUS SLUMPED in the chair behind the massive desk in his office, drumming his manicured fingernails upon the desktop and wondering what would happen if he imprisoned Lord Bartok's son, Atticus, and threatened to inflict upon him all that had been inflicted upon the son of that buffoon Lord Pembleton.

Would Bartok clasp his hands, fall to his knees, blubber and plead for mercy for his son as Pembleton had? Would he be so overwrought at the prospect of losing his only son in such a grisly manner that he'd return the kidnapped king at once and see to it that Mordesius was promptly named heir?

Or would he give an elegant shrug and console himself with the knowledge that he still had a daughter who would be queen? And, of course, with the knowledge that he still had the king?

"*Bastard!*" snarled Mordesius, shoving a short stack of parchment off the desk with such a sudden sweep of his bony arm that he wrenched his back.

With a grunt of pain, he reached around to try to massage the wrenched spot, but it was no use. It was at times like these that he mildly regretted having discarded the plain-as-dirt noblewoman he'd escorted to the betrothal ceremony, for she'd been rather adept at the art of massage. But it had been that or have her teeth knocked out to prevent her from giving him any more of her idiot smiles, and Mordesius had not cared enough about her to go to the trouble. Moreover, he'd thought that such action might not be politic in view of the fact that he might yet need the support of her noble father to get himself named heir. Since the Council meeting several weeks ago, Lord Bartok had repeatedly assured Mordesius that he'd need no such support. Their deal still stood, Bartok had said in his wintry way; his request to have the princess come to Parthania to address Council had been nothing but a regrettable strategic error on his part. According to him, he'd been thinking only of the threat the princess posed to anyone else's claim to the throne. He'd purportedly believed that it would suit *both* their purposes to have her in Parthania where they could keep an eye on her.

Mordesius hadn't believed him for an instant, of course. But as long as the king was still touring the countryside under the protection of Bartok's personal guard—

A knock at the door interrupted Mordesius's thoughts. "What?" he barked.

A nervous-looking servant hurried into the room, set a gleaming silver platter upon the desk, bowed deeply and waited to be dismissed. After casting a moody glance at the youth's graceful hands, Mordesius dismissed him with an impatient flick of his own scarred hand. Then he turned his attention to the two sealed letters that lay upon the platter.

The first was written upon a rather grimy sheet of everyday parchment and bore the seal of a New Man commander from the northern Ragorian prefecture. The second was written on a crisp sheet of quality parchment the color of new cream. It, of course, was from General Murdock.

Setting the latter letter aside with the brooding thought that the message it contained had better be good, Mordesius opened the first letter. It stated that in accordance with the Regent's orders, the commander was writing in secret to report that General Murdock had not only been spotted but had staggered into the New Man training camp located just north of Syon. Though the General had been near death as a result of a putrefying belly wound he'd sustained some days earlier, he'd refused to see the physicians or even sit down until he'd interviewed all New Men recently returned from leave in Syon and subsequently composed a report for the Regent. The grimy letter ended with the commander's groveling assurances that he stood ready to carry out whatever orders his Lord Regent saw fit to issue.

Mordesius knew what *that* meant. That meant the commander would be only too happy to slit his General's throat, slip his perfectly polished boots off his still-warm feet and try them on for size.

Disgusting, thought Mordesius, reaching for the second letter. Unlike the first letter, this one had something written on the outside:

For the Eyes of None but the Regent Mordesius,
Upon pain of Lingering Death

In spite of the evil feelings he'd lately harbored toward his General for his lack of regular reporting, Mordesius could not help smiling. Most people assumed that there was nothing more fearful than the threat of instant death.

He and Murdock knew better.

Flipping the letter over, Mordesius broke the wax seal and unfolded the parchment to see what the General had to say for himself.

My esteemed Lord Regent,
As you know from my latest report sent shortly after the losses incurred upon the Mountains of Pan, the princess and her companions decided to cut through the Great Forest in the hope of reaching the Island of Ru in advance of the coming storm season. I and my remaining two men followed them into the forest but were shortly thereafter set upon by a band of lowborn brigands. In the course of dispatching two of these brigands, I sustained a wound. Though this wound will require some convalescing, I seek to assure Your Grace that I shall yet be able to fulfill my mission. Intelligence gathered from soldiers recently returned from Syon indicates that a man and a woman

disguised as a man boarded a ship bound for the Island of Ru.
I have reason to believe that these two were the princess and
the Methusian, and that they have been stranded on the island
by the arrival of the storms. Assuming this is correct, they
will remain stranded there until the storms abate. By then,
I shall have recovered from my wound, selected fresh troops
and established appropriate surveillance at the docks. When
the princess and the Methusian return to the mainland to resume
their search for that which they seek, I shall be waiting.
 Your Loyal and Obedient Servant in All Things,
 General Murdock

Mordesius leaned back in his chair, his fertile mind racing. Murdock's short message told him many things. It told him that his suspicion of the General had been unfounded since his message suggested that there *had* been other reports. That none of them had reached him told Mordesius that there might be treachery afoot. That the General appeared to have no sense that this was so told him that whoever was behind the treachery was rich and powerful enough to employ exceedingly capable henchmen. This knowledge, combined with the knowledge that Lord Bartok had already expressed a desire to keep an eye on the princess, told him that the smug, interfering bastard could very well be the mastermind.

Even more intriguing than all of this, however, was that Murdock's message implied that the princess and the Methusian had sought out the Panoraki and the Marinese. This suggested that they were not wandering aimlessly about Glyndoria in the hope of stumbling upon the Pool of Genezing—it suggested that they were proceeding with *purpose*.

The knowledge that they'd survived an encounter with the Panoraki, whom he'd have expected to kill or kidnap the princess for being the sister of the king whose Regent had caused them such harm, made Mordesius uneasy. However, the thought that she was proceeding with purpose filled him with excitement. The bastard cockroach had spoken of following clues given to him by his sire, Balthazar. Was it possible that these clues actually existed and that they were leading him and the princess onward from one miserable clan to the next? It was certainly *possible*. After all, the ill-fated Methusian ambassador had been popular with everyone, including the other three ambassadors.

His cold heart beating very fast, Mordesius flexed his shiny pink hands, felt the pain of the wrenched muscle in his crooked back. Though he'd long hoped that he would someday find the healing pool, until very recently he'd never truly believed that he would.

And now that he did believe, there were times when he could hardly breathe for the excitement of it.

Of course, Murdock's message also told Mordesius that the princess would likely be trapped on the Island of Ru for many days to come. If that was so, by the time she got back to the mainland, there'd be precious few white beans left in the pretty little jar he'd given to her as a parting gift. Hopefully, there'd be enough for her and the Methusian to find the healing pool. If there were and they managed to find it, the two of them would die at Murdock's hands and the king would shortly thereafter die in his bed. If, on the other hand, there were not enough beans, the princess would almost certainly return to Parthania to plead for more time. If she did, Mordesius would give it to her—providing she got down on her knees before him and begged for it, that is. Begged for it and promised that she'd do *anything* for it.

If she did that, he'd give her as much time as she needed!

Then she, the king and the cockroach would die.

Mordesius sighed deeply, images of the princess begging and dying and doing other things swirling in his head. Then, feeling the sudden need to talk with someone about all of this, he rose to his feet.

The nursemaid in the dungeon was the perfect confidante. Though her spirit yet refused to break entirely, and though she often made comments that enraged him, Mordesius knew that she'd never breathe a word of his secrets to another living soul.

Because, of course, she'd never be given a chance to do so.

Forty-Four

Seventy-four white beans left in the jar

FOR MORE THAN A WEEK, the storm winds howled, the rains poured down, and Azriel and Persephone had not a single moment alone together.

In part, this was due to the fact that Ekatarina stuck to Persephone like a particularly tenacious burr might stick to Cur's furry ear. Though Roark had offered the girl as a companion for Persephone, it soon became clear that her greater responsibility was to act as chaperone—presumably to ensure that "Daughter of Fey" did not disgrace herself with further lewd behavior. This did not cause Persephone to like Ekatarina less, for the girl was kind and sweet, and when she was out of the sight and hearing of Roark and the other men, she had a bright energy about her that Persephone found most engaging. However, it *did* mean that Persephone was unable to do pretty much anything besides tend to the call of nature by herself, and even this Ekatarina seemed reluctant to allow her to do.

That being said, the girl's chronic presence was only part of the reason Persephone and Azriel did not get a chance to be alone together. The other part was that in the Marinese village, men and women lived essentially separate lives. They did not eat together and only slept together when they sought to "couple for the sake of making children." And though they both worked very hard, they did entirely different things. The men and boys fished, hunted, sculpted, whittled, built furniture, made tools and spears, and repaired the domiciles that were endlessly battered by storm winds. The women and girls cared for the babies, tended the silkworms, spun thread, wove cloth, sewed and embroidered garments, made ropes and fishing nets, and collected roots, berries, fruit and shellfish. They also cooked and served all the meals—a task that annoyed Persephone like no other. Even when she'd been enslaved, she'd detested having to serve men who couldn't be bothered to say "please" and "thank you" when she laid food on the table before them.

The idea that she should have to do so now even though she was an acknowledged princess was galling beyond measure!

Azriel said "please" and "thank you," of course, but he also looked at her as though he'd like to lay *her* on the table before him. Well, once he'd gotten used to the sight of her wearing the unflattering kjole, he did. The first time he'd seen her in the shapeless Marinese garment he'd looked so utterly dismayed that Persephone had nearly started laughing. This urge to laugh had vanished abruptly a few minutes later, however, when he'd made a spectacle of them both by absently laying his hand upon the back of her thigh and murmuring endearments to her while she was serving him. A very large spoonful of steaming mashed tuber "accidentally" deposited into his lap had inspired him to remove his hand, and his startled shrieks had distracted the Marinese from his immodest behavior, but Persephone had been on her guard ever since. She had the feeling that she and Azriel were not going to be granted an audience with the Elders until they'd been judged worthy to stand before them, and she was determined that this would happen as soon as may be. Not only for Finn's sake and for that of Rachel, left to fend for herself in Syon, but also for the sake of the mother Persephone had never known. Though Fey had been dead and gone these many years, Persephone could not abide the thought of bringing shame upon her memory by acting the harlot in the presence of her people.

As she hauled a brimming serving dish of mussels into the dining hall on the evening of the eighth day after their arrival in the village, Persephone thought for the thousandth time that Azriel wasn't making the situation any easier. Though she knew he worked as hard as any man in the village, he'd failed utterly in his attempt to master the Marinese men's habit of ignoring their women. Indeed, during the rare moments when the two of them found themselves in the same room together—like this particular moment, for example—his eyes followed her relentlessly, and the hunger she saw in them seemed to grow fiercer with each passing day. Or was it her own hunger she saw in his eyes? Hunger borne of the memory of lying in his arms, and the feel of his lips upon her throat, and the feel of his hands upon her—

"Careful," murmured Ekatarina as Persephone barreled into a man who had yet to be seated, nearly dumping the dish of mussels down his white shirtfront.

"Sorry," she muttered, bowing her head to hide the flush brought on by her thoughts. Out of the corner of her eye, she saw Azriel smile in a way that made her think he knew exactly why she was blushing.

The thought made her blush harder.

"Daughter of Fey?" said the man she'd bumped into.

"Yes?" she blurted, looking up in surprise at the fact that he'd actually spoken to her.

"The Elders will see you and your husband now."

The man led Persephone and Azriel to a well-lit domicile on the other side of the village square.

"Roark!" Persephone exclaimed in amazement as she shrugged off the heavy cloak she'd been given to shield her from the wind and the rain. "*You* are one of the Elders?"

"I am," he replied with his usual stiffness.

Persephone was about to comment that he was awfully young

to be an Elder when it occurred to her that she'd hardly seen any old men in the village. Hot on the heels of this thought came the thought that this was probably because most of the old men, being the Marinese's finest craftsmen, had long ago allowed themselves to be given to the Erok as tribute in the hope that the rest of their people might be spared.

Just as my mother allowed herself to be given to my father, realized Persephone with a start.

"Are you all right?" whispered Azriel, touching her elbow.

"Fine!" she whispered back as she scurried away from him.

After giving the other Elders a rather pained look, Roark cleared his throat and said, "Daughter of Fey, I have told my brethren of your desire to know what your mother gave and said to us in the desperate days before she returned to Parthania to wed your father the Erok king, Octavio."

"So she did give you something, then?" breathed Persephone.

"Yes," said Roark shortly. "And though some might argue that the gift and the words she entrusted to us should remain in our keeping, the majority of my brethren feel that as her daughter, they are yours by right."

"It was a gift that she gave you, then—a gift from the Methusian Balthazar?" pressed Persephone, who could not resist looking over at Azriel, who looked just as excited as she felt.

Roark nodded. Then, after only a moment's hesitation, he lifted from his lap a small, exquisitely carved box that Persephone had not noticed before.

"What is that?" she asked in a hushed voice.

Instead of answering, Roark lifted the lid. There, lying on a bed of finest silk was a . . . leafy twig.

Before Persephone could feel even a hint of disappointment at how remarkably ordinary it looked, the Elder sitting next to Roark said, "The Methusian Balthazar told your mother that he plucked this sprig from the lone banyan tree he found growing upon the banks of the Pool of Genezing. I cannot say if he spoke the truth, but I can say upon my honor that for more than eighteen years its leaves have remained as fresh and dewy as the day I first laid eyes upon them."

Persephone's chest felt tight. "Could it be a Methusian trick, Azriel?" she asked.

When he shook his head without looking at her, Persephone exhaled softly and put her trembling hand to her lips.

Some part of her had always believed that their quest was a wild goose chase.

This little leafy twig all but proved that it was not.

It all but proved that the healing pool truly existed and that there was hope—*real* hope—that if they were able to get off the island in time, they might find the pool and save Finn's life.

"Do you know if Balthazar told Fey anything that might lead us to the healing pool, Roark?" asked Azriel, tearing his gaze away from the sprig.

"He did not," replied the Marinese man as he reluctantly handed the tiny carved box to Persephone. "However, Fey did say that before he was taken up by the old king's guards, the Gorgish ambassador told her that Balthazar had given him a map that showed the location of the pool."

"*A map?*" exclaimed Persephone and Azriel in unison.

"Yes," said Roark calmly. "According to the Gorgish ambassador, Balthazar gave it to him because he was the cleverest person in all of Parthania."

Azriel snorted and rolled his eyes to show what he thought of this.

"I believe the Gorgish ambassador spoke these words to Fey," said Roark a little testily. "Whether he spoke the truth or not, no one will ever know."

"*I* know—" began Azriel.

"That we are most grateful that you've shared with us all that you know," interjected Persephone, resisting the urge to jab her elbow into Azriel's ribs.

Appearing somewhat mollified, Roark nodded. "I know also that you seek urgent passage back to the mainland," he said to Persephone's feet. "However, I'm afraid that will have to wait until after the storms have passed. Though we have whaling boats at our camp on the north shores of the island, they would be battered to bits in the channel, and since there is no captain in Parthania fool enough to sail from Syon in such conditions, there is no hope of flagging down a passing ship."

"I understand," said Persephone in a low voice as she clutched the tiny carved box to her sinking heart. "And I thank you—for everything."

Looking her full in the face for the first time since finding her on the beach with her clothes barely back on and her lips yet swollen from Azriel's kisses, Roark said, "That you continue to behave as you have these past eight days is all the thanks I and my people require, Daughter of Fey."

After fervently promising that she would do so, Persephone bid Roark, the other Elders *and* Azriel goodbye. Then she threw her heavy cloak around her shoulders and left the domicile. As soon as she stepped outside, she saw Ekatarina gliding across the village square toward her. Waving to get the younger girl's attention, Persephone pointed first to the backhouses half-hidden in the mulberry trees at the edge of the village and then to the silkworm domicile. Though Ekatarina's frown made it clear that she was yet uneasy with the idea of her charge tending to the call of nature unchaperoned, she nodded reluctantly, turned and headed toward the silkworm domicile.

Feeling almost as grateful for the girl's cooperation as she did that the wind had temporarily died down and the rain had slowed to a drizzle, Persephone slowly made her way toward the backhouses. She didn't actually need to tend to the call of nature, but she did want a few minutes to herself so that she could reflect on all that the Elders had revealed. Though she'd been disappointed to learn that there was no chance of her and Azriel making it back to the mainland until after the storms had ended, she'd been expecting as much. What she hadn't been expecting was that she and Azriel would be given proof that the healing pool existed, and that they'd learn that an actual map of its whereabouts might exist.

As she picked her way around the trees that sheltered the backhouses, Persephone thought about the map. In spite of Azriel's skepticism, she thought that if Balthazar had known he was about to be arrested and had wanted to ensure that the location of the pool would not be lost with him, giving a map to the Gorgish ambassador would have been a shrewd course of action, indeed.

Since it was common knowledge that he disliked the Gorgish ambassador, she thought, *no one would ever dream that he might be the one who—*

The sharp snap of a twig directly behind her drove the rest of the thought from her head and set alarm bells clanging. Persephone whirled around to face the threat only to find herself blinking up into the smiling face of her ne'er-do-well husband as he swiftly slid his arms around her and expertly eased them both down onto a surprisingly comfortable bed of moss.

"Azriel!" she gasped, wondering if her heart might burst right out of her chest.

"Hello, wife," he said in a pleased voice. "Fancy meeting you here."

Persephone opened her mouth to tell him to get off her, but he silenced her with a long, deep kiss.

"What was that you were going to say?" he asked as he idly brushed his lips back and forth across her left earlobe before turning his attentions to the one on the right.

"Uh . . . uh . . ."

"That's what I thought," he said with a chuckle. "I know we have much to talk about, but I've missed you too desperately to think about talking just now."

He kissed her again, then, so deliciously that Persephone could not help kissing him back—tentatively at first, then with greater and greater urgency until . . .

"Azriel, please!" she gasped, wrenching her lips away from his.

"Well, all right—since you asked so nicely," he murmured, leaning in for another kiss.

She was just barely able to summon the strength to turn away from him again. "Azriel, we must stop," she pleaded. "We can't do this!"

"I bet we can if we really, *really* try."

"No! I mean . . . Roark . . . he . . . uh . . ."

Persephone knew there was something very important she needed to tell Azriel about Roark, but the feel of his hands on her was blotting out rational thought.

When he slowly started to tug up the hem of her kjole, however, rational thought returned with an unpleasant jolt.

"I said stop!" she snapped.

Azriel froze instantly. Then he slowly sat back on his heels and raised his hands where she could see them. Still panting slightly, he said, "I . . . do not understand what the problem is, for it is clear that you are as eager as I—"

"The problem is that after what happened on the beach—"

"Which was so incredible that I have thought about it every waking moment since," he breathed, his blue eyes blazing down at her.

"That . . . that's not the point," she stammered, trying not to get distracted. "The point is that I cannot even imagine what Roark and the others would think if they caught us here now."

Azriel shook his head and rose to his feet. As he did so, Persephone heard him mutter something under his breath.

"What was that?" she asked.

"Nothing," he said as he leaned over to help her up.

"It wasn't nothing," she said, ignoring his proffered hand. "I heard you say something—what was it?"

"It doesn't matter," he said.

"It matters to me," she insisted.

"Fine," he said with a sigh. "I said that I don't care what Roark and the others would think."

"Well, you *should*," said Persephone indignantly.

"Why are you shouting at me?"

"I'm not shouting!"

"Yes, you are."

"NO, I'M NOT!"

"Daughter of Fey?" came a hesitant voice from nearby.

Looking up, Persephone was mortified to see kind, sweet Ekatarina peeping around the side of the backhouse, her eyes bugging halfway out of her head at the sight of her charge sitting in the dirt with her kjole hiked up to her thighs, bawling at her handsome Methusian husband like a fishwife on market day.

"E-Ekatarina," stammered Persephone, scrambling to her feet. "It's not what you—"

"I waited for you in the silkworm domicile," interrupted the younger girl, who seemed to be taking great pains to avoid looking at Azriel. "When you didn't come, I got worried and came looking for you. I never thought that I would find you . . ."

Her voice trailed off.

"Neither did I," said Persephone hurriedly, cringing at the fact that the girl would not look her in the eye. "Come—let us go to the silkworm domicile at once."

"A good idea," replied Ekatarina, who went bright pink before adding, "You'll need to replace your cloak anyway, for, uh, the one you're wearing has mud stains on the back and I do not think Roark would be best pleased if he saw that."

Persephone opened her mouth then shut it again. Then she started walking.

"Persephone—wait," called Azriel.

But Persephone did not wait.

Mortified, disheveled and on the verge of tears, she walked away from him without a backward glance.

That night, as Persephone lay on the pallet next to Ekaterina, she spent hours replaying in her head both the grapple with Azriel and the fight that had followed. Every time she thought about the grapple, she felt the same hot flood of desire. The longer she thought about the fight, however, the more her view of it changed. At first furious with Azriel for not caring what Roark and the others would think even though it was clearly important to her, she reluctantly came to admit that he hadn't stated his position aloud until she'd pushed him to do so. And that even if it was indeed how he felt, he'd yet gone to great effort not to behave publicly in a manner that would offend her mother's people. And that though the two of them had spoken with raised voices in the end, it was she who'd raised her voice first.

Indeed, Persephone's view of the fight so evolved that by morning, she'd resolved to find a way to speak privately with Azriel so that she might apologize. That the only respectable place for a husband and wife to find privacy in the Marinese village was the "coupling domicile" was daunting—indeed, just the thought of having Roark wish her good luck was enough to make her toes curl with embarrassment. But if there was no other way for her to be alone with Azriel, she would force herself to go there.

For his sake . . . and her own.

Before she could find a way to make amends with Azriel, however, Persephone had to help the other women serve the men their morning meal. As she was hastily splashing her face with cold water so that she wouldn't be late reaching the dining domicile, Ekatarina told her she needn't hurry so.

"Why not?" asked Persephone, halting her ablutions mid-splash.

"Because they're gone," replied Ekatarina.

Like the other girls in the domicile, she was sitting at the edge of her pallet plaiting her white-blond hair.

"Who's gone?" asked Persephone, straightening up from the stone washbasin.

"The men," replied Ekatarina.

Persephone stared at her. "What do you mean?" she asked as droplets of cold water trickled unnoticed down her wet face into the collar of her kjole. "Where have they gone?"

"They left before dawn for the whaling camp at the northern tip of the island," explained the girl sitting across from Ekatarina.

"Azriel never said anything about going to any whaling camp," said Persephone hollowly.

Ekatarina's cheeks turned very pink. "Perhaps he was . . . distracted," she said. "Or perhaps he saw no reason to tell you. After all, men's business is not women's business."

Brushing aside both explanations with a sweep of her hand, Persephone said, "When will the men return, Ekatarina?"

"Not until the hunt is over, the fat is rendered, the meat is salted and the bones are picked clean."

"And when will that be?"

Ekatarina hesitated before replying, "The end of the storm season."

"The end of the storm season!" gasped Persephone. "But . . . but that could be *months*!"

"Yes," said the younger girl, who sounded as though she was not without sympathy when she added, "it could."

Forty-Five

THERE SHE WAS AGAIN—the princess's pretty friend!

The man in meanest homespun wandered slowly through the bustling market with his hood pulled as far forward as it could go, watching her out of the corner of his eye. He'd surreptitiously done so for many days, ever since the disguised princess and the Methusian had boarded the ship bound for the Island of Ru. That the ship had returned to the storm-tossed harbor without them aboard had, of course, caused the man much dismay. However, as there'd been nothing that he could do but wait and see if they turned up after the storms abated, he'd had to content himself with keeping an eye on the princess's friend.

As it happened, he'd come to enjoy the task very much. The princess's friend was so pretty and pleasant and kind to one and all! She favored vendors with such smiles that they could not resist inviting her to sample their wares, and she always had a spare coin or piece of bread for the hungry urchins that others shooed away with brooms and bellows.

At first, the man had watched her comings and goings through the window of the tiny room he'd rented in the inn across the market from where she was staying. Eventually, however, he'd been unable to resist venturing out into the market for a closer look. Before doing so, he'd thoroughly bathed and had the innkeeper's wife launder his clothes, for the prospect of being nearer the princess's friend had made him suddenly, uncomfortably aware of his own stink and of the filthiness of his garments. Indeed, such was his desire to present himself well (even though he *obviously* had no intention of *actually* presenting himself) that the man had been sorely tempted to buy himself an outfit fashioned from velvet and brocade instead of homespun. Though he could easily have done so using only a few coins from the bulging purse his master in this matter had given to him, he'd ultimately resisted temptation. Calling attention to himself by dressing like a peacock might have jeopardized his historic mission and he could not, in good conscience, risk that for the sake of looking good for a girl.

Besides, all the velvet and brocade in the world could not camouflage some things.

That was why the man kept his hood forward now as he wandered through the market, trailing after the princess's friend. As usual, he noted the deliberate way she shopped for her food and the fact that she refused to buy herself even the most trifling trinkets no matter how sorely tempted she appeared to be. The man knew that the care with which she spent her money almost certainly meant that she did not have enough of it. And since he did not believe that the princess and the Methusian would have deliberately left the girl behind to struggle, it most likely meant that they'd not intended to be gone for as long as they had been.

It was something to think about.

The man in *freshly laundered* homespun watched now as the princess's friend selected an apple, counted out a few coppers to give to the vendor and gently placed the apple into the little shopping basket she'd presumably borrowed from the innkeeper's wife. The man was so close behind her that he could see the bruises on the piece of fruit she'd selected, and he could smell the clean, soapy scent of her skin. He knew he shouldn't be following her so closely and yet he couldn't help himself. She was so pretty and her hair was so shiny and the sound of her humming softly to herself made his heart swell in his chest and—

She turned around so unexpectedly that they bumped right into each other. As they did so, the apple was knocked from her basket. Horrified by his clumsiness, the man quickly leaned over to pick it up and promptly bashed heads with the princess's friend, who'd likewise leaned over to pick it up.

"Oh!" he cried as he staggered backward. "Oh, miss! I'm so sorry! I was just . . . I didn't mean—"

"You needn't sound so troubled, sir," she said with a smile. "You didn't exactly inflict a mortal wound, and anyway, I am quite sure that it was I who knocked into you." Ducking down a little so that she could peer into the shadows of his hood, she smiled again and said, "Are you quite recovered from my heartless attack?"

Wordlessly, he nodded.

Smiling for a third time, she bobbed him a little curtsey, bid him good day and continued on her way.

The man in homespun could hardly breathe.

The princess's friend had looked upon him and she'd not recoiled or gasped or shrieked or cried out.

On the contrary, she'd *smiled* at him!

The man was dazzled. Truly, the princess's friend was as pretty on the inside as she was on the outside. Perhaps . . . perhaps he could find a way to do her some small, anonymous kindness.

It was something else to think about.

As he slowly made his way over to the other side of the market, it occurred to the man in homespun that the one who'd sent him had not given him any instructions as to what he ought to do with the princess's friend if the princess and the Methusian ended up dead.

Now that he was in the habit of thinking instead of just following orders, the man decided that he'd have to think about that, too.

Forty-Six

IN SPITE OF THE GREAT luxury in which he'd traveled, Mordesius had found the three-day journey to Lord Bartok's northern estate arduous. Though the carriage in which he and Lord Bartok rode was richly appointed with plump, velvet seats and heavy curtains to keep out the dust, nothing could prevent the endless bumping and jostling that bounced Mordesius around until every muscle in his poor body was screaming in pain. And while they'd obviously not stopped at any flea-bitten inns along the way, instead choosing to enjoy the hospitality of noblemen who'd pretended to be honored to host them in royal fashion at exorbitant personal expense, it was not the same as sleeping in one's own bed.

Most of this third day had been spent traveling through Lord Bartok's vast estate, which consisted of pastures and parklands, orchards and pleasure gardens, wheat fields and forests. Mordesius felt his guts twist into knots every time he nudged back the curtain, gazed out upon the staggering wealth the high-and-mighty bastard had accumulated as a result of his own munificence and thought about how little he'd profited in return.

"Isn't it beautiful, Your Grace?" murmured Lord Bartok, gracefully stifling a yawn with the back of one hand.

"It is," said Mordesius, just managing not to snarl.

Soon, he would have the king back in his possession.

And with a little luck and some shrewd planning, the odds of the game would shift back in his favor.

It was nearing dusk by the time the carriage finally turned onto a long avenue paved with crushed white quartz and lined with apple trees in full blossom. At length, the avenue led them through a set of massive wrought-iron gates emblazoned with the Bartok family crest and into the elegantly manicured courtyard at the front of Bartok's sprawling stone castle. There was no Lady Bartok to greet them, she having died of the dread Great Sickness several years past. However, there were eight footmen dressed in blue and gold waiting to help Mordesius and Lord Bartok alight from the carriage, several lesser servants on hand to tend to Mordesius's large retinue of New Men, and at least a dozen wide-eyed servant girls who bobbed pretty curtseys and breathlessly told Mordesius how honored they were to have the pleasure of serving him.

With the passing thought that one or two might have the pleasure of serving him in more ways than one during the course of his visit, Mordesius impatiently declined Lord Bartok's suggestion that they wash off the dust of the road before calling on the king. Raising a silvery eyebrow ever so slightly, as though he found Mordesius's manners uncouth but was too refined to say so, Lord Bartok nodded, turned and personally led Mordesius to the wing of the castle reserved for visiting royalty. Upon arriving at what was clearly the finest set of chambers in the wing, he ordered the guards to announce them to His Majesty.

Not sure what he'd do if the king refused to receive him, Mordesius decided not to take the chance. Brushing past the guards, he shoved open the door only to be confronted by a sight that nearly caused his heart to stop.

It was the king and Lady Aurelia *naked in bed together!*

"Aurelia!" cried Lord Bartok in a not-quite-convincing tone of outrage.

As the delicate-boned little noblewoman fluttered about trying to cover herself, the king attempted to sit up. The first time he faltered and fell back onto his pillows. The second time he was seized by a violent fit of coughing that caused him to bring up so much black blood that he had to lean over and spit it into a silver bowl already swimming with the vile stuff.

On the third attempt, he finally managed to push himself into a sitting position.

"Do not fret, Your Grace, my lord Bartok," said King Finnius breathlessly, nodding to each of them in turn. "For you see, Lady Aurelia and I are married."

Mordesius felt his mouth fall open.

"*Queen* Aurelia," reminded the shrew with a hint of sharpness.

"Queen Aurelia," agreed the king, appearing not to have noticed her unpleasant tone. Fixing his darkly shadowed, sunken eyes upon Mordesius, he said, "During our weeks spent on progress seeing the countryside and meeting my subjects—"

"*Our* subjects," interjected Lady Aurelia more sharply still.

The king nodded and suffered another wracking fit. "The point is," he wheezed when he'd recovered sufficiently to speak, "we developed such a great affection for one another that we could not wait another moment to wed. Thus it was that three days ago we were married in your family's private chapel, Lord Bartok. The ceremony was appropriately witnessed, the license was duly signed and yesterday a herald was sent to court with the news. You probably passed him on your way here."

They probably passed him on their way here! That meant it was too late to stop him. It meant that even now he might be shouting the news from the Grand Balcony!

Mordesius had thought that "losing" the king had been a disaster. It was nothing compared to this. The Council would never entertain the possibility of naming him heir now, *never*! Why would they, when the king had wedded and bedded a wife who might even now be carrying his royal child? What a terrible mistake it had been to play the waiting game with Bartok. He'd known the high-and-mighty bastard was lying. What on earth had he been waiting for? And the king! The fool—did he really imagine that he could do something like this and not see those dearest to him suffer terrible consequences?

Mordesius was about to demand to speak with the king in private when the king said, "My Lord Regent, I wish to speak with you in private. Lord Bartok, please escort His Grace to the library at once."

"Yes, Your Majesty," said Lord Bartok. Bowing low to the king, he gave Mordesius an inscrutable glance and said, "This way, Your Grace."

And before Mordesius could say a word, the nobleman turned on one heel and walked out of the room.

Mordesius, who was already spitting with rage, nearly had an apoplexy when the one-legged slattern who'd taken over from the nursemaid tapped past him in the direction of the royal chambers from which he'd just been so rudely evicted. Nevertheless, he forced himself to calmly follow Lord Bartok to the library, stopping only once along the way to mention something to a passing servant.

Upon entering the vaulted chamber with its imposing leather armchairs and shelves full of dusty, leather-bound tomes, he fixed Lord Bartok with his dark eyes and demanded to know if the marriage had been his doing.

"No, Your Grace," replied Lord Bartok solemnly.

Liar! shrieked Mordesius in his mind. Out loud, he said, "Well, then, I can only imagine how terribly shocked you must be by your daughter's wanton behavior—"

"It is not wanton for a wife to lie with her wedded husband," interrupted Lord Bartok with a slight smile.

Clenching his hands into fists to prevent himself from raking his fingernails down the bastard's smug face, Mordesius said, "Still, you must be disappointed to have been robbed of the honor of hosting a royal wedding—"

"Robbed of the honor of *paying* for a royal wedding, you mean," said Lord Bartok, still smiling slightly.

Knowing that, at a minimum, he needed Lady Aurelia dead as quickly as possible and that for that to happen he was going to have to get her beyond the protection of her powerful father, Mordesius said, "You may have been robbed of that honor, my lord, but I shall *insist* upon hosting a banquet celebrating the nuptials as soon as the happy couple and I have returned to Parthania and—"

Now, Lord Bartok's smile grew very wide. "Aurelia will not be returning to Parthania," he said. "For you see, the king has advised me he wishes her to remain here with me."

Bristling, Mordesius snapped, "She shall go where I order."

"She is not yours to order, Your Grace," pointed out Lord Bartok. "She is Queen of Glyndoria."

"She has not been anointed."

"She has married the king, whom I believe I hear approaching even now," murmured Lord Bartok with an elegant shrug as the door to the library swung open. "Goodbye, Your Grace. If you still have an appetite following your audience with His Majesty, I will see you at supper."

Turning toward the open door, Lord Bartok bowed low to the king before quietly leaving the library and closing the door behind him.

Impeccably dressed in black leather breeches, a white silk shirt and a wine-colored velvet doublet that looked as though it had been padded to camouflage his painful thinness, the king approached Mordesius slowly. Even so, the tiny beads of sweat on his upper lip told Mordesius that the effort of walking was taxing him terribly.

Good.

Mordesius waited until the king was close enough to threaten without having to raise his voice. Then he hissed, "You have made a grave error, Your Majesty—"

"No, Mordesius—it is you who has erred," interrupted the king, not troubling himself to whisper. "It was convenient for you to see me as a fool entirely in your power and so that is how you saw me. But your vision was a false one. For though it is true that I made mistakes along the way, in the end I accomplished that which mattered most: I have saved the realm from *you*. My queen and I have spent the last three days in bed and I would lay odds that she is already with child. You will never sit upon the throne of my forefathers, Mordesius. Indeed, I'd not be surprised if my new father-in-law has already set plans in motion to oust you from power altogether. I turned your plans to my own advantage by playing the fool to buy time to put my own plans into effect. I played *you*, Mordesius," said the king, breathless but triumphant. "And now the game is over."

With this, the king pressed a handkerchief against his lips and struggled to stifle a cough. As he did so, Mordesius gaped at him the way one might gape at a mouse that has just turned into a lion.

"The game . . . the game is not over until I say it is over," he finally spluttered. "You *will* obey me, or I will leave your nursemaid to starve! I will order my vast army of New Men to slaughter thousands of your lowborn subjects! I will—"

"The thought of the evils you might perpetrate grieves me more terribly than someone like you could ever imagine," panted the king, pulling the bloodstained cloth away from his mouth. "Nevertheless, I cannot allow myself to be held hostage by evil. Moira and all those who die at your hand or by your command will know that they did not die in vain nor because they were not loved by their king."

"I will tell them that you abandoned them," spat Mordesius.

"They will never believe you."

Mordesius stared at the king, malevolence oozing out of every pore. "And what of your beloved sister, the long-lost Princess Persephone?" he sneered. "She will shortly return to Parthania—"

"No, she won't," said the king with certainty, before falling victim to another of his wracking fits.

Mordesius stood heaving like a bellows. He'd hated many people in his life, but he'd never hated anybody more than he hated the sickly boy who stood before him at that moment.

Because Finnius was not a boy anymore, he was a man. And not just a man but a king. And not just a king but a *great* king.

Mordesius couldn't wait to kill him.

Abruptly, he clapped his gnarled hands together three times. Upon the instant, the dozen New Man soldiers who'd been summoned by the servant in the corridor silently filed into the room. Ten of them took possession of the king, who did not even try to fight them off. While they hurriedly escorted him and Mordesius to the waiting carriage, the two other soldiers went to inform Lord Bartok that, regrettably, matters of state had required the king and the Regent to depart unexpectedly. Oh, and also to politely let Bartok know about the two thousand soldiers who were camped just north of his estate. Mordesius had seen no need to have Bartok told that if he did not accept the king's unexpected departure with good grace that these New Men would descend upon the estate, razing crops, slaughtering livestock, burning buildings and murdering every living soul they encountered.

Lord Bartok was many things, but stupid he was not.

Mordesius and the king did not travel beneath the royal standard because Mordesius did not wish to draw attention to them. If news of the king's nuptials had already spread, he did not think he'd be able to resist the urge to have his men beat to death any well-wisher who dared to toss a posy of flowers after the carriage or call out blessings for a fruitful royal marriage.

So, rather than traveling as befits a king—or even a Regent, for that matter—they traveled as fast as they could with minimal escort. The journey was brutally hard on Mordesius but even harder on the king. As soon as they reached the courtyard of the imperial palace in Parthania, Mordesius had the coughing, nearly unconscious fool whisked up to his chambers and put under guard with strict instructions that no one but his physicians were permitted to see him.

Content that the king would not be stolen out from under his nose again since the guards *and* the physicians were all his creatures and clearly understood that they'd be boiled alive if it were to happen, Mordesius lurched to his own chambers and collapsed into his chair by the fire. That he now had the king back in his keeping was not really a triumph because although he possessed the fool's body, he no longer possessed his mind and spirit. Moreover, if his sickly seed had indeed taken root in the belly of Bartok's spawn, nine months hence a royal child would be born and that would change *everything*.

Mordesius had just begun to despair anew that such a disastrous outcome might spell the end of his glorious ambitions when it hit him: A solution so simple and perfect that he could not believe he'd not thought of it before.

For a long moment, Mordesius sat rigidly still—probing for weaknesses, looking for flaws.

There were none.

Though he hadn't realized it until that moment, the simple fact was that he had no need of the king or Lord Bartok or the rest of the worms on the Council, after all.

He could have what he wanted, and they could all go straight to hell!

Hurriedly shuffling over to his desk, Mordesius penned a hasty note to Murdock ordering him to cease following the princess and return to Parthania at once. Smiling to himself, he added a short postscript before bellowing for a messenger. When one appeared a moment later, Mordesius noticed that it was the letter delivery boy who'd so taunted him with his graceful hands some weeks past. Narrowing his eyes, Mordesius shoved the letter at the youth and informed him that if it did not reach the General within five days, his hands would be chopped off and fed to the dogs.

After the trembling imbecile had fled, Mordesius, who was also trembling but probably for different reasons, sat back in his chair. With luck, the storms would not yet have abated and the General would still be convalescing at the New Man training outpost north of Syon. If he was not there but had resumed the hunt, Mordesius would have to take drastic measures to track him down and ensure that he did not kill the princess under any circumstances.

Mordesius smiled again. Knowing Murdock, he would be perturbed at being recalled to Parthania. He would also fret over the possibility that the princess and the cockroach would find the pool but refuse to reveal its location. It was a risk, and one Mordesius had initially hoped to eliminate altogether by sending Murdock after them in secret. Yet Mordesius had never considered it a significant risk. The princess and the cockroach knew that the king would die if they did not return to Parthania by the time the last white bean was plucked from the jar. And since the princess loved her brother and the cockroach lusted after the princess, Mordesius was confident that they would return, either with proof that they'd found the pool or with a plea for more time.

And when they did . . . well, he, Mordesius, would be one step closer to having everything he'd dreamed of having.

And so much more.

Forty-Seven

GENERAL MURDOCK STARED unblinking out the open window of his small chamber in the New Man training camp, slowly chewing a small bite of cooling liver. A message had just arrived from the Regent Mordesius. It had been written six days earlier, and while the exhausted, mud-splattered messenger had appeared most distressed by this fact, General Murdock was not pondering the reason for the young man's distress.

No, what General Murdock was pondering was the reason he was being recalled to Parthania before completing his mission. The Regent's message had given no indication why this should be so. Nor had it given any indication of how the Regent intended to ensure that the princess and her Methusian husband did not abandon their search for the mythical healing pool. Or worse, find the pool but disappear without bringing this information to him.

With a rather detached sense of unease, General Murdock wondered if he might be in danger. He wondered if perhaps the Regent was displeased that he'd allowed himself to sustain an injury, or if the Regent's favor had fallen upon another, or if the Regent had somehow discovered that his last report had not been entirely truthful. In it, General Murdock had said that he had reason to believe that the princess and the Methusian had been stranded on the Island of Ru by the arrival of the storms. What he'd *not* said was that according to intelligence gathered from the docks at Syon, the princess and the

Methusian had, in fact, been tossed off the ship upon which they'd been sailing. While it was possible that they'd drowned or been devoured by sharks, it was also possible that they'd made it to the island alive. And since General Murdock had had no way to confirm what had actually happened, he'd sought to spare the Regent undue worry by omitting altogether the fact that they'd been tossed overboard.

Leaning over to frown at an almost imperceptible stain on the white linen tablecloth, General Murdock decided that he was probably not in danger. He'd never known the Regent to spy upon him, and he'd held his master's favor for many years. Besides, His Grace knew that he was loyal and hard-working, and he'd never asked for anything but to be allowed to continue to serve.

Nevertheless, General Murdock thought that it couldn't hurt to arrange a gift—a small token of his continued devotion to the Regent and his glorious ambitions. Since he was to return to Parthania at once, he would be unable to personally oversee the gift being brought to fruition.

However, he'd send soldiers enough to ensure that the job was done thoroughly, and he was certain that the Regent would appreciate the sentiment.

Pleased with his decision, General Murdock took a small sip of ruby-red claret from the crystal goblet on the table before him. Then, picking up the Regent's note, he reread the postscript that the Regent had added.

It seemed that the commander of the outpost was eager to try his boots on for size.

With a sigh, General Murdock set the note back on the table. The commander had been instrumental in saving his life and had served him tirelessly while he'd convalesced from his belly wound. It was unfortunate that he was going to be required to teach the man a lesson regarding the inappropriateness of trying to supplant a superior.

Sawing off another small bite of liver, General Murdock carefully placed it in his mouth and began to chew. As he did so, he wondered if the commander was going to be able to appreciate the irony of attempting to try on his superior's boots even though he'd had his feet removed.

Probably not.

In General Murdock's experience, most military men lacked the depth and refinement required to appreciate such subtleties.

Pity.

Forty-Eight

Eighteen white beans left in the jar

PERSEPHONE STARED DOWN at the writhing mess of worms, leaves and filth. Taking a deep breath through her mouth, she closed her eyes and tried to imagine a more pleasant sight, but it was no use.

Her gorge rose abruptly. Dashing across the silkworm domicile, she shoved open the door and got her head outside just before she started to heave. Since she'd barely eaten anything for breakfast, it didn't take long to empty her stomach. Even so, by the time she was done, her head and shoulders were rain soaked and she felt thoroughly chilled by the wind. Pulling herself back inside the warm domicile, she began shakily drying off with the scrap of silk she used for such purpose most mornings.

Ekatarina frowned with sympathy and said, "There is a saying among our people, Daughter of Fey."

"Oh?" said Persephone, wiping her mouth with the back of her hand. "And what is that?"

"'Cleaning the silkworm feeding tray is not for the weak-stomached,'" intoned the young Marinese girl reverently.

The other girls who were cleaning trays chuckled at this. Persephone smiled weakly, then slowly made her way back to the long work table.

In the nearly eight weeks since Azriel had been gone, she'd spent every morning helping Ekatarina tend to the silkworms, every afternoon learning how to spear fish and every evening toiling over a loom. In that time, she'd learned that she was no better at weaving than she was at sewing, that she had a natural gift for spearfishing and that everything about silkworms utterly revolted her. From the grating *snip, snip, snip* sound of them eating their precious mulberry leaves to the staggering amounts of excrement they produced to the way the fattest of them wriggled between her fingers when she transferred them to fresh feeding trays.

Indeed, between the silkworms, the foul weather and the high seaweed-and-mystery-tuber content of the Marinese diet, it was no wonder that she felt wretched half the time!

In her heart, of course, Persephone knew there was another reason she felt so wretched, and it was that she'd not seen or heard from Azriel since the night of their fight behind the backhouses. Though he and the other men were camped less than half a day's hike north, it was commonly understood that they were far too busy to return to the village for even a short visit. And when Persephone had recklessly suggested to Ekatarina that the two of them hike up to the whaling camp to see them, the young Marinese girl had looked at her like she'd just suggested opening a brothel.

"Roark and the other Elders would *never* permit such a thing," Ekatarina had whispered, flicking her downcast eyes in the direction of a passing Elder, one of the few men who remained in the village. "Besides," Ekatarina had continued cheerfully, once he was out of earshot, "we are not needed at the whaling camp, and we *are* needed here. Why on earth would we want to go see the men, anyway?"

In response, Persephone had shivered slightly at the memory of Azriel's lips brushing against her right earlobe, but had said nothing.

As the weeks had dragged on, Persephone had tried not to worry, but it had been difficult because there'd been so much to worry *about*. She could not stop thinking about the fact that they'd left Rachel alone in a town teeming with lust-filled soldiers and sailors, and that they'd left her with nothing but a handful of coins and a promise that they'd return in two days, three at the most. And though she'd left the Regent's jar of beans with Rachel, Persephone could count well enough to know that if the storm season did not end soon, all hope of finding the healing pool and saving Finn would be lost. On top of all this, each day while she and her fellow "silkworm mothers" were tending the vile little creatures, the other girls insisted upon incessantly sharing with Persephone the many terrible dangers of the whale hunt.

"Hardly a season goes by without at least one death," said the youngest of the silkworm mothers now, repeating the sobering words Persephone had heard a thousand times over the preceding weeks. "We have ever been a sea-loving people, so drownings are rare, though certainly not unheard of."

"Not at all," agreed a second silkworm mother with a frown as she held a particularly juicy specimen up for closer examination. "However, it is more common for men to be crushed to death by the tail of an angry whale intent upon smashing their ship to kindling."

"Or for them to be eaten by one of the monster sharks drawn by the scent of death in the water," offered a third.

Persephone could feel her stomach jumping again and was just about to ask Ekatarina and the others if they could *please* talk about something else when the door of the domicile burst open to reveal a breathless woman in a rain-soaked kjole.

"Daughter of Fey," she panted, clutching her side. "Roark . . . sent me. It is . . . it is your husband . . ."

Persephone went cold.

"Your husband . . . ," panted the woman, perching both hands on her hips as she struggled to catch her breath. "Your husband . . ."

"What about him?" demanded Persephone, whose clenched fists had begun to shake. "*What about him?*"

Holding up her index finger, the woman took two huge breaths. Then she said, "He has just arrived at the western edge of the village with news of a ship."

Persephone was out the door of the silkworm domicile before Ekatarina could take her rain cloak from the peg on the wall. As fast as she could, she pelted to the western edge of the village. There, she saw Azriel standing near the very path the two of them had followed into the village all those weeks ago.

Without a care for what Roark, the Elders or anyone else might think, she threw herself into Azriel's arms and buried her face against his neck.

"You smell like fish," she whispered, hugging him fiercely.

"You smell like worms," he whispered, hugging her back.

Choking back a burble of half-hysterical laughter, Persephone clutched him more tightly still and murmured, "I'm sorry."

"I'm sorry, too," said Azriel softly. Then, setting her down long before she was ready for him to do so, he said, "Just before dawn this day, one of the men spotted a ship in the channel not far off the northern coast—"

"But the storm season has not yet passed," said Roark with a furtive glance at Azriel's hand, which was holding Persephone tight against his side.

"I know," said Azriel as he let his hand slip from Persephone's waist and stepped away from her. "I cannot explain it. Perhaps the captain is a daring man on a mission of greatest urgency, perhaps he is a madman—"

"Or perhaps he is a New Man come seeking slaves and booty," offered one of the other Elders quietly. "Perhaps he braves the dangers of a channel crossing in the hope of catching us unawares."

"I cannot say that he is not a New Man," admitted Azriel. "However, if he is, perhaps the rescue beacon I lit on the beach at the other end of this path will serve as a warning to him that he has been spotted and that you are *not* unaware."

"You lit a beacon there?" said Persephone in surprise. "Why there? And how did you get from the whaling camp to the beach so quickly?"

"I lit a rescue beacon there instead of at the whaling camp because in the event that the captain paid heed to it, I thought he might not appreciate coming ashore on a mission of mercy only to find himself facing hundreds of harpoon-wielding Marinese. As for how I got to the beach so quickly, at the risk of breaking my neck, I ran—quickly," replied Azriel with his old familiar pirate grin. "Which is what we must do now, wife. When I left the beach, it looked as though the ship was anchoring beyond the reef—but it also looked as though the wind was picking up again. If whoever is aboard that ship is inclined to come ashore to rescue us, they're going to have to do it soon, and we're going to have to be waiting for them on the beach when they do."

Almost before he'd finished speaking, Persephone was running for the domicile she'd shared with Ekatarina and the other silkworm mothers for the past two months. Dashing inside, she shrugged off her kjole, used a length of silk cloth to bind her breasts and hastily pulled on her washed and mended breeches and shirt. She then slipped her treasures—the bit of lace, the rat tail, the auburn curl and the key—into one pocket and slung across her chest a silk pouch containing the tiny carved box in which lay the ever-dewy sprig from the banyan tree. Pleased by the thought that lying next to her heart was proof that the healing pool existed, and that she and Azriel were at last (hopefully!) resuming their quest to find it, she hurried back to him.

Smiling at the sight of her in her boyish clothing, Azriel wordlessly handed her a brimmed cap he'd found for her. As soon as she'd finished tucking her thick braid up under it, Ekatarina handed her a hastily gathered sack of provisions and the spear Persephone had fished with every afternoon. "It has been . . . an experience knowing you, Daughter of Fey," murmured the girl. Casting a darting glance at Roark, she abruptly lifted her head, flashed a smile and added, "A *good* experience—one that I shall treasure always!"

"As shall I," laughed Persephone, giving the younger girl a warm hug.

After hugging each of the other silkworm mothers in turn, Persephone bid goodbye to all the others she'd come to know during her time in the village.

"We need to go now, wife," warned Azriel as Persephone leaned over to pat a small girl on her little blond head.

"I know, I know," said Persephone. Hesitantly, she turned to Roark. Though she'd never particularly cared for the Marinese Elder, and though she suspected that he'd never particularly cared for her, she felt she owed him a great deal more than a simple thank-you.

To her surprise, before she could frame suitable parting words, Roark raised his eyes to hers and said, "Though you are far from being the kind of woman I am comfortable with or accustomed to being around, I have come to think of you as a true daughter of our people, and to believe that your mother would have been proud of you. Best of luck, Daughter of Fey. Know that you will ever have a place among us."

Persephone's surprise at these unexpected words was followed by a rush of gratitude. Resisting the urge to reach out and give Roark's hand a squeeze (a gesture that would almost certainly have utterly horrified him), she said, "Thank you."

It felt like enough.

By the time Persephone and Azriel made it to the beach, there was a flat-bottomed boat struggling through the choppy waves of the lagoon. One of its two occupants had his back to them. He was short, squat, bald and hauling away on the oars for all he was worth. The occupant facing them was filthy, hunched and scowling, with long hair tied back by a colorful head kerchief, a gold hoop earring, a jaunty black eye patch and a bloodstained facial bandage.

Persephone eyed this villain with some trepidation until she noticed his ears.

Or rather, *her* ears.

"I don't believe it," she gasped. "It's Rachel!"

After studying the occupants of the approaching boat carefully for a very long moment, Azriel exclaimed, "You're right! And look how well she's rowing!"

Persephone indignantly began to inform him that she was not referring to the short, squat, bald man. She broke off abruptly, however, when Azriel's smile told her that he was teasing. Shaking her head at his silliness, she smiled, too, and called him a beast in the bargain. And when Rachel's boat was close enough to hail, she followed him from the shelter of the rocks down to the water's edge. Over the howling of the wind, the lashing of the rain and the crashing of the waves, she gruffly called out greetings.

"Arrgh, greetings to you, as well!" replied Rachel in an even gruffer voice.

Perhaps feeling that this response did not sound entirely genuine, the sailor holding the oars eyed Rachel askance. As if to reassure him that she *and* her response were entirely genuine, Rachel snorted deeply and spat noisily over the side of the boat.

Resisting the urge to smile, Persephone jerked her thumb toward Azriel and called, "My, uh, companion and I were shipwrecked before the storms and are looking for quick passage back to the mainland."

"Yar in luck!" boomed Rachel. "For as it happens, yonder ship is bound for Syon. We shall be underway within the hour!"

The sailor looked surprised to hear this. "When you chartered the ship, I thought you told the cap'n that you wanted to search the islands for the dastardly rogue who slashed your face in a duel over a beautiful girl," he said as he irritably picked something out of his soaking beard and flicked it into the water.

"'Tis a man's prerogative to change his mind—" began Rachel.

"Nay, that's a *woman's* prerogative," interrupted the sailor, narrowing his eyes in suspicion.

"Whatever! Arrgh!" said Rachel, who turned to Persephone and Azriel before adding, "Climb aboard, me bonny fellows. Let us return to the ship and set sail at once."

✳

Unlike the trip to the Island of Ru, which had taken only a few hours owing to ideal conditions, the trip back to the mainland took nearly three days. The stormy sea was a savage thing, windswept and rolling with fifteen-foot swells. As it laboriously climbed each swell, the ship that Rachel had chartered listed nauseatingly before righting itself; time and again it was driven off course. Sailors in the rigging shouted and prayed, canvas sails snapped and strained, cargo was washed overboard by rogue waves. Persephone, who'd found the rolling rhythm of the ship and the feel of the wind and spray in her face so invigorating on her trip *to* the island, vomited unceasingly the entire voyage back to the mainland. Indeed, she was so sick that Azriel would not leave her side for a moment, earning him many disgusted looks from the embattled sailors, who clearly believed him to be a useless dandy who had eyes for none but his beloved pretty boy.

It was dusk when the ship finally limped back into port in Syon. Having had no opportunity to speak alone during the voyage, Azriel, Rachel and Persephone debarked as quickly as they were able and headed directly for the little room at the inn by the market. There, Azriel impatiently waited outside while Rachel transformed herself back into a girl. After she'd done so, she headed out to see about supper while he went inside and helped Persephone wash and change. She would have liked to protest, but after three days of continual vomiting she was too weak to give it even a token effort. Sitting limply at the edge of the bed, she allowed Azriel to remove her clothes and gently sponge her clean before helping her into her traveling shift and giving her such a tender kiss on the forehead that she almost started weeping.

As he pulled away with a smile, there was a knock on the door. Half a second later, Rachel strode into the room armed with a wheel of cheese, two loaves of bread and three succulent peaches. She was accompanied by the innkeeper's wife, who carried a cauldron full of steaming stew, three bowls and a large jug of ale.

After the innkeeper's wife left the room, Rachel set the bread, cheese and peaches upon the little table in the center of the room while Azriel served up three bowls of stew, poured three mugs of ale and helped Persephone to a seat at the table.

For a while, the three companions were so intent upon eating that there was no conversation at all. Persephone could feel her strength miraculously returning after only a few tentative bites of nourishing stew; at length, she asked Rachel how she'd paid for all the food.

"Never mind the food," said Azriel as he cut two thick wedges of cheese and handed one to each of the girls. "How did you continue to pay the innkeeper for your room and still have enough money left over to charter a ship? We left you with only a few coins—I can't see how you didn't run out."

"I *did* run out," said Rachel, tearing the crusty end off of one of the loaves of bread. "About a month ago, I spent my last coppers on a bruised apple that one of the vendors in the market was kind enough to sell to me at half the usual price. That night, after removing one of the beans from the little jar as I did every night— just as you asked me to, Princess—I went to bed having no idea what on earth I was going to do. Indeed, I was so worried that I must admit that I prayed for a miracle. And do you know what? The next morning, the very first thing I saw when I opened my eyes was a purse bulging with gold coins. And beside it, a blue hair ribbon and a red rose."

"*What?*" exclaimed Azriel and Persephone.

"All three items were sitting here on this very table," continued Rachel with a smile. "Well, of course I didn't believe for an instant that an *actual* miracle had taken place. In fact, at first I was terribly frightened by the knowledge that a stranger must have crept into my room while I was sleeping. Eventually, however, I decided that I had nothing to fear from any stranger who left such welcome gifts."

"And you never discovered who'd done it?" asked Persephone in disbelief.

"Never, though I've come to think of him as my personal hero. For if he'd not left the purse of gold, I'd never have been able to afford to keep this room and stay fed—not to mention charter that ship and come looking for you. Have I mentioned how relieved I was when I saw you on that beach?"

"Only about a thousand times," said Persephone with a smile.

From her seat across the table, Rachel smiled, too—a mirror image, except for the ears. "Yes, well, the whole time you were gone I kept telling myself that you were still alive, but I don't think I truly believed it until I saw you standing there. Now tell me, for I am simply dying to know: did you meet the Marinese? Did they know anything at all that might be of use?"

Persephone fetched the tiny carved box that Roark had given to her. Opening it, she showed Rachel the leafy sprig and reverently explained where it had come from.

"What's more," Persephone said as she carefully closed the lid of the box, "the Marinese Elders gave us reason to believe that the Gorgishmen may have a map—"

"A map!" exclaimed Rachel in amazement.

"That's what the Elders said," said Azriel before Persephone could answer. "I, for one, do not believe it for many reasons. And even if I am wrong, it will take us four days of hard traveling to get to the Valley of Gorg and four days more to get to Parthania from there. That leaves us with precious little time to befriend the Gorgish, convince them to give us the map—if, indeed, they even have one— then follow the map to—"

"We understand: there isn't much time left," broke in Persephone, trying not to sound impatient. "What is your point, Azriel?"

Azriel hesitated for a long moment before saying, "My point is that I wonder if we might be better off heading straight to Parthania."

Persephone stared at him.

"The journey as I've described it would be taxing in the extreme, wife," he continued. "You're already in a weakened condition—"

"I'm fine," she bristled.

"Moreover, I'm afraid that if we press on, we'll somehow find ourselves unable to make it back to the imperial capital before our hundred days are up," he said, ignoring her prickliness. "If we head there at once it won't be an issue."

"No, but the fact that we've not yet found the pool might," said Rachel, grimacing and shrugging to show that she felt bad about having to point out this rather enormous flaw in Azriel's plan.

"That is true, Rachel," acknowledged Azriel with a faint smile, "but we may be able to bluff our way through if we show the Regent the sprig and tell him that *we* plucked it from the banyan tree that grows at the edge of the pool."

"And if he doesn't believe us?" said Rachel.

"We improvise."

"No," said Persephone with as much vehemence as she could manage in her weakened condition. "I'm sorry, Azriel, but I dare not risk Finn's life on bluffing and improvisation, not while we still have time." Then, before he could offer protest, she said, "Do you remember what you said to me shortly after we left Parthania?"

"Yes," he replied promptly. "I asked if you wanted me to get rid of the leper."

In spite of the seriousness of the moment, Rachel laughed out loud and even Persephone had to smile.

"When I told you that one hundred days was not a lot of time to find something that may not exist, you told me that we did not need a lot of time," she reminded, laying a hand on his bare forearm for the comfort of feeling her skin against his. "You told me that we only needed *enough* time and that if the Fates were willing, we would have it. You said you believed that the Fates were willing."

"Yes, but that was then—"

"And this is now," she said. "And as long as there is *any* time left to us, I say we carry on for the sake of my brother, the king—the *Methusian* king—that he may live to see all people in this realm united in peace."

Forty-Nine

HIS HEAD SPINNING, the man in homespun sidled away from the open window beneath which he'd been crouched listening to the princess's pretty friend talk to the princess and the Methusian.

No, not "the princess's pretty friend"—Rachel.

What a pretty name, Rachel. Almost as pretty as the girl herself!

The man was pleased to know her name at last, and ecstatic to learn that she considered him her personal hero. Indeed, his heart swelled and lifted at the thought. A good thing, too, because it had sunk like a stone when he'd heard her say that she'd initially been frightened by the sight of his gift. He hadn't intended to frighten her—after having accidentally knocked heads with her in the market that day, he'd only wanted to do her a small, anonymous kindness. He knew she'd run out of money, and since he had no real use for the bag of gold he'd been given, he'd decided to give it to her, along with the flower and the hair ribbon. Obviously, walking up and handing her these things had been out of the question, and since they'd surely have been stolen if he'd left them on the ground outside her door at the inn, he'd had no choice but to slip into her room in the dead of night. Even now, he trembled at the memory of watching Rachel while she slept. Her dark hair spread out across the pillow, her long lashes brushing against her cheeks, her full lips slightly parted as though waiting for a lover's kiss . . .

Of course, all of this was not the only thing that had set the man's head spinning. The strangeness of the conversation he'd just overheard had done so as well. Why did the three of them count time in beans? Where was this leper the Methusian mentioned? What pool were they looking for, and why did they think that it may not exist? And what had the princess meant when she'd said that she'd not risk Finn's life? She'd obviously been talking about King Finnius. Was the king's life in danger, and did this danger have something to do with the Regent? The man in homespun could not imagine that it was so. However, when he considered the second part of his orders—the part that involved the princess—he could not help but worry if perhaps it was connected to the danger the king faced. If it was, it made him wonder if the one who'd sent him had been thinking clearly.

Still.

The man was not yet so changed that he could see himself disobeying direct orders, and the part of his orders that involved the princess had been very direct and *very* clear.

Sitting down upon an exquisitely carved stone bench at the edge of the market, the man pushed back his hood. As he sighed and lifted his poor face to the setting sun, it fleetingly occurred to him that his head had never ached half so much back when he simply followed orders without thinking.

And it seemed to him that he had more thinking to do yet, for it sounded as though the princess intended to lead her companions across the realm to the Valley of Gorg in search of some map that may or may not exist. And that afterward, she meant to head back to Parthania, come what may.

And what the man had to think about was this:

How far he ought to let the princess go before executing his orders—and what he ought to do about pretty Rachel after he'd done so.

Fifty

Fifteen white beans left in the jar

AFTER RELUCTANTLY AGREEING that they'd press on to the Valley of Gorg come what may, Azriel joined Persephone and Rachel in settling down for what would likely be their last good night's rest for at least a fortnight. As there were no other rooms to be had at the inn, he insisted that the girls share the bed while he took the floor. Though Persephone would have been much dismayed if he'd suggested any other sleeping arrangement, as she lay in the darkness listening to him toss and turn just as restlessly as she, herself, was doing, she couldn't help thinking that there might have been advantages to marrying a man who was just a little less thoughtful and gallant.

The next morning after breaking their fast, they settled up with the innkeeper, used the last of Rachel's gold to buy food and horses and struck out across Glyndoria. Though Persephone did her best to hide that she'd not yet fully recovered from the channel crossing, she could feel Azriel watching her whenever they stopped to rest and water the horses. And she could feel Rachel watching them both.

By the time they finally stopped for the night at the end of the first day, Rachel had evidently seen enough.

"Well?" she said in a hushed voice as soon as Azriel had left the fire to gut, skin and spit the fat hare that Persephone had earlier managed to spear from her seat in the saddle. "Are you going to tell me or are you going to make me ask?"

"Am I going to make you ask what?" asked Persephone, being deliberately obtuse.

Cocking one eyebrow, Rachel said, "Are you going to make me ask when you decided not to risk regretting the things you didn't do?"

"Oh," mumbled Persephone, flushing.

Laughing with genuine delight, Rachel tucked her clasped hands beneath her chin. "Oh, Princess, I am so pleased for you!" she said. "Tell me: Was he a *very* gentle lover?"

When Persephone could come up with no better response than a gurgling noise in her throat, Rachel laughed again. Then, leaning so close that their nearly identical heads were almost touching, she whispered, "And have you told him?"

"Told him what—that he was a gentle lover?" squeaked Persephone, who could not imagine saying such a thing to Azriel, and who would never have described his lovemaking skills so blandly in any event.

"No, not that," said Rachel, chuckling as she fed another branch into the fire.

"Then what?" asked Persephone, who immediately regretted asking the question.

Rachel gave her a knowing smile. "You know what."

Trying to ignore her suddenly hammering heart, Persephone lifted her chin—and did not return the smile. "No, I *don't* know what," she said, not caring that she sounded rude.

Rachel looked over at her in surprise. "Princess—"

"I'm going to fetch more wood for the fire," interrupted Persephone, abruptly getting to her feet. "Call me when supper is ready."

Rachel asked no more questions that she obviously thought she already knew the answers to. Not on that night, nor on any that followed. Instead, she was even kinder and more thoughtful than usual—taking on extra chores when Persephone was tired, wordlessly handing her a damp cloth to wipe her mouth each time her yet unsettled stomach revolted without warning.

Somehow, that was worse.

As Azriel had predicted, it took four days of hard riding to reach the entrance to the Valley of Gorg.

"This is it," he said, gesturing to the canyon that cut through the red rock face that rose up before them.

Wide enough to allow perhaps a dozen horsemen to ride through it abreast, the canyon was surprisingly long and so straight that Persephone could see glimpses of the grassy valley that lay on the far side. All along its undulating walls were outcroppings that looked like large lumps of pale-red icing smoothed on by way of a giant pastry knife. These outcroppings cut through the beams of sunlight that shone down from above, creating a patchwork of light and shade on the dusty ground and obstructing Persephone's view in a most discomfiting manner.

"Are you sure there isn't another way into the valley?" she asked.

Azriel shook his head. "The rock is too soft to safely climb, and I've never heard talk of another fissure that cuts all the way through to the other side," he said. "We could go around the rock face, I suppose, but that would require us to ride a full day north, cut west past the Mines of Torodania and then hack south through the coastal jungle to make our way back to yonder patch of grass."

"We haven't time for that," said Persephone, who cast another uneasy glance into the eerie shadow-and-light canyon before adding, "I just . . . don't you think this canyon is a good place for an ambush?"

"No, wife," said Azriel. "I think this canyon is an *excellent* place for an ambush."

Nudging his horse closer to hers, he reached his right arm across the gap between them, laid his hand upon her left cheek and gently turned her face toward his. With a soft sigh, Persephone tilted her head so that her grimy cheek rested more heavily against his hand.

"It is not too late to turn back," said Azriel with an intensity that took her breath away. "I do not believe Balthazar entrusted the Gorgish ambassador with a map showing the location of the healing pool. Remember, according to Barka, Balthazar neither liked nor trusted the man. Add that to what Cairn told us—that only the very boldest of slave hunters will go after the Gorgish and that more than half of those disappear without a trace—and I truly do not know if venturing forth is worth the risk."

"It is, for it is our last hope of finding the pool and saving Finn," she said, reaching up to gently cup the hand that cupped her cheek. "However, we are going to take precautions."

"I am glad to hear it, Princess, for I could not bear to see any harm befall you," said Rachel with a tenderness that set Persephone's teeth on edge even though she knew it shouldn't. "What kind of precautions shall we take?"

"The kind that involves you setting up camp and staying put until sunset tomorrow evening," said Persephone.

"*What?*" exclaimed Rachel, clearly torn between relief and dismay. "Why?"

"So that if Azriel and I are not back by then, you can ride for Parthania," said Persephone. "When you get there, pretend that you are me. Meet with the Regent. Show him the sprig of the banyan tree." Slipping the carved box out of the silk pouch at her chest, Persephone held it out to her doppelgänger. "Tell him that Azriel was killed but that you found the healing pool. Promise him that you'll tell him where it is in due course. Insist upon an audience with the king. Tell Finn . . . I don't know, tell him—"

"If you are truly worried that something may go wrong down in that valley," interrupted Rachel, who'd made no move to reach for the box, "then perhaps you should be the one to stay here, Princess."

"No," said Persephone firmly. "Finn is my brother. This risk is mine alone to take."

"Yours alone?" said Rachel, raising her eyebrows.

"Well, not *entirely* alone—" began Azriel, gesturing to himself.

"Yes, mine alone," said Persephone without looking at him.

"And what happens if you get hurt?" asked Rachel. "What happens if you get *killed*?"

"I'm not going to get hurt *or* killed," said Persephone.

"You don't know that," said Rachel. "That is why I wish you'd reconsider—because I don't want you to do something you'll regret."

"Oh?" said Persephone flippantly. "What happened to not wanting me to regret the things I *didn't* do?"

Pursing her lips at Persephone's tone, Rachel said, "Circumstances change."

"Many things change," said Persephone with a deliberately philosophical wave of her hand. "And many things stay the same."

"And some things change everything," said Rachel pointedly.

Though Persephone wanted to shout at Rachel that she didn't know *anything*, she somehow managed to hold her tongue. Thrusting the carved box at the girl with such force that if she'd misjudged the distance, she'd have knocked out her two front teeth, Persephone glared at Rachel (who glared right back at her) until she took the box.

Then, without another word, Persephone kicked her heels into the flanks of her mount to urge him forward into the mouth of the canyon.

"What in the name of the gods was that all about?" asked Azriel in a bewildered voice when he caught up to her.

"I haven't the faintest idea," said Persephone even though what she meant was, *I don't want to talk about it.*

In fact, I don't even want to think about it.

The red-walled canyon was even longer than it looked. Luckily, Persephone was so irritated by Rachel's attempts to meddle in that which was none of her business that she completely forgot to worry about being ambushed. Before she knew it, she and Azriel were safely through the canyon and standing upon the threshold of the Valley of Gorg.

"Oh *my*," breathed Persephone, her irritation vanishing upon the moment.

Tiny had once described the valley as beautiful beyond description—a veritable paradise on earth, fit for no less than the gods themselves. From what Persephone could see, he'd not exaggerated in the least. Before her lay a vast, sloping field of emerald-green grass dotted with patches of fragrant wildflowers. These were doted upon by lazily buzzing bumblebees and butterflies as big as saucers. Just barely visible on the distant horizon was the sea; nestled in between field and sea was a lush, sprawling jungle. Its trees were thickly hung with flowering vines, brilliantly colored birds soared above its canopy and a fine, silvery mist hung over it all—evidence of hidden waterfalls, Persephone was sure. And somewhere in all that lush beauty was the hidden city of the Gorgish and, if they were lucky, a map to the healing Pool of Genezing.

"Dismount," said Azriel as he jumped to the ground.

"Why?" asked Persephone, looking down at him.

Grinning as if to say that some things never changed, he said, "Because, wife, it is well-known that the Gorgish favor pit traps with spikes in the bottom, and if we're going to fall screaming to our bloody deaths, I'd rather not take the horses with us."

"Oh," said Persephone. Sliding down from the saddle, she grabbed her horse's reins and gingerly followed Azriel into the beautiful but potentially deadly field.

His body rigid with tension, Azriel used his toe to probe and tap extensively at the ground before him. When he was satisfied, he gingerly set his foot down and ever so slowly eased his full weight down upon it. Exhaling heavily when the earth beneath his foot remained firm, he cast a relieved smile over his shoulder at Persephone, wiped the sweat from his brow and then stretched out his toe to tap and probe at the next patch of ground.

At first, Persephone held her breath with each step that he took. When they managed to get halfway across the field without being impaled on spikes, however, she felt considerably less concerned. And by the time they'd gotten safely across the field and were standing at the edge of the jungle, she'd decided that his performance had really been rather comical.

"Despite the fact that we did not encounter a single one of your harrowing pit traps, I want to thank you for going to such entertaining lengths to fulfill your solemn vow to protect me," she said with a smile.

Azriel scowled at her. "It was dangerous out there," he insisted, jabbing his finger in the direction of the flowers and butterflies.

"If you say so," she said.

With that, she stepped into the jungle. As she did so, she heard a very quiet but very distinct:

SNAP.

Without warning, the ground erupted in a spray of dirt and leaves and twigs. Persephone was thrown against Azriel with such force that she got the wind knocked out of her. Her feet were yanked out from under her and her already jumpy stomach jumped right into her throat. The next thing she knew, she and Azriel were dangling high above the jungle floor in a very small net watching the badly startled horses, laden with all their packs and panniers, gallop back across the field.

"This . . . this isn't a pit trap," grunted Persephone as she groped for her dagger.

"No," agreed Azriel, who was wriggling mightily.

"Careful!" exclaimed Persephone as he accidentally elbowed her in the ribs before accidentally smacking her in the nose. "Ouch! Quit squirming!"

Azriel quit squirming at once. "We need to cut ourselves loose, but I can't reach my knife," he panted. "Can you reach your dagger?"

"It's . . . in my hand," replied Persephone, who was already sawing away.

Luckily, the net was so old and poorly maintained that it practically disintegrated beneath Persephone's blade. Azriel maneuvered through the hole first and jumped to the ground. As soon as he landed, he held out his arms and nodded up at her. After resheathing her dagger, she let herself drop.

"Oof," he said, pretending to stagger under the weight of her.

"Funny," she said, giving him a light swat across the side of the head.

"Thank you," he grinned.

Then, as if it had only just occurred to him that they were alone together for the first time in months, Azriel's grin faded, his eyes drifted to her lips and his arms tightened around her. Feeling considerably more breathless than she had a moment earlier when she'd had the wind knocked out of her, Persephone waited to see what he'd do next.

What he did next was open his mouth extremely wide, bulge his eyes alarmingly and bellow, "Ow!"

He then spun around with her yet clutched tight in his arms. The wave of dizziness she felt when he did this was instantly replaced by shock when she saw four scowling, sneering Gorgishmen standing next to a deep pit that she could have sworn had not been there the instant before. Three of the Gorgishmen were twirling loaded slingshots above their heads; one was busily reloading.

Slowly, Azriel set Persephone down onto her feet.

"Greetings, illustrious ones," she intoned, folding her hands across her chest and bowing deeply.

In response to this, a perfectly executed version of the traditional greeting of his clan, the Gorgishman on the far left let fly with his slingshot.

"Ouch!" cried Persephone as the walnut-sized rock smacked into her shin.

"Next time, I will take out your eye!" cried the Gorgishman shrilly. "Hand me your weapons immediately or die in agony, female!"

Though Persephone was fairly certain that between them, she and Azriel could take out all four Gorgishmen without losing an eye, let alone their lives, she also knew that such action would utterly ruin any chance they had of obtaining the map that would lead them to the healing pool.

So, resisting the urge to go over and give the one who'd let fly a good kick, she nodded at Azriel to hand over his knife and sword (which were visible) and made no mention of her dagger (which was not). Then she spread her hands wide in an exaggerated gesture of supplication and said, "We have handed over our weapons without a fight—"

"Because you fear us!" cried one of the two Gorgishmen who'd not yet pelted them, twirling his slingshot even harder.

"Uh, yes, and also because we come to this valley in peace—"

"And shall leave in pieces!" hooted the other one.

"To discuss a matter of vital import with the leader of your people," continued Persephone with more patience than she felt.

"Will it make him rich?" inquired the hooter.

"Filthy rich," said Azriel loudly, before Persephone could answer. "Do you think he'll grant us an audience?"

At this, all four Gorgishmen snickered. Then the one who'd interrupted Persephone and Azriel's romantic interlude by pelting Azriel with a rock said, "Oh, yes. Miter will grant you an audience. And if you fail to grovel like the sniveling worms you are or otherwise displease him in any way, he will also grant you a swift and painful passage into the afterlife."

Fifty-One

Eleven white beans left in the jar

AS IT TURNED OUT, the hidden city of the Gorgish was surprisingly close at hand.

During the short hike there through the steaming jungle, Persephone and Azriel's escorts ignored them completely. Persephone ignored them back in favor of trying to figure out what to do about Azriel's lie that they'd come to the valley to discuss a matter that would make the Gorgish leader filthy rich. Though she recognized that the lie was the only reason they were being granted an audience, she also recognized that if the lie was exposed, it could spell her and Azriel's doom.

She'd just come up with a possible solution when the Gorgish city appeared before them with startling suddenness. It was clearly an ancient ruin, with many of the buildings in a crumbling state of disrepair and the jungle having reclaimed much of it. Trees had taken root in the narrow spaces between the buildings and paving stones; vines had crept around weather-beaten pillars and up the sides of walls. That a city of stone had been built in the middle of a jungle was remarkable. Far more remarkable than this, however, was that the city was not just vast but literally *giant*. Everything about it was huge—the buildings, the fountains, the streets, everything! Indeed, it was so oversized that the many Gorgishmen who were hurrying about their daily business looked like ants by comparison.

"Behold the magnificent ancestral city of the mighty Gorgish!" declared one of their escorts proudly, smacking his hand against his chest.

Knowing that there was no possible way the man's ancestors were responsible for building a city of such gigantic proportions, Persephone and Azriel exchanged a furtive glance.

Catching their shared look, the Gorgishman bared his crowded teeth at them and screeched, "What? *What?*"

"Nothing," said Persephone, resisting the urge to sneak another peek at Azriel.

Scowling and smacking his lips at her, the Gorgishman prodded the two of them forward into the city. As they made their way through the broad streets, surprisingly large crowds of sneering, booing Gorgishmen pelted them with rotting fruit, twigs and pebbles.

At length, they came to a building so tall that Persephone could not believe she'd not been able to see it from the field of flowers and butterflies. After ordering her and Azriel up the almost comically tall stone steps, one of the Gorgishmen trotted off to request an audience with the Gorgish leader.

It was granted at once.

The circular chamber in which the Gorgish leader held court seemed more like a massive indoor arena than a chamber. With a ceiling so high that it was lost in the darkness above and a stone floor strewn with sand, the chamber was ringed by banks of stone benches crammed with jeering Gorgishmen.

And every single one of them seemed to be demanding that she and Azriel be stoned to death on the spot.

Though it was clear to Persephone that she and Azriel were in grave danger, the longer she conversed with the Gorgish leader, the harder she found it to maintain any feelings of mortal terror. Miter was short and bald with very big feet, and he had a habit of hissing and baring his teeth when displeased. Even upon short acquaintance, this seemed to be practically all the time. These things, together with his unique habit of referring to himself in the third person and the fact that his big feet barely stuck out past the edge of the seat of the enormous stone throne upon which he sat, made it rather difficult to take him seriously.

For the third time, now, Persephone tried to explain to Miter why she and Azriel had come to the Valley of Gorg. As she did so, she took pains to emphasize that he'd be exceedingly well paid for whatever information he could give them. She thought this prudent not only because Azriel had promised *filthy* riches, but also because she did not think the Gorgish leader would give a fig for helping to set things to right for all people.

In response to her efforts, Miter laughed loudly and threw twigs at her.

"YOU ARE A VERY FOOLISH FEMALE TO THINK THAT THE GREAT MITER WOULD BELIEVE YOUR LIES!" he screeched to the renewed jeers of his tribesmen.

"They're not lies," said Persephone. "Look at the ring I gave you."

Miter lifted his unusually small hand and gazed greedily at the ruby ring she'd presented to him upon entering the throne room.

Persephone watched him admire his ill-fitting new ring for a long, silent moment. Then she cleared her throat and calmly continued. "That ring and the scar I bear are proof that I am sister to the Erok king, Finnius," she said. "It is he who will pay you for whatever information you have about the healing pool"—not a lie, for she was sure that Finn would honor such a bargain—"and he who will die if you do not give us the information."

Abruptly curling his hand into a fist, Miter pounded it against the armrest of his stone throne. "So?" he cried. "The great Miter cares nothing for the Erok king!"

"Well, he . . . that is to say *you* should because—"

"You know, Miter could kill you," said Miter, baring his crowded teeth at her. "Perhaps Miter *will* kill you." When this elicited a frenzy of hoots and cheers from the mob in the stands, he added, "Perhaps Miter will have you stoned to death!"

The crowd went wild.

"Listen, Miter—"

But Miter wasn't listening. "Yes," he mused in a tone that suggested he was talking to himself despite the fact that he could probably be heard in the farthest corners of the echoing chamber. "Yes, Miter thinks he will *definitely* have them stoned to death. He will then send their battered bodies to the imperial capital that they might be laid before the throne of the Erok king who dared to steal the Mines of Torodania from its rightful lords."

"It was the Regent who stole the mines from your people," said Persephone. "And it is he who will murder my brother and steal his throne if my husband and I do not find the healing pool."

"MITER CARES NOTHING FOR YOUR BROTHER *OR* HIS THRONE!" screeched Miter.

"Well, you *should* care," said Azriel bluntly, speaking for the first time, "for it is my wife's brother who will make you filthy rich, and he cannot do that if he is dead. So if Balthazar told your ambassador anything about the Pool of Genezing—"

"What makes you think that our illustrious ambassador would have stooped to involve himself in such drivel?" sneered Miter, throwing a twig at him.

Ducking the twig, Azriel said, "We've been told that your ambassador made claims to another that Balthazar entrusted him with a map showing the location of the pool. Apparently, Balthazar believed your ambassador to be the cleverest person in all of Parthania."

Preening as though this lofty compliment had been directed toward him, Miter said, "Yes, it is true."

"What is true?" asked Persephone, leaning forward a little.

Puffing out his chest, Miter said, "Our illustrious ambassador *was* the cleverest person in all of Parthania."

His skepticism plain upon his handsome face, Azriel folded his arms across his chest and said, "Even so, Balthazar never gave him any map, did he?"

Miter cast a few furtive glances around the room at his listening tribesmen. Then, glaring down his long nose at Azriel, he said, "Yes, as a matter of fact, he *did*."

"He did?" said Persephone in surprise.

"Yes," sniffed Miter, examining his fingernails.

"If that was true—" began Azriel.

"MITER HAS ALREADY SAID THAT IT IS TRUE!"

"Then you'd long ago have found some way to use the knowledge of the location of the pool to your advantage," finished Azriel.

"Ha! That shows what *you* know!" jeered Miter, jabbing a finger at Azriel. "Are you so stupid that it doesn't occur to you that perhaps the pool is located where none are able to get to it?"

"Balthazar was able to get to it—"

"MUCH HAS CHANGED SINCE THAT METHUSIAN FOOL RUINED EVERYTHING FOR EVERYONE!" shrieked Miter, flinging a whole handful of twigs at Azriel.

Seeing that the Gorgish leader seemed genuinely upset for the first time, Persephone gave silent thanks that he didn't know she and Azriel were kin to the Methusian fool who'd ruined everything. "You're right," she said soothingly, in an effort to calm him. "You're right—much has changed. Help my husband and me save my brother so that he can make you rich beyond your wildest dreams and right the wrongs that have been done to your people. Please, Miter—tell us where the healing pool is."

Not seeming the least bit soothed, the Gorgish leader laughed nastily. "Do you think that Miter is as stupid as your hideous companion?" he demanded as Azriel looked around for the "hideous companion" to whom Miter had referred. "Do you think Miter does not know the value of the healing pool? Do you think he does not realize that to reveal its location without first receiving something of equal value is to receive *nothing*?"

Persephone, who was actually beginning to wonder if Miter might be telling the truth, took a deep breath and said, "Miter, I promise—"

The room erupted in shrill laughter.

"Promises are nothing but words!" heckled Miter, clutching his belly and rocking back and forth in a theatrical display of mirth. "Miter does not barter with words, female! Guards, seize them!"

"What?" exclaimed Persephone in alarm as a veritable army of Gorgishmen stormed toward her and Azriel. "No! Miter, wait—"

"MITER WILL NOT WAIT!" cried the Gorgishman, hammering his fists upon his armrests. "Miter has decided that stoning would be too kind a death for you! You will be delivered to Miter's private chambers at once! There, Miter will finish you in a way that will make the gods themselves shudder and weep with horror and fear!"

As he wriggled forward to the edge of his seat, hopped down from his stone throne and trundled off the dais, Persephone and Azriel found themselves swept along behind him on a tide of jeering Gorgishmen. Heart pounding, Persephone made a move for her dagger. Even as she did so, a loud humming noise began echoing throughout the chamber. Looking up, she saw that every last Gorgishman sitting in the stands was twirling a loaded slingshot about his head.

Her dagger stayed sheathed.

In less than a minute, the tide of Gorgishmen had delivered her and Azriel to the threshold of a wooden door at least three times as tall as she was. The door immediately opened to reveal Miter.

"Miter does not wish to be disturbed under any circumstances!" Miter shrilly informed the mob as he stepped aside to allow them to shove Persephone and Azriel into the chamber. "If the female and the hideous one appear before you without Miter by their sides, bury them in a hail of stones the likes of which this realm has never seen!"

Without further ado, the Gorgish leader grunted and strained in an effort to slam the heavy door in his clansmen's faces. Persephone watched in silence as the door slowly inched closed, and when it was finally shut and latched, she said,

"Listen, Miter—"

"Quiet, female," shushed Miter, flapping his hand at her. "Miter has something to show you and the hideous one."

Azriel pursed his lips but said nothing. Folding his arms across his chest again, he impassively watched the Gorgish leader trot over to the fire and kneel down in front of a large piece of parchment so old that four lumps of ore had been placed on the corners to keep it from curling up on itself.

"Come, come!" ordered Miter impatiently, waving his hand so vigorously that his new ruby ring, which was at least three sizes too big for him, nearly flew off his finger.

Feeling more curious than wary, Persephone followed Azriel across the room. When she got to where Miter was kneeling, she peered over his shoulder at the piece of parchment and flinched when she recognized the place that was sketched out in impressive detail.

"That's a map of the Mines of Torodania," she said.

"Foolish female," sneered Miter. "Look more closely."

Leaning over, Persephone noticed that someone had drawn an X in a dead-end chamber at the end of a shaft deep within one of the outer mines. There were words written next to the X in a messy but distinctive scrawl.

As she stared at these words, she heard Azriel inhale sharply.

"That's right," said Miter smugly. "It says 'Pool of Genezing.'"

"We know what it says," snapped Persephone. "And we also know that you wrote it."

"Miter did no such thing!" screeched the little man.

"You did," insisted Persephone, pressing her hands against her belly to keep them from trembling. "You . . . you seek to send us to our deaths and so you ran into the chamber ahead of us and you took out a map you already possessed and you wrote those words and—"

"I don't think so," interrupted Azriel.

Something in his tone brought Persephone up short. "What do you mean you don't think so?" she asked, looking over at him.

"I mean, I don't think Miter wrote those words," said Azriel, pointing to the map. "In fact, I *know* he didn't."

"How do you know that?"

"Because those words were written by Balthazar's own hand."

Fifty-Two

Eleven white beans left in the jar

PERSEPHONE GAPED AT AZRIEL.

"What do you mean, those words were written by Balthazar's own hand?" she exclaimed.

"Just what I said," said Azriel in the voice of one who was having a hard time believing his own eyes.

"But . . . but how can you possibly know that?" blurted Persephone, panicky at the thought that he might actually have an answer. "You'd have been no more than an infant when Balthazar died. When would you have had opportunity to see anything written by his hand?"

"During his time as ambassador, Balthazar sent many letters back to our people," explained Azriel, who could not seem to stop staring at the map. "Not all of those letters were lost during the massacres. Those that were saved have become much-valued pieces of the clan's written records."

"AHA!" cried Miter, sitting back on his heels. "It is as Miter suspected all along—you and the female are Methusians!"

"That's right," said Azriel, eyeing the Gorgish leader with distaste.

"Miter does not care for Methusians," said Miter loftily.

"And they do not care for him," said Azriel.

Much offended, Miter muttered, "Perhaps they do not. But they must admit that Miter spoke the truth concerning the map's provenance."

"Perhaps," said Azriel noncommittally. "How did you come by this map, anyway?"

"Methusians were not the only ones who received letters from ambassadors," sniffed Miter.

When Azriel shrugged as though unimpressed by the answer, Miter scowled and shook his small fist at him.

Feeling sick to her stomach, Persephone stared at the X that Balthazar had supposedly drawn with his own hand. She could not believe it. She and Azriel had searched so long and so hard—had risked death so many times!—only to discover that the pool might be found in the one place she feared above all others on this earth.

Verily, it appeared that the Fates had chosen to play their latest trick on her—*again*.

"Well?" she said to Azriel at length. "What do you think?"

"I don't know what to think," he admitted, his expression troubled. "What I *know* is that Balthazar wrote those words. And that at least some of what we know of his discovery of the pool fits with the mines as a possible location."

"The mines are certainly a place of nightmares," said Persephone bleakly, recalling this description from the conversation they'd had with Cairn and the others on the morning after their wedding. "They are also near enough to the sea that Balthazar could have walked there after being shipwrecked. And they are reasonably close to the estate that Barka said Balthazar won from my father—the estate he'd supposedly sailed off to inspect."

"And the frothing beast that is said to have chased him?"

Persephone swallowed the bile that had risen in her throat. "The New Men who oversee the mines keep huge, half-starved dogs," she said in a very small voice. "The dogs are released if the New Men see workers attempting to escape or shirk or . . . or do anything at all that the soldiers don't care for, really." She licked her suddenly dry lips. "I suppose these dogs could be described as frothing beasts. And, of course, it is very dark in a mine shaft, and according to Tiny,

Balthazar said he was running in the darkness when he fell and suffered the injuries that so badly scarred him."

Azriel's silence told her that though he sensed her great terror at the prospect of returning to the terrible place from which she'd never thought to escape alive, he could not deny that it seemed as though they'd at last discovered the whereabouts of the Pool of Genezing.

"Even so," he said as though they'd been speaking instead of reading each other's thoughts. "There would be no shame in stopping here, wife. We can return to Parthania with the map and the gift that Balthazar gave your mother and offer them as proof that we found the pool."

Miter, who'd been avidly following their exchange, opened his mouth to protest, but before he could say a word, Persephone smiled tremulously and said, "Again with the bluffing and improvising, husband?" She shook her head. "No, Azriel. If we tell the Regent the pool is in the mines, the first thing he will do is dispatch soldiers to confirm that it is so. And if it turns out not to be so, he will murder Finn, and then he will murder us."

"You know that he will probably do that anyway," said Azriel with a gentleness that brought a lump to her throat.

"I know," she whispered, looking down at her hands. "But as long as there is a chance that he won't, I want to press on, for I truly could not bear to die knowing that I'd lacked the courage to do the one thing that might have saved us all."

Though Azriel said nothing in response to these words, Persephone could feel his eyes hot upon her face. Indeed, they blazed so fiercely they seemed to fill her and consume her, all at the same time.

Miter took advantage of the lull in the conversation to clamber to his feet and sidle up next to Azriel. "Listen to the cowardly female," he urged in a whisper that he clearly believed Persephone could not hear even though she was standing right in front of him. "Let us seek out the pool and—"

"What do you mean 'us'?" said Azriel.

Miter gasped in outrage. "Hideous Methusian, are you such a fool that you think Miter would show you the map without expecting something in return?" he screeched, giving his foot a mighty stomp. "You will take Miter with you when you seek out the pool!"

"We will not," said Azriel calmly.

"YOU WILL!" cried Miter, flapping his arms in agitation. "And you will get down on your ugly knees and thank Miter for agreeing to accompany you! Or are you so stupid that you do not know that being beheaded by soldiers or devoured by dogs are the only fates you can expect if you dare to venture forth into the mines without one who knows them?"

"I know the mines," murmured Persephone. "I spent months toiling deep within them—"

"Which means you saw nothing but a minuscule fraction of them," interrupted Miter without a shred of compassion for what he knew she must have endured. "Before the despicable Regent stole the mines from Miter's people and demoted those that remained to little better than tunnel rats, Miter oversaw the entire operation."

"If that is true—" began Azriel.

"MITER HAS ALREADY SAID THAT IT IS TRUE."

"Then why haven't you followed the map to the pool before now?" asked Azriel.

"It would be foolhardy to undertake such an endeavor on one's own," said Miter, rolling his eyes as though unable to believe the stupidity of the question.

"Almost as foolhardy as undertaking it with two Methusians you just met instead of with your own trusted people," said Azriel dryly.

Instead of looking offended, as Persephone would have expected, Miter looked decidedly shifty. "Miter does not wish his people to know the whereabouts of the pool," he explained as he drummed his fingertips together. "He does not even wish them to know that he has a map."

"You just told them you had a map," pointed out Persephone.

Miter rolled his eyes again. "They will assume it was a lie Miter told to trick you. And by the time they realize it was actually a lie Miter told to trick *them*, none will dare to confront Miter. Why? Because if they do, Miter may refuse to sell to them a few precious drops of the priceless healing waters that the hideous one will be hauling back for him," he snickered.

Giving the Gorgish leader a look of utter disgust, Azriel said, "I need a moment alone with my wife."

"Anything you have to say to the female you can say to Miter," assured Miter.

"If you don't give us a moment alone, I'll not haul back a single vial of healing waters for you," threatened Azriel.

Scowling and grumbling mutinously, Miter trundled off into an adjoining chamber.

After he was gone, Azriel asked Persephone what she thought.

"I think our chances are better with Miter along," she replied at once.

"Are you sure?" said Azriel dubiously. "Because I'd lay odds that my new best friend is going to try to kill us the minute we find the pool."

"Even if that is so," said Persephone, "the mines are unimaginably vast, Azriel. If Miter really did oversee them at one time, he knows his way around them far better than I."

"That may be true," conceded Azriel. "But you knew your way around the mines well enough to have escaped them."

When Persephone said nothing, Azriel pressed the point.

"Persephone?" he said, ducking his head so that she could not avoid looking into his beautiful blue eyes. "You knew your way around the mines well enough to have escaped them, right?"

"Not exactly," said Persephone after a long moment. "Though I did escape the mines, it was never what I meant to do." She hesitated again before adding, "What I meant to do was die."

Azriel seemed to stop breathing.

"I'd just found Faust's body," she explained in a weary voice filled with all the old pain. "He was only a rat, Azriel, but oh! He was *such* a warm and clever one. When I was too tired to work but too afraid to sleep, we would chat together, Faust and I. He liked to perch on my shoulder like a furry parrot, and if I had food, he'd sit up on his hind legs and beg like a tiny dog. He had the most cunning little hands," recalled Persephone, smiling at the memory. Her smile faded as another memory crowded out the first. "The sight of him lying in the dirt, ripped apart and half-eaten, his neck snapped and his eyes gouged out . . . it was the end for me. Using the sharpest rock that I could find I hacked off his tail. Then, clutching the tail in my hand, I started walking. As soon as I could, I veered away from the torch-lit tunnels. Groping my way through the darkness, I ventured deeper and deeper into the mine, turning this way and that until at last I was so hopelessly lost that I knew I'd never be able to find my way back again."

"Then what happened?" asked Azriel, his voice little more than a puff of air.

"Then I lay down and waited to die."

"But you did not die."

"No," said Persephone, a little sadly. "As I was lying there, I felt the ground rumble beneath me and heard the sound of screams."

"There'd been a cave-in?" guessed Azriel.

"Yes," said Persephone. "Shortly afterward I felt a breeze on my face. It was so faint that it took me a while to realize what it was—and what it meant. Even after I realized, I yet lay in the darkness for a while longer, waiting for Death to claim me. But He did not come quickly enough, and eventually I got to my feet and forced myself to follow the breeze. Miraculously, it led to an opening beyond the outer perimeter of the mine. All I had to do was to climb out and start walking."

Brushing a strand of hair off her forehead, Azriel sighed softly and said, "I am very glad you did."

"For a long time, I was not glad at all. But . . . I think I am now," whispered Persephone. Looking up at him, she gave a wobbly smile before adding, "And since I am pretty sure that Rachel would kill me if I let Death claim me now, I say we take Miter with us."

"Agreed," said Azriel, smiling back as he gently pulled her against him and wrapped his strong arms around her. "But if my new best friend so much as looks sideways at us, I'm going to string him up by his own damn slingshot."

"Agreed."

Fifty-Three

Eleven white beans left in the jar

THOUGH PERSEPHONE would've liked to have started out for the mines at once, darkness was already falling by the time she and Azriel decided to allow Miter to join them in seeking the healing pool.

After learning of their decision, Miter grudgingly provided a supper of coarse bread, extremely stinky cheese and meat stew. It was late by the time this meager meal was over, so after silently but fervently entreating the Fates to keep Rachel safe from harm, Persephone joined Azriel on the floor by the dying fire. He lay on his back; she lay in his arms with her head upon his chest.

She was asleep before she could whisper goodnight.

They were prodded awake before dawn the next morning by Miter's scratchy toenail. Dropping a dozen empty waterskins on Azriel's head, Miter irritably informed them it was time to go. Persephone got ready in a stupor. Indeed, it seemed to her that she'd barely rubbed the sleep from her eyes before she found herself hurrying through the streets of the still-sleeping Gorgish city and into the jungle beyond.

The pace that Miter set as he led them north through the jungle made Azriel's usual punishing pace seem downright sluggish. For Miter didn't walk, he ran—and not just in short bursts, either, but all the time. Hour after hour he ran, pushing aside branches and letting them go unexpectedly, leaping over heaving roots without calling out a warning to Persephone and Azriel to watch their step, flying through puddles in a manner that left the person directly behind him soaking wet and covered with mud. At regular intervals, Azriel insisted that they stop to catch their breath or have a sip of water; whenever he did, Miter sneered and loudly whispered disparaging remarks about hideous Methusians and their lack of manliness.

By the time they finally emerged from the jungle, it was nearing nightfall and Persephone was shaking with exhaustion.

And fear.

"Are you all right?" asked Azriel as he watched her staring wide-eyed at the distant mountains of excavated dirt and debris that marked the outermost perimeter of the mines.

Though Persephone nodded, she found herself shaking harder.

Azriel grabbed her bicep. "You don't have to do this, you know," he said.

"Y-yes, I do," she stuttered as soon as she'd found her voice. "It . . . it is like I said to Rachel—Finn is my brother . . . the risk—"

"Is not yours alone to take," interrupted Azriel fiercely, pulling her close.

"No," she agreed weakly, leaning into him. "No, not mine alone."

As soon as darkness had fallen, Persephone, Azriel and Miter stealthily made their way toward the perimeter of the mines. Though there were dozens of armed New Men in sight, it was clear from the leisurely manner in which they strolled back and forth that they weren't expecting trouble. Moreover, though they occasionally looked up at the mountains of dirt and debris, they never so much as glanced in the opposite direction.

"Why should they?" whispered Azriel.

"Because the storage sheds are brimming with gold, jewels, ore and weapons forged within!" breathed Miter, his voice brimming with avarice as his fingers strayed to his precious new ring.

"That is true," whispered Azriel. "But unless one had a sizable army, it would be impossible to properly storm such a place. And I'd think that yonder welcoming committee"—he nodded toward the dozens of heads perched on spikes planted at random intervals in the dirt mountains—"would be sufficient to deter all but the most determined lone intruder."

Persephone only nodded, her throat having closed up again at the sight of the heads.

For what seemed a very long time, the three would-be intruders lay in a shallow depression in the earth about fifty paces from the nearest guards, waiting for the opportunity to advance. Persephone was just beginning to despair that such an opportunity would never come when, at the distant sound of a whistle, the guards all began hurrying toward the nearest gate. Realizing that it must be the changing of the guards and that, at best, they'd have only a few minutes before the next shift arrived at their posts, Persephone whispered to Azriel and Miter to follow her. Then, before her courage fled—and without waiting to see if the other two were following her—she jumped up and, staying low, sprinted toward the nearest mountain of dirt. Darting around the head-topped spikes without looking at them, she clawed and scrambled her way up the mountain, not pausing until she'd reached the very top.

An instant later, Azriel collapsed on one side of her and Miter on the other.

"Here's a thought," panted Azriel. "Next time, perhaps we could discuss what we're going to do before we do it?"

Persephone was so dumbfounded by the sight that lay before her that she barely noticed that he'd spoken. Her first fleeting thought upon getting a bird's-eye view of the mines was that Miter had been right: she'd seen nothing but a minuscule fraction of them during her internment there.

Her second thought was that this was surely what hell looked like.

Far below her lay a pit that was vast beyond imagining and so deep that Persephone could not see the bottom. She could, however, see the orange glow of the mighty forges she knew occupied the pit's lowest level—forges that worked day and night to melt and mold freshly mined ore. Dotting the walls of the pit were the jagged mouths of the mine shafts that burrowed into the earth. Over the long decades, as excavation had seen the pit grow deeper and deeper, narrow, uneven ledges of rock had been left behind to allow workers to more easily access the mine shafts. These ledges were crowded with scaffolding and equipment and what looked to be thousands of enslaved Gorgishmen and half-naked lowborns. Some of these pushed carts or carried timber or torches but most shuffled along carrying brimming buckets. Persephone knew that some of the buckets were filled with dirt that would eventually be tossed onto the surrounding mountains of dirt. Others were filled with ore that would be dumped into one of the massive buckets that were continually being lowered to the glowing forges below. In and amongst these unfortunates were the overseers—easy to spot, for they were fully clothed and ever cracking their whips. Why, even as Persephone watched, an overseer on one of the higher ledges laid his lash upon the bent back of a woman who seemed to be holding up the line of those hauling buckets. Obviously startled, the woman stumbled to the edge of the ledge, lost her balance and fell to her death.

This was what Persephone could see.

What she could hear were the belching roars of the forges and the barking of dogs. She could hear the sound of a thousand pickaxes striking rock and a thousand buckets of ore being upended. She could hear screams and droning murmurs; every few seconds, the crack of a whip would be followed by a shriek. Or *not* followed by a shriek—a thing Persephone knew meant that the one upon whose back the lash had landed was beyond pain and just waiting for Death.

Beyond this vast pit was another pit.

And another . . . and another . . . and another . . .

Terrible as these open pit mines were, however, far worse were the mines that were nothing more than holes in the ground. At least those in the open pits occasionally breathed fresh air and saw light. They even had the chance to die beneath the open sky.

In the underground mines like the one Persephone herself had been locked in, the workers got none of these things. Feeling a wave of nausea, she was struck by vivid recollections of toiling in darkness by the meager light of torches, and of delivering great buckets of mud and ore through the bucket-sized opening in the heavy door at the mouth of the mine, each time hoping with pathetic eagerness that she'd done enough to earn her daily bread and ladleful of water.

Wildly now, Persephone's eyes darted around, trying to pick out the particular door that had slammed behind her all those years ago. Though she could not do it, she did recognize the barrack in which her head had been so viciously shaved on the night she'd first arrived. Outside the barrack a group of children huddled close together.

They look so small and helpless, thought Persephone, wondering if she was going to throw up. *They look so—*

The feel of a hand on her shoulder made her jump. Jerking her eyes away from the nightmare below, she forced herself to give Azriel a brisk nod to show that she was all right. He studied her face for a long moment before reluctantly nodding back and gesturing that she should turn around and pay attention to Miter.

"*As Miter was saying,*" said Miter, looking mighty peeved, "the good news is that according to the map, the mine we seek has been abandoned for many years."

"How can you be sure?" asked Azriel.

Looking even more peeved, Miter said, "Because Miter *personally* sealed it off when he was overseer."

"Oh?" said Persephone, trying to sound businesslike. "And . . . and why did you do that?"

"Because there'd been an outbreak of the Great Sickness among the workers in that particular mine," explained Miter. "Rather than risk the entire workforce, Miter decided to seal off the mine."

"You mean you shut up the healthy with the dead and the dying?" exclaimed Persephone, who'd heard rumors of such horrors during her time in the mines but had chosen not to believe them.

"Yes," said Miter unconcernedly.

"So in order to reach the healing pool, we're going to have to enter a mine littered with corpses," said Azriel in disgust. "You call this good news?"

"No, hideous one," sneered Miter. "That is the bad news. As Miter has already said, the good news is that the mine has been abandoned for many years. Are you hard of hearing, in addition to being stupid and repulsive?"

"Now, listen here—"

"The reason Miter is pleased that the mine is abandoned is that although it is true that it is nearly impossible to escape from an active mine, this place is simply too vast to guard all the mines all the time. Though it is a closely guarded secret, very important people like Miter know that abandoned mines are frequently left unguarded."

Azriel whistled softly and said, "So that would explain how Balthazar was able to get inside."

"And how he was able to get out again," added Persephone.

"Yes," said Miter, as smugly as if he'd arranged the whole thing. "Shall we proceed?"

Moving at his usual brisk pace, the Gorgish leader led them up one dirt mountain and down another for nearly an hour before finally taking them down into the heart of the mines themselves. Though the particular area they were in was clearly abandoned, and though she could see no guards at all, Persephone suddenly felt as though she was walking on the knife edge of panic.

This feeling eased a little when Miter trotted onward with great self-assurance but came rushing back full force when he stopped in front of a mine shaft entrance whose iron door was sealed with a padlock as big as Persephone's head.

"This is it," breathed Miter, licking his lips in anticipation. "The mine from the map."

"He's right," confirmed Azriel. "I memorized the map."

Miter scowled. "There was no need to do that," he said in a deeply offended voice. "Miter told you that *he'd* memorized the map."

"Yes, well, I felt that under the circumstances—"

"*I could not care less about the circumstances!*" burst Persephone, feeling as though she was about to take a flying leap off the knife edge. "How in the name of the gods are we going to get—"

"Inside?" said Azriel with a swift, steadying smile. "I'm going to pick the padlock. I'm a thief, remember?"

Biting hard into the knuckles of one clenched fist, Persephone willed herself to stay calm as he pulled out his tools. Before he'd even inserted the pick into the lock, however, from somewhere not far away Persephone heard the sound of scrabbling footfalls. These were immediately followed by a breathless sob. Snapping her head around, Persephone gasped when she saw a woman stumbling along through the moonlit darkness. She was painfully thin, dressed in rags and her hair was shorn; even from thirty paces off, Persephone could see the desperate, hunted expression on her face.

As if sensing sympathetic eyes upon her, the woman stopped suddenly and looked right at Persephone. It was as their eyes locked that Persephone heard it:

The distant sound of many barking dogs. Many barking, *hungry* dogs.

Breaking off eye contact, the starving woman cast a terrified glance over her shoulder and began to run.

Frozen with horror, Persephone watched her go—as sickened by what she knew was going to happen to the woman as she was by the fact that there was nothing she could do about it.

Then, abruptly realizing what was going to happen if she, Azriel and Miter were still out in the open when the dogs arrived, she bolted forward.

"Hurry, Azriel," she blurted, clutching at him in her terror. "For . . . for both our sakes, *hurry!*"

"No need to nag, wife," he said lightly as he poked and prodded at the lock. "I can assure you that I'm doing my utmost to hurry."

"It is likely that the hideous one will fail," confided Miter, sounding boastful in spite of the fact that he was hopping with agitation. "Miter did an excellent job of sealing up the—"

"*Shut up,*" hissed Persephone.

The dogs were now so close that she fancied she could hear their wet snarls and snapping teeth and—

"Got it," said Azriel, the relief in his voice belying his earlier light tone. Leaping to his feet, he grabbed the handle of the door and yanked as hard as he could.

It didn't budge.

The dogs—at least a dozen of them, by the sound of it—were nearly upon them.

Bracing himself, Azriel took a deep breath and yanked again.

This time the door budged, though just barely.

The dogs were only seconds away.

Heaving back on the door with a strength that seemed almost superhuman, Azriel somehow managed to open it just enough for a person to slip through. Whirling, he lifted Persephone right off her feet and shoved her through the opening after Miter, who'd pushed his way ahead to get in first. Just before she plunged into the darkness, Persephone saw the pack of hungry terror dogs bound past about thirty paces away.

And she saw one stop and turn its head their way.

Then she was stumbling over the debris piled at the entrance of the mine. Falling to her hands and knees, she whipped her head around to see Azriel start to squeeze through the crack . . . and immediately get dragged back by the snarling dog. With a leap of horror, Persephone groped in the darkness for something, anything she might use to save him. Almost at once her hand closed around a stick. Scrambling forward, she jabbed it hard through the crack in the desperate hope that if she could hit the dog, it might get so distracted that Azriel would be able to shake himself free.

To Persephone's surprise, the dog not only let go of Azriel but clamped down on the stick and jerked it right out of her hand. The next instant Azriel was inside and safe.

"Are you all right? Are you bleeding? How's your leg? Let me see," demanded Persephone, babbling in her terror and relief.

"I'm fine," panted Azriel, fumbling in the darkness beside her. "The beast only caught its teeth on my breeches, wife. My greater concern is that by saving my life *again*, you have caused yet more damage to my manly pride."

As Persephone gave a laugh that sounded more like a sob, there was a sudden flare of light in the darkness. She exhaled with relief when she saw that Azriel had managed to fashion a torch . . . then gasped when she saw that he'd fashioned it out of a dusty bone and an old shirt.

All at once, she realized that the "stick" that the dog had snatched out of her hand hadn't been a stick at all.

It had been a thigh bone.

Looking around she saw that she was kneeling in a veritable heap of human remains, some larger, some small enough to be children. Biting back a scream, she scrambled to her feet and stumbled away from them.

"M-Miter, after you sealed off the mine, the h-healthy workers must have crowded around the door!" stammered Persephone, staring at the mound of loose bones and partial skeletons. "You . . . you must have been able to hear them pleading for release."

"Yes," said Miter carelessly. "Come. Let us go find the pool whose magical healing waters will make Miter the richest among his people!"

Turning away from both the door and the remains of those he'd condemned to death for nothing more than being in the wrong place at the wrong time, the Gorgish leader eagerly started forward into the darkness. In spite of the horrors of the place and all they'd endured to get there, Azriel gave Persephone a look that could not contain his sudden excitement that their quest was almost over. Grabbing her by the hand, he lifted the torch aloft, and together they hurried after Miter.

For the first quarter hour, all three of them walked carefully in order to avoid tripping over discarded pickaxes, buckets and bodies. As they drew nearer to the chamber that contained the healing pool, however, their excitement overcame them and they began to run. Each time they came to a fork in the mine shaft, Persephone anxiously looked to see if Azriel agreed with Miter's decision as to which tunnel to pursue. Each time, he did, until at last they came to a tunnel that did not fork but instead had a rotting wooden door at the end of it.

"This is it," panted Azriel, gazing at the wooden door as though it were a thing of wonder. "Beyond that door is the chamber that was marked with an X."

"Yes!" breathed Miter, who shook his fist and bared his teeth at Azriel before adding, "Do not forget the bargain you struck, hideous one."

"I won't forget," muttered Azriel, sourly patting the empty skins he'd agreed to fill and haul back to the Gorgish village.

"Attempt to cheat Miter and you and the female shall earn the eternal enmity of Miter and his people," warned Miter darkly.

Azriel rolled his eyes. As he did so, Miter licked his cracked lips and started eagerly trotting toward the door.

"Not so fast," said Azriel, yanking him back by the shoulder. "My wife and I are kin to the Methusian who gave you that map, and the pool is sacred to our people. It is only fitting that we should be the first to lay eyes on it."

Miter stomped his foot and shook his fist some more, but Azriel paid him no mind whatsoever. Giving Persephone a dazzling smile, he stepped forward and slowly reached for the doorknob. Turning it, he pulled open the door and stepped into the chamber.

Breathless with excitement, Persephone stepped in behind him and nearly fell to her knees at the sight that met her eyes.

The chamber was empty.

Fifty-Four

Nine white beans left in the jar

PERSEPHONE HEARD an angry hiss behind her, but she did not turn around.

Instead, she stared blankly at the empty place where the healing pool should have been. "We must have taken a wrong turn," she concluded, looking up at Azriel.

Wordlessly, he shook his head.

"We *must* have," she insisted, sounding as shrill as any Gorgishman. "The words were written in Balthazar's own hand. The pool must be here somewhere!"

As though struck by a sudden and terrible pain, Azriel squeezed shut his eyes and pinched the bridge of his nose with the fingers of his free hand. "The pool is not here, wife," he murmured. "I . . . I should have trusted my instincts . . . should have known that the map was a trick . . ."

"A trick?" echoed Persephone in disbelief. "A *trick?*"

Heart pounding, she whirled to confront Miter for his treachery. But Miter was gone.

"I'll kill him," snarled Persephone, reaching for her dagger. Azriel laid a hand on her arm to stop her from unsheathing it, but she jerked away from him, crying, "He deserves to die!"

"Perhaps," said Azriel. "But not for this."

"What do you mean 'not for this'?" she spat. "He tricked us—"

"No," said Azriel heavily. "The trick wasn't Miter's. It was Balthazar's."

"*Balthazar's?*"

Azriel shrugged helplessly. "He must have hoped that a fake map would throw the Regent off the scent."

"Or perhaps he liked Gorgishmen no better than you do," said Persephone, who could not help sounding accusatory. "Perhaps the map was nothing but a jest played at the expense of the Gorgish ambassador. A jest that has earned us the eternal enmity of Miter and his people—one that has seen Miter abandon us here, no doubt that he might have the best possible chance of escape!"

"Perhaps," agreed Azriel, slipping his hand around her waist.

Violently shrugging him off so that she could stand alone beneath the crushing weight of her disappointment, Persephone stared at the spot on the floor where the Pool of Genezing should have been.

She could not believe it.

Saving Finn was going to come down to bluffing and improvisation, after all.

Fifty-Five

Nine white beans left in the jar

THEY LOST NO TIME retracing their steps to the entrance of
the mine.

Persephone's heart was in her throat the entire time, certain that
if Miter got to the entrance before them, the furious Gorgishman
would close and padlock the iron door, shutting them in to die among
the dusty bones of those who'd died before them. Mercifully, this did
not happen, though the tiny fingerprints on the outside of the iron
door told them that the Gorgish leader had *tried* to make it happen.
Indeed, he'd tried so hard that his precious ruby ring had evidently
slipped from his finger without his even noticing. Fiercely glad to
have Finn's gift returned to her—however inadvertently—Persephone snatched the ring up out of the dirt, dusted it off and slipped
it onto her own finger once more. Then she and Azriel headed for
the mountain of dirt and debris that they'd climbed down to enter
the mines. They encountered no guards or dogs along the way, but
halfway up the hill they encountered the severed head of the doomed
woman Persephone had locked eyes with just before entering the
mine. It was planted on a dripping pike, and though glazed over with
death, the woman's half-open eyes seemed to bore into Persephone,
accusing her.

Persephone stumbled then, and fell.

Azriel's strong hands were upon her before she hit the dirt.

"It's going to be all right," he said as he gently lifted her to her feet. Persephone said nothing, only pulled away from him and kept climbing.

They retraced the path they'd followed into the mines, just barely making it back to the shelter of the jungle before the sky began to lighten. Persephone was shaking with exhaustion and hunger by that point, but she was too agitated to even consider Azriel's suggestion that they try for a few hours' sleep. Tossing back the handful of berries he'd hastily foraged, they set out at once.

Thanks to Miter's tendency to snap twigs and pull off leaves while he ran, they were easily able to follow the trail that led back to the Gorgish city. Worried that if they did not reach Rachel by sunset that she'd head to Parthania to face the Regent alone, Persephone responded to Azriel's protests that she was pushing herself too hard by pushing even harder.

Even so, it was late in the day when they finally reached the Gorgish city, which they skirted before hurrying onward to the field of flowers and butterflies. Racing across it without so much as a passing thought to spike-bottomed Gorgish pit traps, they finally reached the red-walled canyon that would lead them out of the Valley of Gorg.

In spite of feeling more exhausted than she could ever remember feeling in her life, Persephone picked up her pace. She was anxious to see that Rachel was safe and well and still there, and also to apologize for how she'd behaved during their last conversation. Although Rachel's uncanny shrewdness sometimes made her a most aggravating person to have around, Persephone knew that her friend always meant well. And she was so sweet and kind—sweeter and kinder than Persephone, truth be told.

After all, thought Persephone, *it wasn't me who said she'd happily lay down her life to see the prophecy of the Methusian king fulfilled. I wanted to run away and find a destiny that belonged to none but—*

Her thoughts were cut short by the sight of a large, bloody lump writhing on the ground just beyond the far end of the canyon.

It took her brain one endless second to process what it was.

Rachel.

"No," gasped Persephone, breaking into a run. "NO!"

Azriel made a grab for her but missed. He yelled something after her, but the only thing she could hear was *Rachel. Rachel. Rachel. Rachel.*

Something whizzed so close to her head that she felt the air move, but she was too panicked to consider the fact that whizzing projectiles were probably not a good sign. Bursting out of the far end of the canyon, she was immediately attacked from the side by something that sent her flying.

And just before she hit the ground, she caught a glimpse of homespun.

Fifty-Six

Nine white beans left in the jar

SCRATCHING AND SNARLING like a wildcat, Persephone reached for her dagger. Seeing the movement, her attacker moved to disarm her. As he did, Persephone drove the heel of her free hand upward as hard as she could. The blow landed on her attacker's chin with such force that his teeth snapped together and his head snapped back. Before he could recover from this most unpleasant surprise, Persephone pulled her hand back, balled it into a fist and punched him in the throat. Though he started to cough and gag, he was not sufficiently incapacitated for her to deliver another hit. Using his greater weight and strength to easily roll her onto her stomach, he quickly bound her wrists behind her back. When he was done, he bound her ankles and then rolled her back over and lifted her into a sitting position.

Squatting in front of her with his elbows leaning on his homespun-clad thighs, the man, who bore an unusually shaped wine-colored birthmark on one cheek, anxiously inquired as to whether she was all right.

Though she was yet panting from exertion and panic, Persephone managed to find the strength to spit in his face.

Instead of angering the man, her response seemed to make him very unhappy. "I knew you'd not take kindly to what I'd been asked to do," he sighed as he wiped her spittle off his cheek.

Jerking her gaze away from his face, Persephone looked toward Rachel. When she saw that her friend was no longer moving, she felt her gorge rise. "What have you done to Rachel?" she asked with mounting hysteria. "*What have you done to her?*"

"Nothing, nothing!" cried the man. Jumping to his feet, he ran over to where Rachel was lying. Pulling a rag from her mouth, he gently helped her to sit up.

Though her hands were also bound behind her back, Rachel smiled and croaked, "I'm quite well, Princess."

Persephone was so relieved that she nearly burst into tears. "But . . . but I don't understand," she said tremulously. "Your shift . . . it's covered in blood."

"It's not her blood," explained the man hurriedly. He gestured to a dead hare dangling from a branch on the same tree to which all three of the horses they'd purchased in Syon were tethered. "I needed to draw you out of the canyon alone."

At the word "alone," it suddenly struck Persephone that in spite of his solemn vow to protect her with his life, Azriel was nowhere to be seen. Her heart seizing up at the sudden memory of that whizzing projectile, she blurted, "Where is he? Where is—"

"Don't worry about him, either," said the man hastily. "He should awaken soon."

"You put him to sleep?" asked Persephone as her heart started beating again.

"In a manner of speaking," said the man uncomfortably. "I didn't want to hurt him, but I was afraid that if I had to take you both on at once, someone would get killed."

"Yes—you," growled Persephone.

"No, Highness. It is your husband who'd have gotten killed, for you are the reason I am here, and I would *never* hurt Rachel," said the man, who paused before shyly adding, "You see . . . I am her personal hero."

"You're what?" said Persephone blankly.

Rachel scrutinized the man, a look of dawning recognition coming over her as she did so. "I remember you now," she said slowly. "We bumped heads in the market in Syon."

"Yes," said the man, who seemed positively thrilled by the knowledge that Rachel remembered him. "I'd been watching the princess ever since you all left Parthania, but when she and her Methusian husband sailed away and didn't come back, I started watching you instead."

At these words, a shiver ran down Persephone's spine. "Why?" she asked, before Rachel could say anything. "Why were you watching us? Why were you following us? Who sent you?"

"The king," said the man.

"The KING?" exclaimed Persephone.

"Yes," nodded the man. "My name is Zdeno—I am one of His Majesty's personal guards. The night before you left Parthania, the king dismissed all of his other attendants and called me into his chambers. Whispering as though he feared we might be overheard, he told me that he had a mission for me and that if I performed it as he believed I could, poets would someday write verses praising my heroism, and minstrels would sing of how I'd single-handedly changed the course of Glyndorian history."

"Very impressive," murmured Rachel.

Zdeno beamed.

"*And?*" prompted Persephone impatiently.

"His Majesty said that you were undertaking a quest."

"And he wanted you to follow me," guessed Persephone.

"No," said Zdeno, surprising her. "He wanted me to follow whoever followed you."

"No one followed us," said Persephone. "We lost them shortly after leaving Parthania."

"No, you didn't," said Zdeno. "General Murdock and his men tracked you all the way into the Great Forest."

"*What?*"

"Don't worry, Your Highness," Zdeno rushed to reassure her. "In addition to seeing the General and his men dead or as good as, I saw to it that none of the General's reports made it back to the Regent. That was the first part of my orders."

"What was the second part?" asked Persephone, who already had a fair idea what was coming.

"To keep you from returning to Parthania, come what may," he replied, cringing a little in anticipation of her reaction. "The king said . . . he said you'd not be best pleased but that it was vital for the good of the realm."

Persephone heaved an exasperated sigh and let her head fall forward.

Oh, Finn! she thought, affection for him swelling in her breast. *Azriel was right when he guessed that you'd want to keep me away until you were sure it was safe for me to return. I underestimated you.*

But you underestimated me, too.

Slowly, she lifted her head and fixed her gaze upon the man in meanest homespun.

"The king was wrong, Zdeno," she said softly.

"Highness?" he said cautiously, but in a voice that told Persephone he was already having doubts.

She nodded as though to confirm his unspoken misgivings. "The king fears that I may put myself in danger if I return to Parthania, and he may be right," she acknowledged. "But if I do not return by sunset eight days hence, he will be dead."

Zdeno looked horrified.

"The Regent will murder him, Zdeno," she continued bluntly. "Oh, I am quite sure he'll make it look like a tragic accident, but the king will be just as dead for all that. How could that be good for the realm?"

"Well . . ."

"Think, Zdeno, *think!*" urged Persephone, the air around her crackling with the power of her will.

Looking very close to panic, Zdeno bobbed his head convulsively, squeezed his eyes shut and thought so hard that tiny beads of sweat popped out on his forehead.

At last, exhaling heavily, he opened his eyes and stammered, "I think . . . I think that the realm would be the poorer for the loss of either of you."

"But I am only a princess," said Persephone. "And he is the king."

That night, after Zdeno untied the girls and Persephone checked to make sure Azriel was all right (he was, other than a bump on his forehead and a little incidental damage to his manly pride), the four of them supped and slept. The next morning, Ivan arrived with the dawn; shortly thereafter, the four companions and the hawk set out for the imperial capital.

During the long journey south, Persephone, Azriel, Rachel and Zdeno talked of little but the looming confrontation with the Regent. Recalling the evil looks that Mordesius had ever cast at her handsome husband, Persephone tried to persuade Azriel to let her face the Regent alone, but he refused to be persuaded. He said that if anyone were to face the Regent alone, it should be him, and that as long as he spoke the words they'd agreed upon, Mordesius would be fooled, Finn would be saved and all would be well.

Eventually, Persephone gave up arguing with him.

She could not help noticing, however, that in spite of his assurances that all would be well, for once Azriel did not hint at a future beyond the next few days. Each night when the campfire finally died out and the stars overhead began twinkling in earnest, he merely gathered her into his arms and held her as though he never meant to let her go.

When they got to within a day of Parthania, Persephone wound a dirty scarf around her head and bid Rachel to do the same. She did not think she could cope with the scrutiny of being recognized as the king's long-lost sister just now, and she did not see how such recognition would help anything or anyone.

Even with her face covered, Persephone worried that as they passed through the city gates, she might be recognized by one of the New Men whose job it was to scrutinize. Fortunately, she was not given a second glance, the New Men being entirely focused on shouting oaths at a farmer whose cart had broken down just inside the gates, resulting in a large pile of potatoes being dumped in the middle of the thoroughfare. Smiling briefly at the thought of the noisy scene darling Fleet would have made trying to get at them, Persephone chirruped and pressed her heels into the flanks of her present horse to encourage him to catch up with the others. Zdeno had an uncle who owned a storage shed near the common harbor. The plan they'd all come up with called for Persephone and Azriel to drop Rachel and Zdeno at his uncle's shed before proceeding together to the palace. That way, they'd at least have someplace to flee to if their bluff was called.

That was the plan they'd *all* come up with.

As it happened, Persephone had come up with a plan of her own. For though she'd given up arguing with Azriel, she'd never given up her fierce desire to see him kept safe from harm at the Regent's hands.

And that is why, when they reached the shed and Azriel turned to ask Zdeno where they might stable the horses, she slipped off her horse, ducked out of sight and headed to the castle to face the Regent.

Alone.

Fifty-Seven

One white bean left in the jar

MORDESIUS SAT ALONE in the king's outer chamber staring at the nearly empty jar of white beans he held in his scarred hand.

Though he obviously could have chosen to sit in the king's chair by the fire, he'd chosen instead the seat upon which the nursemaid used to plant her fat arse back in the days when she still had a fat arse. She hardly had any arse now. Months spent enjoying Mordesius's hospitality belowground had seen to that. It had seen to other things, as well—the loss of her finger and several of her teeth, the burns and boils that scored her sagging skin and, of course, the many tiny bite marks from the rats that crept out of the darkness to gnaw upon her when she could no longer keep her eyes open to fight them off. Unfortunately, the months had not seen her spirit broken. If Mordesius hadn't been so pleased with the way everything else was unfolding, he might have been enraged by her unwillingness to crumble before him, especially considering all the personal attention he'd given in an effort to make this happen.

But he was pleased.

No, not pleased. *Euphoric.* So much so that it had been difficult not to laugh in the face of that high-and-mighty bastard Bartok when he'd come to the door of the royal chambers demanding to see his son-in-law, the king. Mordesius smiled broadly as he recalled his solemn response.

So sorry, my lord, he'd said in a hushed voice. *But the king—*

A loud knock at the door startled Mordesius out of his reverie. "What?" he shouted.

A liveried guard—not one of the fools personally selected by the king but rather one of Mordesius's own New Men—took three brisk steps into the room, halted and rapped his poleax smartly against the polished floor. "The Princess Persephone is back!" he cried, unable to contain his excitement at the sudden reappearance of the king's long-lost sister. "She's right out there in the corridor and insists upon speaking with Your Grace at once!"

Mordesius stood up, his cold heart beating very fast.

Though he'd been expecting her and the lying cockroach, now that the moment had arrived, he found that he was trembling. Not just at the prospect of seeing her again but also at the possibility that she brought with her the location of the healing pool. He knew that he ought not get his hopes up, because the more likely possibility was that she was here to beg for more time, but *still.* The idea that he might be mere hours away from finding his terrible injuries healed on top of everything else? Truly, it was enough to make him believe that the Fates were on his side.

"Well?" he snapped with a malevolent glare at the broad shoulders of the grinning moron before him. "What are you waiting for? Send her in!"

After once more rapping his poleax on the polished floor, the moron hurriedly slipped out the chamber door.

The next minute, she was there.

She was dirty and dressed like a peasant. Even so, Mordesius felt his loins stir as he drank in the sight of her. Her wild, dark hair hung in waves about her face; her violet eyes glowed like amethysts. She was as delectable as before. More delectable, even. The set of her shoulders and the tilt of her chin reminded him of how different she was from simpering sows like the plain-as-dirt idiot—sows with whom he'd dallied but would not dally again.

"Hello, Princess," he breathed.

"Hello," she replied, lifting that chin of hers a little higher still.

Smiling broadly, Mordesius leaned forward and shook the nearly empty jar of white beans at her. "You were almost too late," he whispered.

"But not too late," said the princess, not returning his smile.

"No," agreed Mordesius. Tucking the jar into the pocket of his fur-lined robe, he said, "Can I assume from the fact that you are here alone that the cockroach got himself squashed at some point during your little quest?"

When the princess did not answer, Mordesius shrugged. It didn't matter either way. A week ago, Murdock had set a special watch at the city gates—New Men whose sole task it was to spot the princess when she arrived in Parthania and thereafter not let her *or* her companions out of their sight.

If the cockroach who'd dared to marry the princess hadn't yet been squashed, he soon would be.

"Don't you want to know if I found the healing pool?" she suddenly asked.

His cold heart beating faster than ever, Mordesius held his breath and willed her to say the words he longed to hear.

She did.

"I did," she said.

"Liar," came Mordesius's automatic response.

The princess shook her head. "I speak the truth," she said. Pulling a tiny, exquisitely carved box from her pocket, she opened it to reveal a *twig*. "Eight days ago, I plucked this from the banyan tree that grows by the edge of the pool. As you can see, it is as dewy and fresh as though it had been plucked only moments ago."

For about three seconds, Mordesius stared at the leafy twig in amazement. Then his handsome face twisted into a scowl.

"You think you can fool me with your little tricks?" he snarled.

"It is no trick," she said, pushing the box into his hands. "Keep the sprig with you for as long as you like; you shall see that it never wilts."

"Even if that is true, it will prove nothing but that the cockroach taught you a Methusian trick or two along the way," spat Mordesius, shaking the box at her. "If you'd truly found the pool, you'd have brought me a vial of the healing waters. *That* would have been proof!"

Nodding as though in agreement, the princess pulled from her pocket a lumpy, folded rag. Laying it in the palm of her hand, she unfolded it to reveal a heap of shattered red glass. "I *did* collect a sample of the healing waters, Your Grace, that I might be able to offer you just such proof," she said. "Unfortunately, I was thrown from my horse on the journey back to the capital and the jar smashed against a rock when I hit the ground."

"How convenient," sneered Mordesius.

"Not really," she snapped. "For if it had not broken, I'd not be standing here having this tiresome conversation with you. A conversation that I'll not continue until after I've seen my brother," she added.

Mordesius stared at her, thinking how delicious it was going to be to tame her and wondering if it was possible that she spoke the truth about having found the pool. Though she sounded utterly sincere, and though her story was plausible enough, he must never forget for an instant that she was a lying whore.

Of course, that did not change the plans he had for her any more than a visit with her dear brother would.

Such a visit might be enough to tame her.

Indeed, such a visit might be enough to *break* her.

And so Mordesius nodded and said, "I think a visit with your brother would be a marvelous idea."

"You do?" said the princess, clearly caught off guard.

"Oh, *yes*," breathed Mordesius as he slouched across the room, flung open the bedchamber door and beckoned her over.

Slowly and, it seemed to Mordesius, with dragging feet, the princess made her way to the threshold of the king's bedchamber.

As he watched her eyes widen in horror at the sight before her, Mordesius pressed his cold lips against her ear and whispered, "As I said, you were nearly too late."

Fifty-Eight

THE KING WAS DYING.

That much was clear to Persephone the instant she laid eyes upon him. Though his hair was as thick and dark as ever, his face was skeletal—his lips pale, his eye sockets shadowed, the waxy skin pulled tight across the bones beneath. The arms that lay upon the covers were blue-veined and thin as sticks; each breath he took was shallow and labored and made it sound as though he was drowning in his own fluids.

Almost worse than any of these things, however, was that Finn's beautiful blue eyes were as luminous as if they were already looking past this world of pain and into the shining light of the next.

"Oh," said Persephone in a choked voice as she ran to his bedside. "Oh, *Finn.*"

Though he was too weak to lift his head, he managed to turn it toward her. A desperate hope leapt into his already bright eyes. "Did . . . did you find it?" he gasped, his bony hand groping for hers. "Did you find the healing pool?"

Persephone opened her mouth but was too devastated to speak. She was too distraught to tell him that she'd failed, too shattered to confess that she'd thought she'd be able to save him by bluffing and improvising.

Finn smiled wanly, understanding everything and wordlessly telling her that she had nothing to be sorry for. "It's all right," he said as the hope slowly faded from his eyes. "It . . . brings me peace just to know . . . to know that you are safe. Especially since Zdeno was supposed to—"

A wracking fit snatched away his words; stringy black blood bubbled at his lips. Jumping to her feet, Persephone frantically rolled him over so that he could try to spit out that which was strangling him. After an agonizing minute, he finally stopped coughing. When Persephone eased him onto his back, she saw that his lips were tinged blue.

"Where are your physicians?" she demanded agitatedly as she wiped the blood away from his lips. "Why have you no attendants to nurse you?"

"I sent them all away . . . even Neeka," he wheezed. "There is nothing they can do for me, Persephone. There is nothing . . . anyone can do for me. Except you."

Her heart leapt. "What can I do for you, Finn?" she asked, snatching up his hand once more. "Tell me! *What can I do for you?*"

"You can . . . promise me that you will be Queen of Glyndoria after I am gone."

This was so far from anything that Persephone had expected him to say that without thinking she loudly blurted, "I can't!"

Smiling faintly as though amused by her lack of tact, Finn said, "You can."

"No, really—I can't," she insisted, struggling to lower her voice. "I wouldn't know how to be a queen, and besides, the Erok would never accept a Methusian as a prince consort—"

"You . . . married Azriel?" asked Finn in surprise.

"Yes!" cried Persephone. "So you see why I couldn't possibly—"

"I'm glad you did," coughed Finn, nodding his approval of her marriage. "Azriel is . . . a good man. He will stand by you."

Persephone grimaced in frustration. "Finn, *please*," she begged, gripping his cold hand tighter. "On that very first day we spent together as brother and sister, I told you that I'd lived my whole life enslaved and yearning for freedom. I told you that ruling a realm was naught but its own kind of enslavement and that I'd not do so for anything. Nothing has changed!"

"Everything has changed," countered Finn, who paused to cough and gag and spit out another mouthful of bloody mucus before continuing. "I am dying, Persephone."

"No," she said, trying to snatch her hand away from his so that she could cover her ears.

"Yes," he gasped, holding onto her hand with surprising strength. "Now . . . stop arguing and listen, for I think that I . . . haven't much time. I've had copies of my will delivered to several of . . . the great lords with instructions that . . . the seal not be broken until after I am dead. Among other things, it names you as my heir."

Persephone ground her teeth together to keep from crying out that what he was suggesting was impossible for a thousand reasons!

"As you may have heard," continued Finn, "I was recently married to Lady Aurelia—"

"What?" exclaimed Persephone.

"Lord Bartok will want people to believe that Aurelia is carrying my child, but it is impossible. I was too sick and weak to perform the act, and even if I'd not been, I'd have found some excuse. Though . . . I'd have liked to know that . . . I had fathered a child—even with her—it would not have been fair to the kingdom *or* the child. For . . . regardless of whom I might have named Regent, it would have turned into a battle between Mordesius and Bartok."

"Finn, *please*—"

Giving her hand a barely perceptible squeeze to silence her, he raggedly added, "You may . . . have to fight for your throne, Persephone."

"Fight for my throne?" she burst. "Finn, in all likelihood I'm not going to be able to fight my way out of this chamber! The Regent is out there waiting for me and—"

"There is . . . a secret passageway," he interrupted, limply gesturing to one of the beautiful tapestries that hung on the far wall. "One that . . . even he . . . doesn't know about."

Feeling something beyond panic, Persephone opened her mouth to tell her twin that even if she escaped the castle alive, she wouldn't have the faintest idea what to do next, but Finn cut her off before she could utter a word.

"You . . . once told me that you were a loyal subject," he gasped as an ominous rattling noise began to issue from his chest. "You vowed . . . to obey me even unto death. I am calling upon you to honor that vow. Take the throne that was yours by right of birth, Persephone. Unite the realm. Finish the job I never got a chance to start."

Persephone stared down into the blue eyes that were growing more luminous with each passing second, even as the hand she held grew colder. In those eyes, she saw the strength, the brilliance and above all the kindness that made Finn the great king he was.

It was no use.

In failing to find the healing pool, she had denied him life.

She could not deny him this.

And so, unable to speak for grief, tears streaming down her cheeks, Persephone nodded and watched as the brother she'd known so briefly but loved so well breathed his last.

Fifty-Nine

PERSEPHONE STARED at the body on the bed in disbelief.

Finn was dead.

Dead.

Dead.

Dead.

Her body felt so heavy she was sure she'd never be able to move again. When she heard a soft shuffling sound on the other side of the bedchamber door, however, the survival instincts that had kept her alive even when she'd longed for death kicked in.

Rising to her feet, she silently ran to the far wall and ducked behind the tapestry. It took her a moment of feeling around, but at last she found the door to the secret passageway of which Finn had spoken. Forcing down her panic at the thought of what might lurk within, she plunged into the narrow, dusty darkness.

Her overloaded mind must have had the mercy to blank out because the next thing Persephone knew she was tumbling out a small door in one of the outer walls that faced the royal garden where she'd first met Finn. She stood transfixed by the sight. Not having any idea that he was her brother and not recognizing him as the king, at their first meeting, she'd flown at him in a rage. She'd called him a beast for trying to get Ivan to behave as a hunting hawk should, and when he'd hopped about in pain after Ivan pecked him in the side of the head, she'd chastised him for his tiresome theatrics.

Tears welled in Persephone's eyes again as she remembered how good-naturedly Finn had laughed in the face of it all and the earnestness with which he'd offered to lecture the horse who'd tried to kill her.

Then she blinked the tears out of her eyes and forced herself to turn away. Any moment now, the Regent would discover that Finn was dead and she was gone.

She didn't have much time.

Keeping her head low, she raced across the courtyard, through the watchtower passageway and into the streets beyond. The harbor storage shed where Azriel and the others were waiting was not far away. Part of her wanted to run to it as fast as she could and hurl herself into Azriel's arms in the vain hope that they might shelter her from her battering grief. She knew that he'd be furious with her for having given him the slip *again*, but she also knew that the moment she told him about Finn, he'd do everything in his power to fulfill his vow to be the rock upon which she might stand in times of trouble.

As tempting as all this was, however, another part of Persephone desperately wanted to run as fast as she could *away* from the harbor storage shed. She wanted to run away from everything and everyone; she wanted to return to being a nobody with no one and nothing but the dream of a destiny that belonged to none but her.

Persephone slowed to a walk, and then she stopped.

Heart thudding against her rib cage, she looked toward the harbor, then she looked in the opposite direction.

Then she started walking again—toward the harbor.

Because even if I could run away from everything else, she thought a few minutes later as she stumbled over the gangplank of one of the many ships anchored along the docks, *there is one thing I would not be able to run away from, no matter how hard or how far I—*

Sudden shouts from up ahead caught her attention and the attention of everybody else in the busy harbor. With a gasp of horror, Persephone saw a small band of sword-wielding New Men running down the harbor front. What horrified her was not the way they were callously shoving aside people and crates as they did so.

What horrified her was that they were heading straight for the storage shed in which Azriel, Rachel and Zdeno were hiding.

Even as she realized this, the door of the shed opened wide enough for Azriel to look out to see what was happening. Persephone saw him take in the sight of approaching danger before abruptly jerking his head in her direction.

For one forever instant their eyes locked.

Then Persephone was grabbed from behind and a pungent-smelling cloth was pressed hard against her nose and mouth.

She remained conscious for just long enough to drive her heel down onto the toe of her captor and to hear Azriel shout her name once.

And then she knew no more.

Epilogue

MORDESIUS WHISTLED as he lurched into the Council chamber to attend the emergency meeting that had been called by Lord Bartok. Though Mordesius had been displeased when he'd realized that the princess had managed to slip away from the castle undetected, thanks to a quick-thinking New Man, his displeasure had not lasted long.

Unlike times past, none of the great lords jumped to their feet when Mordesius walked into the chamber. With the king dead, he was no longer the Regent Mordesius. He was back to being Simply Mordesius.

As he shuffled toward the chair at the head of the table that had been his since the death of the old king all those years ago, Lord Bartok stepped forward to bar his way.

"This is not your seat anymore, *Mordesius*," he said.

Mordesius smiled up at him, his black eyes glittering like polished obsidian.

"It is not your seat, either, my lord," rumbled the ponderous Lord Belmont, who was already seated. Tapping his sausage finger against a piece of parchment on the Council table before him, he said, "I have here a copy of the late king's will. In it, he names his sister, the Princess Persephone, as his heir."

"I am certain he'd not have done so if he'd known that Aurelia was pregnant," insisted Lord Bartok.

"Is she pregnant?" asked someone.

"She thinks it is possible," hedged Lord Bartok.

Lord Belmont shrugged his massive shoulders. "Possible or not, my lord, the king's sister is now queen and that means that the seat at the head of this table belongs to her. All that remains is for her to present herself to us that she may be anointed and crowned."

The rest of the great lords joined in the discussion at this point, nearly all of them agreeing with Lord Belmont. For several moments, Mordesius stood off to one side savoring the sights and sounds of Lord Bartok's ambitions being utterly destroyed.

Then he stepped forward.

Clearing his throat, he smiled at the lords and said,

"I am most gratified to learn that nearly all of you agree that the king's sister is the rightful Queen of Glyndoria because it is with great joy that I bring you the news that I have her safe in my keeping. We shall shortly be married and the royal sons I get upon her will be the foundation stones of a dynasty that will rule this kingdom for all eternity."

M.L. FERGUS's many books for young people have been translated into more than a dozen languages, optioned for television, adapted for stage, and won or been shortlisted for numerous prestigious awards. She writes illustrated books for young readers under the name Maureen Fergus. She lives in Winnipeg, Canada with her family.

More information about M.L. Fergus can be found on her website www.maureenfergus.com.